Anselm Audley is at St J
Ancient and Modern Histo

Also by Anselm Audley

Heresy
Book One of the Aquasilva Trilogy

Inquisition
Book Two of the Aquasilva Trilogy

CRUSADE

Book Three of
THE AQUASILVA TRILOGY

ANSELM AUDLEY

POCKET
BOOKS

LONDON · SYDNEY · NEW YORK · TOKYO · TORONTO

For Naomi

First published in Great Britain by Earthlight, 2003
This edition published by Pocket Books, 2004
An imprint of Simon & Schuster UK Ltd
A Viacom Company

1 3 5 7 9 10 8 6 4 2

Simon & Schuster UK Ltd
Africa House
64–78 Kingsway
London WC2B 6AH

www.simonsays.co.uk

Simon & Schuster Australia
Sydney

A CIP catalogue record for this book is available
from the British Library.

ISBN 0-7434-1503-5

Typeset in Bembo by SX Composing DTP, Rayleigh, Essex
Printed and bound in Great Britain by
Cox & Wyman Ltd, Reading, Berkshire

ACKNOWLEDGEMENTS

As this is the last book in the trilogy, I'd like again to thank all those who helped with the conception of Aquasilva and the writing of the books (some entirely unknowingly). Also, many thanks to my family and my friends in Oxford for support, criticism, arguments, and putting up with my various eccentricities.

Particular thanks for *Crusade* to Dominik Kasprzyk, Darcy Krasne, Katherine Richardson and John Roe for various aspects of the world, to Jenny Soar for endless enthusiasm and to a man called Esteban in Girona, whose loan of a monitor thwarted my computer's evil plots.

To my brilliant agents – James Hale and Rosie and Jessica Buckman; thank you so much for everything.

To all those at Simon & Schuster – in particular John Jarrold, Jane Holland and Darren Nash, as well as Steve Stone for his covers.

Finally, I should mention Languedoc and its people both living and dead, and in particular the cities of Albi, Cordes-sur-Ciel and Carcassonne, for providing the original inspiration.

Equatorial circumference
as calculated by the Oceanographic Guild
65,397 miles

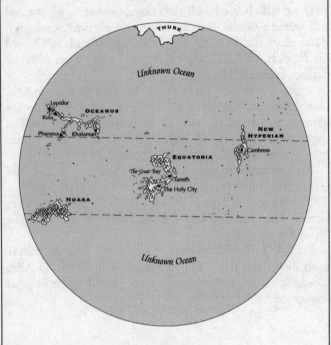

Continents

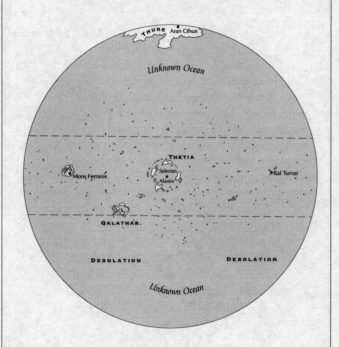

Kreon Eirillia
Cartographer to His Imperial Majesty
Orosius Tar'Conantur

Archipelago

NOTE: Aquasilva is a much bigger world than Earth, with a diameter of about 20,000 miles; the continents are therefore drawn larger than life for legibility.

QALATHAR

Abyssal Ocean

Reach of Unvanquished Sorrows

Ilthys Thetis

ILABI ISLANDS

Phaeronnis

AETIAN ISLANDS

Jaya

Inland Sea

Ta'duris

Ruins of Perdition

Albel

CLOUD FOREST

CEDAR FOREST

Savaitooth

Fortress

Kalessos

Mount Perrantis

PERDITION'S SHORE

TEIHAMA

Lake of Clouds

Dam Ilitu

Ruins of Kerestasi

CLOUD FOREST

Falls of Telmun

River
Road
Ruin
City

QALATHAR: LAND
Compiled by the Oceanographic Guild
from the Qalathar Aether Survey 2170
and the Imperial Cartographic Archives.

PART ONE:
THE DARKENING FLAMES

CHAPTER I

As I watched the Inquisitors walking towards me, I knew that my respite had come to an end.

They might not have looked so terrible to an outsider, to one who had no idea what they signified. Five men in black and white robes, pointed cowls drawn up to hide their faces, they seemed to glide across the granite stones of the courtyard. They had their hands folded inside their sleeves as always, and from where I was standing there was only their shape to tell me they were human.

No, perhaps they would have been sinister even to an outsider – but where across all the wide ocean would I have found someone who had never heard of them?

They cast distorted shadows on the weathered stone of the far wall, elongated until they became tall, thin triangles and then passed below the roof-line of the main building.

Their shapes blurred for a moment as they approached, heading for the main door almost directly below me. It was only a visual effect, a bubble in the thick glass of the window, but it made them more unnerving. I followed their path until they disappeared into the line of arches below me, and the courtyard returned to normal. Only a few people crossing it on one errand or another, and some seagulls preening on the terrace overlooking the lagoon.

I finally looked away as I heard the faint murmur of voices from below. My feet sounded painfully loud on the intricately patterned floor as I walked over to the door between tall rows of shelves, even though I knew I was making hardly any noise at all.

I came out into a wide corridor looking on to the western courtyard, its arched windows glassed in to protect the interior from storms. There was no sun shining in here to make the stone glow, and it was faded and drab by comparison with the outer court.

I heard snatches of conversation floating up from two floors below, but I was too far away to make any sense of them. I left the relative airiness of the corridor behind to descend a flight of narrow steps lit only by a tiny skylight, then emerged on to the floor below. There were no creaks as I walked; the stairs had been carefully tended and maintained to be as noiseless as possible, and there were rugs or stretches of matting on all the open flooring. This was a place of silence.

Silence, but not always secrecy. I slipped through a hidden door, two curtains and into a tiny, dark gallery with three windows of wooden tracery so delicately worked that I could barely fit a finger into the largest gap. There was a sliver-thin layer of muslin stretched across the inside of them, which made everything on the other side, down in the main part of the room, somewhat fuzzy.

There was one other person already there, Litona, a middle-aged woman whose motherly exterior belied her brilliant intellect and a ruthless single-mindedness. She glanced at me as I entered, gave a tiny nod of greeting, but said nothing.

The voices were much clearer here, and after a moment I saw the five Inquisitors enter the spacious room below. There were chairs, but none of them sat, and the two men who followed them in were ill at ease.

The first Inquisitor spoke after a moment, his cowl now thrown back. He was turned away from me, towards the two men who now stood by the far wall.

'As you are aware, Keeper, over the last four years the Index of forbidden books has been revised, and those who have charge of it are concerned that too few heretical texts have been found and purged.'

The Keeper's blunt face showed no signs of surprise.

There was no other reason why the Inquisition would come here, and he knew it as well as they did.

'It does not seem that way to us, *Domine* Amonis. But we are not heretics.'

'Your clan has shown considerable reluctance to surrender forbidden books to us, which is hardly the act of true believers.'

'It is the action of those who collect and preserve knowledge of whatever kind, *Domine*. We have copies of the Book of Ranthas in every language known to mankind, so that scholars from anywhere can study it in their own language. Is that the work of heretics?'

'To preserve blindly is to fall into the snares of evil,' Amonis said. 'Would you stock a horreum with every type of fruit imaginable? Of course not, because some fruit is poisonous. It is the same with knowledge. Your dedication to theological scholarship is valuable, but to keep forbidden books is, nevertheless, heresy.'

'We have already given you our copies of all the books recently added to the Index.' The Keeper's expression was as inscrutable as Amonis's would be, and his all-black clothing was, if anything, more austere. But, even on his home territory, he was only an ageing scholar facing a representative of Ranthas on Aquasilva.

'There are many such books still in existence.' The Inquisitor's tone was cold, precise, without any overtones of menace, though menace was what I sensed from all of them, as I always did.

'As true servants of Ranthas,' said one of his companions more sharply, 'it is your duty to act in accordance with the decrees of the Index.'

'Which we have done,' the Keeper said neutrally, but there was nobody in the room or the gallery who believed him.

Another man slipped through the curtains to join us, watching the conversation in the room below. By choosing to meet the Inquisitors in this room, the Keeper had given tacit permission for anyone to eavesdrop.

'That is for us to decide,' the Inquisitor said. 'We are here on the authority of His Grace the Exarch of Thetia to ensure that everything here is in keeping with the laws of Ranthas.'

'I will not stand in the way of His Grace's decrees,' said the Keeper. His companion shifted uneasily, a motion the Inquisitors no doubt noted. 'Will your stay be long?'

'We will stay until we are satisfied,' said Amonis. 'We will require lodgings for ourselves and our acolytes, and we do not expect to be denied access to any part of these buildings.'

'This is a place of quiet, where scholars come to work away from the bustle of the world,' the Keeper said, far more forcefully than I would ever have dared. 'We will not hinder you, but we ask you to respect the quiet of this retreat.'

'You do not dictate terms to us,' the Inquisitor said. 'The inspection will begin now. My brothers and I will be left alone for two hours to wander the rooms.'

'This is outrageous!' the assistant said, unable to contain himself any longer. Why couldn't he have kept his mouth shut? The man had no grasp of tact whatsoever, he was the model of a self-absorbed academic.

'This is the will of Ranthas,' snapped the second Inquisitor. 'Are you angry that we have come to interrupt your heretical work?'

'We will have no outbursts here,' said Amonis quietly. 'All will be revealed in time. If there is any heresy here, it will be rooted out and punished.'

He pulled his cowl back over his head with a single, graceful motion of his hands and the five Inquisitors filed out. I heard the door shut behind them with a click, and almost immediately my two companions in the gallery left to warn their fellows.

'What did you think you were doing?' the Keeper demanded, rounding on his assistant.

'I could say the same,' the assistant said. 'Just letting them in without a murmur.'

'Where have you been the past four years?' the Keeper said, in disgust. 'Now go and warn people. I'll be in my office.'

I didn't stay any longer, because to stay any longer would risk the Inquisitors seeing me in the corridor. Thankfully, there was another of those tiny boxed flights of stairs opposite, and they wouldn't have had time to reach the second floor yet.

Whoever had originally built this place had had a mania for secrecy rivalling Ravenna's. I'd never seen a place with so many hidden staircases and rooms. It was perfect for hiding books – or people, which apparently had been its original purpose. One of the scholars told me it had been built during a dynastic blood-bath, a place for people to hide from the assassins of Empress Landressa.

I felt a twinge of relief when I reached a short, plain corridor on the top floor, its only decoration a faded key pattern painted on the white plasterwork.

The old woman was sitting inside a small but very well-lit room. Not working, although there were papers open on the desk, but sitting back in a padded chair.

She didn't smile. 'What was it?' she asked, in a voice that seemed to come from a much more robust person.

'Inquisitors,' I said, closing the door behind me. 'Looking for Index books.'

'Carrion,' she said, scornfully.

'They've already started going round, the Keeper couldn't . . .'

'The Keeper couldn't stop a family of mice eating his shoes.' Despite its strength, there was a harshness to her voice, an edge that went with the unpleasant smell in the room. Even with the windows open, it lingered.

'Will they find anything?'

'They'll have to take the place apart. Anyway, we don't have time for this. You've wasted enough going off to investigate, and now those crows will come bursting in here demanding to know what's going on. Put these papers in the safe and then get working on those tables again for me.'

I watched her out of the corner of my eye as I sat down at the chart desk in the corner and went back to the thankless task of checking the new set of current tables she was using against the map of Thetia. She didn't take up her pen again, but propped a book up against the desk and starting reading, a look of concentration on her withered face.

It would end soon, one way or another. I just hoped she didn't live to see the Inquisitors tear this place apart as they had so many others, destroying the books that were the lifeblood of her clan.

I was unsure whether they'd get this far or not, but Amonis was nothing if not thorough. It was dark outside by the time he reached here, and almost time for dinner. I'd lit the lamps and strung the mosquito nets across the window, and my hand was aching from hours of repetitive writing.

The Inquisitor didn't even bother to knock. He simply walked in, to receive an icy glare from the old woman.

'What is the meaning of this?' she demanded, as if I hadn't warned her.

It was the first view I'd had of their faces, and I felt a familiar sensation of dread. I stared at the man with a fear that was totally genuine, for any number of reasons.

Thankfully, he took it as a compliment, his eyes flickering all over the room before he deigned to reply.

'I am Oshadu, my brothers and I are searching for forbidden books.'

'You will find none in here, Inquisitor,' she said, bending down to complete a sentence before she looked

8

him in the eye again. She was too old to be afraid of him.

'I will see. You are?'

Another pause, then, 'My name, Inquisitor, is Dione Ferainos Polinskarn, if it is of interest to you.'

It would have been, had he known that the woman named Dione had been dead for eleven years. But he had no way of telling that.

'And you?' He turned a square, tanned face towards me. Oshadu was – had been – an Equatorian peasant before he took orders, I could tell. He was also the second man to have spoken in the room below, the vehement one.

'A . . . Atho, *Domine*,' I said, transfixed by the man's stare. I was far too good at playing this part, but I'd never been able to suppress my panic at being this close to an Inquisitor.

'He is my copyist, Inquisitor,' the woman who'd named herself Dione said. 'As you have surely noticed, I am too old to transcribe all my research myself.'

'And what are you researching?' the Inquisitor said, but I guessed it wouldn't matter what the answer was. This man was an unwashed fanatic, his stink almost worse than the faint odour of Dione's tumour. A man of no education who should probably have been a Sacrus. Or had I misjudged him?

'Large-scale current change,' she said calmly. I wondered if anyone, anywhere in this building had told the truth once since the Inquisitors arrived.

'A pitiful matter,' the Inquisitor sneered, going over to the nearest shelf full of books and running a meaty finger along their delicate spines. He could read, I realised after a moment – but then, why would they have sent an illiterate?

'You're damaging the books,' she snapped. 'And this *pitiful matter* helps to explain how you can get from Equatoria to here in under six months, and whether you'll be able to do so in the future.'

Oshadu pulled one of the books roughly out of its place and flicked it open, leafing over pages indiscriminately. 'There is no need to study anything other than the works of Ranthas,' he sneered, bending the book so far backwards the brittle glue in its spine snapped. 'See how frail and pitiful it is. Soon it will crumble away and be forgotten.'

'You may be an ignorant lout, but I am sure your superior is not,' she said. I saw her clutch the arms of the chair with claw-like hands. 'No matter how strong your faith, it cannot overcome the currents.'

'That sounds like heresy,' he said, dropping the book on the floor. I found myself biting my lip, hoping he wouldn't provoke her into anger. 'Are you implying that Ranthas cannot overcome the ocean if He so wishes?'

'You depend on it as much as everyone else,' she said, and there was a look in her clouded green eyes that dared him to deny that.

He leaned over the desk, sweeping papers out of the way with a casual gesture.

'Beware what you say, old crone. This will be reported to my superior.' He looked down at the scattered papers on the floor. 'Your work seems to have suffered. I suggest you pick it up and get on with whatever insignificant matter you are pursuing.'

I started to get up to do as he asked, but he spun round with incredible speed, pointing a thick finger at me.

'If you make one more move I will have you flogged. Scholars engaged in such important studies hardly need help.'

The old woman didn't move.

'Pick up the papers, woman, or I will report your heretical words rather than merely remember them for future reference.'

'I have gone beyond fearing man or beast, you ignorant scum,' she said. 'You speak with the voice of an unlettered

10

peasant, not that of God. Now leave me to my work.'

I thought the big Inquisitor would lose his temper, but what happened was much worse.

'Then I am forced to conclude that since you will not obey the emissary of Ranthas on Aquasilva, you are a heretic. To defy the orders of the Holy Inquisition is nothing less than heresy. And since you are obviously too weak to stand up, let alone be questioned, I will have to ask your copyist instead, since he is no doubt privy to your heretical thoughts.'

I saw a slight tremor on her almost bloodless face, the way her hands suddenly grasped the chair.

'Say nothing, Atho!' she commanded, before I could open my mouth. Then she pushed herself very slowly to her feet and hobbled over to where the papers lay scattered on the floor. The Inquisitor kept his eyes fixed on me, and I dared not move as the old woman stiffly gathered up her scattered work and then collapsed back into the chair, her skin like grey parchment. I gripped my pen so tightly it bent in my hand, victim of my utter frustration and anger.

'Good,' Oshadu said softly. 'I will assume that since you have obeyed the instructions of a representative of God, you must still be a believer. Do not give me any reason to think otherwise.'

He didn't bother to shut the door behind him, and I just about heard his footsteps on the stairs.

The woman who'd named herself Dione was shaking, her face only betraying a fraction of the pain she was feeling. I poured her a tiny measure of the medicine that sat in a drawer of her desk, and after a few moments she relaxed slightly. I pulled the bell-rope that hung down beside her desk, but it would be a while before anyone got here, especially if they were preoccupied with other Inquisitorial monsters.

'The book,' she whispered, gesturing weakly at the floor.

I picked it up and almost immediately half the pages fell out.

'They will destroy us,' she whispered. 'I have lived too long.'

A moment later I heard footsteps on the stairs, and one of the house healers came running in. I explained quickly, and the woman's face darkened.

A few minutes later, with the old woman safely asleep, I followed the healer back down to the main part of the building. Neither of us said anything about the Inquisitors; they were probably still around.

I caught the aroma of cooking from the kitchens, and realised how hungry I was. It would be supper soon, and perhaps the Inquisitors would all be gone by then.

Thankfully, they did not overstay their welcome by demanding to be received at supper. The meal in hall was a quiet affair, though, and even the best efforts of the talented chef who had been inexplicably lured far from civilisation to cater to a collection of reclusive scholars didn't redeem the atmosphere.

I had to listen to mutterings of outrage from all sides; it seemed we weren't the only ones to have suffered. Sitting on the table behind me were a group of manta scientists from the shipyard below the beach, who were equally indignant about the way they'd been treated.

'They walk in as if they owned the place,' said the assistant from further up the table, waxing lyrical about the various insults he had received at the Inquisitors' hands.

'It's intolerable,' another man agreed. 'Have we sent word to the President yet?'

'I've been asking them to station troops here for years, but will they listen?'

I stopped paying attention. How could they be so foolish? They had no idea what was going on, no idea of the realities of life outside this remote retreat in south-eastern Thetia. They were still living in the vanished years of my brother's time, when the clans could do what they liked. Even Litona, probably the most hard-headed of them, still couldn't believe the Inquisition had any power to interfere in her beloved clan.

I looked along the ancient wooden tables with their flickering candles, the grandly painted walls with portraits of Polinskarn Presidents and Keepers, the universal black academic garb, and wondered again why I was here.

I knew, of course. It was the price I had to pay for knowing the woman who now slept in her tiny room upstairs, inching towards death with every breath she took. Another month, two at the outside, and then she would be gone.

It would have been kinder if she'd died before the Inquisitors arrived; by her account, her life had been forty-one years too long. For three decades in exile she'd mourned the loss of this existence, and now the peace of her last years would be shattered.

'How is she?' asked Litona from across the table, losing patience with the assistant's bombast.

'She'll sleep until late morning. They won't be able to wake her if they try.'

Litona scowled. 'That one was out to provoke everybody, it's almost as if he was trying to cause trouble.'

'He was,' I said, wondering why she felt the need for the *almost*.

'Maybe he's just obstreperous. He's a peasant who ended up in the wrong order, and they've sent him out to look at books. Obviously they didn't have anyone else to send.'

'He isn't here by accident, they'll have chosen him for this.'

'That's absurd.' She dismissed the idea with a wave of her hand. 'They send educated Inquisitors to deal with books.'

'Why?'

She looked at me as though I was an idiot. 'Why? Because they know their way around libraries and they know what the heretical works are.'

'The Inquisition doesn't care if it makes mistakes. Amonis and Oshadu are fanatics who won't get distracted by notions of scholarship or anything. They see libraries as hotbeds of heresy, nothing more.'

'That hasn't been my experience,' she said sharply. 'Perhaps in the Archipelago, but not here.'

'The difference being?' Maybe if I could make her see some reason at least, realise how serious things were . . .

'This is Thetia. The Archipelago has no libraries worth the mention, and there's nobody to oppose the Inquisition. The Domain knows it's dealing with a different situation here, a much richer tradition.'

I sighed inwardly. It had been sheer presumption to imagine I could change anything, to convince these invaluable guardians of Thetia's learning that they had to adapt. Like all the Thetians, even my politically astute cousin Palatine, they'd believed their country was safe from these men. She hadn't accepted the reality of the new order when I last saw her three years ago, and heaven only knew where she was now. The scholars hadn't either, but they hardly deserved the Domain's wrath for that. Even though I was powerless to do anything directly, at least I could try talking.

'Did that stop the burnings?' I said, being deliberately provocative. 'Did it save Aelin Salassa?'

Litona's expression was suddenly hostile. 'Do not speak of that here.'

'It doesn't change anything,' I went on. 'Aelin was innocent by all the laws of Thetia, but the Domain still executed her. Forgetting it won't change the fact that it happened.'

'Several people here knew Aelin,' she began, but this time I cut her off.

14

'It makes no difference,' I said. 'She was a friend of my mother. I'm just saying that we can't shelter under the old laws any more.' The fact that I'd never met either my mother or the late Aelin Salassa didn't matter. I owed a monumental debt to Aelin's House, and bringing her name up was a way of reminding myself.

'We are still record-keepers for the Imperial Library,' Litona said stiffly, wiping her mouth with a napkin. 'I think you underestimate the favours we can call in, and after six hundred years of guarding the records, no Emperor is going to dispense with our services.'

'So will you obey the Emperor's demands to erase those parts of history he dislikes? As your ancestors erased all the records of Aetius the Great?'

'We preserved those in our own way,' Litona said. 'Perhaps it would have been better if we had obeyed the usurper's commands. There are versions of history that don't stand up to close examination. Even the Archipelago you're so fond of has a darker past than some would have you believe.'

'How can the Archipelagan rulers you dismiss as petty tyrants have rewritten history as well as the Inquisition?' That was something I couldn't believe, and I knew well how poisonous historians could be when they turned their minds to it.

'One day you might find out,' said Litona, helping herself to more rice. There was a finality in her tone that marked the end of the conversation.

I might as well have tried to talk to her about academic politics, for all the good it did, and I excused myself a few minutes later before the meal had ended.

The tiled corridors were deserted – there were few libraries on this level, and anyone not eating supper in hall would be in their private suites, too busy to be dragged away from whatever they were pursuing.

What had she meant? History wasn't something that

concerned me much, except where my own family was involved, and it served little purpose now except as a rallying-cry. In the Domain-occupied Archipelago, there were more pressing things to consider than whose doctored version of the past was more accurate.

I wandered through a strange, staggered hallway where two different stages of building had been awkwardly joined, and up a short flight of steps on to the terrace, looking for some fresh air after the close stuffiness of the hall.

It was a warm night, slightly cloudy, but nothing exceptional. Except for the rainy season, there was little change in the weather in this country where seasons had no meaning. The terrace was a roughly triangular empty space, paved and with a parapet, that looked out over the lagoon on one side and the sea on the other. It would have been more pleasant with trees and a fountain, but it was so windswept no trees would grow out here, continually drenched by the waves as it was.

The sea was a restless mass of small waves tonight, not large enough to be whitecaps, but the breeze came from onshore and was mild, scented with the warm humidity of the island forests.

I sat on the lagoon side parapet, looking down into the water and seeing the ghostly shapes of mantas lit up by their docking lights. Only two, and one of those was tethered outside the shipyard, no doubt while the engineers tried out some modifications that would give it an extra half-knot of speed or make its weapons pack a little more punch. The other must be the Inquisitors' manta. Had they brought a huge staff? It would be impossible to work if their acolytes were in every room, scanning the shelves and the papers for hints of heresy.

Especially since there was so much of it here. While a heretic was anyone who opposed them, the Domain had another term to designate someone even more touched by the taint of evil. To follow different beliefs was bad enough, but to create those different beliefs was much worse. Those guilty of that sin were heresiarchs, and the ghastliness of their punishment was in proportion to how rare they were.

I didn't want to imagine Oshadu or Amonis's reaction if they found out that there were two officially defined heresiarchs here. Especially not because I was one of them, and a very lonely distinction it was too. The old sick fear of being discovered that I'd been free of for more than a year was back, a horrible feeling in the pit of my stomach that was only made worse when I remembered what had happened earlier on. How anyone could be so callous to a dying, seventy-nine-year-old woman should have been beyond me, but I knew what Inquisitors were capable of.

I gripped the stone of the parapet tightly, trying to block out images of her screaming as the fires of the stake engulfed her, or of being bound and helpless while the Inquisitors turned their instruments of torture on me as Oshadu had threatened earlier. I was marked already, and they'd only been here a few hours.

The worst of it was that I needed what time the old woman had left. Maybe it was selfish of me, but I suspected that it was my being here, the knowledge that all she had discovered wouldn't die with her, that had kept her alive these last couple of years. But still she had more to tell me, more to explain. I'd sacrificed so much to come here and learn with her; to know that it had all been in vain would be as bad as anything the Inquisitors did to me.

I stared out at the black silhouettes of the hills surrounding the bay for a few minutes, then went back inside again to finish some of the work I would have done if the Inquisitors hadn't come, the work that would have condemned me simply by being in my possession.

Had I lingered a bit longer, I might have seen the Inquisitors watching me from the sea-terrace of the guest-house further inshore.

CHAPTER II

The Retreat was slow to come alive in the morning, and I was one of only a few people who ate breakfast in the main hall. I liked this time of day here, when the sun shone directly into the courtyard, and the early breezes swept through the arched corridors, wafting away the staleness of the night air. The breezes would be gone soon, but while they were blowing it was wonderfully fresh and airy inside.

It would be a while before I was needed upstairs, and when I found one of the manta engineers working on the fountain in the courtyard, I didn't object to being drafted in.

'Wretched thing keeps doing this, and there's no-one else who knows how it works,' he said impatiently. 'What's more important, the *Sappho* or this fountain? No comparison, of course. Hold this, will you?'

He wouldn't be anyone's image of a shipwright; in fact, he appeared to belong in the book-lined rooms of the Retreat rather than the much more physical world of the shipyard.

'How's the *Sappho* going?' I asked, holding a small hammer for him while he fumbled around with the feeder pipe. I wasn't quite sure what they were doing to the manta, but there was no harm in asking.

'As well as could be expected. Damn this, I keep saying they should build a new fountain, but it was built by the old Keeper and they love it dearly.'

He made me hold the pipe in place while he started repairing it; as far as I could see, there were more repairs than original substance.

'No, *Sappho*'s doing fine,' he admitted after a few

18

minutes. 'Another month or two and we'll be done, and if she works then we'll have half a dozen more in soon. Or else we'll have to teach every shipwright in Thetia how to do the modifications for themselves, and then everyone else would know.'

What were they doing, then? Was it a minor change, or perhaps something bigger?

'Will you be testing it here?' I asked.

'Good God, no.' I saw flakes of corroded pipe sloughing off into the pool as he worked. 'Have to catch those, or they'll wreck the mechanism. No, we'll have to take her somewhere nice and quiet, wouldn't want anyone eavesdropping. Why, Scartaris had this brilliant engineer a few years back, managed to get a look on one of our weapons tests and five weeks later they had exactly the same system. No shame, the Scartarans.'

That I could agree with. The one I'd known well had to have been the most overbearing man I'd ever met, and he saw nothing wrong in making use of anyone else's facilities or plans when it suited him. Mauriz was dead now, had been for four years since he'd aimed too high and run into an opponent far beyond his league.

'Anyway, that should fix it for now. Perfectly simple, and if only they'd let me take it to bits and put a new pipe in, it'd work fine.'

As he gathered up his tools, I heard someone calling my name – or rather my false name, Atho.

'Dione's up and waiting for you,' the healer called from a first-floor window. 'I said you'd be on your way.'

'Will be.'

The healer ducked inside again, and I handed the last piece of equipment back to the engineer.

'Look after her while she's with us,' he said, as I started walking away. 'We'll not see another like her, not for a long time. Credit to the clan.'

'I will.'

Thankfully the Inquisitors were nowhere to be seen – still in their guest-house, presumably – and I wasn't accosted on my way upstairs. The windows up here had been opened for the day, and it could almost have been a normal Thetian palace with its arched courtyards and plants growing up the walls.

I started climbing the last flight of stairs, but her voice cut me off, and I realised she was standing by one of the windows in the huge library at the end, a room with two intricately drawn world-globes in the middle.

'Very domestic, isn't it?' She was observing the court-yard with a clinical detachment, leaning on an ebony stick. I stopped, amazed that she felt well enough to come down; maybe it was the drugs in the medicine, which would virtually remove the pain for a few more hours. They were too dangerous to use continuously, though.

'Domestic?' I said stupidly.

'Not on the same scale as the affairs of nations, really, is it? You fled from the offer of a throne to help with little tasks in this retreat.' She was speaking in the formal High Thetian of seventy years ago, the language of my grand-father's court, but all the Thetian dialects were so fluid that my mind translated it into the High Thetian I knew now, with the nuances of my brother's time. It was a strange language, constantly shifting and with its dialects deter-mined by the age of the speaker, not their place of origin. 'This is the level the world really works at, mind you, small-scale things like this, but it's not exactly worthy of your talents, is it?'

'Is it worthy of yours?'

'I've lived my life, and it's too late to go back and change anything now. But my previous existence was almost as cloistered as this. I went from being a student in Selerian Alastre straight into the faculty, and I spent fifteen years as a professor there and in Castle Polinskarn. A few expeditions out now and then, living on a stipend from the clan – it wasn't really much of a life, although it was what I enjoyed doing. But I've told you this before. What's important is that it isn't the life for you.'

I started to interrupt, but she cut me off with a peremptory gesture.

'Yes, perhaps you've been happy here, but it's as much from not being hunted or used as a pawn as from what this place actually is.'

'I was happy enough at home, before any of this began.' Home. It felt almost as distant to me as it must to her. Did the decades blur into one another for her now, or was her home as far away in time as it had ever been?

'You thought you were,' she said. 'But from what you've told me, talking about it, you were beginning to chafe at the bit. Your father was too protective, you said, and even when you went back, it was only going to be for a few weeks.'

My father had been completely right in a way, I thought, remembering everything that had happened to me since. Still, I had my own life to lead.

That didn't mean I entirely agreed with her. 'The only thing I ever wanted when they offered me that throne was to be somewhere else.'

'Perhaps you did. But why? Because you didn't want it, or because you couldn't face up to it?'

'Because there was no way I could have done what they wanted,' I said, resenting her implication. This was something that had rarely been touched on, and I wasn't sure why she chose to bring it up now. 'Some people are born to lead and organise. I'm not one of them.'

'Some people are born to be told what to do, and you're not one of them either. What does that make you, Cathan? Neither fish nor fowl?'

'Does your philosophy have no middle ground?'

'The Domain will pay, and the world will pay with them,' she said. 'You can kill as many of them as you like.

21

All of them, preferably, down to the last novice. But how many others will suffer too? Even if you try to keep casualties to a minimum, will Ravenna be so careful?'

'You knew what I was planning to do from the first day I was here, but you still taught me.' Her callousness was understandable, and I knew she had as much, if not more reason to hate the Domain than I did.

'And now I'm pointing out that there's a choice, as always. Nobody outside the military or the Domain has any love for the present Emperor, and by the current laws of succession you're his heir.' She held up a hand as I began to object. 'Forget the ancient laws, they mean nothing now. Do you really want to start sending the storms against people?'

I knew I'd never be free of this, as long as I lived. Whatever happened, there would always be someone who opposed the Emperor, someone who believed another member of the family would make a better Emperor.

'If it prevents a Crusade, I will,' I said, making sure I didn't sound in the least bit uncertain. There was no need for her to know.

'Don't set your mind in stone, Atho,' she said. 'Once you've convinced yourself that you're right, you block yourself off from other possibilities. Doubt is always a good thing.'

'The Domain seems to have done fairly well in its ossified state.'

'For a time it has, but that won't last for ever.' A bell tinkled quietly in the corner. 'The Inquisitors are up. I'd appreciate it if you'd help me back upstairs before they arrive. I wouldn't want to give them the wrong impression.'

Thankfully, this time we didn't see Oshadu. A small army of clerks in acolytes' robes swarmed into the Retreat, scouring the thousands of books for any known forbidden

22

titles, while the Inquisitors started their search for hidden chambers.

After rallying that morning, Dione rapidly lost her strength and took to her bed again, attended most of the day by the healer. Coming downstairs had taken a huge effort, and she was listless and exhausted, unable to teach me anything.

Without my privileged status as her 'copyist', I ranked somewhere between a minnow and an earthworm in the hierarchy of the Retreat, especially now that the Inquisitors were in charge. Something I had learnt early on was that oceanographers, being concerned with practical matters, were grouped with engineers and architects as far as the scholars were concerned, on a lower plane. Only in the theoretical subjects – history, philosophy, grammar, logic and the like – could one be considered a true scholar. Dione, being an infamous heretic, was an exception.

So I took myself off to seek kindred spirits in inferiority at the oceanographic station in the lagoon. Ravenna and I were masquerading as oceanographers in any case, and we'd got used to wearing oceanographic blue full-time over the last couple of years.

The Retreat stood on a rocky bluff high above the bay, on what had once been an island. It had been connected to the mainland by a huge breakwater when the place was first built, sheltering the lagoon from the sea and giving protection to ships that anchored there. Over the centuries, as the breakwater had been widened and strengthened, a whole complex of buildings had sprung up along its inner side.

I took the wide path that led down from the Retreat to the lagoon, enjoying the walk as I passed through a gatehouse covered in clematis with birds nesting in the shadows of its arches. It was one of the few genuinely Thetian parts of this building, and it was so ordinary, so summery, that it was hard not to be cheered simply by walking through it. It had been so long since anyone had used the gates that flowers had twisted their way round the portcullis.

The sun shone from a sky dotted with fluffy white clouds, making even the faded white paint on the nearest of the shipyard buildings seem pristine. The dome of the oceanographic station was a little way beyond, so I walked down the path in the shadow of the massive breakwater, a dozen yards or so below the level of the road. It was sheltered enough here for palm trees to have been planted in a line along the inward side, strangely at odds with the otherwise barren shoreline.

A tall man in a very worn blue tunic was making his way towards the oceanodome from the shipyard, and he waved as he saw me. Iulio, he was, an instructor on sabbatical from the Guild School in the capital.

'Tired of being up at the Retreat?' he asked as our paths converged just outside the untidy one-storey oceanodome complex. I stared at him curiously for a moment, wondering why the olive skin of his arms and legs had taken on a mottled green cast.

'We've had some problem with weeds,' he said cheerfully. 'Great mats of some obnoxious seaweed keep getting tangled up with everything. If you're staying, you'll end up looking like this.'

It wasn't a prospect I relished, but I had to earn my keep. 'Dione's ill, there's nothing to do up there.'

He grimaced. 'I heard about that. We'll have the bastards down here soon enough, and what trouble they'll be. Do you think she'll be up and about again soon?'

I shook my head slightly, and he caught the significance of it immediately.

'Why couldn't the vultures have waited a little longer? Just to let her live out her life in peace. Well, I'm glad she had someone to pass it all on to before she died.' He gave me a questioning look, the reserve there as ever. She'd taught me, but no-one else was sure what I intended to do with the knowledge.

I opened the door of the station for him, and we went into an atrium filled with the familiar but indefinable salty tang of oceanographic equipment. It was the same as every station the world over, large or small; only the details varied. Even the fact that this was a research station with no town to serve didn't change things much.

Ravenna came out of a side door a moment later, wearing a wetsilk diving tunic and carrying two whet-stones. Her skin was still its normal tanned olive, so she obviously hadn't started working on the weeds yet.

'Atho, how helpful of you to appear,' she said. Iulio held up a vial he'd been carrying in his right hand and she nodded, pointing down the corridor. 'He told you about the weed, I suppose?'

'Yes.'

'Impeccable timing.' She looked smug. 'Put a diving tunic on and join us outside, you've saved Vespasia and me at least an hour working on those weeds.'

I sawed through another strand of kelp and stuffed it into the bag that floated beside me, to stop it immediately drifting back and adding to the evil tangle of seaweed that clogged the catamaran's rudder. My hands would be stained green for days after this, and not a very pleasant green either, if Iulio's skin was anything to go by. He was darker than me, but not by very much.

The light faded again, and I glanced up at the cold silver surface of the sea a couple of feet above. It wasn't a very cloudy day; why did the sun always seem to be behind a cloud when I was out in the water?

Another evil tendril, this one inextricably entwined with one of the rudder cables. It had been three hours since the *Silverwing*'s unfortunate encounter with just a small cluster of that weed, and I seemed to have made no impact on the debris at all. At least I was doing no worse than any of the others who'd worked on it before me.

I pulled away a few more strands – although not the one on the cable – and surfaced, feeling the need for a break. The sun came out at almost the exact moment I broke the surface, and I trod water in the clear blue of the lagoon. We were in shallow water here, but the sandy bottom was all of thirty feet below me and only a dozen yards or so away it plunged into blueness.

A moment later I saw Vespasia's head appear a few paces away as she swam round the side of the *Silverwing*'s equally incapacitated twin, *Albatross*. They were such beautiful boats, very steady platforms to work from, and built by the shipyard to test at this station. Some copies were already being built to sell to the Guild, from what I'd heard. It would be a long time before my former home in the wilds of Oceanus saw one of them, though.

Vespasia held up green hands and inspected them critically just as Ravenna surfaced a few feet away, brushing tendrils of black hair out of her eyes. 'This stuff is foul, and it takes hours of scrubbing to get off, apparently.'

'Where does it come from?' I asked Vespasia. I'd never seen it before, and from the difficulty they were having getting it off, I assumed none of them had either.

'Heaven knows,' she said sourly. 'Actually, I doubt that. Ranthas isn't concerned with oceans, is He? They're below His notice.'

'Maybe you've got the wrong version of heaven.' It was a joke, but she didn't take it as one.

'They're all as ridiculous as each other, the only difference is that none of the heretic versions come complete with Inquisitors and ready-stoked fires. They don't have the chance.'

That was a little harsh, but the perpetually untidy oceanographer from Clan Estarrin was possibly the most irreligious person I'd ever met. It was quite common in

Thetia, even in these unsettled times, only Vespasia was exceptional. She'd even suggested that magic had a scientific explanation, and while I was prepared to apply oceanographic principles to using it, I felt she was going a little too far.

'Anyway,' she said, 'I've never met this stuff in Thetia before, and if it grows in the sea, we Estarrin should know about it.'

As far as I could see, that was Clan Estarrin's only distinction, and not a commercially lucrative one, but Vespasia was as fiercely proud of her adopted ancestry as if she belonged to one of the great clans, faction leaders such as Scartaris, Canteni or Salassa. There were two other Estarrin in this station of eleven people, but since they belonged to Clan Polinskarn's faction, there was nothing unusual about their presence in this Polinskarn sanctuary.

'It doesn't grow in Oceanus either,' I said, pulling a stray length of it off the *Silverwing*'s hull and holding it up to the light. Nothing remarkable about it aside from its presence here, and in due course a sample would be sent off to Guild Headquarters. In a few months they'd discover its origin and work out how it had got here, perhaps by a tiny current shift or a particularly severe winter storm somewhere a year or two back. One of many. 'Ravenna, have you ever seen this?'

'I've never looked very closely,' she admitted. 'Comes of having only been an oceanographer for a couple of years, but I don't remember seeing anything similar. At least, nothing so evil.'

This was all irrelevant now. The two catamarans were needed, and at the moment their rudders were too clogged for them to go anywhere.

We were relieved half an hour or so later by the next 'shift', and swam gratefully back to the station beach to find Iulio and another oceanographer showing a clump of it to the Inquisitor Amonis. I heard Ravenna's indrawn breath and the brief narrowing of her eyes. Her hatred always seemed to be stronger than her fear, which probably made life easier for her.

It was too late to swim away again, so I breathed a silent prayer and followed Vespasia on to dry land to report progress.

'Atho, Vespasia, Raimunda, I'm afraid your rest will have to be a short one,' Iulio said, a warning look in his eyes that meant *no protests*. 'A lot more of this got in than we thought, and *Domine* Amonis's manta has become clogged with it. We've been ordered to help clear it so they can safely put to sea again.' I knew Ravenna as Raimunda here, something she'd taken a while to get used to. It was her birth name, apparently, but she'd never used it.

So oceanographers did have a use after all, when the Domain couldn't be bothered with menial tasks. My skin crawled, though, at the thought of working in such close proximity to the Inquisitors.

'May we use more powerful tools on the manta?' Vespasia asked.

'There will not be any damage to the hull,' Amonis said coldly. 'Other than that, I do not care. I think they burn it off with flamewood torches, but I believe it is a difficult operation. Practise on the other manta first.'

'You've seen this before?' Vespasia asked, as the Inquisitor turned away.

'It grows off Qalathar,' he said, with more than a faint tone of irritation. 'Your place is not to question, but simply to undo the malice of the elements which have disabled my ship. I expect it cleaned within two days.' He walked off towards the path, seeming to glide rather than actually touch the ground.

'We'd better finish this in time,' said Iulio grimly. 'You three have ten minutes. If *Silverwing* isn't ready, you'll have to take another boat over, but I want you working on that manta before the hour is up.'

'So much for research,' Vespasia said as we headed for the station and something to eat. 'It's hard enough getting a little bit off, and no doubt their manta's totally covered in it. Malice of the elements, indeed. How can it have come from Qalathar, in any case? The only current from there to here is very deep. Very fast, but very deep.'

'I've never seen it there,' Ravenna offered. 'Maybe it comes from Perdition's Shore, it would have to be tough to survive there.'

I stared out at the lagoon entrance, where a net had been slung across the opening to stop any more of it coming in. There were great rafts of the weed floating up the coastline, far more than a freak combination of currents allowed for.

'How did it get ripped up? This stuff is so tough even a kraken would have trouble uprooting it.'

As we rowed over to the Domain manta half an hour later, facing an hour or two of indigestion, we discovered the answer. A small mat of it had somehow slipped past the net and was drifting on the lagoon's surface.

Something had punched a hole right through it, and the weed around the edges of the hole was black and charred.

'Flamewood pulse weapons,' Ravenna said, eyeing the mat as if it was about to swarm on board.

The weed travelled faster than news; it would be a month before I heard another of the few remaining heretic squadrons had been crushed by the Empire.

CHAPTER III

A thumping on the door roused me from an exhausted sleep.

'Dawn, back to work.' Iulio's voice, and he sounded in a dreadful temper. When there was no answer he banged again, and finally I told him we were coming. He barked at us to get a move on, and I heard him a moment later waking up some other poor unfortunate.

'That bloody manta again,' Ravenna said, looking as bad as I felt. And she'd been sleeping on the bed, rather than a thin mat on the floor. It was all very well for some.

I pulled myself up and struggled into a fresh diving tunic, wondering why I'd been so stupid as to stay here last night rather than go up to my room in the Retreat and wake up a little earlier to come back down.

There was no point in taking a shower, I knew, because we'd be in the water soon enough. At least it was a Thetian dawn, and there was none of the grey dampness of Qalathar or the chill of Oceanus. The air was balmy and merely cooler than it was during the day.

It seemed like only a few minutes since we'd stumbled back here for a late supper and into bed after nearly ten hours working on the Domain manta *Obedience*.

I'd been too exhausted to contemplate walking up to the Retreat, so Ravenna had offered me the floor of her small lodging in the station. None of the others would have misinterpreted the offer, because despite all the Domain's best efforts the Thetians held to their principles of equality. I knew that many of the Continentals despised the Thetians for the lack of segregation between men and women, and not even Eshar's Halettite puritanism had changed the reputation of Thetia as dissolute and immoral. And since her injuries, Ravenna had shunned physical contact as much as Palatine.

'Why does he want it in such a hurry, anyway?' I asked, realising I'd put my tunic on the wrong way round. 'He's got long enough.'

'He enjoys tormenting people.' Ravenna rubbed her eyes wearily and tied her hair back so it wouldn't float into her eyes while she was working. She always had the look of an absent-minded academic, but to some extent that was a mask. Unlike most of the Retreat's population, she knew how ruthless the Inquisition could be.

Breakfast was a bad-tempered affair, very different from the slow, leisurely morning meal the scholars at the Retreat enjoyed, especially since all the oceanographers were there.

It was hurried too, because everyone was anxious to finish the job as quickly as possible. Only a few minutes after Iulio had banged on our door, we were loading flamewood torches on to the repaired *Silverwing* and pushing her out into the gentle waves of the lagoon.

I began to feel more alive once I'd splashed some water on my face and was sitting on the catamaran's deck, letting the morning breeze run over my face. It was the last enjoyable moment I'd have for hours.

As we halted above the *Obedience*'s mooring, I heard snatches of chanting on the wind, and glanced up at the sheer walls of the guest-house, perched on the edge of the Retreat's cliff. At least the Inquisitors were up there, out of the way. I looked over the side of the catamaran as we anchored, saw the great dark blue shadow below us, as beautiful as any manta. Even if it was a Domain one. The weeds that covered all of its central section and starboard wing looked almost natural, like a host of tiny remoras on a living manta.

Natural or not, I wished the weeds had never been

spawned. I was working on the front of the manta, clearing weed off the horns and the bridge glass. I didn't expect anyone on the manta to be up so early, but when I started on the windows I saw a single man in an orange-red uniform staring out at me. The shape of his face and the thinning grey hair reminded me of a priest in the temple at home who'd taught me for a while and made too liberal a use of his stick.

I tried to keep my eyes off him as I gently scorched the weed and then pried it off the windows. It was worse because *Obedience* was almost brand new, her surface relatively clean and unscarred. On an old manta any marks we made would have blended in with the pitting that indicated long service in a hostile sea.

I watched the man out of the corner of my eye, thinking how strange it was to be looking into a bridge from outside. Thankfully, he wasn't sitting still in the captain's chair, but moving about. Maybe simply checking that all systems were in order.

I saw another figure loom at the back of the bridge, half-hidden by shadows in the well beyond. The captain, or at least the man I thought was the captain, turned to talk to him for a moment, then the figure disappeared in a flash of red.

It was only then that the peculiarity of all this hit me. There were six Inquisitors and about a dozen acolytes here at the Retreat on what was, despite the degree of vandalism involved, a relatively unimportant mission.

So why did they merit transport on one of the dozen or so mantas that belonged to the Domain? Why hadn't they simply been dropped off by an Imperial warship? There was more to this than met the eye.

The man remained on the bridge all the time I was dealing with the windows and wishing I'd been assigned duty on the engines instead, where I wasn't in plain view of someone. Too many people were seeing me, and even if I registered as nothing more than an underling, I'd still stick in their minds.

I was only given a rest when my flamewood torch, unreliable at the best of times, sputtered and failed. I swam back up to the *Silverwing* and clambered on board, handing the cumbersome thing to Iulio to mend. I sprawled on the wet deck, glad simply to be doing nothing for a few minutes.

'Do we know why this lot have their own manta?' I asked him, wondering if he'd heard anything on the grapevine.

Iulio shrugged. 'Not many ships coming here, I suppose, it's off all the main routes. No reason for Imperial ships to be coming this way. What does it matter, anyway?'

'One manta for six Inquisitors just seems excessive.'

He gave me an ominous look. 'We stay out of their affairs. I don't want to hear this discussed by any of you.'

I could understand his reluctance, but as we floated gently above the *Obedience*, it was hard not to wonder about what else the ship contained.

'What was the point of that?' said an exhausted Ravenna as we staggered up to the Retreat a long day later. The constant vibrations from the torches had given me a headache, and I'd scraped exposed skin several times on the abrasive polyp of the manta.

'I suppose it's not very impressive, travelling in a manta covered in weeds.' I glanced upwards, in case there were any Inquisitors on their way down. She was right, though, the weed wouldn't have impaired any of the manta's systems. So why the insistence, the demand that the entire oceanographic station work on it? Iulio had been forced to postpone his nocturnal study of the bay; he'd intended to see if the weed had brought any new phosphorescent algae.

So much for pure science, I thought. Thetians used

algae for lighting and various other purposes, so discovering a new species would have opened up commercial prospects. He'd have another chance soon, although not tonight. We were all shattered, and I had every intention of going to bed as soon as I'd eaten.

We passed through the gatehouse, the clematis leaves rustling gently in the night wind. The white flowers were very pale in the light from the first moon, hanging huge and distorted, low over the sea.

I hoped we'd get into the Retreat and straight to the hall without delay, but we weren't that lucky. A black and white figure seemed to materialise out of nowhere at the top of the steps, and we stopped.

'How goes the work?' Oshadu demanded. I saw one of his brethren standing a few feet away, conferring with two acolytes. Amonis, from his voice.

'Finished, *Domine*,' I said meekly, hoping he wouldn't recognise me in the poor light. Again, luck deserted me.

'Work for idle hands,' he said, with satisfaction. 'Do we believe you, though? Can we be sure you haven't taken the opportunity to sabotage His work?'

'I have inspected the *Obedience*,' Amonis said, breaking off his conversation. 'All is in working order, these meddlers in knowledge have at least proved useful for something.' He fixed a cold eye on us. 'I hope there will be no more problems with the weed.'

He didn't move, and after a second I realised we were supposed to move out of his way. I bowed and walked around him, through the shadows of the guest-house into the more brightly lit main courtyard. I heard the Inquisitors' voices as we left them behind.

'They are heretics, Brother, you must see that.'

'You say that about all oceanographers.' Amonis's tone was clipped and short, but I knew he held us in as much contempt as Oshadu did; the only difference was that he knew we had a use. 'Patience, patience.'

There was a slightly sinister ring to that last exhortation. Amonis was telling Oshadu to keep his views to himself, not to learn to accept the situation. I didn't like the sound of that.

But when we reached the hall a few minutes later I forgot all about Inquisitors and concentrated instead on the plate of succulent marlin steak in front of me. It was quite full tonight, and the more outspoken critics of the Inquisitors were in full voice, confident that they couldn't be heard.

Ravenna and I squeezed into a place on one of the side tables, near Litona again. She looked a good deal less cheery than she had two days ago, and I didn't have to be a genius to know why.

'I'm beginning to agree with the hotheads,' she said, as if the Keeper's assistant was a fervent young revolutionary rather than a desiccated academic. 'The Inquisitors are a menace, they ride roughshod over everything. They've started going through the Records Library, where we keep all the old correspondence, and it's in a terrible state. Papers all over the floor, manuscripts damaged . . . Why, we have letters in there written by eleven generations of Emperors. A priceless record.'

Her eyes flickered briefly over me, as if she knew my connection with them. Maybe she did, or perhaps she'd guessed it. The resemblance was too strong to be entirely offset by dyed hair and stained eyes, at least to someone who'd seen my brother.

'Including Aetius IV?' Ravenna asked innocently.

'Of course not,' Litona said. 'Unfortunately for historical accuracy.'

I knew she was lying. Clan Polinskarn had used the Retreat to store all the accumulated historical correspondence not judged important enough to be easily accessible in their main library. They'd have preserved their letters from that time as they did for every other reign, and the material would be safely hidden in a vault somewhere.

Was anything safe from the Inquisitors, though?

I listened to her and her colleagues' litany of woes with only half a mind, the warmth and close atmosphere of the hall making me drowsy. I didn't have the energy to complain.

After the meal was finished and Litona went off with the Keeper and some of the most senior scholars for a private discussion, we went upstairs to my small room, buried in the labyrinthine maze of the topmost storey. There were no libraries up here, only stores of unimportant books and the rooms of people without full Scholar status.

It was a very Thetian room, sparsely furnished and painted a vivid, glowing blue that was one of the traditional colours. Not furnished in excessive luxury, because anyone unimportant enough to occupy such a room was here to work, not enjoy life. It probably compared with a garret in the huge, sprawling university quarter of Selerian Alastre.

'If I can beg a floor for the night,' Ravenna said wearily, 'I won't have to go past the vultures in the courtyard again.' She sat down on the hard, uncomfortable chair that stood by the tiny desk. 'How in heaven's name can clearing weeds be so painful?'

'We're not used to hard work.'

'At least not for hours on end. Listen, before I fall asleep . . .' She got up and looked out into the corridor before closing the door firmly behind her. 'I wanted to mention it, just in case I forgot. Doesn't this all seem a little excessive?'

She was echoing my own thoughts of earlier on, and I nodded. 'The manta.'

'Not just the manta, the whole thing. The Inquisition isn't very big, there can't be more than a couple of hundred Inquisitors in the whole of Thetia. The Emperor relies on them more and more, from what I hear. So why send so many? Why not just a couple, and half a dozen acolytes?'

'If they want to swell their bonfires, they should try Karn Madrasa, where the main library is. Not this miserable place.'

'Exactly. I'm sure they must be up to something else, I wondered if you had any idea?'

'Not really.' I felt like I'd have to prop leaden eyes open in a few minutes.

'If it's important, we'll remember it in the morning,' she said. 'Plenty of time, no doubt, while they plot and scheme.'

They'd have had plenty of time to plot and scheme in Selerian Alastre, was my thought, but I didn't want to prolong the discussion. She refused to hear of sleeping on the bed, hating to be treated as other than an equal, and I made her as comfortable as I could in a pile of blankets on the floor.

I closed my eyes not expecting to wake until late morning, but the knocking on the door came many hours before that.

Slow and insistent, it took a while to rouse me from sleep and a few moments longer before I realised what it was. By then Ravenna had already dragged herself up to answer. It was the healer, looking very grave, and I guessed what she was going to say. As it turned out, I was wrong, but not by much.

'She's asking for you – both of you – but there isn't much time.'

I hadn't troubled to undress, so I slipped my sandals on and followed her along the corridor, trying not to stumble into objects. I had better than usual night vision, for reasons the Domain would not approve of, but I was half-asleep and it was a miracle I didn't walk straight into a wall.

37

We arrived in her room to find two torches burning but, to my surprise, no-one was there except the Keeper, sitting beside her bed.

Dione's head was slightly raised on a pile of cushions. I thought she was asleep at first, but as we came in she opened her eyes.

'You're here,' she said. The rasping tone was much stronger. 'Good. I wanted to see you again.' It sounded as if she had to force out every word.

I started to apologise for what I'd said two days ago, but she cut me off.

'Nothing to be sorry for. Listen, I have passed on to the two of you all the work I ever did. I've done it not just to spite the Domain, but because you were the only ones who ever asked. All I ask from you is a promise.'

I felt suddenly nervous, hoping she wouldn't use the sanctity of an oath to the dying to force me on to a path I didn't want to take. I nodded agreement, though, because it would be unforgivable after all she'd done for me to refuse her last wish.

'The two of you already know a lot that nobody else does, you understand now what no-one in history except myself has ever grappled with, and in truth you have taken it further already than I ever could. In a few moments, you will know a little more.' She looked weakly at the Keeper and the healer. 'Could you kindly leave us for a minute or two?'

The Keeper looked slightly offended, but he stood up and left, shutting both doors behind him as he went.

'What is it that they can't hear?' Ravenna asked, moving round to the other side of the old woman's bed.

'First, I want you to promise to live. I know that when you leave here, you'll use what I've taught you against the Domain. But if that goes wrong, you must not lose your lives.'

We stared at her in puzzlement for a second.

'Don't you understand? If you take this knowledge to the grave with you, then it's gone. Tell people you can trust. More importantly, though, even if the Domain destroys everything about you, you must escape. No pointless self-sacrifice.'

'But if the Domain wins, then . . .' It was so bizarre, so unexpected, that I couldn't make sense of it at all.

'Go south,' she said firmly. 'And stop arguing, I don't have very long. You're young enough to have faith in yourselves, and in whatever gods are supposed to watch over us. But I think the Domain will defeat you in the end. Too many people in their hearts believe what the priests have told them as strongly as they believe that the sun will rise. That's something you can't defeat with armies or storms.' She sighed and closed her eyes; it was a moment before she started again.

'So if it comes to that, the two of you will be witnesses and emblems of what has happened. The Domain rewrote history when they were founded, and I fear that this time they'll go further. *If* the Domain crushes whatever resistance there is, I want you to promise to go south, find somewhere they have no power. You won't accomplish anything if you're dead.'

Neither of us said anything for a moment. It was a dangerous promise to make, too open-ended. And a curious one; more than curious.

'What else is it you're going to tell us?' Ravenna asked hesitantly.

'When you've promised,' Dione insisted. 'And use your proper names.'

I took her hand, surprised at how hot it was. 'I, Cathan Eltanis Tar'Conantur, promise in Thetis's name to fulfil the promise I make now.' Ravenna repeated the oath in her birth name, for what it was worth. Then we both looked expectantly at Dione, and I saw my own worry mirrored in Ravenna's face.

I knelt down beside the bed rather than bend over it any more, my back muscles seizing up again because of those hours of holding the heavy torches. I was tired, too, but I banished any sensation of tiredness to the back of my mind and tried to concentrate on what the old woman was saying.

'Two hundred and fifty years ago, Aquasilva's climate was very different. Storms were rare events, and like mild showers compared to what we have now. There's a poem of Maradia's, one of the love elegies, where she talks about what a wonderful time the Festival of Hyperias was for lovers – warm but not too warm, balmy enough to sit out all night. Try sitting out now in the New Year, even in Selerian Alastre.'

I'd read Maradia's poems for pleasure, not for the climate information they contained, but I knew what she meant. Maybe they were all the more haunting for that, capturing a lost way of life.

'You wanted to know when you came here why I called the book *Ghosts of Paradise*, and I've told you that. Paradise is a misleading word to use, of course, because there's no such place. Aquasilva is what we make of it, and while the weather may have been idyllic, the inhabitants were as unsuited to Paradise as humanity always is.' She seemed to be rambling now, wandering off at a tangent, but neither of us dared to say anything.

'In the book I proposed a way of ridding Aquasilva of the storms. It's entirely theoretical, because it requires more power than all the mages in Aquasilva's history could muster. What I didn't say was that the storms will only get worse as the centuries go on.'

'But surely we'd have noticed by now . . .' Ravenna said.

'We have, or rather I have. It's too slow a change for us to notice, and because of the Domain's prohibition on studying the storms, no-one has a chance to do proper studies. Only the Domain has any idea of this. As the decades and the centuries pass, the climate will get worse and worse and the Domain's power will get stronger.'

That made sense, since the Domain was the only defence against the storms. But it was such a bleak prospect I didn't want to believe it.

'Is there no way to change this?' I asked, wondering whether that was the secret.

She nodded very faintly. 'You have to understand them – I've written this down, it'll take too long to explain. I tried to hurry your teaching, but the Inquisitors arrived too quickly. There are opportunities every so often to make small alterations. The only chance anyone had to set the clock back was in the first few years, and the Domain refused to do it.

'Humanity made the storms, and it can unmake them. This doesn't matter to you now, but if you alter the storm cycle too drastically to use it against the Domain, you risk upsetting the balance.'

So to turn the storms against the Domain as we'd planned could be devastating. Too late I saw what she'd been driving at all along. She didn't want us to interfere with the weather.

For Thetis's sake, nor did I! But it seemed to be the only way now to strike back at the Domain, to drive them out of the Archipelago and avenge the dead of the Crusades. There was no way to know which would cause more damage, and if there was she seemed intent on taking it to the grave with her.

'All you are giving us is despair,' Ravenna said, her eyes locked on the old woman's face. 'Is there nothing more? We can't trade a possible victory against the Domain simply for these few words.'

'You would destroy the climate to save your throne?'

'We don't know about the climate. And not just my throne. Thetia, the Archipelago – don't you want to see the Domain thrown out?'

41

'I will be beyond all that,' the old woman said. 'Destroy the Domain's power, yes, but don't sacrifice the planet to do that. If the Domain launches a Crusade against the Archipelago, there will be perhaps a hundred thousand deaths, but that's nothing to what will happen if the storm cycle goes out of control. *You cannot do this.* I hoped when you came that my teaching would show you what a horrific idea your storm-magic is. You haven't learnt.'

'And nor have you,' said Ravenna, the anger showing in her words rather than her face. 'They'll ruin everything that Thetia and the Archipelago have been, turn them into pale copies of Equatoria.'

'What right have you,' Dione demanded, 'to choose between the lives of your own people and the suffering of everyone on the planet? Stop thinking with your emotions for a minute, and start using your head. Think of the famines, the floods, the shipwrecks. If there are no fishing fleets to feed them, your people will die anyway. Are you so monstrously arrogant as to believe you're entitled to make that choice?' She stared first at Ravenna, then at me, but neither of us looked away. 'Go on, tell me you are. Tell me that, to use a weapon which might not even bring you a decisive victory, you're willing to risk so much.'

I felt sick. She was telling me I'd wasted the last two years, that everything I'd learnt had been to no point because the dangers were so intense.

'Why didn't you tell us this at the beginning?' I asked.

'Because you thought *Aeon* would solve all your problems, that you could stay here a few months, have me explain everything to you, and go back to the ship to begin. You wouldn't have believed me. You still don't, which means I've failed. I wanted to pass on what I knew before I died, and the two of you were my last chance. But I taught you so you could understand the storms, so that somebody outside the Domain has an idea of what will happen.'

'So you're going to tell me again that I should follow your advice and seize the throne,' I said. It had all come down to this again, and I just wanted to stumble away and go back to sleep, let the morning bring what it might. The surviving heretics were relying on us to start fighting back, and instead there was nothing we could offer. Except to tell them that we'd been the victims of an old woman's twisted pride.

'I'm beyond advising you now, that's your choice to make. If you use storm-magic against the Domain, you'll be no better than they are. They'll paint you as a monster like Aetius IV or Tiberius, only you'll deserve it.'

'Thank you,' said Ravenna savagely, standing up again and walking round towards the door. 'Thank you for using us as everybody else has, for your own purposes. Thank you for wasting two years of our lives. Thank you for writing a book which proved nothing and ruined the Guild's reputation. Goodbye, *Salderis*.'

'I haven't finished,' the old woman said with a strength I hadn't thought she was capable of any more.

'Do I want to hear it?'

'You will hear it, because you owe that to an old woman with a few minutes of life left in her.' She hauled herself slightly more upright. 'Come here.'

Ravenna moved back to the foot of the bed as if forced to by an armed guard.

'Only those who caused the storms can help you,' Dione said, before slipping back again. She was still breathing, I saw after a moment of panic, but she didn't say anything more.

We called the Keeper and the healer back in, and sat with them for an indefinable amount of time before the old woman opened her eyes again and croaked a few words. A goodbye to the Keeper and the healer, a thanks, and a request for a benediction.

'You want us to call a priest?' the Keeper asked, aghast.

'A Thetian benediction,' she said, and pointed at me.

Because I should have been the Hierarch, the high priest of the old religion. She knew that even as she urged me to challenge the Domain directly, to lay claim to a throne that wasn't mine. I was as certain as I'd ever been that no-one would ever call me Emperor, but as Hierarch I whispered a Thetian blessing for her.

A few minutes later, Salderis Okhraya Polinskarn was dead. Perhaps the greatest scientist Aquasilva had ever known, heretic and heresiarch, oceanographer, citizen of Thetia. My teacher for those last two years, and even if Ravenna considered it a waste of time, there was no way I ever would.

'We'll bury her at sea tomorrow,' the Keeper said, no doubt as he wondered what it had been she'd said to us. 'Atho and Raimunda, you weren't here. If the Inquisitors ask, she died in her sleep.'

A few minutes later, Ravenna and I reached my room again. Every time we'd taken a step it felt like waking the dead, but we didn't seem to have disturbed any of them.

'She betrayed us too,' said Ravenna, closing the door behind her.

I sat down numbly on the bed. 'She was right, though . . .'

'Can you never hold your own opinions?' Her temper hadn't abated, and tiredness only made her more vicious.

'I can listen to what other people say occasionally.'

'You don't have to believe them. She wants you to try and seize the throne, you know that. Of course she'll make the other options as bleak as possible.' She looked at me angrily. 'After all that, what was the point of coming?'

'We know what to do now.' I rubbed my eyes to try and keep myself awake for a few more minutes. 'Where else could we have done that?'

'You know,' she said bitterly. 'We should have gone back to *Aeon*, learnt from watching the weather unfold rather than a theoretical model that we'll have to change anyway.'

'Next, you'll be saying we should never have left in the first place.'

'Of course we should. But once we'd found a healer for Tekraea, we should have gone back, then and there.' It was an old argument, one we'd had several times over the past three years – at least when no-one else was listening – and she hadn't forgiven me.

'We've been over this before,' I said wearily. 'Just admit that you needed the scientific training, even if we didn't have to stay this long.'

She wasn't in a mood to admit anything, though. 'That wasn't why we stayed. It was because you wanted to be an oceanographer, hide here and hope no-one would ever notice you.'

'And they would have on *Aeon*?'

'Sooner or later we'd have had to do something. The day after tomorrow we're leaving on the manta for Karn Madrasa, we'll be back on *Aeon* within the week. I hope you're capable of making at least one decision by then.'

'We can argue in the morning,' I said, knowing she'd see it as an admission of defeat. I wasn't going to win anyway, not in that state.

'Fine.' She slumped down on to the floor as I blew out the candle. I was too tired to mourn now, and I was asleep almost as soon as I lay down, almost too exhausted to take off my sandals. No point getting up for breakfast.

I was too deeply asleep to hear them coming. They didn't knock, simply banged once on the door and then barged in, torch held high. I wasn't sure whether it was dream or nightmare, but I opened my eyes at the crash to see a black and white robed figure standing in the doorway with two red figures behind it.

I panicked, but I was in no condition to resist them. Oshadu simply looked on and smiled coldly as the Sacri tied our hands with clinical efficiency and pushed us out of the room to some of their fellows in the corridor. I was too stunned to take in the pandemonium, the presence of the veiled holy warriors, or anything. Anything except the satisfaction on Oshadu's face.

Every window of the Retreat blazed with light as the red-veiled Sacri moved through it room by room. Occasionally I heard the splintering of wood as they broke through a door, or an unidentified crash, punctuated by sharp orders from the officers. The Sacri themselves worked in a chilling silence, as if they were merely machines behind the red veils.

Every so often a group of them emerged through the broken main doors carrying an armful of books, which they threw on to a pile in the centre of the courtyard. It was a pile that was steadily growing, and no-one could mistake its purpose.

Only half a dozen Sacri stood around it, not to guard the books but the seventy or so staff and scholars of the Retreat who'd been dragged out here when they were captured. They looked too horrified and stunned to try anything – most of them were half-dressed, and seemed frozen to the spot.

I could feel my heart beating painfully loud against my chest as I watched the ransacking of the Retreat. I was kneeling on the stone of the courtyard, surrounded by the other oceanographers. They hadn't bothered securing any of the scholars, but we were all bound.

I glanced over to the right, where the shipwrights had been herded up from below and were being made to kneel in front of the guest-house, facing the pile of books as we all were. They looked as shocked as the rest of us.

No-one had had a chance; the Sacri had swarmed through all three of the main buildings simultaneously, rounding up everyone inside and bringing them here to be kept under guard. Only a couple of night-watchmen had been awake, and there was no way they could have resisted. The entire Retreat was in the Domain's hands.

We'd found out, too late, why Amonis had brought the *Obedience*, but in my worst nightmares I could never have imagined this many Sacri. There had to be a hundred of them, far more than I'd ever seen in one place before.

I closed my eyes, praying instinctively for this to be a nightmare. As usual, it never worked.

My knees had already started aching by the time Amonis came out to inspect the pile, now shoulder-high. Letters, books, manuscripts, papyri were all being thrown heedlessly on to it. I was too far away to read any of the titles, so I couldn't tell whether they were even heretical.

Another two days and we'd have been gone, I thought bitterly. Two days, that was all it had been. Two days out of more than two years. It didn't matter whether they found out about us or not; we were still prisoners of the Domain.

Amonis picked a book from the last armful to be thrown on the pile and opened it, smoothing down the crumpled pages.

'Ah, the *Secret History*. What's this – the fifteenth copy?' He ripped off the spine and threw it back on to the pile, picking up another. '*Arte di'ammoreze*, of Florianus. This book is a catalogue of sin, Keeper. What is it doing in your library? Letters from the foul Emperor Tiberius to his monster of a father.' The last two suffered the same fate as the first, although since the letters had no spine he simply ripped them in two and threw the pieces back on to the fire.

He spun round, glancing at each group of his prisoners in turn. 'This place is an abomination! It is a lair of evil, and you have permitted it to go on existing. Worse, you have all co-operated in its preservation. Let me hear one of you deny that you knew about these books! You said nothing!'

There was a terrified silence, broken only by a thunderous cascade from one of the upper storeys, an entire shelf of books being hurled on to the floor.

'Every last one of you is guilty in the eyes of Ranthas. You have committed mortal sin, and by allowing these books to be undisturbed you have exposed another generation to their perfidies. It is grave enough to fall into the ways of evil, but far worse to lead another on to that path.'

I stared down at the stones as he ran his eye over us, not wanting to do anything to catch his attention.

'We have come to purge this place of heresy, to purify it with the holy flames of Ranthas. When it has been cleansed, we will turn our attention to those who have stained it with sin.'

He said nothing more, but stood watching as the pile grew. It took forever, and I hardly dared look up in case he saw me and picked me out for one reason or another. No Oshadu, yet – presumably he was inside supervising the chaos.

I was bone-tired and my arms and legs were aching, while it no longer seemed as warm as it had been. The cold was seeping up from the flagstones through my legs, and my hands were going numb.

They didn't let us move for hours, until the commotion in the house had died down and a vast heap of books lay in the middle of the courtyard, surrounded by a wide open space. How many books were there? Two thousand? Five? It couldn't be anywhere near the whole contents of the Retreat.

Oshadu took a torch from one of the Sacri guarding us, as the others assembled in the doorways and windows.

'Look kindly upon us, Lord of Fire, as we consign these works of evil to Your cleansing flames, that through burning the world may be purged of its heresy. Bless this pyre and lend it Your aid to utterly consume all that is

48

written therein, so that it may be removed from the world for ever. In Your name, Ranthas, Lord of the one true Element and of Your people on Aquasilva,' Amonis said, and stepped back.

Then Oshadu held his torch high and threw it on to the pile, and a moment later the three other Inquisitors followed suit. I saw the nearest one land and remain where it was for a moment, before the flames caught the open pages of a book lying on its spine and started spreading, from one to the next.

It was only a few minutes before the whole pile was engulfed, devouring everything indiscriminately. A stricken cry from one of the scholars was cut off by a blow from the Sacri.

Then more books came raining from the upper windows as the Sacri threw them down, singly and in bundles, to add fuel to the fire. The oceanographer to my right looked away, only for a Sacrus to grab his hair and wrench his head back to look at the appalling sight in front of us.

How much that was priceless were they destroying? How many of those books were unique, the last copies of works hunted to extinction by the Domain?

Had they found the notes I'd made over the past two years, my copy of *Ghosts of Paradise*? It would have been safer to leave them where they'd simply be caught up and burnt, rather than discovered on their own. Why? I wanted to scream defiance at them, to vent my helplessness and frustration in a torrent of magic, but I couldn't. That was the worst thing of all – they had a mind-mage.

I'd seen him as we were hustled down the stairs, a bearded figure in black with a hammer by his side directing a pair of acolytes. He could negate anything I did with a single thought, and all I'd do would be to give myself away.

It wasn't until hours had passed that Amonis spoke to us

again, silhouetted against the still-fierce flames of the book fire.

'Soon your learning will be gone, and this place will be clean again. This place is no longer the territory of your pathetic clan, it has become a stronghold of Ranthas. By the edict of His Grace the Exarch of Thetia and the Emperor himself, it now comes under our jurisdiction. As do all those who inhabit it.'

His voice took on the tone of one pronouncing judgement, as Inquisitors now had a right to do within Thetia – and certainly on Domain territory.

'You are all guilty of heresy for protecting and har-bouring the evil of this place. However, you will serve your atonement as penitents under His representatives on Aquasilva, to undo the damage you have done to this place and to the lands of the Archipelago and by your efforts make them places of sanctity and piety once again.'

I gave an inward sigh of relief, thankful for small mercies. They weren't sending us to Selerian Alastre. By the time they marched us from the square and herded us into makeshift cells in the basement of the Retreat, it was almost too much effort to untie Ravenna's hands and wait to be freed before I fell asleep.

We emerged in the morning to a very different Retreat, a huge orange banner flying over it in place of the black and gold of Polinskarn. The fire in the courtyard was still going, periodically fed by more loads of books. They intended to burn the entire library, as we'd feared last night.

From the look of it, they'd begun feeding the fire with bookshelves and equipment, too; I saw wooden orna-ments, clothes and even the great portraits flung into the flames.

There were wreckers at work in the antechambers, too, pulling down every last Polinskarn fitting and ripping the black velvet curtains to shreds. When we came into the hall I stared around sadly, remembering what it had been like only the night before. All the portraits were gone, and it was bare except for the tables and another huge banner with the Domain's flame signal hanging behind what had been the dais.

One of the Sacri barked at us to kneel, and in my sleep-deprived mind I saw the hall overlaid with other images, other times.

My father's hall in Lepidor on the day the Domain had captured it, when a Prime had condemned me to the stake. It was so eerily similar I could almost see the ghostly shapes of everyone who'd been there – the Prime on my father's throne, with a man I'd once called a friend beside her. A bearded Tanethan – Lord Barca, troubled by the first stirrings of a conscience; and Admiral Sagantha Karao, who'd gone on to become the last independent Viceroy of the Archipelago.

We waited, and my thoughts moved on to the hall of the temple in Ilthys, a similar banner dominating the scene – Inquisitors too, though no Prime. That was a much happier time, and I wished Ithien Eirillia was here now, to stride into the hall and set us free in the name of the Assembly. But Ithien was gone too.

Where was Amonis? What was he waiting for?

I tried to concentrate on the present, but all I could think of now was the Imperial apartments on my brother's flagship, of kneeling there while he toasted his new alliance with the Domain.

And then, as footsteps sounded from somewhere close by, another scene, hazy and insubstantial as if I was looking through the muslin above the reception chamber. Thirty years ago in the palace in Vararu, the day Ravenna's grandfather had expelled the Domain and sparked off the Crusade.

It was only Amonis's voice that dragged me back to the

present, as he appeared on the dais with Oshadu and another Inquisitor. Two acolytes had taken up station on chairs to one side and were holding writing implements.

'We're taking an audit of the Retreat's assets,' the third Inquisitor said, coming forward while the other two watched with aloof detachment. 'You will give your names and former clan allegiances to Acolyte Haferus.'

It was like being a herd animal, I thought, as we gave our names one by one. Register of assets for Polinskarn Retreat: forty-two sea turtles, ninety goats, twelve fishing boats, eleven oceanographers. Twenty thousand volumes' worth of ashes.

'This island is now governed by religious law,' Amonis said, as the third Inquisitor walked back to join his fellows. 'In not reporting the presence of so many heretical texts, you are guilty of heresy of the third order.' The other two voiced their assent, which was all that was needed; three Inquisitors constituted a tribunal, empowered to pass any sentence allowed under the Domain's code. 'Your penance will be as I specified, to serve the Domain as penitents in whatever capacity we see fit. First, though, are any of you aware that the oceanographer Dione Ferainos Polinskarn died last night?'

I did my best to look shocked, and prayed that they took it as genuine.

'We knew she was ill, *Domine*, but . . .' Iulio was cut off.

'It is of no concern to you. I merely wish to verify what I have been told. She was a suspected heretic and we were unable to question her.'

Oshadu looked directly at me and I felt a sensation like needles in my chest.

'Should we uncover any more evidence connected with this, all connected with her will be put to the question. For the time being, you will work as you are directed in the Retreat. More penitents will be drafted in before we begin work on the larger projects.'

He looked about to dismiss us when the door by the dais opened and the mind-mage walked in.

I'd only caught a brief glimpse of him the night before, but somehow in daylight he was much more menacing, and I repressed a shiver. Had these two years here made me so timid I was jumping at shadows?

I looked at him again and thought not. At first glance he looked Thetian, but there was something about the set of his face that made me unsure. And that beard – close-cropped and pointed, not long and curled as Halettites and Tanethans wore their beards – wasn't a Thetian affectation at all.

'*Illuminato*,' Amonis said, with the faintest inclination of his head. This man was his superior, though not by much. *Illuminato* must be a mage's title, although I'd never heard it before.

'There is a matter we need to discuss. Have you finished with these?' His eyes flicked over us, eyes so dark they seemed almost black at this distance. He lingered for a second on me, and then Ravenna. Then he looked back at the Inquisitor, dismissing us. His wasn't an accent I'd ever heard.

'Put these to work, Decurion,' Amonis said to the Sacrus guarding us. 'Treat the women as you treat the men, they're only Thetians.'

To my surprise, there was no reaction on the mind-mage's face at this remark, but I didn't see anything more as we were led out again. The decurion left us in the courtyard, perhaps to find his superior.

Ravenna tugged my sleeve and I turned round, saw the tense look on her face.

'Cathan, in case they separate us, be careful of that mind-mage.'

'Why?' I would anyway, but why the concern?

'Because he's Tehaman,' was all she had time to say.

PART TWO:
THE MEMORY OF WATER

CHAPTER IV

One year later

Billowing grey clouds overhead warned of an imminent cloudburst. The sky, which only a few minutes ago had been all blue, was now more than half-covered, and in another minute the sun would disappear as well. The warm, humid air that the clouds carried with them had already arrived, and it had become increasingly uncomfortable to work over the last few minutes.

Tehama was supposed to be the Island in the Clouds, not the whole of Qalathar, but it didn't seem that way when we kept having these cloudbursts. I glanced over to the west, saw the clouds building up around the purple smudge across the horizon that marked the mountains of Tehama. Ravenna's Tehama, where she should have been months ago – no, it was more than a year now since I'd helped her escape to join the Tehaman mind-mage she'd decided was a friend after all. She'd be safe from the Domain there at least, something I envied desperately.

'They'll keep us working until the last minute,' Vespasia said bitterly. 'We're so far behind with this they're getting desperate.'

I tried to reply but could only cough.

'Don't try,' she said. 'Can you tell me whether I've got this straight?'

We were a few dozen feet from the front of the workings, part of the team levelling up the trench to its final shape. It was better at least than being part of the earth-cutting or moving teams, but slow and frustrating work for those doing it. I at least had the advantage of being a surveyor, so I didn't have to do manual work, but the conditions were terrible. There was little point anyway, because the storm would turn the whole place into a lake.

I glanced up a couple of times while we measured the trench, and each time the amount of blue sky was markedly smaller.

Only when the first raindrops began to fall, and the noise of the wind began to drown out the sound of picks and shovels, did the overseers call a halt. I picked up my tools, pushed them into a canvas bag and stumbled to the nearest ladder; they wouldn't let us leave tools in the trenches during these storms, in case they were buried too.

Ten or eleven people were already clustered round the base of the ladder, and I had to wait a minute or two before it was my turn and I could scramble up and out.

The mountains above us had vanished behind sheets of rain, and I could hear the sound of distant thunder.

'I'll take your tool bag,' said Vespasia, emerging from the trench behind me. I shook my head, but she wrested it out of my hand and started running back to the camp. The overseers had disappeared as soon as they'd stopped work, and by now would be safely in their half-buried, stone-built hut.

Vespasia had the edge on me as usual, and by the time I reached the low, broken wall at the edge of the camp, gasping for breath, she was already inside the tent we shared with four other people.

It couldn't really be called a tent — just a large piece of worn fabric stretched between three walls of a ruined room, in the lee of the wind. There wasn't even enough headroom for me to stand up in it.

Two of the others were already there by the time I arrived and collapsed against the back wall, and the rest weren't far behind. Vespasia had stacked their spades in one corner and had brought out our hoarded water-gourd from its hiding place.

'Have a drink,' she ordered. 'No argument. You need it today.'

The others nodded consent, I took the gourd and took a few swigs – even the warm, stale water inside was nectar to my parched throat.

As I passed the gourd on, Vespasia propped our make-shift wind-shield against the mouth of the shelter – even though we were facing away from the wind, some rain would still get inside.

Then there was nothing to do except sit back in the gloom and wait while the cloudburst saturated the island of Qalathar, drenching both the cedar forest around us and the cloud forest of the highlands, making hours more work for us while the water was removed. And even though the water had fallen from the sky, the lake formed in the trench would come ready-equipped with insects and the odd leech.

'The overseers won't like this,' Vespasia said. 'Another delay, and it'll take us a couple of days just to drain all the water.'

'I heard there's a high-up coming to visit in a couple of days,' said another man. Pahinu was quite taciturn and kept to himself, but had his ears open. He seemed to be right far more often than the rumour mill; we thought he was probably an informer, promised a reduced term of service here in exchange for letting the overseers know what was going on. But since he'd once been an oceanographer like the rest of us, we tolerated him.

'Someone in Tandaris wants to know why this is going so slowly, so he'll shout at the overseers and they'll shout at us,' Vespasia said. 'Bastards.'

Even after more than a year, she'd never quite managed to curb her tongue, which had earned her more beatings than the rest of us.

'Anything else you've picked up?' Vespasia asked Pahinu.

'Two more men taken by animals last night,' Pahinu said, a hint of fear on his face. 'They must be hiding somewhere in the ruins; heaven knows why they came here in the first place, when there's no wildlife for miles around.'

'They're getting bolder.'

'Of course they are,' Vespasia said. 'The overseers are too scared to go and hunt them out, ever since that guard went for a walk and never came back. These man-eaters are on to a winner.'

'Maybe that's why the high-up's coming,' I said, my throat moist enough to talk again. 'You know how much some of the priests like hunting, and I doubt they've had a chance to do it in an abandoned city before.'

'I'm surprised. Heaven knows, there are enough ruins in Equatoria, let alone here.'

That was too true. I remembered the miserable journey here a year ago, when we'd disembarked near the ruins of Poseidonis, a far larger city than Ulkhalinan. It had been the first time I'd seen Poseidonis, famous though it was, but seeing the expanse of ruins had brought nothing but sadness.

'Or maybe,' said one of the other men, 'they're bringing their novices up here to show them what misery looks like. "My pupil, I want you to send us even more penitents than we already have here".'

'They've got enough penitents elsewhere, I think,' Vespasia said. 'I heard some of the guards talking today; apparently their rations have been cut too, because the fishing fleets have been hit so hard. What do they expect, if they arrest all the oceanographers and half the fishermen, and send untrained convicts to do their work?'

We glanced at each other uneasily. If the crisis was as bad as it looked and the project wasn't getting anywhere, the first to go would be the slaves – or penitents, as the Domain liked to call us – building it. Useless mouths to feed.

'They can't, not yet,' Vespasia said, echoing my thoughts. 'Yes, this is taking a long time, but if it works they should have enough food for a while to come.'

Would they? It had been three years, apparently, since they began construction of a network of canals in the interior to bring water down from the cloud forests into the plain and make communications easier.

One day, Sarhaddon had proclaimed, this could all be fertile farmland, irrigated by water from the hundreds of little streams that trickled down from the hills. Qalathar would at last be made useful and productive – but that was a long way in the future, and another year's planting opportunities had gone.

All of which explained why almost a thousand dissident Archipelagans and Thetians had been drafted in to dig this huge canal, diverting the water from the river Unul and the nearest lake to where it was more useful. Digging in through the stony soil of the cedar forest and the deposits left by the storms, like this one, that actually dropped rain down here rather than all in the mountains.

The air inside the shelter, already close, grew more and more stuffy. There was nothing we could do, not with the pelting rain outside. The roof began to sag slightly as water collected in it. I hoped we'd piled enough bricks on the edges to hold it in place.

After an hour or two the keening of the wind grew softer, and eventually we heard the ring of a bell summoning everyone back to work. Back to a few more hours of soul-destroying work, redoing everything we'd accomplished this morning, before dusk put an end to it for a day.

When the sun finally set and we staggered back to the camp for a meagre meal, there was still waist-deep water in the trench. I had a weal on my arm from where a bad-tempered overseer had lashed out indiscriminately with a whip. It was hard to tell sometimes who was more unhappy with the situation, the slaves or the priestly overseers who'd been assigned the thankless and arduous duty of watching us rather than preaching holy war.

Supper was a thin soup and some stale bread, served roughly in proportion to size – an unusual act of logic on the part of the men in charge, although I wasn't sure how good an idea it was. We ate it in the shelter, drank our evening's ration of water as the last traces of the tropical sunset faded from the sky, and went to sleep covered by rough, ragged blankets. Thankfully, despite the lack of trees in the area immediately around the diggings, Qalathar was never very cold, but we had no clothing other than the tunics we worked in, and so we were glad of any extra warmth.

I woke in the night to a terrifying sound from not very far away, a scream abruptly cut off, then the roaring of what was, unmistakably, a tiger. I heard the guards cursing, the sound of several of them trying to find it, but then the noise died away and I went back to sleep. I'd pay for it tomorrow if I didn't get enough rest.

I never learnt the name of the man they'd taken that night, as I rarely did; there were more than five hundred people and a hundred guards in the camp. The Domain was trying to keep us alive to finish the project, but heat, exhaustion and the animals were taking a constant toll. Sixty people or more had been lost since we started, twenty in the last two months.

It was that day that the 'high-up' mentioned by Pahinu arrived, near the end of the break for midday meal. We were sitting in the shelter to eat, making sure that no-one stole what few possessions we'd managed to hoard, when we heard a shout in Halettite from the wooden watch-tower erected on the tallest of the broken walls.

'Maybe he's seen one of those wretched tigers,' Vespasia commented. 'The entire guard force will go and every last one of them will be eaten.'

'If only the soldiers were that incompetent,' I said.

Thankfully for the large number of women here, the men guarding us were Ranthas soldiers, inferior Sacri who were bound by the same vows of poverty and chastity.

'I think a hundred guards failing to deal with a single pack of mangy tigers is quite incompetent.'

'They aren't mangy now, not after the meals they've had,' said someone else, but no-one was in the mood even for black humour.

There was an answering shout from another guard down below, and a brief, loud conversation. A moment later, the bell began to ring, and shouts from the overseers urging us to get to work.

'Someone coming to visit,' Vespasia said, bolting the last of her food. 'Here, quickly, finish the water.'

By the time the dignitaries, whoever they were, arrived, we were back at work in the sweltering heat. They gave us the bare minimum of two hours in the worst heat of the day, the least they could get away with and not lose far larger numbers. Rumour had it that they couldn't afford to ship any more slaves up. Or that they couldn't spare any more soldiers to guard increased numbers. Or, worst of all, that all the other slaves had been killed to save food. That was something I didn't want to contemplate.

As I marked out the straight line for the crew to dig along, I heard the sound of chariot wheels and horses' hooves: quite a few, by the sound of it. Midian, the Halettite Exarch, had surrounded himself with fellow-countrymen who insisted on bringing their chariots to Qalathar despite the unsuitable terrain. Priests were exempt from the vow of poverty, but not from complaining about the lack of a hippodrome in Tandaris.

As the chariots ground to a halt and I heard snatches of Halettite, I tried to make out what was being said but failed. I knew a little Halettite, enough to translate commands, but nowhere near enough to understand what they were saying. Someone wasn't happy, if I was any judge; I thought it was the Presbyter in command of the camp, a Halettite like several of his men.

After a few moments the sound of hooves came again, at a more leisurely pace this time – they must have been taking the horses over to drink at one of the springs in the ruins.

There was no time to listen for more, though, as an overseer approached, squelching through the mud in the middle of the trench. He was a bad-tempered brute normally, a Qalathari who'd turned religious fanatic to survive, but now he was the picture of hawk-eyed competence and kept a disciplined eye on everything he saw. He was only wearing a kilted robe, but I didn't envy the soldiers up above us in their scale armour.

Wooden bridges had been erected across the trench at intervals to allow passage across and, more importantly, give the overseers a place to stand and watch; it was on to the nearest of these that the party of dignitaries strolled a few minutes later. I made sure I was facing away from them, because it was too likely that one of them might have met me.

As I moved along the line of the trench, sinking cane rods into the ground to mark the edge of the flat bottom, I heard voices raised in argument on the bridge; definitely the camp commandant, but at least one of the people he was arguing with didn't sound like a Halettite. The voice had a peculiar inflection that I knew well: the accent of a Thetian aristocrat who'd been taught the courtly Archipelagan of forty years ago with all its different nuances.

But what was a Thetian doing here? The Thetians were allied with the Domain, but what reason would any Thetian have to visit these irrigation works, for Ranthas's sake? The Emperor had signed over Qalathar's interior exclusively to the Domain, so why would he or his Viceroy want to interfere?

The commandant became more and more irate, but the Thetian's tone never wavered. I heard the words 'penitents' and 'survey teams' but couldn't make out anything more.

Until, that was, the argument came to an end and another voice broke in, a voice which I definitely knew, speaking in Archipelagan.

'Fifty penitents are needed who have experience of working underwater,' he called down. 'There is some urgent work to be done on a dam in the west. It's no more dangerous than what you're doing now, but it's under-water, and you get a couple of months away from this.'

Vespasia and I looked at each other. *Never volunteer for anything.*

There was silence. There wouldn't be that many here who could do what he asked. All Thetians and Archipelagans had the ability to breathe underwater. It required acclimatisation as a child, which only the Thetians considered essential. But experience of working underwater was quite different. Marines, masons, ship-wrights, coral divers, oceanographers – there weren't many other trades which gave that experience. And I doubted there'd be many of the first three trades repre-sented here; they were too valuable to be sent somewhere like this.

'Yes, I know what you're thinking,' the voice said again. 'None of those who volunteer will ever come back. As it happens, this project is more than usually urgent. If the dam fails, I can guarantee you'll be stuck here for the next five years.' Another man interrupted in Halettite, and after a brief pause the voice resumed. 'So those of you who can work underwater have only yourselves to blame, and everyone else will know whose fault it is.'

Could we believe him? I stared at the mass of dirty, mud-caked slaves in the trench, the earth walls that ran on for miles behind us and the untidy face of the workings in front. I could breathe underwater as well as I could in air, and Vespasia was the same, half Archipelagan but brought up in Thetia.

'Cathan,' Vespasia whispered with an urgent note of warning, 'never trust them.'

'Why else would they want water-breathers?'

'To find the wreck of some treasure barge at the bottom of the Inland Sea? To infiltrate some secret heretic hideaway? I doubt this has an ulterior motive, like killing anyone who can breathe underwater, but even if they're telling the truth, what next? There are stretches of water where no-one in their right mind would swim.'

'Vespasia, listen to yourself,' I said, 'Yes, maybe they're lying, but is it any worse than being here? Do we have any guarantee that there won't be another crisis the moment we finish this canal, or even that he's telling the truth and we will be stuck here?'

'You just want to get back to some water,' she said, with a resigned look on her face. 'I agree with you on that one, and at least wherever they take us will be new for a while.'

I didn't mention that the man who'd called us knew my face, and that if he was here he'd almost certainly changed sides since I last met him. We turned round to look up at the bridge.

'We can,' Vespasia shouted.

Slowly, four or five other men and women that I could see raised their hands. One, rather worryingly, was Pahinu.

'All of you, climb out of the trench then,' the second Thetian said. 'Bring your tools. You too, surveyors.' He pointed at Vespasia and me.

Leaving the canal for what I hoped was a long time brought no feelings of elation, only a sick feeling in my stomach as I wondered whether I'd done something terribly wrong.

At the top I looked round, saw a group of unlimbered chariots in the lee of the ruins and a group of about twenty slaves with a detachment of soldiers standing by them. Most of the soldiers were Halettites, but two of them weren't, and I blinked more than once before I convinced myself I wasn't imagining things. I suppose I should have expected them, given the presence of Thetian emissaries, but finding scallop-helmed Thetian Imperial Guards with no admiral or minister in sight was unexpected, to say the least.

The party of visitors walked off the bridge and came over to us, giving me a first good look at them. The commandant and his adjutants I knew, but with him were two imposing Halettite priests with magnificent oiled beards. Noblemen, I could have told at once, even without seeing the servants fanning them.

The last two men were undoubtedly Thetians, looking more at ease than the Halettites, even though we were quite a way inland. Thetia was wet and humid – like Qalathar – and virtually no Thetian cities or towns were inland. Both the Halettites looked rather unhappy, but I didn't feel any sympathy for them.

'Many thanks,' said the man I recognised, sweeping a perfunctory glance over us. It was the first time anyone other than a fellow-slave had thanked me for anything in four years. 'We've got two more sets of workings to go, so you'll ride in the chariots. Don't try to escape, you know it's pointless.'

He turned away and went to a bridge further down. Meanwhile the soldiers led us over to stand with the others. These weren't the second-rate timeservers of the home army who were guarding the workings, but elite guards, their armour and weapons much better quality. The two Thetians kept apart, looking uncomfortable even though their scale armour was much lighter than the Halettites'.

The slaves already gathered there acknowledged our existence but didn't talk. At least we were in the shade here, and I was glad of a few minutes out of the sun. If we were really going to the highlands, it would be much cooler, and with any luck wetter. For all the luxuriance of the cedar forest, it rained little here and the soil was dry and dusty. I loathed being dirty, too, the way the dust worked itself in everywhere.

Our respite from the sun was short-lived, and it wasn't long before the dignitaries came back leading another group of four slaves – they had thirty now, by my count. The charioteers led the horses back out of the ruins and hitched them to their vehicles; I wasn't much good at judging horseflesh, but they seemed sturdy animals, almost all of the commonest bronze-maned kind. The most richly decorated chariot had a team of four silver-maned whites, and I guessed that belonged to one of the Halettite officials. This obviously wasn't a particularly important group.

'Three of you in each chariot now,' the second Thetian said, transmitting the important Halettite's orders.

It seemed a cumbersome way to do things, I thought, as they divided us up and secured us by our wrists to the chariot rail. Not, one of the other slaves said, in case we escaped, but because it would stop anyone unused to chariots from falling out.

'These are infantry chariots,' Vespasia said, as a Halettite soldier climbed in and gathered up the reins. They were much larger than any chariot I'd ever driven. 'Some of their infantry drive into battle on these, then disembark after the first charge. Quite an effective tactic.'

I was jerked backwards as we started moving, but managed to keep my balance as the horses accelerated. Within a few minutes, the workings were lost to view and the ruins of Ulkhalinan hidden behind the trees. Then we headed northwest along the line of the valley, riding down the narrow, trickling stream that provided the water for the whole camp.

As we went on to an unknown fate in the mountains, I

couldn't help wondering whether fate had dealt me a good hand or not in allowing my path to cross again that of Ithien Eirillia. And what the defiantly republican Governor of Ilthys was doing in such company.

CHAPTER V

By the time we reached the shores of the feeble River Maktau, there were fifty-seven slaves riding in the chariots, and the Halettite priest in charge was therefore in a good mood. His name, I'd found out, was Shalmaneser, a minor Halettite noble who'd risen by joining the Domain and now held a chapter post at the Temple in Tandaris.

He apparently didn't know the first thing about dams, but this wasn't seen as a problem. The first Thetian and the other Halettite were engineers — the technical matters were their business.

The Maktau valley was like every other in the interior of Qalathar; quite narrow with very steep sides covered by cedar interspersed with scrub bushes. Most of them were slightly yellow or brown from the heat of high summer, and didn't seem in very good condition. The only thing that looked healthy was the substantial stone fort on an artificial rise close to the river, its walls impressively high.

As I realised when the chariots halted outside the narrow front gate, which seemed far too small for the wall that contained it, the fort was actually quite old; it had been destroyed or knocked down once and rebuilt recently, with much smaller stones.

We loosened the ropes ourselves and climbed out of the chariots before being herded round the side of the fort to a wooden quay, to which were tied two barges and a smaller passenger craft. Shalmaneser made a great show of inspecting them, although from the look of it he didn't really care, and then barked an order before disappearing with the fort's commander through a small gate in the riverside wall.

'It'll be an hour or so before we leave,' Ithien said, pausing a moment as his other companions followed. 'The river's quite safe, there's nothing living in it any more, so if you want to wash you may.'

It was the first time in fourteen months that I'd been immersed in water, and even though it was the cloudy, tepid water of a life-starved river, it was still wonderful. It washed away my mud-caked anonymity, but Ithien was sure to recognise me sooner or later. As he'd once said, I didn't belong in a crowd.

Judging from my reflection in the water, I didn't even belong in the kind of civilised places one would find a crowd. I was gaunt and haggard, and even though I'd managed to keep my hair fairly short, it was still a mess. The last traces of anxiety at leaving Ulkhalinan vanished; I would rather be anywhere than there.

When we came out the guards herded us on to the first barge. It was large, shallow-bottomed and driven upstream by a single, huge sail. There was barely enough space for us to sit, let alone lie down when it was time to sleep, but a moth-eaten old sail gave protection from the midday sun, and the sound of water lapping around the edges was something I hadn't heard for far too long.

Only once we were all inside did I get a proper look at my fellow-captives for the first time. About half looked pure Thetian, probably renegades or victims of the Emperor's Inquisition, while the rest were an assorted bunch of Archipelagans, some with flattened southern features. All of them had the same worn look, the resigned faces of men and women with no future. They'd been betrayed or handed over to the preaching Venatics for the most part; in many cases their towns or villages had been whipped up by rhetoric, their fellow-citizens anxious to avert the threat of a Crusade that constantly hung over the islands.

Their expressions began to change once the barges cast

off and began to make their progress upriver. Ithien, Shalmaneser and the others travelled astern on the smaller passenger boat, which had the luxury of cabins; it was also upwind of our barge and its fellow, which had been loaded with horses and pack animals.

'Why do they need those two Thetians to repair this dam of theirs?' one of the men nearby asked when people had begun talking again. 'There aren't any dams in Thetia, you'd think the Halettites would be able to do something for themselves.'

'It's not a dam,' said another despondently. 'They want us for something else, something they're not telling us about.'

'Tehaman treasure,' said a short, burly man who'd managed to keep his beard vaguely neat and pointed. 'There's only one set of mountains west of here, and that's the Tehama range. Stands to reason that the Tehamans couldn't have taken everything with them when the Thetians drove them out. Now the Domain is short of cash, they'll go to any lengths. If it's that kind of diving they want us to do, it explains why the Thetians are here.'

'Look, whatever they want us to do,' Pahinu said, 'we're not back in cursed Ulkhalinan any more.'

'I'd rather stay in Ulkhalinan than burst my lungs in some godforsaken lake so the Domain can buy itself out of the mess it's made,' the first man said.

There was a chorus of dissent, and five or six people started arguing with him at once. The burly man looked at the last speaker in vague disgust. 'Then why did you leave it, if you're so fond of the place?'

'They all knew I used to be a pearl fisher,' he muttered. 'Couldn't have stayed.'

'And now you're here, so stop complaining. Do something useful like listen to the guards, see if any of them have a clue where we're going.'

That night the barges stopped on a low, marshy island

in the middle of a small marshy lake, just below where the river became unnavigable. Most of the lake was shallow enough to wade through and there were a few scraggly reeds growing in it. It was a place devoid of charm.

We disembarked and on Shalmaneser's orders built a fire with some of the wood from the stores boat, so that he could have a proper meal. We ate a lukewarm, thin soup on a patch of clumpy ground by the fire, watching the priests and the two Thetians eating on a low table on the deck of their boat.

Vespasia and I found ourselves sitting with Pahinu and the burly man, whose name was Oailos.

'They don't get on all that well, do they?' Oailos said, staring at the small party of dignitaries. In this desolate landscape, the little boat with its high stern and awning-covered deck seemed an outpost of civilisation. 'Shalmaneser thinks the two engineers are beneath his notice, and as far as he's concerned the other Thetian is an effeminate nobody.'

'He does like showing off, rather, doesn't he?' Vespasia remarked. Even out here Ithien's clothes were well-made and in bright colours, not entirely suitable for the circumstances. 'I get the feeling he doesn't approve of slavery.'

'None of the Thetians do,' Oailos said scornfully. 'They pass laws against it, but all the Domain needs to do is call it "penitence" and it's fine with them. Did the Thetians in Ilthys protest when two dozen of us were shipped off as penitents? I did some work for them there, helped rebuild a courtyard in the Jontian consulate and some other stuff besides, but when someone told the Venatics I was a heretic, they didn't lift a finger to help me.'

Oailos didn't bother to hide the hatred in his voice. If he was as bitter as he sounded, and not another stool pigeon, he'd be in danger from Pahinu. If Pahinu was indeed an informer. But if he'd been promised a reduced term of service, why would he risk volunteering?

'It doesn't matter if they don't like each other,' Vespasia said. 'All that means is that Shalmaneser will sit around all day while the other three do all the work.'

'And take the credit, you're right,' he said. 'Well I for one would like to know where I'm going, so if you pick up any titbits and pass them on, I'll remember the favour.'

Oailos finished off his supper and started looking for a place to lie down that wasn't too uneven.

'I hope the guards are awake,' said Pahinu. 'This place is probably infested with crocodiles.'

I felt a pinprick on my arm and slapped my palm against it. The insect I'd killed was tiny, it looked hardly large enough to inflict any damage at all. Clouds of midges swarmed above our heads, just visible against the afterglow.

'It's infested with bloodsuckers, at least,' I said, lying down and wrapping myself in the rough blanket I'd been given. 'Heavens, I hope we're out of this swamp soon.'

The next morning we left the boats behind and began marching westwards. Our sandals hadn't been designed for this kind of treatment and my feet were blistered by the time we'd gone a few miles, the terrain growing steadily more extreme. The leaders were all right, of course, mounted as they were, but the rest of us marched along in the dust kicked up by their horses and surrounded by bad-tempered soldiers. They were governed by the discipline of their order, but even the leaders were eager to be involved in some fighting for a change, the chance to win a place among the blessed.

Shalmaneser's companion, the engineer whose name I finally discovered was Murshash, seemed very concerned that we were properly fed to build up our strength, something I found rather ominous. Others concurred, including Oailos, who had become our leader by some unspoken agreement.

Once Oailos had found out Ithien's name, I disclosed as

74

much as I was willing to about Ithien: that he had been Governor of Ilthys for the old Assembly, and an ardent republican. I didn't mention that I'd met him.

'Why did the Emperor let him change sides, then?' Vespasia asked. 'It's not as if there was a shortage of men he could rely on.'

'It means he's a slippery customer, not what he seems,' Oailos said firmly. 'Shalmaneser's a fairly straightforward arrogant Halettite and the two engineers are fairly inconsequential. Ithien's probably anxious to show the Emperor how loyal he is, so he won't care how much damage he does, as long as he's successful.'

So far Ithien and the others had kept very much apart, hardly paying us any attention as they guided their horses up the tortuous paths into the mountains. That had to change when we reached our destination, and sooner or later he was sure to notice me. I had to be careful, and since Vespasia already knew much of the story, I told her all of what she'd missed before – which wasn't actually that much.

I'd seen the mountains of Tehama from the river, a grey line in the distance, and they grew higher and higher during two days of walking, at least when we could see anything through the canopy of cedars and then, increasingly, jungle trees. They were titans compared to the hills around us, rearing too far up to see their peaks. Far too tall for an island the size of Qalathar, but they were there, grim and towering as we came nearer and nearer.

The place we were going to was right at their foot, and it wasn't until we thought we couldn't go any further without a steep climb that we reached the dam.

It was totally unexpected; I topped a rise in the path and found myself looking down into a chasm, the ground dropping away a few dozen yards in front of me down to a frighteningly distant blue water. It was somehow familiar, but I didn't remember being anywhere like this, and at first I only looked at the dam.

It blocked the end wall of the canyon in front and to the left, a smooth arc between two massive spurs of rock. White stone glistened in the sunlight, rearing high above the surprisingly placid water below. I remembered the cliffs of Tehama as dropping down into raging white water, not the bowl-shaped lake below us – or was it a lake? Not a lake, a channel, I realised as we went a little further along; it bent abruptly a mile or two to the right.

'Now I believe Ithien,' Pahinu said, staring at the stone-built edifice. 'I don't remember any mention of Orethura building something like this, though.'

'He didn't,' was Oailos's answer when I mentioned it. 'This wasn't part of Orethura's realm. This must be Tehaman work, at least two hundred years old.'

'So something's gone wrong, and the Halettites don't know how to repair it,' I said. 'That explains why they needed Thetians, people who build in stone rather than mud brick.' But not why it was so vital.

'Sounds right. At least they told us the truth there. Now we have to hope that whatever's wrong with the wretched thing is near the top, because the lake on the other side must be a hundred feet deep if it's an inch.'

· 'Ithien's Thetian, he knows we can't dive anywhere near that deep.'

'Ithien's not in charge,' Oailos said. 'You're far too willing to trust that man. He's a turncoat and an Imperial officer. Just because he seems pleasant, it doesn't stop him being one of the enemy.'

The procession was halted in an open space above the water, below a narrow path that was only wide enough for one man at a time. It was then, as the soldiers started to organise everyone into single file, that the moment I'd been dreading came. Ithien, who'd been sitting on the beach talking to Shalmaneser, walked over to supervise the arrangement.

'Murshash wants to speak to all the surveyors now; I think there are six of you.'

I stepped out of my allotted place behind a pack mule and moved cautiously round the animal, as the other five detached themselves from the crowd. I was the only man, and all but one of the others were Thetian. I wasn't really surprised, given that Thetians tended to be shorter and were more likely to be properly educated. Especially the women, but education in the Archipelago hadn't been the same since the Crusade and the destruction of all the universities.

'Good,' Ithien led us over to where Murshash and the Thetian engineer waited with two other men, both Thetians, in the shadow of a pile of rocks. 'These four men are in charge of the project.'

One of the two newcomers, tall for a Thetian and quite cadaverous-looking, fiddled impatiently with his dusty tunic. 'Are these all the surveyors you could find?'

'I'm afraid so.' Ithien glanced back at us, and his gaze rested on me for a second. I saw his eyes widen in shock, and he caught his breath, breaking off without saying anything. I felt my heart beating wildly. Please let him not say anything, in Thetis's name.

'Are you all right?' Murshash asked in broken Archipelagan.

Ithien coughed awkwardly. 'Yes, it's no problem.' He went hastily back to his original subject. 'The overseers were very bad-tempered, they wouldn't let me have any surveyors who didn't have the experience we asked for.'

'They'll be still more bad-tempered when they've had to spend another decade digging irrigation channels through that godforsaken forest.' He stared imperiously at us. 'I am Sevasteos Decaris, Imperial Architect and in charge of patching up this dam before it bursts. You're all competent enough to have been appointed surveyors by the idiots who are running the canal project. That doesn't cut any ice with me. If you can do your job, I'll leave you as surveyors. If not, I'll go through until I find some people who can.'

He introduced the other two Thetians – Emisto, Ithien's companion, and Biades, who presumably had already been at the dam. Then he ordered us to follow him up to the dam.

The path zigzagged up the side of the spur, just good enough for a horse or a mule, but very uncomfortable for us. The narrowness of the enclosing cliffs trapped the air and turned the path into a cauldron. Walking in the dust kicked up by the horses' hooves didn't help either.

The heat reflected by the bare rocks rising steeply on one side of the trail was intense, enough to give me the beginnings of a headache. At least the pack animals would carry everything up, not the penitents.

At one point we passed through a small dip in the ground, passing out of sight of the dam entirely, but when we emerged we were slightly above and behind the dam.

Exhausted as I was after the climb, I gasped when I saw the long, winding lake trapped by the dam, a sheet of water glinting silver in the sunlight and surrounded by green vegetation on the far side, out of place amidst the bleak grandeur of the cliffs. It looked so much like a shard cut from the sea and transported up here that, for a moment, I could almost imagine it was the sea. A lot of the far shore was hidden, but I thought I could make out the shine of falling water on the Tehaman side, where after a few hundred yards of foreshore the cliffs reared sheer for more than a mile.

After the tepid water of the rivers, it was a vision of Paradise.

The path switch-backed one last time down to the level of the parapet, where a broad walkway, wide enough for five or six men to walk abreast, led in a smooth curve across to a cluster of weathered stone buildings in a fairly flat open space on the other side. The cliffs weren't quite as close as I'd thought.

'Why do we need the pack animals?' asked Emisto. 'I know it's a bad path up, but surely if we brought the stuff up little by little it would save on fodder.'

'We'll be needing raw materials,' Sevasteos said bossily. 'There's a quarry about three miles away, and grazing grounds on the way.'

They dismounted and led their mounts along the top of the dam, talking amongst themselves as we looked spellbound out over the lake. I couldn't help noticing markings on the inner side of the parapet and ropes fixed to it at one point near the middle. I thought they would stop and examine it now, but Sevasteos kept on going, perhaps uneasy about having the horses up here for more than the shortest possible time.

Thankfully, it was blessedly cool up here, and the water looked surprisingly clear − peering over the parapet, I could see the pale stone wall extending down quite a distance, although it was far too deep to see the bottom.

'Who built this?' one of the others asked Sevasteos.

'The Tehamans,' he said. 'Sometime before the Tuonetar War. It bends further round, so you can't see the ruined cities at the edges where there's enough flat ground for agriculture. This was all part of Lower Tehama. Quite impressive, actually.' For non-Thetians, was the unspoken subtext. Murshash didn't pick up on the veiled contempt, or chose to ignore it.

At the other side, the Architect handed his horse to a groom and led the way inside one of the nearest buildings. A single room took up most of the space inside, and two men were bent over tables in the middle, hard at work on plans.

'The Emperor sent an engineer out after the storms last year,' Sevasteos said, unrolling a plan on the large central table. 'There are some serious flaws in the central section which need to be repaired, otherwise it'll give way with the next set of serious storms.' He glanced out of the window at a cloudless blue sky. 'No sign of those at the moment, and the weather's been set for a while, but you can never tell. This is actually only the first stage in a larger project, later there'll be some work down below but I doubt that'll happen for a few years. What's important is that once the dam is secure, the Viceroy can start sending farmers up here to start work on the old orchards and market gardens. There's probably fishing potential in the lake, too, but it can't be risked unless we can be sure the dam will hold.' Viceroy indeed. Charidemus was Sarhaddon's mouthpiece, as everyone knew. But, according to the Domain, Sarhaddon and his Venatic Order were only *spiritual advisers* to the secular rulers – Thetian Viceroys, Governors and Archipelagan puppet presidents. Individual Venatics didn't hold any official power.

He spent the next half-hour, as the pack-trains from below began arriving, elaborating on the technical details of what he intended to do. Most of it I didn't understand, but he made it clear at the beginning that we weren't expected to. We were here to do all the mundane jobs the architects couldn't be concerned with and to act as technical overseers: this was an order of magnitude more complicated than canal-building.

Once Sevasteos had finished explaining, we went back out on to the dam to the place with the ropes on it, where the most serious flaw apparently was.

'How far underwater do we have to work?' I asked, staring down into the greenish-blue depths.

Sevasteos looked irritated at having to consider such a mundane thing.

'Shouldn't be more than fifteen feet,' he said. 'Perfectly possible. If the cracks go deeper, we might arrange to let a little water out.'

I was no engineer, but surely any cracks to worry about would be those in the bottom of the dam, not the top. If something went wrong with the upper section, it would cause a small flood, but not on the scale Sevasteos had suggested.

Oh well, he knew more about it than I did. At the moment all I wanted to do was get into the water, the first chance I'd had to swim properly in such a long time. It was a desire that would seem irrational, maybe even weak, to someone who wasn't Thetian. The Halettites would never understand it in a thousand years, but it was in every Thetian's blood, and in mine, perhaps, more strongly than most. Even though I'd grown up tens of thousands of miles from Thetia, I was still every bit as much one of the People of the Ocean as Ithien or Sevasteos.

'Wouldn't it be better to put up a coffer dam?' Emisto said, looking down at the lake with a calculating eye. 'Then we could see if the faults go deeper. We don't want to patch up the cracks near the parapet and then find out it's only a cosmetic repair.'

'There isn't the time,' Sevasteos said flatly. 'Or the materials, or the people. Our original engineer surveyed the front face and couldn't find anything wrong.'

Not that Sevasteos would have taken the man's word for it; he would have gone over all the work with a fine-tooth comb. I wondered how the original surveyors had discovered the flaws on this side, under ten or twelve feet of water. Had they used slaves as well?

'But if the base goes, there'll be more than just a flood,' Emisto went on doggedly. 'If we only do half the job, there's still a disaster waiting to happen.'

'I said, there is not a problem,' Sevasteos said, turning harsh grey eyes on his subordinate.

Murshash looked vaguely troubled, and spoke before the architect could change the subject. 'I'm not happy, Lord Architect,' he said slowly. 'If there are flaws on the inside up here, there might be more further down.'

'But there's no way we can do anything about them,' Sevasteos said with considerably more politeness than he'd given Emisto; the Halettite was a priest, if only a lowly one. 'If the Exarch will give us the wood and the extra slaves we need, it might be possible. As things stand, we're doing the best we can.'

'I will talk to Shalmaneser.'

I saw, but Murshash must have missed, the momentary eye contact Ithien and Sevasteos made. There was more to this than there seemed to be.

'Talk to him when we're done surveying,' Sevasteos said. 'I need you with us now, Murshash.'

I wondered which of them would get to Shalmaneser first, and suspected it would be Sevasteos.

We walked along the bridge, examining each place in as much detail as was possible without going into the water. He intended to fix the cracks with metal clamps and water-setting concrete, something the Thetians had mastered centuries ago and passed on to the rest of the world. Murshash seemed to know a little about stone, but even though he was the most qualified of the Domain priests in Qalathar, apparently, for working on the dam, he still possessed only a fraction of the Thetians' technical knowledge.

He was one of the few bearable Halettites I'd come across, and seemed not to resent his ignorance, though I could see he was worried by the thought that they wouldn't do a proper job. That was a professionalism I hadn't expected to find, given that it concerned him very little and wouldn't affect him very much. The food crisis was, I supposed, an important matter, but the dam had no strategic importance. There couldn't possibly be anything of value in that chasm.

'There are still a few hours left today,' Sevasteos said, squinting up into the sky, when he'd finished the tour. 'We can start building the scaffolding at the first two points. Biades, take the surveyors and show them what's to be done, then gather up the workers.'

Neither he nor any of the other Thetians ever mentioned the word *penitent* if they could help it, and even then it was easy to see their distaste. Perhaps they hoped that by denying the reality it would go away, but I was grateful that all of them, even the abrupt Sevasteos, treated us as human beings – unlike most of the priests I'd come across since my capture at the Retreat. Many of Murshash's people had difficulty seeing even free Archipelagans as entirely human.

What Sevasteos had called the 'scaffolding' was simply a framework supporting planks that would be suspended over the damaged areas to make work easier. Lightweight cane poles had been brought from somewhere, and the other surveyors and I were left to supervise their assembly into the structures Biades had specified.

A few soldiers watched from a distance, but they'd obviously been ordered not to intervene, and we were entrusted with saws and proper, sharpened knives to cut the poles and the vine-rope that secured them together.

By the time the sun disappeared behind a jagged peak to the west, casting the huts and the ground around them into shadow, we'd nearly finished both sets of scaffolding. But even though Emisto took the trouble to congratulate us on a good day's work, and the soup we were served for supper was considerably better than in the workings at Ukhalinan, I still felt on edge.

It wasn't that I hadn't been into the water yet, though as I finished the last of my soup, sitting on a rock looking out over the still water of the lake, I felt more grimy than ever with the water so near, but that was merely a physical discomfort.

'Glad to be here?' said Oailos, wandering up to sit down beside me, brushing little pebbles away with his hand to make the ground more even. Vespasia was over at the fire trying to wheedle some more soup out of the surly cooks.

'It's much better than the canal,' I said, musingly.

83

'But not perfect?'

I shook my head.

'Something still doesn't fit,' Oailos said with a grimace. 'One of the other surveyors told me most of what we'll be doing. I used to be a mason, and I can tell you, it doesn't fit.'

'Our repairs? With the concrete and clamps?'

'Nothing wrong with those. No, it's bringing all of us out here for a few cosmetic repairs. For heaven's sake, the Imperial Architect working on a pathetic project like this? It's ridiculous. That's the highest post any architect can hold, and with the Emperor's fort-building programme in full swing it makes even less sense.'

That was something that hadn't occurred to me, and Oailos noticed my surprise.

'Architects and masons have pecking orders like every-one else,' he said, with just a hint of scorn for an aristocrat's careless assumption that only in court circles did one find politics. Unlike most of my former class, though, I had experience of more than just the intrigues of the powerful. The politicking in even a small oceanographic station was every bit as intense as in the Imperial court – it was just the stakes that were different.

'Yes, of course. But if this is as vital as he said, surely the Emperor's just demonstrating how seriously he takes the alliance?' I suggested. 'He leaves everything outside the military to his Domain advisers, so this may not be his work at all.'

'But if the damage is only to the top of the dam, and the lake isn't doing anything at the moment, there's no need to send such an important man.'

'He denies there's anything more wrong.'

'I know, and our Halettite friend Murshash isn't happy. So one of them – Sevasteos, Ithien or Murshash – has an agenda of his own. Or maybe all three of them. Whoever is involved, though, we're the ones caught in the middle.'

So keep your ears and eyes open.' He stood up and walked off, exchanging a brief greeting with the returning Vespasia.

'What did he want to talk about?' Vespasia asked in a low voice, sitting in the space Oailos had vacated.

'Things,' I said. There was no need to be more specific; Vespasia knew what I was talking about.

'Oailos has ambitions.'

'Yes, but I'm beginning to agree with him. There's something wrong here.'

'Of course there's something wrong. But I don't think it's as important as he makes out, and nothing more than there usually is where the Domain's concerned. If you could find out why Ithien changed sides, we'd probably clear most of it up.'

I watched a Halettite sentry making his rounds down by the shingle lakeshore, carrying a flickering torch. I'd seen the look that Ithien and the architect exchanged, and I wasn't so sure.

But I had nothing to go on. What was certain was that tomorrow I'd get to swim properly, and I could hardly wait.

CHAPTER VI

We were roused at dawn, because Sevasteos was eager to get the job completed, but I was glad to see that he and the other engineers were all up and dressed as early as we were. We were lucky to be in the tropics in some ways; it meant the nights were always long, never less than eleven Thetian hours. Neither the Halettites nor Sevasteos could afford the expense of lighting during the hours of darkness.

There was a torrent of swearing an hour or so later as we manhandled the first scaffolding frame awkwardly along the parapet. It wasn't particularly heavy, and there wasn't much of a problem with splinters, but it was too tall to be easily portable.

In the end we fixed ropes to the upper sections, and the surveyors took turns to hold the ropes – thus keeping the frame more or less steady – and guide the whole apparatus to where it was needed.

'This hasn't really been thought through, has it?' one of my colleagues said as everyone stood around the ungainly construction.

Another shook his head. 'They showed us what they wanted, but not a word about how to attach it.'

They sent me along to the large central hut, where the engineers were standing around discussing plans. Sevasteos seemed most put out that something as minor as the scaffolding should slow things down, and sent Emisto and Biades back to supervise. There followed nearly an hour of painfully slow progress, as we slung weighted lines over the parapet. A few of the bigger men brought sacks full of stones to secure the lines to.

'Not a man for practicalities, Sevasteos,' Emisto sighed

as the architect stalked away, having asked for the second time why nothing was being done. 'He works in big concepts, leaves the small matters to everyone else.'

'Isn't that what the man in charge is supposed to do?' asked Oailos, standing nearby.

'As long as he understands that the small matters take time as well.' Emisto was a rotund little man, no taller than me but round where I was slender – or thin, now. 'He itches to get on with what he thinks is the proper work.'

Impatience didn't sound like a virtue in an architect.

'Where's the proper work here?' Oailos said. 'Patching a few holes in a dam, it hardly seems a big concept.'

Emisto rolled his eyes, a gesture cut short as he barked a command at one of the men securing the sacks. 'Ranthas only knows what he's doing here. He's at least the third Imperial Architect in four years, the Emperor keeps on sacking them. I didn't even know his name until he dragged me off my nice quiet project near Ilthys to come and work in this godforsaken wasteland.'

Now this *was* interesting, if only he'd go on with it.

'Why you?'

Emisto shrugged. 'I'm an expert in underwater masonry. He didn't have one when he reached Ilthys, so I was conscripted. I'll probably get back and find that my splendid harbour has been abandoned and turned into a quarry.'

A careless man on rope duty let go and fathoms of weighted rope began unfurling into the lake. Emisto jumped forward, shouting at anyone in the area to secure the dry end, and that was the end of the conversation.

A central feature of their highly sensible way of securing the gantry with weights and ropes involved more or less throwing it into the lake. It was a procedure which, even done under Emisto's eagle-eyed supervision, proved highly entertaining and required about a dozen men to jump in more or less immediately to prevent the whole thing floating away.

It was at this point, finally, that Emisto decided he needed a surveyor in the water, and ordered me to go in and make sure everything was attached in its proper place.

'You've convinced me you need proper rations without even needing to say anything,' he said, as I clambered on to the parapet. My skin, prickly with the irritation of dry heat, suddenly seemed ten times worse, and I could hardly wait for him to finish speaking. 'Everyone gets more food from now on, I'll make sure of it. Heavens, what barbarians the Halettites are!'

Emisto's concern, like that of the other Thetians, seemed entirely genuine, but I was profoundly heartened that he was concerned enough to do something about it, and polite enough not to mention that it was in his interests for us to be well-fed.

Then Emisto's concern was temporarily forgotten as I plunged the eight or so feet from the parapet into the cool, clear water of the lake.

It was like diving into heaven, the feel of water on my skin again, proper water even if it wasn't salty and there weren't any waves. I opened my eyes again almost the moment I was underwater, looking through a cascade of bubbles at a blue, sunlit world that stretched away below and in front of me. I could clearly see men swimming around below me, adjusting the ropes, and the half-shadow of the scaffolding breaking through the silvery sheen of the surface.

Elements, it was wonderful!

I gave myself the luxury of diving a little further down before twisting round to come up again close to the framework, breaking surface again and pushing wet hair away from my face. There were smiles on the faces of many of the men in the water, and I saw some sympathetic nods.

There was no time to celebrate further, but I didn't mind being asked to work. Emisto threw a measuring stick in and I dived downwards, checking that the ropes were long enough and that the framework would be attached in the right place. I didn't have to do much in any case; while the other men attached weights to the end of the gantry and moved it into position, I simply had to ensure that it was placed correctly, and at the right depths.

When I finally surfaced to report that everything was in position, Emisto was the only person left up above except for two men fixing a rope ladder for us to get out.

'I sent the others off to collect the next frame and the planks,' he said. 'It should go more quickly now we know what we're doing – I'll leave all of you down there to fix the planks and finish the job. You've more than earned a long stint in the water.'

There were no complaints about that task, and when we finally had to get out half an hour later, feeling immeasurably better and four years younger, everything was ready for work to begin on the first crack.

'A couple of months?' Oailos said, pulling his tunic on without bothering to dry himself first. 'I can't see how this will take more than two weeks.'

As the first couple of days progressed, I couldn't help but agree with him. By halfway through our second full day all six gantries were in place, and work had begun on the first of them. Even that included the time we'd taken off to build two large rafts for the architect and the other engineers to direct work from; say what we might about Sevasteos, he wasn't averse to getting his hands dirty.

Breathing underwater had taken almost no readjustment even after such a time, and it didn't take long before I forgot the canal totally, forgot everything else but the lake and the work we were doing – which, I had to admit, I was rather enjoying. I was no architect and never would be, but I tried to pick up what I could from Sevasteos and his engineers – especially Emisto, the friendliest of them.

Still, I had enough awareness of what my legal status was and enough concern about the rate of progress to milk my privileged position for all it was worth. Never with Ithien; thankfully, he'd gone off with Shalmaneser to the nearest inhabited town, at the other end of the lake, to arrange for supplies. I became one of the principal conduits of information between the engineers and the slaves, as did the other five surveyors; Oailos seemed particularly interested in what I told him, though.

'You're an aristocrat, which none of the other surveyors are,' he said, when I asked why. 'I know I said everything has a pecking order, but Shalmaneser, Ithien and Sevasteos are all politicians of one stripe or another. You'll pick up a lot more nuances than the others will.'

So I listened, and passed on what I heard. My initial unease had died down somewhat but on the third day something happened which revived it with a vengeance.

I was working alone on the endmost of the cracks, marking out the exact positions where the metal clamps were to go. Most of the others were right at the other end of the dam, on the side nearest to the huts, so I had this half of the lake to myself.

Although I could breathe underwater as easily as in air, it wasn't something I could do for ever; after a few hours my head started to spin and I lost coordination. I was fairly sure that if I stayed in longer I'd eventually pass out and drown. So I came to the surface for a few minutes, and was surprised to hear voices from the parapet just above my head. After more than an hour in underwater silence it took me a moment to identify them as Sevasteos and Ithien. They were speaking in Thetian, a language I only half-understood.

'. . . getting to Shalmaneser again,' Sevasteos was saying. 'The pig-headed idiot has suddenly developed an intense concern for the dam and he's starting to listen to Murshash.'

'Can't we send Shalmaneser back to Tandaris to pay a visit to the Viceroy?' Ithien asked, his words becoming clearer. They must be walking towards me. 'Sideline him?'

'I'll try, but I can't guarantee success.'

'Try,' Ithien said, his tone very much one of command. 'Of all the problems we could have encountered, a Halettite noble who takes his work seriously must be the most unlikely.'

'*Barbarissimi!*' Sevasteos's voice, now just overhead, carried more than just contempt; it was hatred. 'I can't even feel guilty about this.'

'You will,' Ithien said. 'Just remember why we're doing it.' Then he said something which sounded like *In the Emperor's name*, but I wasn't quite sure of the case. It could have been *For the Emperor's name* or something else entirely.

'I'd sell my soul to get out of Qalathar, go somewhere you can move without bumping into a priest.'

'It is ghastly, isn't it? Oh, for a secular city and some sea. I can't imagine how horrible it must have been for those poor wretches we've got working on the dam. Four years away from the sea. And they're the lucky ones – think how much longer all the others might wait before they see open water.'

'You call this open water?'

Their voices became too faint to make out, as they passed by without ever having glanced down and noticed me. I was especially glad not to have had any contact with Ithien.

On the surface, I thought, diving again in case they saw me from further along, there was nothing abnormal about that conversation. Murshash was concerned that the Thetians weren't doing enough on the dam, which was entirely understandable. If it failed, his life would be forfeit, so he was trying to persuade Shalmaneser to send for more men and investigate more thoroughly. The Thetians wanted only to finish the work and get home.

That was very much the tone of the conversation, but it still struck a jarring note. Sevasteos was senior to Ithien, surely? The latter was no longer Governor of Ilthys, and always deferred to the architect in public.

And why should they feel guilty, if they were so sure there was nothing seriously wrong with the dam?

As soon as I finished marking up, I swam halfway along the dam before surfacing near another scaffolding, in case Ithien and Sevasteos noticed where I'd been. I wasn't sure why I was so nervous, because even after that conversation I had no rational grounds for suspecting them of anything.

As luck – or Fate – would have it, I ran into Oailos when we were deputised to mix some concrete on the walkway later that afternoon, and told him about the conversation without thinking about whether it was a good idea. The burly mason looked thoughtful.

'We need some more red dust,' he said to one of the others. 'We'll go and see if Sevasteos will dole out some.' He gestured to me to accompany him, which I did. It was a reasonable pretext; the red dust was something we had to add to the concrete mix in small quantities to compensate for the lack of salt. There were virtually no rivers or lakes in Thetia, so even Emisto had little experience of working in fresh water. The red dust, as we called it, was Sevasteos's idea and he was the only person allowed to dispense it, heaven knew why. Emisto wasn't happy, I could tell, but he'd obviously lost the argument, if there'd been one.

'This is the same as some of the others have heard, but yours is the clearest thing I've heard so far,' Oailos said. 'Ithien is senior to Sevasteos, he's senior to all of them, and he's high up enough in the Imperial hierarchy for even Shalmaneser to treat him as an equal.'

'Do we still have no idea what he's doing out here?'

'Not him nor any of them. Emisto reckons the dam's good for another decade even with the freak weather we've been having, so why bother sending the Imperial

Architect and a high official out here to make cosmetic repairs to a Tehaman dam?'

Very cosmetic. Shalmaneser had been insistent that the repairs look as inconspicuous as possible, and blended in with the otherwise almost pristine face of the dam.

'A cover for something else?' I suggested. 'Some plan of the Emperor's that he wants to keep quiet?'

'We're back to that Kemaraean treasure,' Oailos said. 'I think that's why they're here, to see if they can get their hands on it.' He'd seemed very keen on the idea ever since someone had first suggested it on the journey up here.

'So why keep it quiet?'

'Because if it's in an Archipelagan lake, it belongs to the Archipelago. Even if they make the Viceroy or the clan president tithe some of it to them, they still wouldn't get as much. The Emperor found out where it was, and he's going to split it with the Domain. They can't send off to Tandaris for help, or people might find out.'

'And if we're retrieving treasure for them, they won't want us around afterwards.'

'Exactly,' Oailos said, with a grim look. 'Once we've served our purpose, that's the end of us. Now can you see why I'm so eager to find out what's going on?'

I nodded, but didn't have time to say anything as we were approaching Sevasteos, who was studying a set of plans on a rickety table outside the hut, shaded from the sun by a makeshift awning.

'We've run out of red dust on the second working, Lord Architect,' Oailos said, putting a respect in his voice that was entirely absent otherwise. Oailos was careful to conceal his true feelings.

'Use it sparingly,' was Sevasteos's only comment as he handed us four small, rough bags of the substance, not even asking why two of us had come.

'I've never seen this used before,' Oailos said, once we were out of earshot and walking back on to the parapet. 'I know Thetian concrete only works properly in salt water, and that they add something, but from what I remember it isn't red.' He sniffed one of the bags. 'Smells funny, too, though I can't for the life of me remember what it reminds me of.'

I followed suit, and recognised the slightly acrid smell. 'Flamewood.'

'*Flamewood?* Thetis, what on earth are they doing to this concrete?'

Flamewood was more or less the most valuable commodity on Aquasilva, used in every engine ever constructed and a lot more besides. Its dross, which was what the red dust at least contained, was virtually worthless – but why? Surely there were cheaper substances to add?

'At least it doesn't burn underwater,' he said.

'I don't think it burns at all any more, does it? Not after it's been through a furnace once.'

'Oh, it does. I've seen a couple of fires from dross, the circumstances just need to be right. You're right, there shouldn't be a problem underwater.'

We reached the working again after a couple of minutes' walk in silence, and Oailos tipped the first of his bags into the next batch of concrete. The red made very little difference to the colour of the final mix, and would have been invisible to someone not actively looking for it. The vital point as far as this concrete was concerned was that it had to be applied underwater as well as set properly.

Once we'd mixed it, I joined the others in the water to supervise the application. The flaws in the dam were a series of very thin vertical cracks running along the lines between the stones, mostly due to the changing water level, the heat of the sun and, quite simply, the age of the dam. It was an astonishing work of civil engineering, given that it had survived substantially without repairs for nearly a century.

The Tehamans must have been incredible stonemasons

– still were, for all I knew. Ravenna claimed they still existed, that the mind-mage at the Retreat had been one. I wondered why the Thetians had chosen to seal them off as punishment for siding with the Tuonetar, rather than conquering them. My ancestors had had no qualms about conquest, and the Tehamans seemed far too clever a people to leave to their own devices.

We made what felt like exceptionally good progress once again; there was no question that this was taking far too short a time, and it was nowhere near difficult enough to require the services of the Thetian Imperial Architect. Previous holders of the post had been responsible for the Hall of the Ocean, the Acrolith of Tandaris and a chain of glittering monuments in the cities of Thetia. Sevasteos didn't belong here.

But as we worked, I also spotted a flaw in Oailos's reasoning. Sevasteos quite obviously *was* an architect, as was Biades. So why send them to recover treasure? Wouldn't the Navy have been more effective, with trained divers and expertise in recovering sunken objects? I was fairly sure that none of the Thetians were naval officers masquerading as architects.

It was a problem that still hadn't solved itself that evening. I avoided Oailos, unwilling to talk to him until I'd worked out a better solution, and went off as far from the main group as I could for some privacy. A pile of rocks reared up from the ground like the bow of a sinking ship, twelve or fifteen feet tall, and I went and sat on top of it, staring out over the lake.

Tropical sunsets are very sudden, and the mountains to the west blotted out the western horizon, so the light from the torches around us was all there was. I could see more or less the whole bowl-shaped little valley from up here – the buildings, the beach, and the only two paths that led out of it.

And the stars. They were one thing that didn't change between here and the Archipelago, that retained their grandeur wherever I was. I could see one moon, a thin crescent; another would rise later over the mountains to the south, but otherwise only stars and the brilliant coloured sheets of nebulae were visible.

'Still the dreamer, Cathan?' said a voice from just behind me. I turned, startled; I hadn't even heard him come up.

'Dreams are all I have, Ithien,' I said, shifting round to face away from him. 'Whereas you haven't done too badly.'

'Oh, I still dream of a better world.' He sat down a foot or two away. 'But this is the one we have to live in, and it still has its surprises for us. How did you survive?'

'I pretended to be someone else,' I said shortly, unwilling to reveal too much. 'I wasn't given the opportunity of switching sides.'

'You wouldn't have been executed if you'd surrendered.'

'Oh really?' I put as much venom as I could into my voice. 'I've heard this before. Everybody's always keen to tell me that despite being a convicted heretic, an elemental mage and a few other things besides, my life would have been spared when I was captured.'

'It was once,' Ithien said mildly. 'You were born under an unlucky star, Cathan, like the rest of your family. Too strong to accept the path other people wanted you to take, but never strong enough to successfully defy them.'

'Why bother? Surely I could have deserted my cause at the earliest possible opportunity and gone over to the enemy?'

'You don't know what you're talking about.' His tone was offhand, still not irritated. 'I'm alive, in good health, and free. I survived the Emperor's purges. Why is that worse than resisting and ending up a heap of ashes?'

'The Emperor just let you change sides? Didn't he test your loyalty at all?'

'I've been outside Thetia since your brother died, shuttled from one diplomatic post to another helping the ambassadors. I have my watchdogs, but he only worries about success. As long as I get what he wants, he doesn't mind.'

'So you have no problems working for that butcher?' A lot of bitterness that had been bottled up for too long was coming to the surface. So many people I'd known had been burnt, reduced to the level of penitents or killed by Domain treachery, yet Ithien had survived and prospered. Why?

'I work for the Empire,' Ithien said. 'I'm Thetian. No matter who sits on that throne, or even if nobody sits on it at all, I'm still serving Thetia.'

'How noble of you.' I wasn't prepared to give him an inch.

'How sensible of me. I don't like death, not anyone else's and certainly not my own. What would you have had me do – declare Ilthys an independent state? Start the revolt in the name of the Assembly? Tell me, what would you have done?'

He was too quick, and too smooth for me. To be honest, I couldn't think what I would have done, it just nettled me that he had betrayed all his allegiances and was working for the Halettite murderer who now ruled Thetia.

'Of course,' he went on, 'I could have run away and hidden, launched irritating little attacks on outposts and behaved like a petty bandit, as so many of your heretic leaders have done. Would that have been better?'

'It would have been too difficult that way, wouldn't it?'

'Cathan, this is pointless. If you want to vent your anger, find someone else because I have better things to do. I came to talk because you're someone I thought was dead who turns out to be alive, which is something all too rare these days. More often it happens the other way round.'

'So you just came to make conversation with a casual acquaintance.' I wasn't ready to let him off the hook, not by any means. 'Who I am has nothing to do with it?'

'Who you are has a great deal to do with it. I won't pretend otherwise. When we met before you stood for everything I hate. The Imperial throne, the royal blood — heavens, I even hated you because you proved that not all your family were deranged and vicious.'

He was speaking very fast now, the words almost tumbling out on top of each other. I said nothing, waiting to hear if he would reveal anything. It was cynical, but there was no other way to survive as a slave.

'For me, it's as if you've been transported through time from then, only now I've realised that there are things I hate more than monarchy.' He shrugged. 'And seeing you reminded me of the day we met in Ilthys, the last time when all my friends were still alive. Everyone else has changed since then, or died.'

'Is *that* my value?' I said, pride submerging my common sense.

'No. I'm genuinely pleased to see you. And your being here also means that from all this,' he gestured round at the camp and the dam, 'at least one good thing has come. I'm not going to leave you here, how could I? I owe someone a very old debt, and I'll repay her if all the priests in the world stand in my way.'

I knew who he was talking about without him having to say, but in the torchlight I couldn't make out enough of the expression on his face to be sure of something else.

'Alive or dead?' I asked softly.

'Palatine is alive, Cathan. That much I can tell you.' He stood up and put a hand on my shoulder for a second. 'And unlike me, she never doubted you were.'

It was too much to take in. I felt as if my heart had suddenly expanded to fill the whole of my ribcage, beating wildly and incredibly fast.

I learnt the meaning of hope again.

CHAPTER VII

Ithien's footsteps receded into the distance, leaving me alone on the top of the jutting rock. Alone in a world that suddenly seemed worth living in again.

Somewhere out among the unconquered islands, Palatine was walking and breathing under the same stars – or the same sky, given that she could be halfway around the world. And maybe with her there were other survivors of the mobs and the Inquisitors, other friends I'd long thought lost.

I can't leave you here. Did he really mean that? A favour owed to Palatine, Palatine who had been his oldest and closest friend, maybe more if that was possible for her. It was fine for him to say that out here in the wilds of Qalathar, but would he make good on his promise?

And I was no closer to finding out the truth.

My mind drifted away from him again, back to Palatine. My brilliant, forceful cousin Palatine, her loyalties that had never wavered. I remembered her in Hamilcar's airy house in Taneth, in the sun-dappled seas and forests of the Archipelago, the garden of Ithien's palace in Ilthys. Even in winter it had been beautiful.

All that was part of a world that I had hardly seen for four years, one that seemed almost mythical as I sat alone below the cliffs of Tehama, remembering how wonderful it had been. Even the worst moments of my old life seemed better than this.

I looked blindly down into the chasm, fixing my eyes on two points of yellowish light over by the far shore, wondering how there could be people down there.

If Ithien made good on his promise to take me home,

then there was nothing else I wanted to do now except leave here and find Palatine. Find her and the people who would undoubtedly have gathered around her, find the ruins of my old life and the machinations of those who saw me as a pawn in their own power struggles. Only now many of them were dead, and the world they knew was being gradually twisted beyond recognition by the unholy power of Sarhaddon and his Venatic Order.

This time I did hear the footsteps, and knew who it was from the shape of her silhouette against the lighted windows of the huts.

'Did he tell you why he kept quiet?' Vespasia said, then her tone changed, and a note of concern came into her voice. 'Cathan, what is it?'

I looked up at her. I was on the brink of tears, although I wasn't sure why.

'Palatine's alive, Vespasia!'

She stared at me unbelievingly for a moment, then smiled, a broader and more heartfelt smile than I could remember her giving in a long time. She knew Palatine only by reputation, the icon of the republican movement and the infamous commander of some of the heretic forces that still tormented the Domain out on the fringes.

'Then the Domain hasn't won yet,' she said. 'Somehow we still have a chance, and you shouldn't stay here and waste it. They need you, Cathan.'

'Do you really believe that?'

'Of course. They'll need all the help anyone can give them. The Inquisition hasn't extinguished all resistance, much as it would like to have done. All the people who mattered most managed to escape, and you're one of them.'

I'd said nothing about Ithien's promise, but Vespasia's certainty was total. She was like Palatine had been, always so sure of herself, with none of the indecisiveness that had always dogged my steps. Tonight, for once, my mind had been made up from the moment Ithien told me.

'What are those lights over there?' Vespasia asked, momentarily serious again. 'I haven't been up here before, this is the first time I've seen them.'

I followed her pointing finger to the twin lights I'd noticed earlier – surely they had moved, though? They were much further over to the left, nearer the dam, than before.

'No idea,' I said. Come to think of it, the lights were too near the water to be from a hut; I didn't remember there being any buildings down there when I looked in daytime. Maybe the sun's glare had hidden them.

We watched the lights for a minute. They were quite faint, too steady to be torchlight. Flamewood lamps, then, hardly common up here.

'They're definitely moving,' Vespasia said, a few moments later. 'A boat, then. But what's it doing down there, do you suppose there are villages in the canyon?'

I remembered Oailos's warning. Nothing up here was what it seemed; that was too logical an explanation. Elements, I was growing paranoid!

After a while first one light, then the other, disappeared, and the chasm was dark again. By then most of the rest of the encampment had gone to sleep. But even after I'd wrapped myself in my blanket and closed my eyes, it took me a long time to fall asleep.

During the next midday break I talked to Emisto, and discovered the little he knew about Ithien. The rotund engineer had no idea when or why Ithien had changed sides, had never met him until he arrived with Sevasteos and an Imperial warrant to conscript any useful people for the dam project. Ithien belonged apparently to the Emperor's personal staff and derived his current authority from the warrant; there was little more I could ask Emisto without seeming overly inquisitive.

We were kept too busy during the next few days for my

thoughts to wander far as, under Sevasteos's relentless pressure, work on the dam gathered pace. By the eighth full day, five of the six flaws had been fully repaired, the concrete injected and the clamps properly fixed.

With the result that virtually every one of the slaves was working on the sixth and last when Shalmaneser appeared with a visitor whose very presence seemed to drain the warmth from the midday sun.

On this working as one of the others, the cracks extended all the way up to the parapet itself, and I was supervising the addition of clamps to it when I heard the clatter of hooves and four men came into view, walking down the last stages of the pathway. I heard indrawn breaths from around me as we saw the third, just behind Shalmaneser. The buzz of conversation died instantly.

'Vulture,' Oailos muttered under his breath, making the sign against evil – a sign associated with the Wind-goddess Althana, I noticed – with one hand.

'What's he doing here?' someone else hissed. It was as if a blanket of fear had suddenly descended on everyone.

As the men moved briefly out of sight behind an outcrop of rock, someone took the opportunity to warn the men working in the water. I grabbed my spirit level and knelt down facing the wall, checking for the second time whether the clamps we were installing would be level.

'Clear the way for his Reverence the Inquisitor Amonis, representative of His Grace the Exarch of the Archipelago,' a voice intoned, and people moved out of the way as if the centre of the walkway had suddenly become too hot to touch.

Amonis? I felt a shiver of horror. What on earth had led my path to cross his again, for Thetis's sake?

There was no way I could stay facing away from him. I shifted round to face the approaching party and bowed as low as I could, my head almost touching the stones. There was a rustling around me as others did likewise.

'Continue with your work,' said a dry voice in uninflected Archipelagan. It was a grotesque parody of the language, given that, like Thetian, Archipelagan was a musical tongue that relied on inflection to carry nuances of meaning. It was also a voice I knew.

We needed no second bidding, and the fear that was buried not very deep in me had risen to the surface with a vengeance. I shuffled round again fast enough to scrape some of the skin from my knees.

The Inquisitor's robe brushed the skin of my leg as he glided noiselessly by, enough of a touch for me to feel how rough and heavy the fabric was. I didn't want to think how uncomfortable it was in this weather.

A few paces beyond me the Inquisitor met Sevasteos and Ithien, who must have come from the other end of the dam; they'd been nowhere near here last time I looked. Which meant, I reflected, that they hadn't known of this in advance.

'*Domine* Amonis, we had no idea you were coming,' Sevasteos said. Out of the corner of my eye I saw both drop to one knee for the Inquisitor's murmured benediction. His cowl was up, which meant I couldn't see anything of him except the black robe slashed with white and the pointed hood.

When the Thetians stood up again, their faces were carefully composed.

'It is no fault of yours,' the Inquisitor said. 'I and my colleague have been sent on the orders of the Exarch to fulfil *Domine* Shalmaneser's request. I do not believe I know your names.'

Ithien and Sevasteos introduced themselves. Knowing him as I did, I could hear the edge in Ithien's voice; for some reason he was profoundly nervous. Now why? What did a loyal servant of the Emperor have to fear from a loyal servant of the Prime?

I wondered who the colleague he referred to was. So

did Sevasteos, aloud though in a more circumspect way.

'*Domine* Shalmaneser is concerned that this golden opportunity to repair the dam may not fully be utilised,' Amonis said. 'He requested enough men to examine the whole structure, a major engineering challenge. However, this request was passed on to the Exarch, who in his infinite wisdom found an alternative solution.'

Shalmaneser shifted position slightly, hiding my view of Ithien's face.

'I have therefore brought with me an elemental mage captured by one of my brothers. She will be able to hold back the water of the lake from the dam so that you and your surveyors may make a full inspection.'

'Th . . . that is very kind of His Holiness,' the architect stammered. 'It is very kind for us to be allowed to utilise this. Is there any way we might repay his generosity?'

'By using his gift wisely and in the service of Ranthas,' Amonis said. 'I and my retinue will require accommodation for the duration of our stay. Four walls and a roof will be quite sufficient.'

'And the mage?' Ithien asked.

'The mage has a handler, a mind-mage who prevents her from turning her destructive powers on true believers. A secure place will, however, be required for her confinement.'

The thought of a captive mage was bad enough; his last words chilled me to the bone. Mind-mages were dangerous, especially since they could detect the presence of other mages who would rather remain hidden.

Like me.

Sevasteos issued a string of orders, pulling more than thirty slaves off this section of wall to prepare quarters for the Inquisitor and accommodation for his captive mage. A woman I was almost certain to have met at some point, given how few elemental mages there had been even before many were caught in the purges.

Sevasteos and Ithien led Amonis and his party along the dam, but it was a long time before any of those left dared to talk again.

'They're serious about this,' said Pahinu, looking like a frightened rodent. 'What happens if they find something?'

'What happens if that Inquisitor decides to make sure we're all of the true Faith?' said another man. 'I've had that happen before, and believe me, it can be painful.'

'No, I mean we'll be here for ever,' Pahinu said. 'Working eighty or ninety feet down behind some makeshift dam.'

'We'll be doing that anyway once they get their mage here,' I said. 'We'll be doing all the grunt-work.' Whoever the luckless mage was, the Inquisition would have broken her spirit and bent her to their will, otherwise she'd never have been allowed out of the Holy City.

'I thought they executed mages,' the second man said.

'Not all of them.' I shot them a warning glance as I heard the sound of more people coming up the path.

We were still working there an hour later, very close to finishing, when the rest of the Inquisitor's entourage came up. They were almost as unnerving as Amonis himself had been: four crimson-robed men with swords at their sides, faces veiled except for a slit for their eyes. Even the armour they wore was lacquered red.

Sacri. Sacred Ones, soldiers of the Faith.

Murderous fanatics, the men responsible for the worst excesses of the Crusade thirty years ago, at least as far as brutality went. The Sacri did not pillage, loot and rape. They simply burnt and killed.

In the centre of the guard of Sacri a bearded Thetian wearing entirely black robes and a black cap, with a hammer by his side, was hardly taller than the captive mage he led on a chain. His name was Memnon, and he wasn't Thetian, I corrected myself; Ravenna had told me at the

Retreat that he was Tehaman. As soon as I saw his captive, though, half-hidden behind him, he ceased to exist except as an obstruction.

But in that moment, as I saw first his face and then hers, everything changed. I felt as if someone had drawn the air out of me in a single instant, and my throat was too tight to breathe. I must have gone completely white, and out of the corner of my eye I saw Vespasia start violently and then turn away.

Elements, *no!* Oh, Thetis, how could you have done this? I screamed silently and turned back to the wall so that no-one would see my face. I rested my head against the wall for a moment, not even pretending to read the spirit-level, and tried to breathe. Of all the people, all the things that could have happened now, this was the worst. Memnon had betrayed her, been working for the Domain all along. She'd been so certain he was loyal to Tehama rather than the Inquisition.

The pain in my gut was so strong I wanted to drive a knife into it, just to be rid of it, but it was only my stomach seizing up from some emotion I couldn't name. I stayed huddled against the wall until they'd gone past, too vulnerable because of the feelings I knew would be written on my face.

The quiet confidence I'd had since Ithien told me about Palatine drained away as if it had never been there. It was even worse than if Palatine had been the captive mage – although her magic was entirely latent – because there was only one person who meant more to me than Palatine.

All this time I'd thought her safe with her own people, ever since I'd helped her escape from slavery at the Retreat to contact Memnon and earned myself a savage punishment in the process. I'd been sure that she'd come back and find me, helped by her reclusive people, to finish what we'd begun four years ago.

Ravenna must never have reached Tehama; Memnon

must have turned her over in Thetia or on the journey, before she reached the safe haven of the plateau she'd left seventeen years ago. She'd been a prisoner of the Domain for almost a year, and who knew what they'd done to her?

She hadn't looked at any of us as she passed, not even acknowledged our existence as she walked along in chains behind the mind-mage. Like a bird with its wings broken.

There must still be a spark of life left in her, I thought, clutching for straws, or they wouldn't have chained her. I'd seen captive mages before, docile automatons walking behind their handlers, their spirits crushed to the extent that the priests felt no need to chain them any more. A demonstration of the strength of Ranthas's will.

Why had they brought her out here, though? She was an incredibly valuable prisoner, the Pharaoh of Qalathar, and I'd have expected them to use her as a figurehead. And she was an air-mage, while surely whatever the Inquisitors were proposing would need a water-mage. Actually, I wasn't so sure about that, but it didn't matter.

Nothing could change the fact that she was a prisoner of the Domain. That was as much of a living death as slavery, and especially for someone as mercurial as she was. And with the mind-mage here, I was helpless to act, restricted almost as effectively as she was. That was something I couldn't bear, and the pain of seeing her like that would only get worse and worse.

'Cathan?' It was Vespasia, shifting over as if to help me with the work.

'Did you see her?' I croaked, trying to breathe properly again. My throat would ache for hours.

'Yes. We'll talk about it later, though. We'd better finish this. Sevasteos won't be in a good mood, and he'll take it out on any target that comes into his sights.'

'In other words, get a move on,' someone else said, breaking the tension.

*

Sevasteos was indeed in a foul mood, but he was doing his best not to show it. We cleared up and walked back to the huts as the sun was setting to find that the Inquisitor's 'four walls and a roof' meant the best available accommodation. For all that they were technically the same rank as priests everywhere, this was the Archipelago, and so the Domain's people had precedence over all secular authorities except the Viceroy's. Even his authority was more or less nominal.

Consequently the architects and the engineers had all been moved down a level, having to descend to the unspeakable indignity of sharing rooms – Ithien and Sevasteos; Emisto, Biades and Murshash. Another of the better huts had been reserved for the mind-mage and his charge; Oailos told me that he and some of the others had hastily erected a wooden cage in a corner of the room. Vespasia must have said something to him, because there was a guarded sympathy in his voice.

The atmosphere in the camp that night was very different; people were less willing to talk, and there were frequent glances at the two buildings occupied by the newcomers. Not a single person spoke of the Inquisitor with anything other than dread, but I was largely indifferent to it all.

Amonis didn't waste any time. The next morning, soon after dawn, we were assembled in the largest open space so that the Inquisitor and an uneasy-looking Sevasteos could tell us what would be happening. Over to one side, wrists and ankles chained and wearing a grey shift and sandals, Ravenna looked more like a condemned prisoner than anything else. Especially beside the angular-featured mind-mage who guarded her – wearing nothing but black as was traditional, he looked more like an executioner. For him to have turned up here as well was more ominous, and it put me in more danger.

I found myself conjuring up visions of throwing him into the lake and crushing him under the weight of the water, keeping him alive just long enough to know why he'd been killed.

'This will be quite simple,' Sevasteos said. 'The mage will just push the water back from the dam about twenty cubits, slowly decreasing the water level. We'll use the two rafts and some distance-glasses, and scan the face of the dam for any further cracks. Ignore anything that's obviously just weathering.'

'The dam will be covered in weeds and mud near the bottom, *Domine*,' Emisto pointed out. 'How are we supposed to see through that?'

'The action of removing the water should scour the face clean, Engineer,' the Inquisitor said, resting his inscrutable face on Emisto. 'If not, other ways will be found.' He raised his voice slightly and turned to address all of us. 'As there are two rafts, Murshash and myself will each join the crew of one to aid the engineers in charge.'

So Ithien and Shalmaneser would be left on the top, along with all the Halettite soldiers. And as many slaves as they didn't want on the rafts.

'The Book of Ranthas frowns upon the employment of twisted powers,' Amonis said, his gaze sweeping over all of us. 'The miserable creatures who use them pay the full penalty for their crimes when in death they are cast into Ranthas's fiery furnace to burn in agony for eternity. Yet sometimes the powers of evil may be used for the greater good, and it is for this that we now beg His forgiveness.' We lowered our heads for his brief prayer, one I'd never heard before but which sounded entirely standard and canonical:

'Ranthas, Lord of Fire, Bringer of Life, we ask you to forgive this employment of base powers for the safety of Your worshippers and the preservation of Your message. For as Your fire gives life to us, so we work to preserve that life and turn the forces of evil against themselves for Your Greater Glory.'

My luck, which had undoubtedly soured with the arrival of the Inquisitor, got even worse; to my absolute horror, I was assigned to the raft with Sevasteos and the Inquisitor on it. Why on earth did the man have to come with us? Why couldn't he be like any other Inquisitor and leave everybody else to suffer? He was going to recognise me, I knew it, and it was only a matter of time.

Until the mage, standing submissive on the beach, raised her hands, there would have appeared nothing out of the ordinary. Two rafts out on the lake, as still in the windless morning sun as it ever was, and a few figures clustered on the shore.

The raft was only about fifteen feet long and ten wide, with a rope handrail around the edge. All of us except for Sevasteos and Amonis were secured to the planking with ropes around our waists; I sat at the bow holding a paddle. Wet, but there was nothing wrong with that. At least I was looking away from him.

I was the only one who felt the exact moment Ravenna began her spell, a familiar tingling feeling on my skin. All around me, the apprehensive faces of the other slaves stared over at the shoreline.

It began almost imperceptibly, a slight delineation on the water behind us, which grew into a step, a barrier as if there was a pane of glass stretching clear across the lake with different water levels on either side. Then a bulge, behind the barrier, as water was drained out of the damwards section.

I heard a sharp, indrawn breath from someone, a gasp and a curse. The power was building – how much could she take? Not until now had I thought about how much power it needed to move this weight of water, even for a water-mage. Hundreds, thousands of tons of water flowed *uphill* from around us, a blue wall of water growing foot by

111

foot behind as we watched. And she was doing it with Air, too. I could feel the heaviness of it on my shoulders, and there was a slight distortion in the sky above the lake, a space free from birds.

'Ranthas will protect and preserve us,' the Inquisitor said calmly, fixing his eyes on one of the more panicked slaves. 'You work in his name.'

The man nodded feverishly. I heard a series of sharp cracks from along the face of the dam as the scaffolding, now left entirely out of the water, fell back against the newly-reinforced ropes that held it in position. The crescent-shaped wall of water that towered over us was now at least twenty feet high; on the other side, the dark stone of the dam, unbleached by the sun and underwater for more than two centuries, was almost as imposing.

I felt a cold sensation in the pit of my stomach. This wasn't right. We were pushing the laws of nature too far, and sooner or later, surely, something had to give. This wasn't what magic was about. It was supposed to be manipulation, the bending of forces we didn't understand for our own purpose. This was something else entirely. And I had no idea where Ravenna had learned to do this, to work on an order of magnitude so far removed from what we were used to.

Even Sevasteos looked nervous, but his tight-lipped composure held.

'Start looking out for cracks,' he ordered. 'Row towards the shore, then back when it gets too shallow.'

So we rowed, which was hard work against the eddy currents thrown up by the physical impossibility we were witnessing. The four men in the centre of the raft, two of them equipped with distance-glasses, began scanning the face.

We were thirty feet below the water's surface now, and it was draining out at a slower rate now, to allow both rafts to examine every inch of the dam's face. It was like being in one of the river gorges I'd seen in the mountains of Oceanus, a great dark tunnel with walls rearing high above us, cutting out the light. We were entirely in shadow, had been almost since we began the descent.

They hadn't spotted anything serious yet, which I was glad of. I sincerely hoped they'd find nothing wrong at all, no reason to keep us here for another six months, or a year. The end had been very much in sight until Amonis arrived with his captive.

The power she was channelling into this was, incredibly, enough to make the tingling become almost an itch, an active discomfort that was impossible to ignore. What if the Inquisitor noticed? Would he see it for what it was? Please, let him just assume I was as unhappy as everyone else with what we were doing.

'Is it possible to build a coffer dam this deep?' the Inquisitor asked Sevasteos, at about fifty feet below the parapet.

The architect shook his head slightly. 'We'd have to bring in proper underwater equipment – repair searays, construction bubbles, people who knew exactly what they're doing. It'd be a long job, very difficult to bring supplies up here.'

'Time is not what matters, Architect,' the Inquisitor said sharply. 'What matters is the damage that will be done to Ranthas's cause and the maintenance of orthodoxy. You have been told many times how important this dam is. His Imperial Majesty puts as much value on its survival as His Grace the Exarch. If its upkeep requires the things you have specified, they will be found, as will an architect sufficiently committed to his duty to Ranthas.'

'Are you accusing me of professional negligence?' Sevasteos asked, eyes blazing.

'Your willingness to ensure that you leave this dam in perfect health does not seem to be very strong. I am informed that you were opposed to the decision to ask for help.'

'I was under the impression that it would be far more difficult to inspect the lower reaches of the dam,' Sevasteos said. 'The use of heretic mages and dark powers was not a solution I contemplated.'

'Such solutions are best left to those who know what they are fighting against,' Amonis said, his eyes gleaming. 'The heretic scum on whose services we are relying will at least have been some good to the world in her miserable existence. Unlike the rest of her people, I might add.'

'I wasn't aware that you were starting another purge.' There was a smooth tone to Sevasteos's voice suddenly. 'After all, you have already dealt with more heretics than you ever thought lived in the Archipelago. How can you have missed any?'

'Heresy is always a threat.' There was an unholy vehemence in Amonis's voice. 'There are still those who cling to their evil ways, despite the best efforts of my Order, and they are constantly trying to bring in help from outside. We captured the mage and some of her kind aiding dissidents, and those who were put to the question have given us useful information.'

Put to the question. The Inquisitorial euphemism for interrogation – or torture, because as far as Inquisitors were concerned the two were identical. Somehow, despite being captured more than once, I had been spared, but I'd rather it had been done to me than Ravenna. His words only made my misery worse, and my sense of guilt at her capture was already a load on my mind. I should have known that Memnon couldn't be trusted, that he had, for some reason, genuinely defected to the Domain. He was an old friend who'd never betray her, she'd said, son of a high official in Tehama.

I stared down into the malodorous green water, as if there could have been some help in its depths, or a kraken that could have come and put an end to Amonis's loathsome existence. And the mind-mage; perhaps being eaten by a sea-creature would be more appropriate.

What did it matter? I had no way to strike back at them, not with a few tattered slaves and the mind-mage preventing any use of my magic. The appearance of Amonis and the sinister mind-mage only reinforced our feelings that there was something strange happening here. And the tension between Amonis and the Thetians suggested a possible window of opportunity, because while I didn't trust Ithien, he was more than just an enemy.

'Have you been able to wipe the heretic fortresses from the face of the seas yet, then?' Sevasteos said, sailing dangerously close to the wind. He outranked Amonis, but not by a huge amount, and the Emperor was more or less controlled by his Domain advisers. There was no position so high and so safe it was impossible to fall. Not even Emperor, as my brother had learnt.

'It is only a matter of time,' Amonis said confidently. 'The Archipelago is ours for good, we have all the time in the world to destroy what resistance remains.'

'I expect your faith is well justified,' said Sevasteos.

'Is that a crack in the dam over there?' was Amonis's reply.

CHAPTER VIII

It was indeed a crack that Amonis's sharp eyes had spotted, the first of several. Every time one was sighted we had to paddle towards it until the raft was as close as we dared bring it to the stones of the dam, so that Sevasteos and Emisto could examine it in as much detail as possible. I found myself silently urging them to hurry up, but under the Inquisitor's accusing glare, they had to be thorough.

It was like something from a nightmare down here now, hemmed in on one side by the weed-streaked stonework and an impossible wall of water sixty feet high. A blue barrier, only sunlit at the top, with occasional shapes moving inside it – it was as if the lake itself had been stood on its side.

'These cracks are superficial, Your Reverence,' Sevasteos said testily, after the seventh or eighth we found. 'They don't stretch more than a few courses and they're hardly wide enough to mend.'

'They are flaws in the dam, and who's to say they won't get bigger?' said Amonis.

'There is such a thing as stress, Brother Amonis. No-one's ever done this before, we don't know what the bottom of a dam should look like after two centuries underwater.'

'And I suppose all your great monuments can go for ever without repairs? Of course they can't. The Hall of the Ocean would fall down if you left it untended that long.'

'We've made no alterations to the dome in two hundred and fifty years. What repairs we do are simply to keep it in good order and preserve its grandeur.'

'This dam isn't here to be grand.' Amonis snapped. 'It's

here to prevent the lake from draining away and losing us all that farmland. It may not matter to you, but Murshash is right to be concerned. I will recommend to my superiors that all the necessary equipment be requested for a full repair. I'm sure we can find everything that's needed in Tandaris.'

'Everything except the expertise.'

'You rate yourself far too highly, Sevasteos,' said Amonis harshly. 'Your land has still not recovered from its decadence. It will be a long while before the last of the dead wood is purged.'

'You mean before it turns into a proper military dictatorship.' Sevasteos's anger had overwhelmed his common sense. 'What an appalling thought.'

'Do you oppose the idea of your people becoming true servants of Ranthas?' the Inquisitor asked, very quietly. I saw the architect blanch, realise he'd gone too far.

'Of course not, Your Reverence. However, not all ways are like the Halettites'.'

'To His priesthood alone is it given to decide that. It is the Halettites who have served His purpose most faithfully.'

A telling point, as revealing about the Domain as those who served them. Of course Amonis admired the Halettites, even though he wasn't one himself. The Inquisition was subtler, but thought very much along the same lines.

A tense silence prevailed on the raft for the next few minutes until a shout floated down from above; one of the Sacri saying something in Halettite. Amonis paused to listen, then called up a reply, and the Sacrus's crimson-veiled head disappeared.

'The mage is growing exhausted. A weak vessel indeed, but it goes to show how puny she and her powers are. She will begin returning the lake to normal.'

I sensed a collective feeling of relief from everyone on the raft. A feeling which the Inquisitor noticed.

'I am pleased with your performance,' he said to us, smiling thinly. 'We will need to do this again; better to use an experienced crew than learn all over again. I will find some use for the slaves who remain above; they shall not be idle while you work.'

I stared down at the dark water in silent frustration.

It was three horrible days before we were finished, and on the last we were so deep my paddle kept catching in the mud. The whole lake had lost its clarity since we began stirring it up, and the water was a murky green at the surface, an unpleasant brown-black down here. The wall of blue from the first day had darkened, too, and I was profoundly glad when the call came telling us that the lake would be returning to normal.

We were almost in the centre of the dam, and Murshash's boat was as close as it could be to the farther shore, not very far away given how much narrower the dam was near its base. Ahead of us the tops of the low arches which allowed passage to the water were just visible, dank and coated with mud that hadn't seen the light for two hundred years. The foul stench that it gave off was the hardest thing to bear: a foetid, dead smell that hung around us even after we disembarked.

'The survey can be considered complete,' the Inquisitor said with satisfaction. 'I will recommend to my superiors that equipment is sent up here as quickly as possible. Along with some architects who have the necessary staying power to ensure that all due attention is paid.'

I saw Sevasteos glance up at the blue sky above us as Amonis was talking. His expression was bleak, but hard to read; he didn't seem as fearful as he ought to be.

We began to rise at quite a considerable rate, but at half-way up I suddenly heard shouting from above, cries of alarm.

Amonis looked up in irritation, called up something in Halettite. I looked fearfully up at the face and saw in a moment what it was: the fifth gantry had come loose, was hanging drunkenly from its ropes. The sacks of broken stone we'd used to keep it underwater were swinging ominously from its underside.

Someone on Murshash's boat shouted a warning, which echoed hollowly through the tunnel of stone and water. I saw paddles on his boat digging into the water, people working desperately to move it out of the way in case the gantry fell.

'Quickly!' Sevasteos called across, urging the second boat on.

Above us, the ropes below the gantry were being blown to one side as if by a strong wind, and I heard an ominous creak.

Then the last of the fastenings gave way, and the gantry with its weights flailing plummeted down the side of the dam, bouncing off the walls. Where the weights hit the dam, gouges appeared in the surface. But the worst was to come. The gantry landed in the water just behind Murshash's raft.

A few more feet and they might have made it, but I watched in horror as two of the rock-filled sacks smashed the end of the raft to matchwood. Screams resounded off the walls, and the raft tipped crazily on its side.

'Abandon ship!' That was Murshash's voice. The raft was disintegrating, wood flying out of all sides. The slaves manning it needed no bidding, and poured off, swimming towards us as fast as they could.

'Steer towards our shore!' the Inquisitor ordered.

'But the survivors,' Emisto protested.

Amonis turned an icy glare on him and pointed up at the fifty-foot wall of water towering over us. It was rippling, as if waves were running along it, and a shower of water broke from the top, just enough to soak us.

'She's losing control,' said Amonis, a look of fury on his thin features. 'I'll see her scourged for this.'

The ripples grew larger, the water distorting like the undulations of a giant snake. But it held, for now.

'Row, you scum!' Amonis shouted at us. 'Or you'll go the same way!'

I wasn't sure whether he meant to a scourging or into the lake, but I dug my paddle into the water, helping to pull us frantically in towards the shore. The water level was rising much faster now, far too fast for comfort. As if we were being pushed up by a giant hand, a sensation I knew only too well from previous encounters with magic underwater.

Screams echoed through the rising tunnel from those left behind. If they could just survive until we were fifteen or twenty feet below the normal surface, they might be all right. Thetis, preserve them. Lady of the Sea, protect them.

Another scream, an animal cry of desperation, from the shoreline. We were thirty feet below the line where the dam's stone changed colour, marking the normal surface. I glanced behind: there was no sign of the other boats, only debris and heads bobbing in the dark water.

The water was rising at a dizzying speed now, the water undulating wildly. A white crest appeared at the top, a fountain of water falling down to drench everything on the raft, covering the deck in water.

Then we were literally thrown upwards as the barrier subsided to form a giant wave, and from being below the surface of the lake we were pushed well above it. The men standing up in the centre were thrown against the handrail on one side, and I heard a splash as someone went in. Not the Inquisitor; I could see a flash of black and white out of the corner of my eye.

Then we were safe on the swell of the lake, our only motion that of the three-foot waves that stretched away in every direction, breaking against the stone of the dam. We weren't bow-on to the waves, so the raft was pitching at a crazy angle, and for a moment I was underwater, only hanging on by the rope around my waist. I didn't dare open my eyes, not with the amount of mud in the lake.

'Paddle!' Sevasteos was shouting. 'Even her out.'

By the time I'd clawed myself back into place at the cost of several splinters in my arms, the waves were beginning to subside. There was nothing to show for the disaster except a pair of loose ropes where the gantry had been and a few heads bobbing in the water.

Seven people had died during or after the gantry's fall. Murshash, it was discovered, had been unable to swim and had drowned in the waves on the surface. Biades had been hit by one of the weights and died immediately; we never recovered his body.

I felt a pang of regret at the Halettite's death, something that would have been unthinkable a few weeks earlier. I'd had little close contact with him, but he'd been exceptional for one of his people, more than just an arrogant, uncivilised boor. Perhaps it had been his dedication to his trade, a trade which for once wasn't conquest.

His was also the only death Amonis seemed to regret. Biades was hardly worth a mention, and the five dead slaves were beneath notice.

He'd wanted to have everyone who'd participated in building that gantry whipped, but Sevasteos refused to let him — as did Shalmaneser, surprisingly enough. The Halettite nobleman probably didn't want damaged slaves. I was profoundly relieved at their stand, given that I'd been involved with it.

My relief vanished, though, when I found that the Inquisitor wasn't going to be cheated of his blame so easily, and had Ravenna punished instead. The work of Ranthas had been set back because of her failure to hold the wall steady and save Murshash by calming the lake.

It felt like the most hideous experience I'd ever had,

being forced to stand helpless among the other slaves while one of the soldiers laid open her back with a whip, criss-crossing the older scars left by my brother. It would have been less painful if I'd been the one tied to the makeshift wooden frame, because I knew what this felt like and it was nothing compared to the pain and the anger I felt now.

Oailos kept a vice-like grip on my arm all the way through, but I might as well have been alone there for all the difference it made. If it hadn't been for my time in the ruins of Ukhalinan, learning to avoid being noticed, I'd have betrayed both of us doing something monumentally stupid. She never cried out, and that at least was one less spur to my temper; I knew she wouldn't feel the whipping itself, hiding in the void of her own mind. Only the aftermath.

And it was the first time the reality of the Domain occupation had come this close. This had been done to me when she escaped, but never to Vespasia or Pahinu, or any other friends I had among the slaves. Never to someone who meant anything near as much to me as Ravenna did. This was what the Crusade and religious rule meant in the end, having to stand by helplessly while someone I loved was whipped – for no crime at all and on the word of a man who could not be gainsaid because his authority came from a god.

This was what the Archipelago had endured for the past four years. Ravenna had fought the Domain, had used her magic to kill its people – but so many of those who suffered at the hands of the Inquisitors were innocent of any offence against them. Amonis claimed to be acting by the divine law of Ranthas, but this was the opposite of law, too far to be even a parody of it. Where the Inquisition was concerned, no-one was ever innocent.

On the lake shore below the cliffs of Ravenna's home-land, listening with numb horror to the sickening sound of each stroke of the whip, I finally learnt how to hate. Not simply the strong dislike that many people called hate, the dislike that one clan might have for its bitterest rivals, but hatred of the kind that had sustained Ravenna for the seventeen years since her brother was murdered by the Sacri.

It wasn't a pleasant lesson, but it gave me the will to watch and wait, instilled in me the kind of passion that drove the ancient Thetian tragedies. As soon as it took root, it fed off all the terror and misery I'd lived through or heard of in the last four years. What I wouldn't realise for a little longer was that I'd finally grasped my true family inheritance, that it wasn't the looks, or the temper, or the magic that made the Tar'Conantur Emperors what they were. None of those were enough to explain the intensity that had driven Aetius and Carausius in their long, bitter war against the Tuonetar.

It wasn't until after the Inquisitor had delivered a sermon and Ravenna had been dragged back to her cage, sobbing with pain, that I moved again, finding my eyes unexpectedly and totally dry.

The Inquisitor and the Thetians walked back into their huts, and we were pushed into the guarded section of open ground that was set aside for us. I made my way over to the ship's prow rock and sat down in its shade, positioning myself where I could see the huts as well as everything else. I wasn't alone for long, as I'd expected.

'Now you know what it feels like,' said Oailos without preamble, sitting down on a flat outcrop to my left.

I nodded, still not trusting myself to say anything.

'There were things I saw when the Venatics arrived in Ilthys that were worse. To have your own people, your friends and neighbours, suddenly turn against you and shriek for your blood, hand you over to the Inquisitors . . .'

'I never had to go through that.' But I was the one who'd persuaded Sagantha, then Viceroy, to give the Venatics a chance. When it had seemed as if they came with a message that promised peace for most of the

Archipelago, a message which only the most dedicated heretics would turn a deaf ear to.

'That wasn't my meaning. I wouldn't come here to tell you how much worse it could have been. Those people in Ilthys believed they were acting justly, righteously, in the name of Ranthas. After all, the Venatics had told them so many times how evil heretics were. Amonis believed he was meting out divine justice, and that's the only law that rules us now.'

I felt as if my insides had been scrambled by a mad cook, but it wasn't the queasiness of an upset stomach – more like a twisted elation, and I didn't like it at all.

'He can do that to any of us, but it's much worse when it's someone else, someone you love.'

I hardly noticed Vespasia joining us, sitting on the ground because there wasn't any room left on the ledge. Oailos knew what it felt like as well as I did, only his loved ones, whoever they'd been, had been separated from him when he was shipped off as a penitent. I could dream of rescuing Ravenna, but he didn't even know where the rest of his family were.

'In their eyes, they have the right to do that to any one of us,' said Oailos. 'That's no different from any occupying power in history. What makes it so terrible is that they've sanctioned it by divine right, not simply use of force. If they did it simply on a whim, they'd be no better than beasts, but they can turn a whim into an article of faith and inflict it on everybody on Aquasilva.'

'Wasn't that just a whim?' I asked, wondering why my voice sounded so strange. 'He wanted somebody to blame for the accident.'

'Maybe it was, but you heard the sermon, his justification for it. It's not his need to lash out that's scarred her for the rest of her life, it's the will of Ranthas.' He paused. 'Was it the will of Ranthas that put the other scars there?'

I shook my head. 'No, that was just pure malice, and it

wasn't even a priest who put them there.' And unlike ordinary whip scars, they'd continued to hurt and burn, so savagely that sometimes I'd heard her cry out in her sleep from the next room, begging for her tormentor to stop. She'd never let anyone touch her skin since, not even allowing the healers to apply the balm when we finally found some but insisting on doing it herself.

'She'll survive,' Vespasia said, but that only sparked some of my suppressed anger.

'Will she go on surviving?' I demanded. 'Ithien said I was born under an unlucky star, but she's had a far worse time than me. And I take back what I just said. My brother may have held the whip, but the priests were just as responsible for him as they were today.'

Even Oailos looked shocked this time, and I realised I shouldn't have said that. Another slip of the tongue which I could ill afford.

'Your brother did that?' he said.

'My brother was a monster. He was torturing her to hurt me.'

'What happened?'

'He's dead,' I said, my satisfaction only clouded by memory of his last moments, when the person he had once been displaced the monster he had become.

'Whatever happened in the past, today was unforgivable.'

Vespasia nodded in assent. 'It was more important for him to punish her than to mourn the dead. Even for a Halettite, Murshash deserved a better epitaph.'

'He's gone,' Oailos said firmly. 'Maybe he was the best of them, but to him we were still slaves. I'll grant you it was a pity that he died instead of Amonis, but no more.'

An hour or so later Amonis announced that he was going down below the dam, into the chasm to investigate the ruins there. He took only his Sacri and the mind-mage

125

with him, and we were all glad of their absence – all except Sevasteos and Ithien. He apparently left instructions that we were to begin preparing for the next stage of the work; we'd finished what we came to do, but obviously there was a larger project here. And what were the ruins he talked about? I'd never seen any.

Sevasteos waited until the Inquisitor and his guards were out of earshot before losing his temper.

'The bloody vulture expects us to stay here and wait on his pleasure!'

I could make out his words, in Thetian, from half a camp away.

'Clear the road to the bloody quarry, more huts, a wooden jetty, who does the arrogant bastard think he is?' He stalked out of the house, gestured around at the expanse of broken ground with its shingle beach and a few huts. 'What does he think this is, an abbey?'

Ithien didn't look any more pleased, but he'd managed to keep his temper in check, and I heard him reasoning with Sevasteos in a low voice. Obviously he didn't want Shalmaneser, sitting unperturbed under an awning, to hear what he was saying. After a while I saw the architect's normal composure begin to return, then he went back inside. Ithien came over to me.

'Atho, I'll need you and four other people for a trip to the quarry, see what we can get out of it without restarting operations in earnest. Choose four people you can trust.' He said the last words without moving his lips more than the minimum.

I didn't quite manage 'trust' because the first person I saw was Oailos. He was our unofficial leader and there was no way I could have left him out, but even after our earlier conversation I was wary of him. Oailos was the kind of man who started slave revolts, and that was something I didn't want. There was no conceivable way we could win.

The others I found were Vespasia and two oceanographers I knew quite well, a man and a woman who seemed reliable. One was another Ilthysian, who like Oailos knew Ithien's reputation and something about him from earlier.

Ithien lost no time in saddling up his mount and ordering us to follow him; although it was the heat of the day, the fresh southerly wind made the temperature bearable even away from the lake.

The trail to the quarry climbed eastwards into the mountains, following a small canyon away from Tehama on the far side of the lake. There were trees on either side of the path, part of the blanket that covered the lower slopes of the Tehaman mountains until the slopes grew too sheer for them to survive.

It was an impressively large quarry, an almost circular bowl reached through a narrow defile at the end of the path, cut away to allow enough room for a cart to pass through. The bowl was overgrown now, the lines of half-cut whitish stones softened by the ravages of time.

'You have to respect the Tehamans,' Ithien said as we stood in the centre, looking around. 'They knew what they were doing. Too bad they had to side with the Tuonetar. Anyway, see if you can find any piles of cut stone. Fan out, look under mounds and at the base of cuttings. Atho, stay with me.'

As the others separated to follow his orders, Ithien led me over to a spur which projected from one side of the quarry, near a couple of huge blocks resting on the remains of wooden rollers.

'This spur is all the right kind of stone, apparently,' he said, in a voice loud enough for any of the others nearby to hear. 'I need a rough estimate of how big it is.' Then he lowered his voice as we passed out of Oailos's sight.

'Sorry for the charade, but I couldn't do anything back at camp, not with those Sacri watching everything we do. Not to mention those watchdogs I mentioned.'

'The Imperial Guards?'

He nodded. 'Every high official has them, the Emperor calls it an escort of honour, claims it'll give the Legion some experience of real conditions. In fact, they're there to stop any of us wandering out of line.'

'So you're not actually finding life under the Emperor as comfortable as all that? Tell me, is it the Domain's atrocities you don't like, or simply the fact that you don't have the freedom to ride roughshod over everybody?'

I bent down to hammer a peg into the ground and brought a ball of twine out of my surveyor's bag. Not the most advanced method of doing what he'd asked, but slaves weren't entrusted with sophisticated tools.

'I have more chances to do that than ever before,' he said coldly. 'If that was what I wanted, I'd have followed your brother instead of the Assembly. I suggest you stop wasting my time, we can't talk here for ever.'

'So what do you want to talk about? Why you and Sevasteos are behaving so stupidly to that Inquisitor? Are you going to tell me what's happening here?'

'I don't know,' he said flatly. 'The Inquisition has plans for this place that neither of us are aware of. We were sent out here to do some minor repairs which would allow the lake to be developed, only it turns out there's a lot more to it than that.'

'You think I believe that? The Imperial Architect sent out here to work on a project as pathetic as this?'

'He's in disgrace. Not dismissed, but banished from Selerian Alastre until the Emperor's advisers deign to recall him. As penance for something he said to the Exarch, he has to work for the Domain for a while. That's why he's so bad-tempered when Amonis is around.'

I wondered how much of this I could believe. It was all too dangerous to take at face value, but the best lies were those which were closest to the truth, and Ithien was a politician. He knew that as well as anybody.

'Amonis is looking for any excuse to charge Sevasteos with heresy, and you know what that means. As far as Amonis is concerned, there's no other way Sevasteos could be so dismissive of him and the Halettites. The fact that Sevasteos might resent being seen as a treacherous incompetent for not wanting a full survey doesn't seem to have crossed his mind.'

And if Sevasteos was arrested and interrogated, they'd put all of us to the question. Standard practice: if a traitor was found in Haleth, all his slaves were tortured in case their evidence could cast light on his activities. The torture was compulsory, I'd been told – no evidence from a slave could be accepted otherwise – with the result that guilt was virtually guaranteed.

'But what can we do against him?' I reached the point where the spur shelved inwards, and drove another peg in. A rectangle and a triangle, it would have to be, then I'd measure the height. There was an abacus in my bag, but I was educated enough not to need anything except space to calculate on. An oceanographer had to be comfortable with equations, although my grasp of simple figures could be shaky.

'That's what I need you and the others for. Can I trust them all to value their own skins over whatever reward they think they'll gain?'

Was Ithien mad? An Imperial officer relying on slaves to protect him from the Inquisition? This stank to high heaven.

'I think so,' I said cautiously. 'But they don't trust you. They know you changed sides, and they don't like you for it.'

'Too bad.'

'They won't help you if the risk is too great. What do you want them to do?' I drove another peg in, at the apex of the triangle. We were in full view of the others now, and Ithien sat on one of the blocks as if to watch their progress.

'Nothing that risks their own lives. Just to be ready for what I intend to do.'

'Which is?'

Ithien paused. I wasn't taking that for an answer.

'You explain, or we don't help.'

'You pick up the old ways very easily, Cathan,' he said, with a faint smile. 'I wouldn't be surprised if this has toughened you up, too, made you less willing to go along with what others want of you.'

'That includes you, Ithien,' I said, my mind racing. There was something more going on here, something he didn't intend to tell me. 'I don't have the time to play word-games either.'

'I know you don't. But at the moment you have no freedom, no weapons and no way of rescuing her with that mind-mage around.'

'You want to get rid of the mind-mage.'

'If I can rely on you afterwards. Will you and Ravenna be able to deal with the guards if the mind-mage is out of the way?'

'Not Ravenna. The chains they've put on her will block her magic even without the mind-mage's help.'

'Can you, then, or will you need her to be released?'

I looked up at him as I unrolled the ball of twine, moving slightly away from him along the side of the spur.

'If I use magic here, every mind-mage in Qalathar will feel it. The only way to escape is by the coast, and they'll catch us long before we can get there.'

'I wouldn't be so sure about that. The water down below the dam is the end of an inlet, it comes out on the north coast about thirty miles west of Tandaris.'

So that was why it seemed so familiar. We couldn't be more than a dozen miles from the house where Ravenna had been imprisoned, where the Emperor and Sarhaddon had captured us on that ghastly night four years ago. But Ithien was on a hiding to nothing with that idea.

130

'Then the inlet leads out on to Perdition's Shore,' I reminded him. 'Where my brother died. It's almost impossible to get a manta through that safely, let alone a small boat.' And where was he planning to get transport from, I wondered? There wouldn't be any boats down there.

'You managed it, though.'

'In a small manta, yes, one which was built to survive in the middle of a battle.'

He paused for a moment.

'There's a manta down there at the moment,' he said, finally. 'That's what Amonis has gone to see. It must be a Domain manta.'

'But how do you know this?'

'I saw its riding lights a few evenings ago, and then yesterday I saw the wing. They've anchored very deep, but the water's quite clear.'

So that was what those two strange lights had been, the ones I thought had been a shepherd's hut or a small boat. Surely not, though – it had only been my brother's magic that had allowed his ships to enter four years ago, and the Domain wouldn't let any of their captive mages near a manta's controls. The currents were what made Perdition's Shore so lethal, and it wasn't even enough to be able to see them with a water-mage's eye. My brother had used brute force, magic vastly more powerful than anything I possessed, while I'd relied on my oceanographic experience.

'You don't believe me,' he said after a moment, clearly impatient and disappointed at my lack of faith.

'I don't think the Domain could have brought a manta up here. And in any case, you're living in a different universe if you think this has a chance. Will we be able to kill the mind-mage, eliminate all the soldiers and the Sacri, then get on board that ship, disarm whoever is on board, and get out through Perdition's Shore and the odd Imperial squadron?'

'Do you have a better idea? Or would you rather stay like this and lose Ravenna again? Or watch that happen to her a third time? You don't really have a choice.'

'So why do we need you and Sevasteos at all?' I demanded. 'Everything you've just described we could do as well on our own.'

'Do you suppose you could deal with the mind-mage, lure him somewhere far enough from the others that you have time to kill him and still stop the others?'

It had been windy for the past couple of days, which might or might not indicate the approach of a storm. For all I knew, it could be normal for this area; the presence of the Tehama plateau would play havoc with the weather around its base. 'It'll be slightly more tricky, but we'll all feel more comfortable if we don't have to rely on you.'

'And you're sure you can trust all of your fellows? There are no informers, no people of doubtful loyalty?' He saw my hesitation and pressed home his advantage. 'We gain nothing by inciting revolt and then turning on you. You'd simply accuse us and it would be all the evidence the Inquisitors needed. I changed sides to save my family, because our beloved Emperor Aetius doesn't believe in threatening people directly. He works through those who are closest – parents, children, lovers. He may be a jumped-up Halettite thug, but he's obviously learnt subtlety somewhere.'

Though, to be honest, we couldn't blame the Halettites for much more than his lack of scruples. He was Thetian by birth, with all my family's less attractive traits, and at first he seemed to have come out of nowhere. I hadn't believed it when I heard the first rumours that he was well-known under another name, a mangling of his own, but as the months had passed it had become increasingly obvious that he was who he claimed to be.

However impossible that seemed.

'But now . . .'

'My father died a few weeks ago, and he was the last of

my close family. We managed to keep it secret from the Emperor, pretend he was merely ill.' There was a shadow of repressed grief on Ithien's face briefly, the look of someone denied the chance to mourn and whose loss would only get worse as he was unable to acknowledge it. 'So I have this little window to escape him before he finds some other hold over me.'

I hoped Ithien didn't believe that. From what I'd heard of him, the Emperor would be more likely to shift his vengeance to the next degrees of kinship. No wonder there were so few dissidents left. Only those who, like Oailos, had nothing to lose were free to act.

'Can I talk to the others?' I said finally. 'Send Oailos over to help me or something, just in case you're being watched.'

He nodded and moved away, leaving me with a couple of minutes of grace, but it was too little time. Ithien had at least been right about his own denunciation if we accused him of anything – even under torture – so, unless this was all a fantastically elaborate plot to catch me, he stood to lose out by it.

And if we didn't act, Ravenna would stay a prisoner of the mind-mage. It was only his life between us and freedom, in the end. I might not like it, but Ithien was the only one who could help us.

'You need help?' Oailos said.

'No, but look as though I do. Ithien claims he wants to help us.'

Oltan Canadrath to Hamilcar Barca
Greetings.

I hope this letter finds you in good health as ever, and not suffering too much from your stay in Selerian Alastre. I am sorry for the length of time it will have taken to get to you, but as ever I cannot afford to have my letters opened and read by the Thetian intelligence service. I had to wait for an official courier ship and pay the captain a substantial sum of money to have it delivered without interference.

You chose a good time to go away, as little has happened in Taneth these past four weeks or so. It is unnaturally hot, which has made me grateful for the money I spent on having flamewood-powered fans installed in the mansion. I have been taking the opportunity to inspect your island as you asked me to. The cool of the water and the quiet is a blessed relief from the baking heat in the city, and this is the first opportunity I have had to see the buildings you ordered renovated; the rooms are light and very spacious, and many have views over the Straits or towards the city; you shall at last be able to house enough of the House staff out here to make running its affairs practical. I must look to my own island now, or I will find yours overtaking it in splendour.

The exodus at least has given rise to some small amounts of gossip; Lord Ithobaal took the opportunity to marry that Southern Archipelagan girl he has been so besotted with while his mother was out of the city. A dreadful woman she is, I hope she gets apoplexy when she finds out. She had had her heart set on an alliance with Banitas, as you know, but I feel Ithobaal will be better off this way. The new Lord Banitas is as worthless as his father, and seems not to have inherited any useful qualities. I predict it will be six months before his cousin deposes him, and good riddance too.

However, there is one more important piece of news that I felt I should pass on to you, given that you're heading to the Archipelago when you finish your battle with the Thetian customs inspectors. Sarhaddon passed through yesterday on his way back to Tandaris, accompanied by an unusually large number of his Venatic monks. I have it from a reliable source – and I would not trouble you otherwise – that a new wave of preaching is to begin soon.

It will mean trouble principally for the secular schools, which will not interest us, and for the Oceanographic Guild, which is of more concern. I believe they have some grand design for it, which will inevitably involve large amounts of upheaval, and probably some danger to shipping from storms that have gone unnoticed. I suggest you warn your factors and contacts as soon as possible.

I still have not been able to discover quite why Sarhaddon so loathes the Guild. It has been years since anything was heard of Cathan or Ravenna, and as we have despaired for their lives, so Sarhaddon must feel that they are safely out of the way. I have seen no signs of his persecution slowing down, though, and have heard rumours of food crises in some areas. It might be worth looking into these, as there might be a market for Equatorian or perhaps Thetian foodstuffs, provided we can cover the transport costs.

Other than that, the business of House Canadrath goes well, as does that of House Barca. I enclose Mardonius's monthly report for your attention, and he assures me that all is fine. I venture to suggest that one of us, perhaps both, should call in our loans to House Setargon. Their promised neutrality in the Senate is beginning to wear thin, and they show ambitions to gain a seat on the Council of Ten at the mid-year elections.

Elassel has succeeded in finding a bass viol for her quintet, and they already have several performances lined up. Your house is as full of musicians as ever, and when she arranged a recital there the other day for one of her friends, you would hardly have known it for the mansion of a Great House. Your sponsorship of her activities seems to have brought you a fair amount of popularity among the urban population, so at last you have something to congratulate yourself on when other Lords mock your interest in the arts. She has imported several Archipelagan musicians who were in danger of being arrested, which I suspect will give you another small headache but is worth it for the music they play, which should inject a little life into the city over high summer.

I wish you luck in your affairs, as ever,
Oltan

CHAPTER IX

The next morning, I emerged from my ramshackle hut to find a chillier world. The breeze had become a wind, whipping the water of the lake up into wavelets, and the pale blue sky was dotted with white puffy clouds. There was no trace of the hot, dry heat that we'd grown used to – if anything, the air was humid and heavy. Ithien had been right, then.

'There's a storm brewing,' said Vespasia, looking around.

I nodded. No question about that. What I didn't know was how big it was going to be. There had been a steady wind from the southeast for the last three days, which we now realised had been an unusual advance warning.

I looked round at the Thetians' hut to see Ithien and Sevasteos standing in the doorway; from their gestures, they were talking about the same thing. Neither looked especially worried.

We'd guessed what our tasks for the day would be even before Sevasteos gave them to us. The gantries were useless now that we'd finished work on the top of the dam, and far too dangerous if they blew away in the storm; everything else from the pack animals to the one remaining raft had to be put somewhere safe.

Out on the parapet the wind was gusting straight down the valley, strong enough to make the poles of the gantries creak ominously.

'No point trying to dismantle the wretched things in that case,' Sevasteos said, when we pointed out how difficult it was going to be. 'Weight them so they sink, and then cut them loose.'

In the event, the most practical weights proved to be the concrete, so while bigger men did all the dangerous work of preparing everything, I crouched in the lee of the parapet mixing enough concrete to weigh the gantries down. I was instructed to use Sevasteos's red dust, and every time I ran along the walkway to get some more from him, there were more clouds and the wind seemed stronger.

It was amazing how much the mountains changed when the sun wasn't shining: they became dark, glowering, and their sandy-grey colour grew darker, closer to black. The lake was a dark grey-green now, its blue colour totally gone.

'That's the last of this lot,' I said, lowering a bag of concrete down to the men on the gantry, with the wind blowing my hair into my eyes. 'Is it heavy enough now?'

Standing precariously on an upper plank of the gantry, Oailos nodded. 'I think so. Wait a second.' He jumped in and I saw his form swimming down, becoming indistinct very quickly. It was a couple of minutes before he resurfaced to confirm that the raft was sufficiently weighted.

Sevasteos had given instructions that no gantry was to be cast off without him inspecting it first, so I ordered everyone back on to the walkway and went to fetch him. At the second working, a couple of dozen feet away, another team was close to finishing.

The architect brought a leather bag with him when he came back, and it wasn't until he'd confirmed Oailos's verdict – without entering the water, of course – that I discovered the reason why.

'Warning lamps,' he said, pulling two brightly glowing objects each about the size and shape of a watermelon from the bag. 'They'll glow for a few hours and then go out, but in the meantime they'll warn us if any of the gantries float to the surface again.'

Two men had to go down the ladder again into the

unsteady waves to fix the lamps on before Sevasteos pronounced himself satisfied. Casting the gantry adrift was a relatively simple matter of loosing the ropes that held it and then throwing the anchoring sacks over the side. Simple in theory; in fact, the sacks were very heavy indeed and required almost everyone's combined strength to lift them without breaking the ropes that held them.

The gantry had begun to slip away even as we lifted, and so we flung the sacks outwards before stepping back out of range. They fell outwards, reminding me of the flailing weights on the fourth gantry that had sunk Murshash's boat, and then I watched the orange sparks of the warning lamps fade into the water until they were gone.

Although it wasn't quite midday, it was as dark as sunset, and the white clouds that covered the sky were darkening too, turning to an angry grey. To the south, they were almost black. There wasn't much time; it would hit before nightfall, and it could go on for three days if we were lucky – or unlucky. I wasn't sure whether a long or a short storm would be more use.

There was a frantic rush to prepare the last gantry in what was by now a huge swell, and I was extremely glad not to have been in the water. Several men were injured by being thrown against the wall and had to be helped up; in the end we were throwing the concrete down, and Sevasteos let the warning lamps be fixed even before work was finished.

To my surprise, the gantry fell as planned, the lights vanishing into dark water, and we ran back along to the far side. My tunic was half-soaked from the spray, and everyone else was dripping wet and in a hurry to get back to the fire. Ithien had ordered it lit to cook a hot meal, probably the last chance we'd have in three days.

The weather would make things easier, I thought as we walked back, falling in step beside Oailos. It would be more difficult for everyone to see what was going on, and the rain and the darkness would add to any chaos.

'When we've got time, remind me to have a word with you about this,' he said, gesturing down at the lake.

'What?'

'The lamps,' he said. 'Warning lamps are half that size, just a flamewood ember, and nowhere near as bright.' He looked puzzled for a moment. 'We still don't know what this dam thing is all about, and I wouldn't be inclined to trust anyone.'

'Any refinements?' I said, gesturing up at the sky.

'One or two.'

The plan we'd made yesterday in the quarry would involve perhaps twenty of us, the people we thought most trustworthy, but half of them only knew the barest skeleton, and had no idea how ambitious the plan was. It had to end in the mind-mage's death, and while I didn't want to kill in cold blood, there was no other way. Knocking him unconscious might serve, but it was too uncertain.

I couldn't be the one to strike the blow, because I was far too vulnerable. Mind-magic worked in a strange way, at its most effective on those who had magical talent. A single mind-mage could paralyse a whole army of conventional mages, but would struggle to deal with half a dozen ordinary men. And the more disciplined the minds of the targets, the less effective mind-magic would be. Facing Sacri or Imperial Guards, or even a citizen soldier whose trade required huge mental discipline – a jeweller, for instance, or a lens-maker – mind-power would be useless.

The soup was almost ready when we reached the other side, and once we'd been given our bowls, Oailos moved discreetly among the people who knew the most, telling them the small changes we'd agreed, and the difference that the rain and the gloom made. We tried as much as possible to keep ourselves away from those who didn't know without being ostentatious, but people like Pahinu were bound to notice something was amiss sooner or later.

I looked over at the huts and saw the mind-mage standing under the awning, talking to Sevasteos and Amonis. Half a dozen or so of the soldiers waited expectantly nearby, and after a few moments they moved over towards us. They were the key; even if Ithien failed to drug them as he'd promised, I'd still be able to deal with them.

'Everybody inside, and don't leave anything out here,' Emisto called. 'Make sure your tools are dry, we can't afford to lose any.'

The huts were overcrowded but not yet too uncomfortable, as they would be later if the storm went on for more than a day or so. No guard could have stayed outside in this kind of weather, so they secured the door and left us in the gloom. Ithien wasn't going to make his move until nightfall when the mind-mage would be on his own in the hut with the cage, so we had a long time to wait.

It was a nerve-wracking few hours, sitting in semi-darkness talking to Oailos and Vespasia about things which had nothing to do with this, and for much of the time my mind was elsewhere. Worrying about Ravenna and remembering the last time I'd been here, the night Ravenna had received those scars and my brother had died. The night we found *Aeon*, the great ship hidden in its cavern below the rocks, only to abandon it again two days later. Ravenna and the ardent rebel Tekraea had both needed medical attention badly, and there was none to be had on the cavernous, empty ship. She'd been right, though: we should have gone back rather than to Thetia, but it was easy enough to see in retrospect. I only hoped *Aeon* still remained hidden, protected from the Domain by the treacherous sea of Perdition's Shore.

We kept a desultory watch, more for form's sake than anything else, to stop us feeling too cut off from everyone else. We were close enough to the next hut to signal across, and there was a view of the Inquisitor's building and some others.

None of us expected to see any movement, so it was all the more surprising when, during Vespasia's stint at the high, slitted window, a cloaked figure made his way down between two of the guards' buildings and into the Inquisitor's. Only five of us saw him, and we all agreed that it was the wrong bearing and wearing the wrong clothes to be a guard.

So who was it?

'Someone from that ship down in the bay, I reckon,' said Oailos quietly, careful not to let anyone overhear. Only six of us knew about the manta, although we hadn't been able to confirm its presence yet.

'Why are they coming up, though?' Vespasia asked.

'Perhaps they're putting out to sea.'

I shook my head. 'They're safer in the inlet. Perdition's Shore will be lethal in this weather.' This was summer, so it wouldn't be as bad as it had been when we were last here, but I doubted that the manta would have a water-mage on board or be as strongly built as my brother's flagship.

'That's the part of the plan I don't like.' I could sense the unease in Oailos's voice even though his face was in shadow. 'We don't know what's on that ship. It could be a regiment of Sacri or half a dozen mind-mages. And how are we supposed to board it in any case?'

'This is our only chance,' I reminded him. 'Before anyone else arrives.'

'It may be, but I'm still not entirely comfortable. Better to have done this on our own than with his help.'

'Would you rather he'd been another priest?' Vespasia said, and I was glad of her voice of reason. Oailos's pride was threatening to get in the way, which was something we couldn't afford. I didn't care how we escaped this or with whose help, as long as it worked.

'Better anything than a priest,' he said grudgingly. 'Keep your eyes open, anyway, in case more of them appear.'

In the event, two more shadowy figures appeared, moving down from the small path at the top of the clear land and going straight to join the first, with the Inquisitor. There were worried looks among the people who knew what was planned. We hadn't anticipated anything like this – would Ithien have the sense to wait for another night, a better opportunity? As far as we knew, no message had yet gone off – unless the manta in the inlet had taken it.

Where was the mind-mage? We hadn't seen him since we were locked in here, and there was no way to tell if he was in the Inquisitor's hut or his own. Surely the former – he wouldn't have been left out of any plans, whatever they were. But we could only see one corner of his hut, and there was no view of the side with the door in it.

Time dragged on, and still nothing – no more activity, no signal from Ithien. The rain drove against the walls in great sheets, slackening or growing more intense with shifts of the wind. Sometimes we could see all the way down to the crashing waves by the shore of the lake; other times it was hard to make out the shape of the nearest building. There wasn't much lightning yet, and the thunder was sporadic and half-hearted – eclipsed by the constant drumming of rain on the roof – but it would get worse before it got better.

Once, this would have been considered severe, two or three hours a long time for the weather to keep up this ferocity, but two centuries ago they'd measured the storms in hours, not days as we did.

It was bad enough inside, as the rain had very quickly found its way through numerous holes in the roof and the ceiling was leaking in a score of places, soaking the floor. We had to keep moving to find dry spots as new waterfalls appeared, and every time there was a scramble to move blankets out of the way. We started alternating the watch-men more frequently once the only comfortable watch position got wet as well.

It was Pahinu's watch, unfortunately, when something finally happened, but he lost no time in calling attention to it. I craned up to see what was going on, but couldn't make out anything more than a vague shape through the rain.

'Oailos is taller, let him take over,' someone urged; Pahinu was having almost as much trouble as I was. He moved out of the way with bad grace but just when Oailos was in position, an exceptional gust blew the rain sideways into his face, and the figure was gone by the time he could see again.

'There!' he said again, a moment later. 'By the mind-mage's hut. Someone coming out of Amonis's door now, running over . . . He's fallen, he must have tripped or something. He's not moving.' Another gust, and he moved back from the window, face and hair completely drenched. 'Try lifting someone up rather than selecting the tallest,' he suggested, and there was some uneasy laughter. 'Atho, you're fairly light.'

He and one of the other men lifted me up on to their shoulders until my head was level with the window. It took me a moment to see the place he'd been looking at, where someone else was now bending over the man who'd fallen. I couldn't see his face, because of the water-proof cloak he wore, but I assumed it was either Ithien or Sevasteos, and that the fallen man was the mind-mage. No signal, yet, though.

I blinked, trying to keep the water out of my eyes, as the kneeling figure rose to his feet and began turning towards us.

Then there was a rattling on the outside of the door, the noise as someone drew back the bolts, then footsteps receding. The person nearest to the door pushed at it uncertainly, and it flew open. I saw expressions of incredulity, but at the moment I looked back to the scene outside, saw a Guardsman appear by the figure I thought was Ithien, his scallop helm too distinctive to miss even

144

though he was bundled in his dark blue weather-cape.

'Atho, hurry,' Oailos whispered. 'Now!'

The opening of the door was the signal. I started to blank my mind into the void I needed for magic, but then the Guardsman knelt down beside the prone man – and the standing figure drove a knife through the eye-hole of the helmet. I couldn't hear anything, just saw the Emperor's elite legionary slump over the other man's body. That had been far too smooth – surely no-one as well trained as that should be so easy to kill?

I reached for the void again, closed my eyes and felt myself floating in the blank space of my mind, the sensations of my body falling away. I started to draw on power left unused for four years, feeling the tingle of magic on my skin.

And then it was cut off, as if someone had slammed a door in my face. I slipped out of the void and leaned dangerously backwards as Oailos and the other man staggered, feeling myself falling until Vespasia caught me and the two men could drop my feet to the ground.

'What happened?' Oailos demanded, furious.

'The mind-mage is still there, he blocked me.'

There was a gasp from some of the others, but Oailos took control before anyone could say a word.

'Quickly, everyone out. We can still win if we can get hold of the mind-mage. Someone get that Thetian's sword, we can take the Inquisitor's hut before they can call the guards.' He pushed the nearest woman towards the doorway and barged after her.

'But how . . .' another surveyor began.

'He's a mage. If you want to escape, this is your chance.' He grabbed my arm and pulled me after him as there was a sudden, frenzied surge to the door. I was almost pulled off my feet as he started running towards the dead Guardsman and his murderer, who had to be Ithien. He'd already taken the sword.

'Quickly,' Ithien said, handing the knife to Oailos. 'Pick up a stone, anything you can use as a weapon. Cathan, your magic!'

'He's not dead,' I said, desperately trying to reach my power and failing again.

Ithien swore, turned over the first dead man with his foot. He was dressed in black, and bearded – but he wasn't the mind-mage.

'Too late to go back now. I dealt with the guards, at least.' he shouted, to make himself heard above a crack of thunder. 'Sevasteos, get Ravenna out.'

The architect, a dark figure in the rain, started running over to the engineer's hut. He had a cloak, but the rest of us had been drenched the moment we left the hut, and the rain was running down everyone's faces and clothes in a constant stream, too heavy for the fabric to absorb all of it.

None of us gave a thought to Pahinu until we heard the door of the Inquisitor's hut slam open and saw someone disappearing inside. A moment later there were raised voices, cries of alarm, but I wasn't sure whether the guards could hear them. They had to be keeping watch, so they'd be on us in minutes.

'Move!' Ithien shouted covering the few yards to the Inquisitor's hut at a run, with the slaves following in a ragged band behind him. Oailos had sent one man off to open another hut, in the faint hope that some of the other penitents might arrive in time.

Yellow light spilled out of the open doorway, and Ithien paused on one side, swept his sword down across it. I heard the twang of a crossbow, but didn't see the bolt fly. Then the Thetian and two slaves crashed in through the door. One was Oailos, holding my wrist with his free hand. I was still unarmed.

I saw the faces of the men inside frozen as we rushed into the main room, which was lit by a pair of flamewood torches. Amonis, his face a mask of cold fury; Shalmaneser, with a slack crossbow in one hand, and two men in black and dark green, flanking the mind-mage in his gold-trimmed black. None of the last three held weapons, although there were knives at their belts.

'Kill them!' Oailos screamed, and moved aside to let the rock-throwers hurl their missiles into the room. But they'd had a second to move aside, and only two of the seven rocks hit their targets. Amonis staggered back, clutching his arm, while Shalmaneser grunted in pain and dropped the crossbow, suddenly gasping for breath. The rock had hit him in the stomach, large enough to wind him but nothing more.

'Guards!' Amonis shouted. 'Heretics, I will see you burn for this.'

The other slaves grabbed the nearest pieces of furniture – drawing boards, chairs – and hurled them down to the other end, as the priests ducked behind the table.

'Get the mind-mage!' Vespasia shouted, as Oailos let go his grip on my arm to charge forward and attack, shoulder to shoulder with Ithien.

The mind-mage drew his hammer and points of golden light sped across the distance towards us. The two men seemed to slow, as if they were fighting their own muscles, but they kept on.

Two of the others were frozen in place as the light hit them, but I didn't have time to do more than register it as I was hit.

It was as if I was on the verge of falling asleep, my head packed with wool, and the air seemed suddenly to turn to treacle, then to stone as my muscles locked up. I remembered this happening before, and I was powerless to do anything about it.

The two men in black and green moved forward to protect the mind-mage, and Oailos suddenly veered off towards the Inquisitor, crashing into the table. Ithien brought up his sword, but it was a blow that never connected as he slumped backwards without any apparent reason, colliding with Oailos.

It looked for a second as if it was over, but Oailos managed to reached out and grab Shalmaneser, falling on top of him. A moment later, I saw very clearly that he was holding the knife to the priest's throat.

'Let them go or I kill him,' Oailos growled, his burly shoulders set as if he could somehow ward off the mind-magic.

I saw only indifference on the mind-mage's face. 'If you kill him you've lost your bargaining tool.' He motioned to one of his protectors. 'Go and bring the guards here.'

The man gave a nod of acquiescence and left by the other door, more or less behind the mind-mage. His comrade moved forward to divest Ithien of his sword.

'Let them go, I said!' said Oailos.

The mind-mage glanced across at Amonis, who had now regained his feet. The Inquisitor shrugged, and the second man leant down and grabbed the back of Oailos's tunic, hauling him to his feet.

He wasn't quick enough, though. Shalmaneser gave a strangled gurgle as Oailos reached down and rammed the knife into his throat. The priest convulsed and I saw blood pouring on to the floor, then gave what might have been a scream. I shut my eyes, too sickened to watch the third murder in five minutes. Killing in battle was one thing, but none of the three men had had a chance to defend themselves.

'You have just made your end infinitely more agonising,' Amonis said, as Oailos was likewise pinned by the mind-mage's golden spark. He knelt over the dead man's body and murmured a quick benediction.

I felt a sick churning in my stomach as I realised that we'd all been dealt with. I heard footsteps outside the back door – Ithien must not have dealt with all the guards.

'Guards, secure these people,' Amonis called. 'They are heretics and . . .'

A perfectly aimed stone struck him on the forehead, and then I heard an ear-piercing shriek as a drenched fury hurled itself on the mind-mage from behind. I saw a chain looped round his throat, and suddenly the fog surrounding my mind was gone.

'Move!' Oailos shouted, reaching for the mind-mage's protector as the mind-mage himself was forced to his knees, his face turning red. I could barely see the face of his attacker, her black hair plastered to her face, but I knew who it was.

'Vespasia!' Ithien shouted. 'Get all the penitents out and down to the dam, now.'

Sevasteos appeared in the doorway, an almost animal snarl on his face, and flung another rock at the fallen Amonis.

Then the protector managed to get free of Oailos and hurled himself straight at the mind-mage, pushing him to one side and loosening Ravenna's hold on him. The man slumped forward, unconscious but still alive, and I wasn't in time to prevent the second man from pushing Ravenna out of the way. As I stumbled across the room, he dragged the mind-mage away from her, almost throwing him past Sevasteos and out into the night. I could dimly see him haul the prone figure on to his shoulder and start to stagger away.

'Go after him,' Ithien ordered, standing up. 'Oailos, go and secure the guards. Take their armour and weapons, we'll need all the help we can get.' He'd slipped effortlessly into the commanding role, and to my surprise Oailos acquiesced.

But by then I wasn't paying attention any more. Her chains caught in an overturned chair, Ravenna was struggling to get to her feet again. I rushed over but managed to stop myself from hauling her upright, because

I knew her pride well enough to realise she'd hate it. Instead, I pulled the chair away and held out a hand. She brushed the hair away from her face with one hand and stared up at me, her eyes very tired in a gaunt face.

She said nothing for a moment, and I heard Ithien's impatient finger-tapping behind us. Then she stretched up a hand and took mine, using it to pull herself to her feet.

'He got away,' she said, glaring out of the open rear door as if she could stop him in his tracks, medusa-like. Then she looked back to me and let go of my hand. 'Cathan. I've missed you. Can we kill him first and talk later?'

'Who was he?' Ithien asked. 'Do you know what this was all about?'

'Tehaman,' I said. 'His name is Memnon.' I hadn't trusted him with the information before, but we were on the same side now for sure, and he could know.

'It's appalling,' was all Ravenna said, a stricken look on her face. 'We must get away from here. They want to keep it secret, and they'll kill anybody to protect it.'

'What is it?' Ithien demanded. 'Tell me, we haven't got time.'

'*Aeon*,' she said. 'And my . . .'

Vespasia appeared at the door, out of breath. 'We've released everyone, Ithien. I've sent the strongest to help Oailos.'

'What about the mind-mage?'

'I don't know. They were still chasing him.'

'They won't catch him,' Ravenna said. 'None of you can. Cathan, we must catch him, we must!'

'You're in no condition to go after him,' Ithien began, but she cut him off, shaking the chains on her wrists and ankles.

'He's got the key, and these are magical, there's no other way.' She was doing her best to appear in control of herself, and even if the tremor in her voice gave her away, it was more than I could have managed after what she'd been through.

I turned to the Thetian. 'Ithien, get everyone armed and take the ship. Dress your men up as soldiers, Inquisitors, whatever you like, but get out. We'll catch the mind-mage and join you later.'

'How are you going to chase him like that?'

'He can't run either,' was Ravenna's reply. 'Ithien, please! Do as he says, and get away.'

The rain drove into our faces as we made our way up the slope, scrambling and walking at the same time. Ravenna was barefoot and hampered by the chains, but she drove herself harder than I did, not letting me help her except to stop her falling. I could hear shouts, utter confusion behind me in the intervals between the thunder, but we kept on, making our way up to the narrow defile at the top of the foreshore, a path that led heaven knew where. This was the way he'd gone.

There was a path of sorts, earth and crushed stone, winding its way along a miniature gorge between the rocks. It was barely wide enough for two, and slippery with water. The rain was beating down on my back and my head, running into my eyes so I could hardly see where I was going, even making it hard to breathe sometimes.

We stopped at the end of the first rise to suck in huge gulps of air, but only for a few seconds, then Ravenna started again. Her wrists and ankles must have been rubbed raw by now, but she wouldn't show any discomfort, only hobbled onwards with the awkward gait that was all the chains allowed her.

The noise of the storm had long since drowned out anything we could hear from behind, but as we followed the next set of bends in the path, I heard sounds from further ahead that surely weren't natural. Were the four penitents Oailos had sent ahead of us still on track, I wondered, or had they missed their way somewhere?

I stared into the murk ahead for a moment, wondering if I could make out anything, then stumbled and had to look back at the path. Had that been a faint glimmer of light ahead, or just the harbinger of a lightning strike?

Then we rounded another corner and I could hear laboured breathing quite clearly.

'It's him,' Ravenna said, and plunged on again. I glanced up again. Surely that was a torch ahead? The mind-mage hadn't been carrying a torch, but what if there were more of them.

The second man must have heard us scrambling up behind him, because he drew his knife and turned to face us, shouted something that sounded like the Thetian for *help*. His voice was lost almost instantly in the hissing of the rain, but he was still armed, which neither of us was. And behind him the mind-mage was slumped on the path, his black robes sodden but very definitely conscious.

No magic, then. I looked around wildly, trying to find some inspiration and wondering where the other slaves were.

'You'll have no help,' Memnon said malevolently in his peculiar accent. 'And we do, just a little way ahead. They'll be here soon enough.'

'But they're not here now,' Ravenna said, picking up a rock from beside the path. It wasn't very effective, but it was all we had, and I saw a look of worry come on to the other man's face. Even armed and fit against a pair of bedraggled slaves, we had the advantage of range.

As Ravenna flung her rock he ducked under it and ran down the few paces towards us, knife held ready. I dived at him a second before he reached us, hitting his knees and bringing him to the ground. Far stronger than I was, he kicked me in the shoulder and started to twist his knife round – then went limp. Ravenna held another stone in her hand.

'No time to waste,' she said, and we dragged ourselves

the last few yards. 'Pin him down, I'll get the key.' She brought the hilt of the knife down savagely on his head before he could move, then dropped it for a moment until she retrieved the key.

Neither of us noticed his 'help' coming until they were almost on top of us.

'Leave him alone!' a voice said, as Ravenna lifted the knife again. 'Kill him, and your own lives are forfeit.'

'Move away!' Ravenna said, her voice almost a sob. 'Move away, or I blind him.'

The tall figure in the black cloak, his features similar to those of the fallen mind-mage, motioned to the men behind him, and they took two steps backward. 'You will accomplish nothing with this.'

'You're not capturing me again!' she screamed. 'Traitor!'

'You're the traitor, *corvita*. Doubly condemned by the company you keep.' *Corvita* – little crow, it meant in Thetian. But he wasn't Thetian. The resemblance was unmistakable – this was Memnon's father, the Tehaman official Ravenna had believed would help her.

'After so many years we have one of your family at our mercy,' he said, the words directed at me this time. 'I expect every member of the Conclave will be present when we decide how to kill you, Tar'Conantur.'

I tried again to form the void in my mind and draw on the magic, expecting to feel it cut off – only it wasn't. I was too exhausted to handle very much, but knew what I could do.

I drew on my dormant shadowsight, looking up the path to find where they'd come from. A cave entrance, just behind the next bend. Water. There was water all around us, more power than I could tap even if I was fresh. I gathered the rain as if into a funnel, drawing it from yards away into a curtain that surrounded the unnamed man and his followers. I spoke without dropping out of the trance.

'Walk back into your cave.'

I could sense the fury coming from all of them, but after a second's hesitation they did as I'd asked, walking back up and into the cave, surrounded by a rippling wall of water several inches thick, constantly replenished by the rain. Once they were inside, I thickened the curtain and moved it across the entrance, where for a few minutes it would behave like a real wall. I set it in place with the most powerful construct I had left, a magical framework which would disintegrate within a few minutes, and then slipped out of the void.

'They're out of the way for a while,' I said, almost collapsing on to the unconscious mind-mage. 'We need to get back now.'

'You'll have to untie me, though,' she said, handing me the key. 'The keyholes are on the outside of each wrist, I can't reach them.'

She held out her hands; it took me a moment to find the lock, twist the key through the two complete turns it required, and then the manacles came off. My hand brushed against her wrist and I could feel how raw the skin was, but she insisted on unlocking the rest herself.

I heard more shouts, thought for an awful moment that the wall of water had given way. Then I realised they were coming from the other direction. They weren't voices I recognised.

The Sacri. We were cut off, and I had hardly enough energy to hold them back, let along deal with them.

'There must be a way down to the lake,' she said. 'If we go up and then see whether there's a path down, maybe we can get round on the edge of the cliffs or something.'

We ran up the last section of path to an open space in front of the cave. I saw furious faces behind the wall of water – all except the leader, whose words I could hear quite clearly even against the rain.

'You may run, but we will find you and bring you back

here to be tried before the Conclave,' he shouted. 'You can't hide from us any more, either of you, and one of us will catch up with you before very long. Enjoy your freedom while it lasts.'

More shouts from behind, and we turned and ran down the path at the far side of the open space, following it between twisting rocks and sheer cliffs until we had no idea where we were.

And as we fled below the cliffs of Tehama, further and further from safety, we could hear the cries of the hunters until the fury of the storm drowned everything else.

CHAPTER X

We had to stop eventually, an hour or so later, too exhausted and footsore to go any further, and we spent a drenched night huddled under an overhanging rock. It protected us from the worst of the rain, although not from the run-off that was cascading down the cliffs. We'd found a small beach, but the waves had been too severe even to think of swimming and we'd had to go on.

Somehow we managed to sleep for a few hours, having abandoned any hope of getting back to the dam in time to rejoin the others. The Sacri had called off their pursuit when the storm grew too savage, but they'd already chased us for hours, and they controlled the only route back.

It must have been the thunder that woke me again, because when I opened my eyes, the sky was still black and the storm continued unabated. It wasn't as ferocious as it had been earlier, but this wasn't going to be another mere cloudburst.

I stretched and wished I hadn't, because every muscle in my body seemed to have its own ache, an ache which the dampness had carried through to my bones. There hadn't been space to lie down, and I was leaning against a relatively vertical piece of rock, my head resting against Ravenna's.

My stretching had woken her up, and she groaned, no doubt feeling even worse than I did. She moved away from me, pushing half-dried hair away from her face.

'We have to go on,' she said wearily. 'They'll be hunting us again.'

'Already?'

I couldn't see her expression as she looked at me in the

darkness, but her tone was clear enough.

'They'll never let go of me. I know all about Tehama's alliance with the Domain now, and they know if they don't catch me all their secrecy will be pointless.' She crawled out from beneath the rock, leaving me with no choice but to follow her. The parts of my clothes that had dried were instantly drenched again, and the constant, numbing feel of the raindrops on my head was as bad as before.

'Won't you at least take the sandals?' I offered, as she started to walk off. Neither of us was used to going barefoot, but at least I'd been working and mobile the last year, while she'd probably spent most of it in Inquisition cells. 'Ravenna, please! You're not weak or anything, just show some common sense.'

'We'll alternate,' she said finally, and I pulled off my thin, badly made sandals and waited until she'd strapped them on. I was hungry, and we were still a long way from the forest, where we might be able to find something edible.

Then we were moving again along the path in the darkness, collecting scrapes and abrasions on legs and feet as I followed her along its tortuous, unpredictable route between the cliffs and the raging lake. We got occasional glances of the water over to the left, a seething mass of whitecaps lit up by lightning flashes, a nightmare for anyone to swim in since the dam inspections had filled it with mud.

There was no sign of anyone behind us, but in these conditions it would have been a miracle to have heard them fifty yards away. Had Ithien managed to take the manta? Had they even made it past the guards?

Either the penitents were holding tight in the inlet, or they were all dead. I didn't want to think about it, but in either event there was nothing the Inquisitor and the mind-mage could do except hunt us down.

'How big is the lake?' I asked at one point, as we rounded yet another bay and I realised we'd have to climb at least two hundred feet to cross the spur of Tehama that jutted out in front of us.

'Ten miles, perhaps more. I think the end shore is jungle, the forest comes back down to the lake somewhere before then.'

And if she was wrong, then we'd face another trek through furnace-like hills on empty stomachs.

Dawn came very suddenly, as it should, but without any immense change in the light – the sky changed quickly from black to dark grey, and I could make out the silhouettes of the hills on the far sides of the lake. Their sides were hidden by sheets of blinding rain, and there was nothing behind us to indicate a pursuit.

The terrain around us was becoming monotonous, an unending procession of jagged outcrops dominated by the impossible bulk of the cliffs. We were approaching the falls now, and I wondered how the path would bypass those. Presumably this was a route once used by the Tehamans, but not a very practical one – they must have had more efficient ways of communicating between the cities around the lake.

We stopped for a rest beneath another of the massive spurs, hiding ourselves behind a rock out of sight of the path, just in case the Inquisitors were closer than we feared. It offered almost no protection from the rain, but I was glad of the chance to sit down for a few minutes.

Sitting opposite me, Ravenna looked even more bedraggled now than she had the night before. I remembered her as lithe and slender, but that slenderness had almost become emaciation. Her face hadn't changed, except for the haunted look in her eyes – the tense resolve, the composure was more marked.

'Who was that man?' I asked, finally. 'What was he?'

'He's a Tribune of the Tehaman Commonwealth,' she

said, almost as if she was reading from a muster list. 'His name is Drances, Memnon's father. All those people in black are Tehamans.'

'I thought your people hated the Domain,' I said, beginning to realise what had happened.

'I thought they did too. But then they found out about the *Aeon*, and they decided that the Domain was much the best . . . ally. We've stopped long enough.'

It was like trying to squeeze blood out of a stone, because she simply wouldn't tell me any more. But what she'd said was bad enough.

I knew very little about Tehama, apart from the ancient history we were all taught, of how the Commonwealth had been the first civilisation on Aquasilva. But that was all past now, and most of the world thought the Tehamans were extinct. But not only were they still around, but thirty years ago they'd been important enough for Pharaoh Orethura to marry his daughter, Ravenna's mother, to a Tehaman of some rank.

And Ravenna had left her homeland when she was seven. She'd told me so little that I didn't even know her parents' names. True to form, she was unwilling to open up now.

I crested the next spur to find her standing on the other side, just hidden by the ridge-line, looking down on to what was unmistakably a Tehaman city – and beyond it, the edge of the forest.

The city itself was half-overgrown, the wide avenues clogged with small trees and the stonework half-buried under greenery. I couldn't see any houses still standing, and there were broken stones piled everywhere, stones washed a dark grey by the sweeping curtains of rain blanketing the city.

The path became a flight of wide stone steps here, less painful underfoot than the loose stones of the path but more slippery. Looking downwards all the time to make sure I didn't slip, I noticed that each step was a single mammoth block; heaven only knew how much labour it had taken to manoeuvre them into position.

The ground was more open here, and I felt painfully exposed until we reached the ruins of the first houses.

It was a very different place from any of the Archipelagan cities I knew, I realised, as we moved along the street past angular, monolithic buildings. Even the ruins of Poseidonis had been nothing like this; perhaps it was the total absence of arches anywhere here, of anything to soften the straight lines that made it so alien.

Many of the paving stones were cracked, and centuries of water running down from the surrounding heights had worn them absolutely smooth. It was almost like trying to walk on ice, except that here the surface was covered by an ankle-deep stream.

I followed Ravenna through the heart of the city, skirting heaps of rubble and fallen monoliths, and trying not to get caught by the snakelike creepers that had infested some areas. They were sticky and clung to my clothes, too tough and stringy to break.

The main street was a torrent with a viciously strong tow, more than strong enough to have swept either of us away if we'd lost our footing; as it was, we reached the other side a street or so nearer the lake.

The forest was thicker on the other side of the city, and I began to feel more comfortable as the trees became taller, the vegetation thicker. These houses were much more seriously decayed, and it wasn't until we were almost at the far side that I realised the city extended into what I'd thought was only forest.

We paused for a moment at the last house, my stomach growling with the anticipation of the food we were sure to find somewhere. I turned round and looked back, wondering how much of a lead we had.

I could just about make out the three or four figures at

the top of the steps, only half an hour or so behind us. Ravenna took my hand and we broke into a run, trying to put as much of the forest as we could between them and us. The road grew steadily more and more overgrown until it was no longer worth following – there was no point, better to move off into trackless jungle where they'd have a harder job following us.

When we finally stopped, somewhere in the darkness of the forest proper, and sank exhausted into the muddy earth near a tree-trunk, neither of us had the faintest idea where we were.

'What now?' I asked when I'd got my breath back, listening to the eerie dripping around us and the noises of a place that was never quiet. There was no sun to give us directions, no way of knowing where the hunters were any more.

'I don't know,' she said. 'We should have gone back straight away, dealt with the Sacri. There's no point now, it's too late.'

'It was too late the moment the Sacri started after us. But where now? The Domain controls the whole island.'

'Away from Tehama.' She rolled over on to her back, her grey tunic now almost completely covered in mud. I didn't want to stay here too long – the evil flying insects would have sought refuge from the rain, but who knew what the mud harboured? I was used to the relatively gentle rainforest of the small islands, not the immense cloud forest that still covered half of Qalathar. 'Cathan, I really don't know. Just so long as we get away from Tehama,' she repeated.

The energy that had sustained her this far seemed to have drained out of her, and she lay in the mud like a rag doll, utterly limp and exhausted. We were almost at the head of the lake, so we must have made nearly ten miles. How far was it to the south coast from here – thirty miles, thirty-five? We couldn't expect help from any villages –

the punishments for helping penitents escape were draconian, and in any case we were oceanographers, not popular since the Venatics arrived.

'Do you know of anywhere that's still holding out?' I asked. 'Did they mention any heretic strongholds?'

'None on Qalathar. They're all in the far south or west, I think.'

So we had to get off the island somehow, make our way past any patrol mantas that might be offshore, and find a place of refuge.

Thetis, why hadn't we turned back and simply used our magic on the Sacri? We could have been on a manta in a few minutes, with enough people to crew and sail to safety anywhere in the world. And instead, we'd fled in blind panic from the Tehaman and his few men.

'Ravenna, you know this island better than I do. Where should we be heading for?'

'Does it matter? We've no way to navigate in the forest, certainly not while this storm is still going on. If we head away from the mountains . . .' She sat up again.

'We can't see the mountains,' I cut in. 'I don't want to be recaptured any more than you do, but this isn't helping. What will they be hunting us with, are they any good in forests?'

'Tehama is all forest,' she said, hugging her knees. She was a sorry sight, bedraggled and with the rain carving streaks through the mud on her clothes. 'They know this area quite well, they haven't been as isolated as people think.'

'So we aren't safe even here?'

She shook her head. 'Not here or anywhere. The further we get from Tehama, the less advantage they have. Until we get off the island, they can hunt us with jaguars.'

Jaguars? Why jaguars? Hunting dogs weren't common in the Archipelago, as big cats were much better suited to the jungles – but I'd never heard of jaguars being used before, they were too elusive and hard to tame.

'Isn't there a way to avoid them?'

'We'll have to find out, but first we need to find some food.'

We trudged on, pushing already abused muscles further still, walking through the endless hissing of the rain. A few hours later we found something to eat, a small group of fruit palms growing in a clearing left by a fallen canopy tree. I recognised them as palaya palms, far larger and less kempt than those the Thetians grew in glasshouses, with leaves bent by the force of the storm — and clumps of orange fruit growing beneath the fronds. They were delicious; the only problem was that they were ten feet up, and neither of us was in good enough shape to climb a palm tree.

'If you could lift me, I'd probably be able to pick some of it. You're in better shape to be able to support me.'

It was an unexpected admission of reality, and I went over and stood by the tree trunk, cupping my hands for her to use as a foothold. She jumped up and made a wild grab at the trunk, the sudden weight almost knocking me over, but somehow she managed to reach the fruit and pull a clump off. The sudden shift in her weight made my lose my grip, and we both fell over, toppling into the thin, straggly weeds that covered the ground here so hard that I was winded. But there was a whole bunch of the slightly overripe fruit lying between us. Even after we discarded the one or two half-eaten by insects, the rest tasted like the food of the gods.

Once we'd eaten, we managed to detach another couple of bunches at no more cost than a few extra bruises, and slung them over our shoulder on creepers, to eat later. They wouldn't last very long, but at least they'd assure us of another meal, and neither of us could afford to be choosy.

As we made our way deeper into the forest, we

followed streams running down the centres of valleys in the hope that they'd lead us away from Tehama. Somewhere to the south of us was the main road connecting Tandaris and Kalessos, the only east-west highway in the interior, and the only landmark we'd be able to find in the rain. But at the moment there was no prospect of finding anything, and we could have been walking fifty yards away from the road and not seen it.

Ravenna's words echoed in my head, and whenever I was bringing up the rear I kept tensing at sounds behind us. But of course we had no way to tell where our pursuers were, or how far away, not in this numbing, endless rain with its occasional bouts of fury as the thunder and lightning grew more intense.

Four years ago I'd ridden along the highway and along the valleys above the inlet to rescue Ravenna from what I'd thought was the 'safe-keeping' of an Archipelagan noble. Only to find when I arrived at the house that Alidrisi Kalessos was dead, and my brother in control. That was the last time I'd been outside in a storm, though not the first. It had never been like this.

The sheer monotony of it was awful. There was no change in the scenery, just a procession of trees in one steep-sided valley after another, reaching upwards to a swaying canopy and a glowering sky rent by lightning.

By the time exhaustion forced us to stop for the night, anything more than a few trees behind felt like a distant memory. The dam, the fight, everything that had happened might as well have been a year ago. Everything except the brooding figure of the Tehaman and the long shadows cast by his hunting jaguars.

I'd wanted to stop in a small cave at the bottom of a sheer, vegetation-free cliff as darkness fell, but Ravenna insisted that we were still too close to Tehama, it was an obvious refuge and they'd expect us to stay there. Instead we'd plunged on until we found a far less satisfactory place, and one that was moreover difficult to reach. It was another overhang, half-hidden by trailing jungle ivy, twelve feet off the ground and barely seven feet deep.

It should surely have been the haunt of several unpleasant creatures, but it was as abrupt as if cut by a knife, and there were no nooks or crevices for anything to lodge in. It was still very close and very confined, though, with barely three feet of headroom at its highest, and we had to perch uneasily on its edge to finish our palaya fruit.

They weren't enough to ward off hunger any more, not after walking for so long, but we hadn't found anything else edible except for a solitary taraca globe on a fallen branch, its fellows far too high to reach. At least thirst wasn't a problem.

Small mercies were all we had to be thankful for, and at least we were out of the rain, could lie in the dry closeness of our tiny refuge and listen to it falling endlessly outside. There would be decks and decks of cloud in the sky far above us, clouds that wouldn't dissipate until they'd dropped all of their load.

I was tired enough to fall asleep quickly despite the discomfort of lying on bare rock, but it was an uneasy sleep, broken every so often when the thunder intruded into unsettling dreams.

I found myself wandering through a forest of stone trees, like the living trees in every respect except that they were made of the rain-swept grey stone of the Tehaman city. There were even stone leaves and creepers, as if an entire forest had been petrified in an instant. Everything was grey, without the slightest hint of green, and the sound of the rain was different, as it should be on stone. For a few moments I was puzzled, then I heard someone cry out indistinctly to the south, and ran through the forest towards the cry, only it kept shifting.

And eventually I reached them, and saw Ravenna lying there, crying out far too softly for me to have heard her from such a long way away. I dared not approach her, because a jaguar was standing over her, or rather the black shape of a jaguar made from the total absence of light, like a hole in Creation. The only real thing about it was its slitted golden eyes, watching me and drawing me into them while it held one shadowy paw hooked into the front of Ravenna's tunic.

I wanted to run away, because there was no way I could fight something which didn't exist, but instead I found myself held by its eyes, and lay down beside Ravenna on the mud-stones like a victim for the sacrifice.

Only when it moved its paw did I start away, and banged my leg against an obstacle which wasn't there — then I was back in the tiny rock space, and found myself looking around in the darkness for those eyes.

There was someone crying out, though, a few inches away; I couldn't see her face but I could hear her moving, whispering to herself and to people who weren't there.

I listened for a moment, but after a few words wished I hadn't. She was pleading, endlessly, the words running into each other, only it wasn't my brother she was talking to, it was people whose names I'd never heard.

I tried to slip back into sleep again, hating what I was hearing and feeling as if I was prying into her mind, a mental violation far worse than reading someone's diary. But I couldn't sleep, and I couldn't block out the words. She was so strong, so resilient, it was dreadful to know that all this was real, that she was dreaming of things that had happened to her.

Only at the end, as I finally managed to drift off to sleep, did it sound as though she was talking to my brother again, only without the utter panic in her voice that I remembered.

Sleep was no better, with more horrible images of shadowy jaguars filling my mind until everything broke down as if I'd been watching the scenes through glass, and someone had shattered the glass and let shards of darkness in.

It was rest, and I needed it, but when I woke up in the morning I felt no better, and still ached from head to foot. I shook Ravenna awake when I realised it was light outside, and we inched out of the hole and clambered back down the cliff to the stream, resumed our path from the night before. Ravenna looked pale and haggard, but I said nothing. Aside from one brief comment in the hut, neither of us had spoken about anything other than our hunters since we met. It was as if we were two runaways thrown together by fate, chance companions whose only common ground was the enemy who pursued us. It was impossible to keep up a conversation while we were walking.

I had no desire to encounter the Tehamans again, but as the day dragged on without any change I began to worry, wondering why if they were so fearsome and expert we'd seen no sign of them. I didn't dare to hope we'd escaped them, because that was too much.

At some point that day, close to nightfall, we came, totally unexpectedly, to the road.

It was in much the same condition as I remembered it, paved with large irregular stones and wide enough for two carriages to pass each other. Nothing particularly remarkable about it, other than it being the longest road in the Archipelago.

For us, though, it was like seeing a fountain in the desert, and we stumbled to the forest at its edge and looked at it in disbelief. Somehow we'd managed to get here, to avoid being lost in the wastes of the cloud forest, and all these hours we'd been heading in roughly the right direction.

We had no idea where on it we were, or even which way headed towards Kalessos and which towards Tandaris; we guessed, going by the feeling that one side of the sky was much darker than another and hence east.

'Do we go along it?' I asked Ravenna, and got the answer I expected.

'No, it's too exposed.'

'But there won't be anyone on it in this weather, what will it matter if we go a little way?'

'No,' she said firmly.

'Can we at least follow it on the far side, so that we're going in the right direction.'

'Where is the right direction?' she demanded. 'Where is this mythical place that we ought to be heading to?'

'The south coast,' I said, a little desperately. 'Anywhere there might be a ship, some way we can escape. You didn't suggest anything, so this is the way we've been going.'

'There are only fishing villages there mostly, except for Kalessos and Carcaizon, and only the towns will have mantas.'

'Then tell me where to go, and I'll follow you! We can't go north or east, we'll end up in the Desert again. This way at least we're partially hidden.'

But she didn't offer any alternatives, so we crossed the road and plunged into the forest again on the far side. For a few moments, out in the open, we were exposed to the full force of the rain, and I was almost glad that Ravenna had insisted on not taking it. I was so tired, though, and so hungry again. My legs felt shaky, as they could only stand a little more walking or they would melt.

There was a stream on the other side of the road, knee-deep and very fast-flowing. There was something wonderfully refreshing about being in running water instead of rain, though, so I threw caution to the winds for a moment and immersed myself in it; I was utterly drenched so it made no difference, and it made me feel much cleaner even if that wasn't actually the case.

Ravenna followed suit, and then we pressed on through the forest parallel to it, about ten yards above on the slopes of the valley. After only a few minutes I knew I had to stop, and it was just then that Ravenna, ahead of me, abruptly halted.

'What is it?' I asked tiredly.

'Feel,' she said, pointing down at the ground beneath her. 'Oh, you've got the sandals, so you won't. It's stone, like part of the road.'

I took a couple of steps forward and bent down to touch it, confirm what she said.

'Does it matter?'

She was already sounding out the area around it, sinking bare feet into the mud to see if she could find any more traces of it.

'It goes on,' she said, pointing to the left. 'Up, that way.'

'But not in the right direction.'

'Away from the road, it must go to the coast. That's the way you want to go, isn't it?'

'You said . . .'

'Forget what I said. It's obviously been forgotten, so the Domain isn't using it. Who knows what it is, perhaps it connects to the old coast road or something. They won't expect us to go this way, they'll think we're following the highway.'

'We've only just found a landmark, and you want to move away from it again.'

'Cathan, if they can follow our minds, it'll be much easier for them to catch us by riding along the road than if we're miles away in deep jungle.'

I was too weak to resist, so after a brief rest we set out along it. I wasn't happy with leaving the sure path of the main road that would eventually take us to Kalessos, but for once on this journey she overrode me.

The road ran almost straight across the next valley and through a notch in the ridge beyond, by which time darkness had fallen again and we were going much more slowly than usual, to ensure we stayed on the road.

We didn't see the fort until we were almost on top of it.

CHAPTER XI

The huge stones of a wall loomed out of the jungle just to the right, separated from the road by a mass of vegetation that probably hid a ditch, and a few less pleasant things besides.

We both froze for a second, stunned by the sudden appearance of this rampart from seemingly empty forest, and I looked up to the top of the wall, unsure whether it was occupied or not. There was no sign of life, and when the next flash of lightning lit up the scene I had time to notice that there was a small breach in it further along, and the top was irregular, while the nearest tower was missing a corner.

'It doesn't look kept up,' said Ravenna cautiously. We took a few more steps along the road, virtually blind in the intervals between strikes.

'A gate!' Ravenna said, a few moments later, at the same time as I noticed the ditch on the other side of the road.

It didn't look as if there was anyone here, certainly not with the road in such bad condition, but we couldn't be sure. Only when we reached the gate and found it an eerie open space with the door smashed in did I feel a little easier.

I was still wary, not sure why there should be a fort in the forest, and why anyone would build one in the bottom of a valley. Except . . . the walls stretched away in both directions, curving upwards as if it was the valley itself that was walled in.

The road led directly to its gates, so this must be its destination, not the coast we'd been hoping for. Ravenna took a few steps into the blackness beyond the gates, and after a moment I followed her.

'Are you sure this is a good idea?' I said, wondering whether I sounded cautious or merely cowardly.

'No. But there might be somewhere to rest.'

'It looks Tehaman, see the size of those stones. No Archipelagan built this.'

'It's Tehaman, but it won't be occupied,' she said confidently. 'They don't keep any garrisons outside the plateau, so it's a relic, two hundred years old.'

We came up against a blank wall, so we followed the stone floor round to the left, to another broken gate. I didn't like this, heading into an unknown structure in the jungle when we'd been walking all day and were exhausted. And who knew what lived inside? I could probably use magic against anything that attacked us, but that would tell the hunters where we were as surely as if we'd lit a fire in the desert.

The walls had gone when we next got to see anything. There was only more vegetation, tall jungle trees – and a stone building ahead of us.

Determined not to let my nervousness show, I walked beside Ravenna as we advanced towards the building, which was considerably larger than a house. An administration building of some kind, perhaps? But for what? There was nothing here to administer, it didn't defend any vital route, and there was nothing to protect in the middle of the jungle.

Whoever had built it obviously felt a need to protect themselves against something, though, because I could see few outside windows, and there was another courtyard in front of the doorway, surprisingly free of trees and vegetation.

Two flights of stairs led up on either side to a colonnade, while in front of us another door led on to the ground floor. We took the stairs, hoping that it would be safer the higher we went.

The colonnade was rain swept but, again, surprisingly clear except for the ivy growing down its pillars. I could imagine people standing here looking over the courtyard towards the walls, keeping watch over activity in the courtyard.

The colonnade was still cold and wet, so we went inside. The lightning was much less helpful here, but the first room we found seemed to be empty enough of debris and vegetation to sleep in. The floor was stone, which was strange at this height, but it meant we wouldn't fall through the floor in our sleep, and neither of us complained.

I'd thought the previous night's dreams had been bad, but the scenes that played out in my mind that night were much more vivid and realistic, and much more unpleasant.

I was running desperately through a forest, hearing the coughs of jaguars and the shouts of hunters behind me. The ground was steeply sloping, and I was frantically trying to gain height, only the sounds of pursuit were getting closer. Then there was a snarl behind me, and a moment later the hideous sensation of jaws closing around my ankle. I stumbled and was dragged down, falling into the soil. I tried to drag myself upright, but the jaguar only tightened its jaws and I felt blood on my skin. Then another of the creatures appeared in front of me, beautiful and terrible, and started circling as if I was wounded prey. I screamed . . .

. . . and then the hunters themselves appeared, and the jaguars moved away. I looked fearfully up but couldn't see who the hunters were, as if they were only mirages. All I knew was that I'd trusted them. They stood over me and shouted, doing nothing until another man appeared a few moments later. I could feel his eyes boring into me, and after a moment he said, almost sadly, 'What a disappointment. You could have done so much.'

The scene blurred and changed in an instant, as it did in dreams, to somewhere very cold, a stone room where I was chained to a stone table. My whole body was shivering, but for some reason I couldn't see any of it.

'Go deeper,' said the same voice, and terror seized me again as I felt the ghastly presence of an intruder in my mind. Then the brief scene repeated itself over and over again, merged into more, and always I was helpless on the slab.

'In the caves . . .' a second voice said; there was something like a talon in my head, sending bolts of agony lancing through my skull. 'In the caves . . . below the shore.'

'Which shore?' The first man again.

More agony, like the worst headache I could imagine.

'Lost . . . below the shore where ships are lost, under the ledge. Death, hell, something like that . . . *Perdition*!'

The agony abruptly faded, and I could hear satisfaction in the voice of the man I knew. 'In the caves below Perdition's Shore. So kind of you to tell us that, you've outlived your usefulness. We won't kill you, though. I have a better idea.'

Then, what seemed like a few moments before I woke up, there was a completely different image, very clear and vivid.

Two men and a woman were standing on the colonnade we'd come through, looking down into the courtyard. I was seeing them from behind, and although I couldn't see his face, the young man on the right was very familiar. Who was he, though? I couldn't pin him down.

'I want every last scrap of evidence cleared out,' said the stocky, grey-haired man in the middle. 'Let the forest take everything, as he ordered. This place would be more value to them than a whole fleet.'

'Sir, the prisoners . . .' said the man I recognised, but his superior cut him off.

'They're too dangerous. Kill them, but make it quick.'

The young man and the woman exchanged an uneasy glance behind their superior's back, but frustratingly his face was still hidden.

'You have a problem, Lieutenant?'

The man shook his head. 'No, sir.' He turned to go, but then I heard hooves and a voice shouting up from the courtyard.

'Sir! They're coming south.'

The legate swore, and then the scene abruptly faded. I woke to see Ravenna leaning over me and terrible hunger pangs in my stomach.

'It's past dawn, we have to move.'

'Still raining?'

'Yes, just as badly. Nightmares?'

I sat up painfully, trying to clear my aching head of the images of the room with the stone table. 'You were awake?'

'I had them, and you didn't look happy a minute ago.'

The room was even less welcoming in the cold, grey morning light than it had been in the darkness of the evening before. The houses in the Tehaman city must have been like this inside, only more cheerful. No-one could have lived in a building like this and not decorated it.

'I had a look round,' she said, sitting back against the wall and looking gravely at me. 'All the rooms are like this, at least up here. I don't think it's been unused for two hundred years though.' She held out her hand with a little object in it, something metallic.

'An officer's rank pin,' she said, as I took it and held it up to what light came in through the small, square window. Two wavy lines and a crescent, on a pin which would once have been attached to an officer's collar. 'I don't know what level, but I'm fairly sure this belongs to my grandfather's time.'

Presumably a naval officer, from the wavy line, and not a very senior one.

'It might just have been dropped here by someone, maybe running from the Crusaders.' A thought struck me. 'I thought Orethura's Navy was tiny.'

'Not so tiny as all that, just not on a level with anyone else's.' She stared around at the bleakness of the room. 'Maybe my grandfather used this fort for something. It doesn't really matter, anyway. We'll need to be on our way and find some more food.'

Even tired and dirty, her face still held the intensity and intelligence that made her stand out. So difficult, but so beautiful.

Neither of us said anything, and for a second we held each other's gaze, acknowledged that we weren't strangers thrown together by misfortune. Then, as it wavered, I moved over and pinned the rank badge on to the front of her tunic, since her square-cut slave's tunic didn't have a collar.

'Thank you,' she said, and stood up. There was a slight edge to her tone – had I offended her somehow by doing that? Elements knew, her mind worked in such strange ways.

We left the room without a backward glance, but I paused on the colonnade, trying to work out where the three figures in the dream had stood. Such a strange dream, and so different from all the nightmares. Except it had been a nightmare in a way, and I wondered who that grey-haired legate had been, the one so casually ordering the deaths of unnamed prisoners. Annoyingly, I couldn't remember the uniforms, so they could well have been been Crusader Knights.

If only I could remember who that man on the right had been, the one I thought I recognised, I'd probably know whether the whole episode was a construct of my imagination. It couldn't really have been anything else, come to think of it. How could I have dreamed something that I didn't know about, had never experienced? I could just as well have been wrong, and the whole thing had happened centuries ago.

'What are you doing?' Ravenna asked.

I started. 'Nothing. Time to go.' I followed her back out into the rain, down the stairs into the dismal courtyard. The doors on this level, I realised, were two giant slabs of stone swung into place in grooves. They were open, and I could see how thick the slabs were. Had there been a beast pen underneath, perhaps, with stone doors to stop elephants from escaping? But why keep elephants in airless stalls?

I walked over to the door and looked inside, saw only a vaulted hallway and three passages leading onwards at a lower level. No doubt it would be infested with bats and other animals, but that didn't stop me wondering what it was for.

'Which way are we heading?' I said.

As we left the courtyard Ravenna started walking round the side of the building.

'We'll see if there's another gate, and if not, then go round. No point in retracing our steps.'

We passed more buildings as we trudged down the small valley, none as large as the first and all of different shapes, distributed without any rhyme or reason. There wasn't another gate, but we managed to climb the wall and abseil down the other side on some tough creepers.

Things to eat in this forest were few and far between, and we ate anything that we could confirm as edible, forcing ourselves not to notice the taste. The worst, actually, was a totally tasteless and unappetising brownish fruit, but Ravenna said it was used as the base for a very spicy dish which needed something cool and bland.

The hours wore on with no change, no sign of pursuit, as they had for the past few days. I hated this endless forest with its morass of mud, worse with every day the storm went on, and I hated the rain constantly beating down on my head and shoulders, just hard enough to be uncomfortable.

Despite the discomfort, the rain was the last thing I expected to be dangerous. It happened just as we were crossing a wide stream, swollen and fast-flowing with the water that had drained into it over the last day or two. As we approached it the rain began to slacken off, and I looked up into the sky, hardly daring to hope that the storm was coming to an end. But there was no change in the colour of the clouds, only a strange blurring overhead. I dismissed it as a trick of the light and the water in my eyes, and slithered down the bank into the stream, a pace or two behind Ravenna.

The only warning was a sudden change in the light as I felt for footing underwater, and then something slammed down into my back, pushing me forward on to my face with stunned force. Winded, I lost my footing and felt myself being pulled along by the current. I tried to surface, but I couldn't, and panicked. Where was Ravenna? I couldn't see her or anything else, only feel the roaring of the water in my ears.

I reached out blindly, totally disoriented, but I couldn't even find the bottom to hang on to. The stream was only waist deep, I should be able to find it.

Where was it? Thetis, what was happening? I opened my eyes but all I could see was a whirl of dizzying grey. I screwed them shut again, but the lifting, turning sensation didn't go away.

I tried to form the void in my mind, but something jolted me and I lost it, tried again. I was being whirled round and round in a huge circle, totally encased in water – there was something terribly wrong. Who was using water-magic against me?

I was moving faster and faster now, and my head felt as

if it would burst, unable to cope with the speed I was going round at.

I tried to summon my magic a third time, only the void was terribly unstable, and I wouldn't be able to sustain it if I lost consciousness. I pushed against the water around me, and found that something else was pushing back with stunning force. As I thought my head would split from the pain, I managed to push the water away – and found myself falling through the rain, falling with someone else close by. Falling where? I wasn't underwater, but I was still spinning. I reached out to the rain again, started to draw it back in to protect me only to have it close in again and trap me a second time.

Then there was a sickening impact as I was hurled into something much harder than air or water, hard enough that I wanted to black out again. My head was on fire, and I willed myself to lose consciousness, for the pain to slip away.

It didn't, and for long minutes I lay unable to move or escape, until the pain finally faded and I dared to open my eyes.

I shouted Ravenna's name, but there was no reply. I had no idea how far I was from where we'd been struck; she could be anywhere. The great trees were still standing, but their branches had been ravaged by whatever had seized us, and the floor was covered in broken vegetation.

There was that ominous blurring in the sky above me and I looked around with mounting panic. If I didn't find her this time we could be separated even more, but surely she'd fallen with me?

'Cathan?'

I called back, and a moment later she came sliding down the embankment, an even sorrier sight than before.

Before she had a chance to say anything there was a *crack* above us and one of the trees exploded in flames, all hundred and fifty feet of it. It was like a monstrous stake, a torch in the forest.

'They're chasing us,' she said, her calm wavering. 'Cathan, they're using our own magic against us.'

'Just the individual elements.'

'No!' she shouted. 'They're using Storm. Can't you feel it? They're trying to bring us into the open, to force us to fight against them.'

The light became stranger and stranger, filtered through that unearthly ceiling in the sky. 'We have to try and ride with them, they can't keep this up for ever.'

Another lightning bolt lanced *through* the water and torched a tree well out of sight, then, an instant later, the ceiling dropped.

Ravenna threw herself on top of me just as it hit, and as the water engulfed us I felt her go limp. Whatever part of my mind was still capable of thinking rationally made me clutch on to her as tightly as I could before the water carried us off again, and we were lost in a maelstrom of bubbles and the furious torrent unleashed by whatever demonic power was controlling the skies above Qalathar.

This time I did lose consciousness, only it was more like falling asleep, with just the grinding pain in my head as we were flung around.

When I finally opened my eyes again it was to see a forest stripped of at least half its vegetation, lying beneath a mess of broken branches with the rain filtering down through them. Thetis, why didn't this endless storm go away, vent its fury over the ocean instead of on us?

Ravenna seemed to be in one piece, although her clothes were in as bad a state as mine and the sandals had been ripped off her feet.

Her feet. It must just have been a trick of the light, the covering leaves, but I saw on her ankle what were unmistakably teeth-marks. Not deep, just enough to have left a scar, and exactly the imprint that would have been left by a jaguar seizing her from behind without trying to hurt her.

I ran my fingers over them to check that they were real, that I wasn't imagining them. I knew she wouldn't have liked it, but I had to be certain.

Certain that my dream last night had come straight from her mind? How could it have done, she wasn't a mind-mage or anything . . .

But some of the Tehamans were. All those horrible dreams hadn't been my own mind dredging up nameless fears. That had been Ravenna running through the forest, chained to the stone table while they ripped her secrets out of her mind. Her own people, the leaders of the Tehaman *Commonwealth*, which obviously still clung to its democratic traditions.

I looked down at her, lying unconscious in a tangle of branches, and wondered how anyone could be brutal enough to hurt her when she was capable of so much. Had no-one ever tried to gain her loyalties instead of simply torturing her? Probably not, because she was a fanatic in her own way.

It was hard not to feel protective, and easier still to feel hatred. Hatred for the people who'd done this to her, who'd raped her mind so they could steal our ship, the key to understanding the storms.

I half-carried, half-dragged Ravenna into the nearest shelter I could find, beneath a pair of huge branches and some broken foliage which would at least shield us from the worst of the next deluge, and waited for the inevitable, crushing force of the water.

When it came, it wasn't as bad as I'd feared. The vegetation was pressed tightly on top of us, and I found water and mud pooling at the bottom of the shelter as soon as I could raise my head again, but we stayed where we were.

Then, finally, there was silence. I waited and waited for the next onslaught, but it never came. Whatever mind was behind the storm, whoever had been hounding us with our own weapons, seemed to have paused. I squinted up between the branches but couldn't see anything unusual in the sky above, and even the rain seemed to have stopped.

It was too much to hope that we'd be left alone – but as I pushed some of the branches aside and looked out into the devastated forest, I could smell the freshness of the air, the wonderful sensation that always accompanied the end of a storm. It had been three days, after all, time enough to blow itself out.

Not being strong enough to carry Ravenna, I had to wait until she regained consciousness before we could set off again, and for the time being I didn't mention what I'd seen. If I was ever going to. It was a horrible thing, to have your memories laid open for someone else to see in all their ghastly detail, and especially memories like that.

As we trudged through the forest, hoping that we were still heading southwards, it began to come alive again, the trees echoing with the shrills of birds and other animals. Not all of them were welcome, and after we nearly stepped on a curled-up snake I started watching out for constrictors and anacondas as much as the jaguars hunting us. The insects came out to feed too, starved like everything else through three days of isolation, and I found myself almost wishing for the rain to come back as clouds of blood-sucking midges floated round me, too small to see and slap away.

Then, finally, the clouds became thin enough for a watery sun to filter through, shining down through the patchy canopy and on to the undergrowth surrounding us. It gradually burned its way through the clouds until they were gone, and the blue skies of summer stretched over the island again. Everything began to steam, as the water that still coated trunks and leaves started evaporating. It was like that for another warm, sticky day until we finally reached the coast.

I picked up the sound of the sea long before we reached

it, the rhythm of the surf growing gradually louder and more insistent. Ravenna didn't hear it until much later, but by then I was running through the forest, squelching through the ever-present mud and the sticky creepers until the trees stopped abruptly and I skidded to a halt, clutching on to a branch for support.

Below me the black, green-dotted cliffs looked almost welcoming in the sunshine, plunging down from the forest into the blue of the ocean. A blue stretching as far as I could see into the haze of the horizon, dotted with small waves and bringing a fresh, cooling breeze with it.

Ravenna caught up with me as I stood there surveying it, out of breath and, if anything, wilder and more desperate than she'd looked when we began this flight four days ago.

'Where now?' she said, gulping down air as we stared out over the bay. 'What's happened to the coast road?'

'I don't know.' I scanned what I could see of the cliffs and the bay below, staring down into the inviting water, sand and reefs just below its surface. It was so lovely, so inviting, but it didn't lead us anywhere.

I heard a rustle behind us.

'Would you care to explain what this is all about?' said a quiet, menacing voice.

CHAPTER XII

My breath caught in my throat and I turned round slowly, hoping perhaps that it had only been an illusion.

It wasn't. I stared at the black-clad figure standing a few paces away, taking in the mind-mage's hammer hanging at his waist, the angular cast of his face and the slanted violet eyes.

I hadn't given this man a second thought in the four and a half years since our brief meeting in Ral Tumar. I should have done, I knew now. I should have wondered what happened to him after his master's death.

'You have a lot of answers to give me,' Tekla said coldly, 'but it seems somebody else wants them as well.'

I started to move, but felt the air thickening, and my own muscles refusing to obey me as they'd done in the hut above the lake.

'Have you joined their side too?' Ravenna said, and although I couldn't see her, the anger in her voice was clear – and very understandable.

'I could ask that question of you too. You're supposed to be dead. Both of you, and yet I find you very much alive and active.'

That, and more.

'Did you betray Mauriz . . .' I began, but he cut me off.

'*I* ask the questions. Or rather, I will when I've taken you somewhere more secure.' He glanced over at the edge of the cliff, just behind us. 'I'll trust your instinct for self-preservation. There are rocks below this section of cliff, so I wouldn't try jumping off.'

I wouldn't try jumping off. His words rang in my head for a second before I realised why they were so familiar. Not the words, but the way he said them. It was like an echo, as if he'd been wearing the same clothes as someone I knew.

'And in case you think of doing anything . . . foolish, I have nothing to do with the people who've been chasing you.'

'You expect us to believe that?' Ravenna said. 'So that we'll go easily, and make your life more comfortable?'

'It makes no difference,' he said calmly. 'I control you anyway. Now, we've wasted enough time.'

Tekla was much more subtle now; there was no way he could have physically manoeuvred us down the path I took of my own accord, as if I'd heard the sounds and smells of a celebration at the bottom. It led down a cleft in the rock-face, hidden by a tangle of vegetation and steep enough that I had to climb rather than walk in places.

I reached the bottom and moved out on to a stretch of white sand, saw the waves breaking gently a few yards away.

I'd been away from the sea so long, so terribly long, and the blue-green water that stretched out into the bay was hard to resist.

I ran the last few yards, my feet sinking into the sand, and ran into the surf. Water surged around my legs and splashed around me as I ran deeper and deeper, laughing just for the sheer joy of being in the sea again.

It was over my knees now, and as the next wave crested I fell forward into it, immersing myself in the water and tasting the salt on my lips. It was so cool, after the unpleasantly warm rain and the sweat of being in the forests, and I could feel all the dirt and mud being washed off. I waded further out, letting each wave hit me head-on, and only when I found myself out of my depth in the limpid waters of the bay did I realise where I was, and looked back.

Ravenna was just running into the sea at the edge, a wave breaking over her. The look on her face matched my own, even though she couldn't possibly feel the same way. Tekla stood a few paces behind her, not looking pleased at all. Then I dived, looking out into the blueness of the water towards the fish I'd sent scattering. The bottom shelved quite steeply, and there were reefs a little way out, across a swathe of neptune grass waving gently with the current.

For a moment or two I floated, content just to stay where I was, until I realised that the mind-mage's hold on me was gone.

I started to swim further out to the reef, then I saw the arrowhead-shapes along the reef, their four flippers moving lazily up and down as smaller fish darted in all directions. Infant leviathans, only three or four feet long, not dangerous of themselves, but they were warm-blooded creatures and didn't leave their parents until they were much bigger than this.

Then I found myself swimming back, *knowing* I had to get away from the young leviathans before the adults arrived and decided I was a threat. It was only as I broke surface that I realised the water there was too shallow for a full-sized leviathan to have reached me, and by then it was too late.

'You've had your swim,' he said, a little testily, when I emerged, but there was a tension in his words, in the way he was standing, that surprised me. Ravenna was looking sideways at me. 'Follow.'

I tried to think why I'd followed him, but my mind kept slipping away from it, on to the need to stay close behind him and go where he led. It was a sensation like being infatuated with someone, the way every path seemed to lead back to that same thing no matter how hard I tried to put it out of my mind.

So I trudged through the sand, only now feeling the burning sensation where salt water had come into contact with the cuts and bruises on my skin. He wouldn't let us go close to the shoreline, and I noticed he was wearing boots, not sandals.

He led us to a cave that was very different from the one we'd sheltered in two nights ago. I didn't see it until we were almost on top of it, hidden in a jumble of dark grey rocks and dead creepers that had fallen from above. The stench of rotting vegetation was so strong that I tried not to breathe as he led us between the rocks and into the mouth of the cave. There was dead seaweed in here, and pools of water left behind by the storm.

The 'secure place' was above and to one side, a hole in the rock with a few uneven breaks letting light in, very much longer than it was wide. It reminded me of the secret clan warehouses beneath Ral Tumar, where he and Mauriz Scartaris had taken us to escape from the Inquisition. And, from the look of it, someone had had the same idea; there were ring-bolts screwed into the walls and a crude stone shelf running part of the way around the edge.

What was the point? Why smuggle here, miles from any city and nowhere near a road? Anything small enough to be easily transported across that kind of terrain could be concealed in clothes.

It took my eyes a while to become accustomed enough to the gloom to see all this, by which time he'd told us to sit down on the floor towards the landward side of the cave. What daylight there was came from behind him, so he was sitting in front of the light and barring our path to the door, as if we stood any chance of getting that far.

'How come,' he said finally, 'you are still alive? How come you lived when so many better than you perished?'

'Orosius's lapdog,' Ravenna said contemptuously. 'You even speak the same way after so long. Is it so difficult to learn to be your own man?'

'I won't argue with you. As it is, I'm doing you a favour by not taking what I need to know. I'm perfectly capable of doing that.'

Ravenna said nothing. Did he know what the Tehamans had done to her?

'I expect you to answer me,' he said. 'How did you survive?'

'We saw the attack before it hit,' I replied, trying to be as obstructive as possible. As I long as he was asking for information rather than taking it forcibly, I had the upper hand, and there were things I could keep secret. He couldn't read my mind without violating it, only influence me as he'd done so far.

'Who fired on you?'

'*Furnace*. The Domain manta.' Why was it so important to him? A lot of people knew how Orosius had died, or heard rumours at least. My brother was dead; surely that was all that mattered?

'With its armament?'

'No.' Ravenna answered him this time. 'The terror-weapon, the one they used off Ilthys. They boil the water underneath your manta and destroy the insides.'

'Yes, yes, I know.'

'What's so important? Does Eshar want to know what happened?'

'Eshar isn't a subtle man. If he wanted to know, he'd beat the truth out of you. He has a soldier's hatred for anything devious, especially mind-magic.' That actually rang true, given what I knew of my uncle Reglath Eshar, officially titled Emperor Aetius VI.

'So you're not working for Eshar?'

'Silence! You irritate me. Tell me, how long have you been running? Where from?'

He fired a string of questions at us, sometimes jumping abruptly from one topic to another without ever revealing where he was going. I tried to give as little away as I could, but this man knew what he was doing. How many times had he stood at Orosius's shoulder while my brother interrogated his opponents and reduced them to mindless shells? I remembered the dreadful remorse of Orosius's last minutes, his descriptions of what he'd done to people.

Including Ravenna.

Who was Tekla working for now, though? I found it hard to believe his personal loyalty had been to my brother, given how unworthy Orosius had been. So who was his new master? Eshar, perhaps? To trust anything Tekla said would be stupid, so what he'd said earlier didn't rule the new Emperor out. Maybe he'd moved to one of the military intelligence agencies, or perhaps even the Domain. The Domain was supposed to have a monopoly on mind-magic, even if the Tehamans and the Emperor thought otherwise.

Finally I couldn't stand it any more. I'd become more and more aware of how hungry I was, after five days' flight through the jungle on only the odd cluster of fruit.

I was surprised when he stopped, and brought something that he claimed was field rations, designed to stay edible for a long time. That, I thought as I tried to chew the hard wafers of unidentifiable food, was probably because it had been stale to start with and couldn't deteriorate any more. At least it was filling, even if it wasn't the most appetising meal I'd ever had.

'Why does all of this matter to you?' Ravenna asked before he could start interrogating us again. 'Couldn't you just take us back to whoever you work for and be done with it?'

'I work on *my* terms,' he said, annoyed. I still couldn't see his face, just a faint halo of light around him from the brightness outside. 'And surely someone astute would have noticed that this is an ideal place to ask awkward questions. And where were you running to?' he said suddenly, as if asking the time of day. 'Qalathar is entirely controlled by your enemies, and wearing those penitent tunics you'd not have got far. Perhaps you knew of . . . helpers . . . in one of the south coast cities. People who still think you worthy of respect. *Heretics*.' He laid a peculiar emphasis on the last word.

'No,' I said, as Ravenna shook her head fiercely. I shifted slightly, for the hundredth time. It was much cooler in here despite the sunlight filtering through, and I was beginning to feel the chill seeping up through the slightly damp floor, aggravating the ache in my limbs.

'If you have to model yourself on Orosius, you ought to do it well, at least,' Ravenna said, but his words had nettled her, and I found myself wanting to hurl his smug insults back in his face. My brother had been in a position to look down on us, but who did this jumped-up informer think he was? Unless he'd become Eshar's spymaster, he'd lost a lot of his old authority.

'You're in a position to judge, of course.' He sounded as if he was smiling. 'Why don't I see how I match up in other ways?'

My eyes followed him as he reached over and withdrew a coiled whip from the ledge. I shuddered as he held it up to the light and I saw the tiny, thorn-like spikes running along its length.

'I should be able to reopen every single scar he gave you four years ago,' said Tekla, getting smoothly to his feet, but not even Ravenna's resolve was firm enough now.

'No! Please!' she said, scrambling away from him.

'You scare easily. More easily than I forgive an insult.'

Ravenna froze and then slumped limply to the floor. I couldn't let him do this. Not after what she'd been through. As he passed I started to move sideways to block him – then found myself frozen too, as helpless as when I'd watched her being whipped by the lake shore.

'Leave her alone!' I said desperately, but he ignored me. He rolled her over and jerked the tunic up to her shoulders – then stopped, staring down at the fresh, livid scars on her back.

'Who did this?' he asked me, in a voice that was suddenly very soft and dangerous.

'Amonis,' I blurted out, confused by his hesitation. Maybe I could still stop him. 'The Inquisitor at the dam.'

'Why?'

I told what had happened when the lake was drained, the accident that had killed Murshash and Biades, nearly swamping the other raft. Not satisfied with that, he demanded full accounts from both of us, a complete sequence of what had happened. He seemed particularly interested in the Tehamans, and contemptuously dismissed Oailos's idea that there had been Tehaman treasure in the lake.

When we finally finished, he coiled the whip again and put it away. I breathed a sigh of relief.

'She's too weak,' he said to me, before I could congratulate myself on having spared her that. 'I'll suspend that demonstration unless either of you insults his memory again.'

Why was he so concerned about it? He'd given us a way to manipulate him. Not that it would help, but it was something. He was far more vulnerable than I'd thought.

'This could be important,' he said finally. 'Important enough to justify not handing you over quite yet.'

Ravenna and I exchanged glances; she wasn't even bothering to conceal her contempt for him. Neither of us intended to be 'handed over' to anyone.

'The Tehamans will be here shortly,' he went on. 'Or, I should say, they'll reach the top of the cliff shortly, and they'll be able to tell that someone used mind-magic here. As far as they're concerned, all mind-mages are on their side, but I'll have to be quiet while they're going past. Either I can tie you up, or just trust to your common sense that you'll not try to escape – because if you do, I'll make it very clear where we are.'

I didn't ask how he knew, but I was heartened that he gave us a choice. He wasn't with the Tehamans, then, I was sure. It would have been simple to immobilise us until we were secure, and then he wouldn't have *needed* to use any magic.

'We'll stay here,' I said, after a moment.

Tekla demanded our word for it, and we gave it; sitting back against the cold rock of the cave while we waited was preferable to being tied.

I watched him as time dragged by, wondering what he was up to, how he'd found us, and who he was working for. The Domain? Tehama? Who could tell?

Again, I thought of Ithien and the others, hoping that they'd managed to navigate the inlet and reach the open sea, and so vanish into the southern Archipelago where heretic strongholds still held out. Palatine was somewhere out there, and maybe some of the others who'd escaped the purges: Persea, Laeas, Sagantha.

Devious Sagantha, the wily politician, always playing both sides against the middle. Why had I thought of him? He wasn't really a friend, and there was too much I didn't know about him. But I hadn't heard that he'd changed sides, as I surely would have done if that had been the case. The Retreat might be isolated, but news of events had reached there eventually, and the scholars hadn't been entirely unconcerned with the outside world. Sagantha was at least someone people would follow, more because of what he stood for than what he was. He wouldn't trust Ithien at all, only Palatine might because she knew him . . . wherever she was.

It was growing dark when Tekla announced that the Tehamans had gone, and it would be safe to talk and move around again. How did he know? I felt frustrated at how little I knew about mind-magic. My teacher Ukmadorian had focused at the Citadel on how dangerous mind-mages were and how to avoid detection by them, yet he'd never explained the basics of mind-magic that might have allowed us to come up with new ways to stay hidden. That had been the problem with the Citadel, in the end we were only vessels to pass on the traditions and the knowledge. Nothing new was ever developed there, at least not that I ever heard of.

'We're not staying here,' Tekla said. 'This is just a bolt-hole, a shelter from the weather. I'm taking you some-where I don't have to waste time keeping an eye on you. Somewhere I control, before you start trying to escape.'

I hoped there was a healer in this place, or at least someone with enough medical training to deal with the cuts on Ravenna's back.

'How are you proposing to get there?' I asked.

'Don't worry, you won't have to endure the trauma of another trek through the jungle. For the moment, you're worth something and I don't intend to waste you.'

Spoken like a good commodity. My brother's words rang in my head and I shivered, scanning the mind-mage's face for any traces of emotion. Any other reminders of my brother.

Before the quick tropical sunset, Tekla gave us more of his ration wafers and then took us back outside to wait on the beach. For what, he didn't say, but I guessed it would be a boat or a searay.

The sand was still warm, although the last light had faded from the sky. I sat down and ran handfuls of sand through my fingers, looking out over the bay. The dark, looming cliffs robbed it of so much of the magic of the lagoon at the Citadel, or even the shoreline by Lepidor. There was no phosphorescence in the water, only the white streaks as line after line of waves broke a little way away, and it was too dark to make out much more.

This was the third time Ravenna and I had sat together on a beach like this at night-time, and I supposed that was significant, given what we'd said the last two times. But Tekla's presence robbed the scene of any remaining glory it might have had, and neither of us said anything.

We didn't have very long, because after a few minutes Tekla spotted something out beyond the breakers and ordered us into the waves. For once I was happy to comply, and as I waded in, I saw the hump of a searay and two riding lights a little way out over the water, then the glow from the pilot cabin windows.

It was a place of safety, my mind told me, a place I had to get to before the leviathans in the lagoon decided it was time for a snack. But somehow the imperative wasn't as strong as it should have been, and I was more than happy to linger, to duck underwater and swim under the waves.

The searay could wait. It had been too long since I'd done this.

I struck out into the dark water, veering off to the left until I couldn't make out Tekla or Ravenna any more, dived and swam a little way down into the blackness. I could see a little after all, enough to avoid hitting the sharp coral spines to my right, or the urchin-encrusted rocks a little way below.

Then I floated to the surface and lay on my back, letting the waves gently sway me up and down. The stars were so beautiful out here, somehow even better for being in the water, and the great rippling blue sheet of the Tethys Cloud looked like an ocean in the sky, surrounded by the royal blue and maroon of the other dust sheets surrounding it.

I heard Tekla's voice calling, but he had no hold at all on my mind now. I was free of him, protected by my two elements of Water and Shadow. That had been what made him so angry earlier on; he'd lost control of me when I ran into the ocean, because my desire to be in the water had given me, momentarily, the strength of mind to break free of him.

And then, as I lay drifting in the sea, I saw something that I'd only glimpsed once before, on that magical evening six years ago when Ravenna and I had swum at night on the island of the Citadel.

It moved too fast and the wrong way to be a star, lasted

too long to be a shooting star. As I had before, I tracked its strange flight across the sky until I lost it in the billows of the southern ocean.

For a moment or two I puzzled over it, then something made me sit up – or the equivalent when I was floating on my back in the water.

It wasn't a vision from the gods or anything so far-fetched. The scientific part of my mind took over as I trod water, not caring that I was being swept back in towards the beach. Its path had been different here, but then we were further north than at the Citadel. It was linked to the planet somehow, yet at the same time it wasn't.

For me to have seen it tonight was too much of a coincidence. There had to be some meaning behind it, a pattern that could be predicted and followed. Other people must surely have seen it at some point? Why had I never heard any mention of it?

I tried to imagine myself flying high above the planet's surface, like some impossibly huge and high-flying bird. I would have a view in every direction, see the ocean stretching away beneath me, a vast blue sheet. Like standing on the summit of the Citadel's hill, only much more exaggerated. Maybe the mountains inland from my home in Lepidor, the spine that ran down the continent of Oceanus, broken only by rifts where water had broken through to form the three northernmost islands.

There were higher mountains, I'd been told, in the mostly uncharted continent of Huasa and Tehama – yes, of course.

I'd drifted slightly, and a wave almost swamped me, throwing my train of thought away as I tried to get the salt water out of my eyes. Where had I been? Mountains – Tehama. The Island in the Clouds.

From Ravenna's description, I wasn't sure that I could have seen the ocean at all from the summit of the Tehaman mountains, only the clouds from above – although I couldn't think what that would look like from such a height. And of course there were higher levels of clouds over Tehama itself, so to see above all the clouds you'd have to go higher still.

Higher and higher, and so the horizon would get further and further away and – would it curve, eventually? Could you go so unimaginably high that you could see it curve, see everything?

Everything including the storms.

For a moment I didn't believe it, looked up at the sky for reassurance, but the light had gone. Gone, after it had moved across the sky, going from north to south as before. Circling us, seeing far more of the world than we ever could.

But not quite the whole planet, because even if it – whatever *it* was – could see the world as a ball, half would be hidden, so perhaps there would be another one, and between them they should be able to see all of the surface and the clouds that covered it.

And the more I thought, the more logical it became, rather than suddenly collapsing under the weight of its own impossibility. There might still be something I hadn't spotted, though, something too abstract for me. Ravenna. I had to tell her, see whether she agreed, whether I had indeed stumbled on something even the *Aeon*'s last owners had failed to detect.

Whether I had indeed been the first human to recognise the Skyeyes for what they were.

I started swimming again, ploughing through the breakers until I saw the shuttle, heard Tekla's angry voice, and submerged myself to swim the last stretch underwater. This bay wasn't the place to be stranded, although I knew that once I was inside the searay I'd be in his power again. It didn't matter, I could slip away from him given the right circumstances.

Tekla said nothing once he'd dragged me in through

the searay's hatch, just ordered the pilot, invisible behind the curtain of his cabin, to get going. We were simply told to sit in the cabin and stay there.

I shouldn't have become so absorbed with that problem of the moving star, and after trying to run through figures in my head – which wasn't my strong point – it was all the more horrible when the searay docked.

There was a gentle thud as the craft settled on the floor of the searay bay, and I saw bright lights outside the windows. Tekla led both of us out of the hatch and down the steps as the door opened and two priests stepped inside.

CHAPTER XIII

They stopped a few feet away, surprised at the sight of us, but neither of them threw back the hoods of their robes. I stared at them for a moment, taking in the familiar surroundings of a manta's searay bay, feeling the familiar hum of a reactor through the deck under my feet

'The world isn't such a safe place after all, then,' said the figure on the right slowly, pushing back his hood. An Equatorian, grey-bearded and with sunken eyes like a falcon's. Ukmadorian, Provost of the Citadel of Shadow. 'As you have found out.'

I felt such a surge of relief I almost collapsed on to the deck, and I saw Ravenna shut her eyes for a moment. I kept mine open, and I saw the satisfied expression on his face.

'Don't be so harsh on them,' said the other man. Younger than the first, of a very different origin with his golden-olive skin, his slightly flattened face and the military bearing he held himself with. I could have told he was a naval man even if I hadn't known him. His expression was much kinder than the other man's. 'They're injured.'

'Harsh usage, that's all,' Tekla said. 'I've done what you asked, brought them to you in one piece. We can discuss your side of the bargain later.'

'Gone mercenary, have you?' Ravenna said, her confidence returning. 'Do you make them pay you in blood?'

'No, it's a simple transaction,' Tekla said, walking almost to the door before he added, 'I sell you to the highest bidder.'

'I hear you've changed hands a few times,' Ukmadorian said, showing no trace of warmth towards his former ward. 'You left the Citadel to find your own way in the world, but it seems you failed beyond your worst nightmares. Well, you're safe again now.' He turned to the other man. 'We should be under way again. I'd rather not run into some over-zealous patrol captain who's out looking for fugitive oceanographers. These two will need to be cleaned up and attended to.'

'I'll look after that,' said the second man, and then Ukmadorian was gone, black cloak trailing behind him. Both of us turned our attention to the admiral.

'It saddens me to see you like this,' said Sagantha Karao softly. 'Ukmadorian has lost too much, and sometimes he forgets that others have suffered as badly. Come with me, and I'll see what we can provide.'

His clothes were nondescript, made of poor quality silk, and hardly fitted his status as the Viceroy of the Archipelago he'd once been. He'd been removed by the new Emperor, troops sent to arrest him in Tandaris, but he'd been too quick for them and had disappeared, taking most of the government's papers and all its remaining assets with him. I hadn't heard anything of him since.

'Where are we?' I asked, not wanting to ask anything else yet.

'This is the *Meridian*,' he said, as we followed him along the corridor and upstairs to the main deck, leaving the pilot behind to power down the searay. 'She was Imperial once, we managed to ambush her and take her intact.'

We came up into the well, the circular space behind the bridge which linked the parts of the ship together. Sagantha didn't stop, but led us up the curved staircases with their guard-rails to the next level, along a corridor which could have been on any manta of any nation, and into an empty cadets' messroom. Familiar windows looked out on to a dark ocean from a large room with four smaller chambers leading off it.

'We're undermanned,' Sagantha said, gesturing for us to sit. There were still trappings of the Imperial ship this had once been – the dust shadow on one wall where a dolphin banner would once have hung; the intricately worked border at waist-height that seemed to belong in a civilian house. 'We had people in here for a while, but they've disembarked now.'

I sank down into the cushioned softness of one of the chairs, staring out into the blackness of the water. The engine's sound had changed to a hum, and I could just about make out the movement of the wings as the manta gathered speed.

Sagantha called an order to a passing sailor before closing the door behind him. He pulled off the dark cloak and slung it over his arm. 'Sorry about the disguise, but if you'd been someone else, we didn't want to take any risks.'

'Are you still an admiral of Cambress?'

'I was, for a while. Then one of my enemies became Suffete and had me stripped of my titles and ranks in absentia. I don't even have the Viceroy's title now. Still, I've fared better than some.' He smiled, but there was a sadness in his eyes.

'I'm sorry,' Ravenna said softly.

'What should you be sorry for? I knew what I was doing when I tried to help you, and I'd make the same choice again.'

The sailor came back, bringing with him a rich aroma of cooked fish and vegetables. It must be supper time in the mess hall, I thought, and then postponed thinking until I'd finished eating. It tasted like the best meal of my life, the first proper food I'd had since the night of Salderis's death nearly one and a half years ago.

Sagantha went out while we ate and came back a few minutes later when the sailor took the plates away. He brought a flask of Thetian spice spirit with him, and poured each of us a measure in tiny bowl-shaped glasses.

'Have you had this before?' he asked, stoppering the flask again.

'Once.' It had been in the dark, though, without ceremony, and I hadn't known it was this astonishing coppery-red colour. The colour of an Exile's hair, I thought suddenly, not quite sure why. My mother had been an Exile.

'The glasses are made so you can't put them down without spilling it. You have to drain it all in one go.'

That was always the way, somehow, from Oceanus to Thetia to Cambress.

Sagantha held up his glass. 'I salute you,' he said gravely, and drained it. We stared at each other for a moment, unsure what the protocol was, then returned the compliment. It was strong but so rich, so spicy, and I felt a warm glow in my chest. I remembered being told that it wasn't especially alcoholic, although the spices made it taste stronger.

'I don't like to think what you've been through,' he said after a moment. 'Tekla's idea of "harsh usage" is what anyone else calls torture.'

'Why do you employ him, then?' Ravenna demanded.

'Because at the moment the world depends on such men. I didn't call him to our service; he came himself.'

'Don't trust him. He's betrayed so many.'

'For his master, who's thankfully dead. There are a lot of people now who feel we need more of Tekla's kind again to fight back against the Domain. Men who can fight, hide, run, slip in where an army might have trouble. I won't say I disagree with them.'

'*Again*?' Ravenna said, leaning forward. 'When was the first time?'

'They were used a lot until thirty years ago. Orethura had his own special guard, the Ring of Eight they were called, although there were more than eight of them.'

Eight for the elements, that made sense.

'They were *nothing* like Tekla.' She looked suspiciously at him. 'You grew up with the Domain version of history.'

'I grew up with both versions. I think he has a lot more in common with them than you realise.'

There was a knock on the door, and a large black man in a green naval uniform came in, a healer's bag slung over his shoulder.

'Commander Malak Engare,' he said, in a deep, mellow voice, his accent suprisingly southern. 'Mons Ferratan Navy. If you'd excuse us, Sagantha?'

The Viceroy nodded and left, taking the spice spirit and the glasses with him.

'Just give me something I can put on the scars,' Ravenna said, getting ready to refuse his help as she had with all the other healers. 'I'll be fine.'

'No, you won't,' Engare said with the voice of absolute authority. 'I'm a healer. We don't have any female healers on the ship at the moment. Now take your tunic off and lie down so I can have a look at your back.'

The tall, barrel-chested Mons Ferratan refused to brook any more protests, and to my surprise Ravenna gave in and lay down on a blanket he'd spread out on the floor. Perhaps she was too tired to argue. His hands looked big enough to count as two pairs, and it didn't inspire me with confidence for the delicate work a healer was required to do sometimes.

'Holy Ranthas, what a mess,' he said, opening his case. 'This will scar, but I can reduce it a little. I have to ask, do you know if the whip was leather or fibre?'

Ravenna shook her head. I tried not to look at the livid welts across her back, but I couldn't avoid seeing the angry blackish scars that covered so much of the rest of her. Especially on her sides, rarely exposed to the sun. Her skin was quite dark, but beside him she looked as pale as an Oceanian.

201

'It helps, that's all,' he said. 'Some jungle fibres unravel if they're not properly treated, they leave material in the wounds which can fester. But I think we'd know by now.'

I wouldn't have believed that his stubby fingers could be so gentle or so nimble, or that Ravenna would acquiesce so meekly after refusing to let anyone touch her for four years. I think she resented my being there, but I was helping Engare, so she couldn't really complain.

Whipping was still a punishment in the Cambressian Navy, so it was something he must have had experience of. But when he'd bound up the wounds inflicted by Amonis and used a little of the earth-magic in his healer's talisman – they were the only exceptions to the Domain's ban on magic – he turned his attention to the older scars. Those were of a different order.

'What did these?'

'There's nothing you can do about them,' Ravenna said. 'If you've finished, then go.'

Engare wouldn't be moved, though, and in the end she gave in and admitted what had happened. Nor could she disguise the fact that they were still painful, even after so long.

'This will take longer to treat,' he said. 'The pain won't go away, even if you ignore it. In fact, it may get worse. The human body isn't designed to come into contact with aether.'

'I thought aether didn't leave residue,' I said.

Engare's eyebrows went up slightly, as if he hadn't expected me to know that.

'No, it doesn't, but the initial damage never heals properly.' He ran his fingers along one of the scars, and she winced.

The door opened and Tekla came in, clothes slung over his arm and looking irritated at having to deal with us again. 'Haven't you finished yet?' he said, looking surprised to find the healer still here.

'No, I haven't,' Engare said evenly. 'I'm only just beginning. These scars need treatment if she's not to be crippled. Do what you came to do and go.'

'I have to see that they're secure.'

'I can do that. The Provost wants them in good shape, and I'm going to do my job properly.'

He waited while Tekla left the clothes nearby, before leaving in bad humour. I wondered how Tekla had known about Ravenna's older scars. He hadn't been there that dreadful night on Perdition's Shore, although he must have been involved. So how did he know the Emperor had tortured her?

'There's something wrong with that man,' Engare observed as the door closed behind Tekla, but he wouldn't be drawn on the subject. 'Ravenna, I'm going to do a more thorough examination. Please lie still.'

The technique he used was one any mage was capable of, although I couldn't feel the surge of magic. He'd be able to see all of her in his mind, an image that would show how deep the scars went. It was a long time before he opened his eyes again, and I waited tensely until he spoke again.

'I'll do what I can,' he said quietly, and met her eyes. 'Given some time, I should be able to remove the scars, take the pain away. But there's some damage I can't do anything about. You'll never be quite as strong as you once were. And you'll not have any children. I'm sorry.'

'Thank you, Commander,' she said, then paused. 'Please do what you can.'

'I intend to.'

He insisted on cleaning all the cuts we'd acquired in the jungle, and then we changed into the sailors' tunics Tekla had left for us before he went, leaving the two of us alone and drained in the otherwise empty mess.

'Cathan,' she said, sinking back in the chair and closing her eyes, 'I don't blame you for any of it. Orosius will answer to Thetis for what he did.'

'Orosius doesn't have to suffer any more,' I said, uncertain where she was heading.

'This isn't some backward barbarian state where the only duty of women is to get married and wear themselves out bearing children, waste their lives bringing them up to go and get killed in some pointless war.' The bitterness in her voice was something I hadn't expected, but then, this whole issue was something none of us had ever mentioned.

After Orosius died, it had become clear to me that neither Eshar nor Palatine, for their own reasons, would carry on the Tar'Conantur line. Eshar had never, as far as anyone could tell – and the Domain had searched *very* carefully – fathered a single child in all his years campaigning with the Halettites, not even after the King of Kings had allowed him to take several concubines. It seemed he had been afflicted with the same sterility as my brother, something that affected an extraordinary number of the Tar'Conanturs, and had caused breaks in the direct line more than once.

As for Palatine – she was more complex, and there were depths to this that she'd never revealed. I'd only caught hints, but it was enough to suspect that she had no time for sex, and maybe that it was deliberate, imposed by her own strength of will to prevent her ever carrying on the line. She hated the family at least as much as I did, if not more – and she had considerably more reason to.

Which meant that carrying on the line was theoretically a duty I probably had now, but there'd been nobody around to remind me of it. For once.

'There are other things I can do,' she went on. 'It's not as if I was even planning to have any children. Oh, Alidrisi and Sagantha went on about it from time to time, telling me it would be my duty at some point to carry on the family line. But now I can't, and there's nothing anyone can do about it. Did you ever think about it?'

I thought for a moment. Had I? Not really. Not in the way that some people seemed to. It had never been mentioned while I was growing up, and once I'd been to the Citadel, once I'd begun to think of myself as an Archipelagan and a Thetian, it had rarely occurred to me again. There were oddities to Thetian society that I'd never fathomed – the clans worked in a completely different way from the Continental ones – and it was far less based on families than I'd thought. Not to mention that as the Thetian citizen I was by birth, I couldn't have married until I turned twenty-five last year.

'It's never been important,' I said. I couldn't have imagined what her reaction was to this, and I still wasn't sure.

Perhaps that had been another reason. I still loved Ravenna, as I had since that evening on the shore below the Citadel. And the thought of Ravenna as a mother, no matter who she was married to, was . . . unthinkable. It always had been, and maybe that was why for me this wasn't so strange.

'I thought you'd never cared,' she said, musing. 'Odd that, isn't it? I'm just thinking that whatever I do now, even if I managed to win back my throne and everything else, by some standards it would all be pointless. There isn't a single one of my family left alive, you know. So I'd have no-one to pass it on to.'

'Is that the best way to do it? Hand over power to someone just because they happen to be related to you?'

'You're quite the republican, aren't you?' She hadn't opened her eyes, and her arms were limp on the sides of the chair.

'Only going by my family.' They'd managed to avoid the imbecility that royal houses seemed so fond of, this obsession with keeping the blood pure by marrying generation after generation of cousins. No Tar'Conantur had ever married another; instead, they'd turned to the

Exiles, and managed to retain the same features and the same traits down the centuries. Intelligence, viciousness, madness. Hubris, if that could be called a trait. And some other side-effects, such as the Exile bias towards twins.

'And going by mine?' she asked. It was a dangerous question to answer, and, again, I had to stop to think.

'The Archipelago needed a symbol,' I said carefully. 'How else could it have got one?'

'Don't you think my people would have been better off without me? They made me into something I wasn't, a great leader to come and rescue them. You know how that feels.'

'I was lucky. No-one ever believed in me.' It wasn't what I'd intended to say, and it hung in the air for a moment after I'd said it. Was that really something to be proud of, because I knew that I'd been born without a talent for leading, in the same way I'd been born without a talent for, say, carpentry?

'Your people at home did,' she said, after a pause. 'Don't forget them, just because you've left them behind.'

'I achieved something there, or they thought I did. But when Mauriz and Ithien wanted to make me Hierarch, it was only as a figurehead. No-one thought it made any difference whether I was up to it.'

'So am I the same? A name, somebody to wear a crown and revive memories of my grandfather's time?' She shifted slightly, resting her head to one side as if she was planning to go to sleep there. I was more than ready for sleep myself.

'You decide, Ravenna. Only the two of us and Engare know there won't be any heirs. He'll say nothing, because he's bound by his oath. If you still think there's a chance of restoring the crown, then I'll help you. I would have helped you before, only you didn't trust me.'

'Before – you mean the night I drugged you so I could escape?' She sounded more wary now, and her eyes opened slightly. 'How can I believe that?'

'I can't prove it to you. But you know it was because I was too weak to refuse them.'

'No-one who can admit that is too weak at all. And yes, I think you would have come if I'd asked you. But then we'd both have been taken by the Emperor, and no-one would have come to rescue us. It was your idea, even if Palatine planned it. And even if the Emperor knew from the start.'

'I think it was Tekla who betrayed us,' I said, after a moment's wavering. 'Mauriz thought he was a double agent, but he must have been Orosius's man all along. He must have been the one who forced Mauriz to change sides . . .'

'And the one who told the Emperor where I was,' she finished. 'It makes sense, doesn't it.' Her voice hardened. 'And it means I can take my revenge on him. Orosius is beyond me, but Tekla isn't.'

But at the moment, Tekla was beyond us too.

That wasn't something to talk about here, and nor was the matter of the Skyeyes, though I was itching to tell her. We might be overheard, and I still wanted to work things out in my mind, to assure myself that it was more than just a theoretical construct.

Neither of us said anything more, and I hardly had the energy to walk over into the nearest cabin and close the door behind me before I fell asleep on the narrow bunk.

I woke to find myself sprawled in a tangle of sheets, a soft blue light illuminating the room. I looked out and saw the blue emptiness of the open ocean, a netherworld stretching away into the indigo abyss and up to the surface a couple of hundred feet above. This was normal cruising depth, deep enough to be able to manoeuvre in every direction, but shallow enough to give a sense of night and day.

I wasn't sure what the time was, although judging by the empty shower room, I'd slept well into the morning. I got back into the mess room to find someone had left breakfast on the table and Ravenna just emerging from her sleeping chamber.

Not until we'd finished did Sagantha reappear, to show us across to the great cabin on the other side of the manta and a meeting with Ukmadorian.

There was no trace of personality in what had once been the captain's cabin, none of the decoration that a captain would have brought with him. Only standard naval furniture, a table and some chairs below the windows, with Ukmadorian sitting in one of them, still wearing only black. A silver chain hung round his neck, bearing a pendant with the constellation sigil of the Order of Shadow.

Sagantha offered us chairs before sitting down beside Ukmadorian, but it was very clear that they'd been carefully arranged, the two of us facing Ukmadorian with Sagantha slightly over on the Provost's left. Having lived in the Retreat with its unspoken but complicated academic protocols, I knew what it meant, why Ukmadorian was wearing that pendant. To him, we were still members of his Order.

'You were wrong, both of you,' Ukmadorian said slowly. 'You defied me and went off to find adventure like simple fishermen in some epic. All you found was danger and captivity. All you've done for the true cause of the elements is to bring Eshar down on us all, lose the throne and drive your people to destruction.'

'We didn't start the purges,' Ravenna said.

'Yes, you did. By your actions, your open defiance and your meddling in affairs that were far beyond you. You let Sarhaddon begin his preaching. Who knows how many true believers have died? We of the Citadels can't count our own losses, let alone those of our Orders.'

He'd never forgiven us for leaving him and the stagnating Elemental Council behind on the Citadel islands, openly defying him until he gave way and stopped trying to prevent our departure. But could he really believe that the purges, the Venatic-inspired purges that had gripped the Archipelago, were all our fault? Sarhaddon had come up with the plan and put it into action; it was nothing to do with us.

'Your friends, many of the people you learnt with, are dead,' Ukmadorian went on. 'Of my own pupils I know a little. Mikas Rufele went down with the Cambressian flagship at Poralos Atoll, fighting Reglath Eshar. Ghanthi Akeleneser was burnt by the Inquisition along with the rest of his family.' He went through more names of people I'd known, each one more painful. I remembered them as they'd been at that last night there, the party to celebrate the end of our training. Mikas and Ghanthi had been friends, people I'd spent time with and expected to see again some day.

'You understand now?' he said as I blinked back tears.

'They're dead,' I said, trying to ignore the sudden emptiness, 'but not by my hand. Are you so vindictive, that you blame us instead of the Domain?'

'The Council has preserved the true path free from the Domain all these years. Now the Archipelago is in the grip of the Venatics and we cannot pass on the true beliefs to any more generations. Everything we have guarded over the centuries has gone.'

'So you turn to scum like Tekla instead?' Ravenna said. She always gave less away than I did, but I could see the list of deaths had affected her too.

'Tekla has already been invaluable to our cause,' Ukmadorian said coldly. 'He has brought with him the loyalty of many who once served Orosius, and they have disposed of dozens of Inquisitors across the world, provided much-needed information on Domain plans, sabotaged several mantas. What have you accomplished since your lucky escape in Lepidor?'

Tekla had followers? I remembered others of Orosius's secret police on the *Valdur*, but they wouldn't have been the only ones. More must have survived. Why serve the heretics, though? Why on earth hadn't they transferred their loyalty to Eshar instead, as would have been normal? If Ukmadorian was telling the truth, then there was no way they could be double agents, because from what I knew of him Eshar wasn't that kind of man. He was a fanatic and a soldier, and he wouldn't allow the murder of so many Inquisitors even as part of a trap. As Orosius might have done.

After everything that had happened, I was in no mood to be treated like a wayward novice by anyone. Nor was Ravenna, and she got in first.

'Tekla is as worthless as his master,' she said, not bothering to specify whether she meant Orosius or Ukmadorian. 'Why do we have to use their weapons?'

'You speak as if we were somehow above such things. We have no fleets, no marines, so how else do you expect to fight the Domain?'

'I thought you were all for opposing them without fighting them. For keeping things the way they always were, teaching each generation and not bringing down retribution on your own immaculate head. Not for employing hired thugs and assassins.'

Contempt came through clearly in the Provost's voice as he replied, 'You think this is new? We're at war, as I'm sure you've noticed, but since we don't have the advantage in ships and equipment, we have to use more covert means. Is there anything wrong with stealth and cunning?'

'No. But that's not all, is it? Murder, torture, where do they come in? My grandfather managed without them.'

It was the wrong thing to say, and all of us knew it as soon as the words were out of her mouth. Orethura was important to her, I knew, but Ukmadorian, in his sixties now, must have known him.

'Your grandfather was killed,' Ukmadorian said, but I'd caught the slight hesitation in his voice. As if there was another answer he could have given, but thought better of.

Something that would have given her an opportunity to regain the advantage? 'And no leader can manage without those tools, distasteful as it seems. You'd have a hard time as Pharaoh if you couldn't bring yourself to use men of Tekla's calibre.'

'Use them for what? To betray and capture people to bring them before me so I could torture them in person? After all, it's not as if Tekla ever did that for Orosius, is it? Orosius had his fleet and his marines. He had Tekla and his cohorts to murder and inflict pain, but none of that saved him from being assassinated.' Her eyes flashed as she leaned forward, glaring at the Provost. 'Tekla failed the *Emperor*. An Emperor who had more power than you could ever dream of, and he was murdered on his own flagship.'

'I'm well aware of that,' Ukmadorian said stiffly. 'The Emperor may have been powerful, but he was a fool. You exaggerate his abilities, in any case. He made the mistake of trusting the Domain. You did too, Cathan. Does it run in the family?'

His remark stung me, but not into submission as it might have done once. I made myself sit back and appear relaxed, although he'd almost certainly see through it.

'I wouldn't bring up what runs in my family, Ukmadorian,' I said, careful not to use his title. 'After all, they've hung on to the throne for four hundred years. Even the greatest general the Halettites have ever produced turns out to be a Tar'Conantur.'

'That's not something to be proud of,' Ukmadorian said stiffly. 'I cut my ties with Haleth a long time ago. I'm Archipelagan now, and the Halettites are as much my enemy as the Domain.'

I'd forced him back on to the defensive. 'So your first allegiance is to what? The Archipelago, or the elements?'

'You make differences where none exist.'

'Oh, they do,' I said softly. 'Not all Archipelagans are heretics, and vice versa. Do you think Thetians who still

211

follow Thetis would bow down to an Archipelagan Pharaoh if the Domain was driven out?'

'This is about freedom to worship, Cathan.'

'But it's not. You've made very clear, it's a war between the Domain and its opposition. A war fought with, as you say, all the usual weapons of ships and men and spies. The balance may be unequal, but that's the way it is. You can't win a religious war simply by secular means. You can't win it with the weapons you have at the moment, and not even Tekla can change that.'

'Does this mindless word-play have any purpose?' he demanded, and with that I knew I'd succeeded in turning the meeting round, because now he was waiting to hear what I had to say, not the other way round.

'If you're fighting a war over territory,' I went on, 'then you have to take the Archipelago back, and give its people what they want: their own government under their own Pharaoh. If you're fighting it over religion and freedom to worship, then you have to break the Domain's power across the world. There's no need to free the Archipelago, but no amount of intrigue and assassination will break the Domain's power on its own. You, and everyone who opposes the Domain, have to know what you're fighting for, and you have to have a way to win.'

'We know what we're fighting for!' he interrupted. 'You know as well as I do that the Domain needs to be defeated.'

'And the rest of the world can go its own way?'

'Such noble sentiments . . .' he began, but I interrupted him.

'Not noble sentiments. If you throw out the Venatics by murder and revolt, the Domain will launch the Crusade they've been talking about for years. By killing and destroying you'll forfeit the sympathies of even moderate leaders. That path can only lead the Archipelago to defeat, unless you can find from somewhere else the strength and

212

the support to resist.

'On the other hand, with the Domain as powerful as it is now, breaking its power across the world is a hopeless dream, there's simply no way to accomplish it. Not at any rate by weapons, and murder, and torture.'

'Are you saying that we can't win?'

'No, I'm saying that you can't win without us. There is a third way, but whichever path you take, you need Ravenna, and you need me. She's the descendant of the man you all revere in the Archipelago. I'm the only person on Aquasilva who has any claim to be Hierarch. Either way, you owe obedience to one of us.'

'And the third path?' Ukmadorian said, looking me in the eye for the first time, without his previous contempt.

'The Domain know about it, they've used it, but they don't understand it. We do. Whoever controls the storms will win this.'

I thought I'd trapped him, but there was no way I could have predicted the violence of Ukmadorian's reaction. He leapt to his feet, staring down at me with the cold anger I remembered from before, the same anger he'd displayed when we defied him at the Citadel.

'You speak of an abomination! You would bring destruction down on us all and wreck the planet for your own glory! Playing for power with the lives of millions, but you condemn yourself out of your own mouth.' He turned to Sagantha, who looked more than a little troubled. 'I will stop this terror before it happens. You've heard what he says, you can see she agrees with him.'

'It is as we were told,' Sagantha agreed.

'This must go no further. They can't be allowed to spread these seditious ideas; keep them isolated from the crew. I have all the proof I need to lay the matter before the rest of the Council now.' He turned back to us.

'I would rather see the Domain rule us all than loose your evil on the world.'

213

Hamilcar Barca to Oltan Canadrath,
Greetings,

My stay in this city has not been an easy one, despite its
brilliance. I cannot adequately describe it on paper, and I
doubt I will be able to convey anything of its scope
and grandeur even in writing. It is no wonder, with
such a capital, that they consider themselves a superior
race.

There are more similarities to Taneth than one might
think – the huge harbours, the clan palaces, the commercial activity – but it is blighted by the military rule that
Reglath Eshar has subjected it to. This is not a city that
should be treated so, and its inhabitants have never come
to welcome the presence of troops in the streets.

I can, of course, understand why Eshar has put them
there. The machinations of the clan factions do not seem
to have been dampened with the complete sidelining of the
Assembly – I am told that they are worse than before, if
such a thing is possible. In two weeks I have been
approached by representatives of every faction at least
three times, and even by individual clans seeking my
backing in bids for power of their own. You would feel at
home here, and I would certainly not advise it as a place
for a rest cure.

I have of course stayed out of all internal affairs, but I
have made contacts inside the clan hierarchy – alas, not on
any scale inside the Navy, which seems to be utterly loyal
to their thug of an Emperor. Clan links will come in handy
in the future, and I have discovered that several of the
smaller clans in each faction have more enterprising spirit
than we gave the Thetians credit for. It appears that the
Emperor is deliberately strengthening the hold of major
clans over their more restless dependencies, which

suggests that some help in the right place to certain of those dependent clans might cause our mutual enemy a lot of trouble for a very little cost.

I am being terribly indiscreet, but I have every confidence in my courier's ability to get this letter through.

I have also succeeded in making friends among the Oceanographic Guild. In this city they are not regarded, as in the rest of the Archipelago, as pariahs. Thetians worship the sea, whatever the Domain may claim – and the Venatics have been unable to convince Thetia that the oceanographers are heretical and dangerous. This has meant that the Guild's higher officials have little idea of how bad the situation is in the Archipelago, and hence are unwilling to offer support.

My negotiations have not gone well; the Emperor is determined to keep us out of Thetia and his hatred for Taneth has not softened. His officials are no more polite, and it seems that he has ambitions to develop his own, state-run merchant marine, which could prove disastrous for Taneth. Of course, the clans are violently opposed to this, and it appears the threat to their existence has overcome their mistrust of Tanethans.

I will of course send a detailed report to the Council of Ten detailing how this has gone, but for the foreseeable future we have no chance of breaking into the Thetian trade. I suspect that if the Emperor were able to extend his power over the Archipelago, we might encounter similar problems there. The man has his eyes set on the restoration of the Empire to its former glory, and the Archipelago is an obvious first target.

I will at some point move on, with more success, I hope, to deal with my existing routes and exploit some of the concessions I have been able to gain from various islands. It is rumoured that there is a vast source of lapis lazuli in the hills above Ilthys, which could bring in huge profits. I have no idea who owns the rights or whether they have ever been given away, but I shall stop off in Ilthys on the way to Qalathar to investigate.

I trust all goes well with you, and hope to hear from you shortly.

Hamilcar

PART THREE:
THE SANDS OF HISTORY

PART THREE

THE SANDY CLAUSTRA

CHAPTER XIV

I couldn't believe Ukmadorian's reaction. Was it only our old teacher who thought like this? Or could the 'true' heretics, the Elemental Council that had carried the mantle of Carausius for two centuries, share his views?

Sagantha had locked us in the cabins. I glanced around at the walls, wondering if there was some way Sagantha or Ukmadorian could listen in, and decided probably not. Ukmadorian was Shadow, and it would take mages of Air to eavesdrop on us other than through listening holes. And why would anyone have bothered to put those in a cadets' mess? Anyhow, I'd have to risk it, I had to discuss what had happened with Ravenna.

'It's the Council that worries me,' I said. 'Think about it. The Citadels have their own warships, their own marines, a level of organisation capable of getting all their recruits to each Citadel and back year after year with complete impunity.'

'So?' Ravenna said. 'We know all that. What does that have to do with Ukmadorian's outburst?'

'It's never occurred to me before to wonder where they get their backing from. And what about the money? Orethura's Archipelago was bankrupt half the time, and most of its treasure was plundered by the Crusaders. Why was he so poor – didn't the Council ever help him out?'

Ravenna wasn't impressed. 'They've had plenty of time to build up funds and to acquire the expertise to run an organisation like that.'

I was still following my train of thought. 'So why, with all that power and organisation and money at their disposal, didn't they use it against the Crusaders?'

'I don't suppose they're as rich and strong as you seem to think, that's all there is to it. There's no mystery.'

She was being exasperating. There so obviously was more to the Council than we realised, yet she seemed to be dismissing what I was saying without really knowing anything about it.

I knew I wasn't making much sense, but I was growing more certain that something was being hidden from us. 'Are you claiming to know everything about how the Council works?'

'Of course not. But I know enough not to suspect some grand conspiracy.'

'It's not just a question of conspiracy. Can't you see that it affects us? Ukmadorian as good as wants us tried for heresy. If the Council is just what we always thought it was, then we can probably deal with them. But if Ukmadorian has supporters, people who are arming and funding him, then we're in more trouble than we suspected.'

That, finally, got her attention. Perhaps she knew Ukmadorian too well, was too used to thinking of him as no more than an irritation, one of the obsolete Council of 'old goats' that Palatine had criticised, Criticised for their ineffectiveness, their stagnation – but never thinking to ask how they had been able to stagnate.

'I've had enough of people doing this to us,' she said, suddenly angry – or maybe she'd been on the verge of anger anyway. 'Ukmadorian is determined to control us, but he can't afford to waste us.'

'He doesn't need to,' I reminded her. 'We don't have to agree, not with Tekla and his kind around.'

'Ukmadorian wouldn't do that,' she said, but I could tell she didn't believe what she was saying.

'This isn't black and white any more. We're prisoners again, and we don't know exactly who Ukmadorian really represents. You may be right, it may only be the Council, the Council as we know it, but what if it isn't? What if the Council isn't what it seems?

Ravenna shook her head. 'I still don't understand what Ukmadorian wants.'

'He wants us under his control.' I was silent for a few minute, lost in thought, and then I burst out, 'Why does everyone hate the whole idea of Storm so much? They all think it'll bring nothing but disaster.'

'Including Salderis,' Ravenna reminded me.

'Salderis had her own agenda.' I stared out into the blue, the featureless expanse of the ocean. There was no way to tell where we were heading, but I supposed it would be south, towards the last heretic strongholds.

'Ukmadorian is doing to us exactly what he says the Domain shouldn't be allowed to do,' Ravenna said. 'Storm is a new way of looking at things, and, for whatever reason, he hates it, he wants to prevent us from spreading the idea. Isn't that exactly how the Inquisition behaves?'

'It's no threat to him.'

'He sees it as one.'

'And how can he resort to murder, recruiting someone like Tekla?'

'He obviously sees nothing wrong with murder.'

I was thinking hard, trying to put the pieces together, to make sense of so many contrary bits of information. There was something important we were missing here. 'Murder isn't new to Ukmadorian, when you come to think about it. After all, they taught us the assassin's trade at the Citadel,' I said bitterly. 'We just never imagined they'd use it – least of all against us.'

'There isn't any sense in killing off odd Inquisitors here and there, even if they are evil,' she pointed out. 'It achieves nothing. There are always reprisals, and it feeds the Domain's propaganda, makes it easier for them to present us as mere pirates. It might satisfy the Council, but that's all.'

What else, though, could heretics do, with neither ships nor men? This wasn't a war that could be won by resistance or even clever tactics; this wasn't a slave revolt out of some ludicrous epic where a band of ragged escapees brought down a powerful empire. I sighed. Confusing epic and reality was a common Thetian failing.

'One thing is clear,' I said after a long silence. 'If we want to use the storms, we have to work together. Unless, of course,' I added, only half-joking, 'you want to teach me wind-magic and in return I gave you water. If we did that, we could go our separate ways.'

'What did you say?' she asked. She was frowning, but from concentration now, not anger.

'We could teach each other the third element, then we wouldn't need the partnership at all.'

In theory, just the two elements were needed, because the storms were a mixture of Water and Air, but the Tuonetar spells which created the storms had left a taint of Shadow in the atmosphere and some of that element's magic was needed as a safeguard.

'We can't do that — can we?' Ravenna said.

She was right, in a way. Most people could only use one element, but because my Water was inborn and she'd been to two Citadels, we were unusual. So Ukmadorian had said.

Ravenna was prowling about the cabin, thinking aloud. 'He's been wrong about things before: we shouldn't have been able to join minds in Lepidor. What if we *can* learn a third element as well – and, if a third, why not a fourth and so on?'

I had an answer to that. 'They all use different techniques, that's why. You'd have to learn each one from scratch.'

'But would you?' She said nothing for a moment, lost in concentration. 'Listen, we could test it now, if only we were able to get away from Tekla, out of his mind's reach.'

'That should be possible. I did it when he took us out to the searay and I swam off. I came back of my own accord, not because he made me. So there must be a limit to his range.'

'And if we got far enough away from him, it might work.' She gave an unsettling smile. 'Then it's our turn, because he has no other way to defend against our magic. I think strong emotion would work against him, like your strange attraction to the sea, or more conventional emotions. Such as anger.'

'In which case, mind-mages aren't much use against the Domain's mages; they're full of emotion – all that passionate religious zealotry.'

'Never mind them.' She was still for a moment, then moved a little bit away, pushing up the sleeves of her borrowed tunic to show the scars on her shoulders, old and new. 'Anger should do fine, after all this,' she said, letting the folds fall again.

'The only problem is, even if anger broke Tekla's control over us, where would we go? Even without the Council and the Tehamans hunting us, the Domain rounds up refugees to work on Imperial construction projects. We'd be back as penitents as soon as we appeared, looking the way we do.'

'We can worry about that later. The main thing is to get away from Ukmadorian and Tekla. As long as we can stop him dragging whatever he feels like out of our minds . . .'

'I don't think he can do that,' she said, a little too quickly. 'At least, not without seriously damaging his victim's mind.'

I wondered, for the first time, if that had happened to Ravenna, as it had to Palatine when she'd lost all memory of who she was and where she came from. 'At the moment,' I said, 'the people with most of the mind-mages are the Domain. The Council can't have that many.'

As I spoke, I heard the sound of the door being unlocked, and swung round.

'If we did,' Ukmadorian said, 'we wouldn't have told you.' He moved into the room, accompanied by Tekla and another man, an inscrutable Qalathari whose poise and carefully blank expression put me on edge. 'You're too dangerous to be left together.'

Ravenna gave him a contemptuous look. 'Feeling more confident now with your Imperial lackey to protect you?'

'I don't need much more to deal with the two of you, not in this state,' he said curtly. 'I don't have time to waste. You're prisoners of the Council, and you belong in the brig, not the guest quarters.'

'I am your Pharaoh.' She didn't look very impressive in her overlarge tunic, her hair still wild and tangled, but she had as much poise as she'd ever mustered. I felt a surge of pride, or perhaps happiness that her old spirit was still there. 'You're sworn to me.'

Ukmadorian shook his head. 'No. I'm sworn to the Faith, to the Shadow I've believed in for sixty years. It's our faith that will bring us through this, not you. Not you or your unclean magic, or anything you learnt from that witch Salderis.'

How did he know we'd learnt with her? Only Palatine had known where we went – had she told him? I tried to suppress a twinge of unease at that thought. Palatine wouldn't have expected this vehemence.

'You flew the flag of the Archipelago above the Citadel every day,' she said, facing him directly. She was almost a head shorter, but the Provost seemed to shrink beside her. 'My grandfather's flag.'

'Your grandfather was a great man. Foolish, but still great. He died having held firm to Althana, having put the survival of the heresy above his own life.'

'As I would have done. I've never forsaken our gods any more than he had.'

The Provost's face darkened. 'You've used the powers they gave you to create a monster, and now you plan to unleash it on us. Those aren't the actions of a Pharaoh.'

'And all for what? To free us from the Domain! That's what matters, not maintaining the purity of our Faith, but ending the persecution. How many have already died? How many more are going to? I took an oath to protect them, and since I don't have fleets or marines, magic is the only way.'

'Magic such as I taught to you, the magic our ancestors used against the Tuonetar. Not this blasphemy, not meddling with the planet itself. Last time that was tried, it turned Paradise into *this*. It was a warning from the gods not to meddle with their world. The Tuonetar were destroyed for what they did. You in your pride would repeat their mistake, bring down the anger of the gods on us.'

'So you've taken it on yourself to betray me, without even considering what I've proposed?'

'The Council has debated this. You have been deposed.'

She shook her head ever so slightly. I could tell from the set of her shoulders, the way her fingers had curled into a claw, how tense she was, but I wasn't going to interfere, not yet. I didn't know if there was anything I could do, anyway. If he'd rejected her authority, he'd reject mine just as quickly – and claiming the Hierarchate was almost the last thing I wanted to do.

'The Council has no power over me,' she insisted.

'This is wartime. You failed to lead. Instead, you ran away to that woman and her apostasies. You're not fit to lead anything. Neither of you are. The Council rules the Archipelago now.'

'No!' Ravenna's voice cut across his last words. 'The Council rules nothing, not even the few pathetic islands you're still clinging on to. No-one believes in you. Most Archipelagans don't even know you exist.'

'They know Admiral Karao exists,' said Tekla, breaking

his silence so far. 'As usual, you have an exaggerated view of your own importance. He's actually a tried and tested leader, while you're simply a temperamental and rather childish woman who's so far shown a total inability to do something for herself.'

'Temperamental and rather childish?' Ravenna said, her voice wavering. 'Wouldn't that be better applied to an Emperor who has nothing better to do with his supreme power than personally torture members of his own family?'

'Silence!' Ukmadorian said, his tone verging on the apoplectic. He motioned the two men forward, and without thinking I moved over to stand beside her, resting my hand on her shoulder. 'Gag them and take them to the brig.'

'Be quiet, old man!' I snapped, turning all the contempt I could muster on him. 'Tekla, this miserable worm isn't worthy of your loyalty. How can you stand taking orders from a bleating old goat?'

Before anyone could move, heavy steps had sounded in the corridor and Sagantha ducked through the doorway, pushing the Qalathari out of the way.

'What's going on?' he demanded.

'Treason,' said Ravenna flatly.

Tekla began to move, but the Viceroy held out a warning hand. 'Ukmadorian, I thought we agreed we'd leave them.'

'Leave them to hatch more abominations, you mean. They should be confined separately.'

Sagantha shook his head. 'No. You *will* hold to what we agreed. You don't have power to override me. They're to be left here until we have a quorum of the Council, but we're operating under Imperial law.'

'You never bothered with the law as Viceroy, did you?' Ukmadorian said. 'Now it suits your own agenda to use it against me.'

'What agenda might that be?' Ravenna's eyes flicked briefly over to Sagantha.

'You might imagine your guardian angel is protecting you out of the goodness of his heart. That isn't the case, I'm afraid. You'd be a useful pawn for him and his allies to use against some other leaders of the Council. He doesn't care for the storms or your crown any more than I do – the difference is that I'm not bothering to pretend otherwise.'

'What he means is that I'm still a royalist,' Sagantha said levelly. 'I'd prefer to see you ruling the Archipelago once this is over.'

'But you prefer the Council to conduct the war.'

'There were many who thought you were dead,' Sagantha said.

'So, have you officially written me off?'

The scowl on Ukmadorian's face was enough to show they hadn't, that Ravenna was still nominally Pharaoh. Why not, I wondered?

'Take your hired thugs away.' Ravenna said. 'Ask Tekla who he once was, perhaps he'll remember a time before he was Orosius's pale projection. And maybe he'll tell you what happened to make him like this.'

For long moments the Provost said nothing, as Sagantha and Ravenna waited for him – one wary, the other disdainful and every inch the monarch her grandfather had been. Then, finally and with ill grace, he motioned the others to leave.

'You will remain here, under guard at all times,' he pronounced. 'You fled, you abandoned your people, and yet you expect to return and assert your claim as if these years had never gone by. It is time you learned what are the realities of this war.'

He left, locking the door behind him. My mind wandered back to the Citadel on its green island in the far south, the huge white building above the lagoon, the incredible blue of the Ocean. Ukmadorian had been our instructor, head of the Citadel – most of the others had rarely seen him. But he'd taught me most of the magic I knew.

His turning on us now seemed to sully the memory of everything – the night exercises in the jungle, sailing, celebrating the Festival of Thetis in the lagoon. Our defiance at the end had come back to haunt us after all this time, but the worst part was that all the others who'd been there with us would still trust him, still look up to him as a leader of the heresy.

A leader, but not the only one, as Sagantha had just demonstrated. And there was still something that didn't ring true about the Council, some things the two men had *not* said. Neither of them held a dominant position in the Council, which meant – unless it was an exception to every other effective organisation in history – that another faction, perhaps another individual, did. But who?

CHAPTER XV

I drifted out of an uneasy sleep, not sure what had woken me. There was no noise at all except for the quiet humming of the reactor, more a vibration than a sound. After three nights on the manta, I still couldn't get used to the quiet, so different from the noises of the night outside, above the dam or in the jungle.

I'd spent too much time as a slave not to come awake instantly, but I couldn't hear footsteps, or any sounds of someone creeping up on me.

Only a minute or so later I heard a muffled clang, then a shudder of the engines. It was either another manta, or we were about to dock with a gantry. Unsure of our speed, I couldn't guess which.

'Cathan?'

There were no lights – Ukmadorian controlled them from the bridge so we had no way to operate them ourselves. I couldn't use shadowsight either, not with Tekla's stranglehold on our magic.

Ravenna padded over to the side of the bed. 'They'll need time to talk before they come to get us. Presumably they're joining up with their allies.'

It was strange, hearing her disembodied voice in the blackness. We'd been almost half a mile deep at sunset and there was total darkness outside. Most of the crew were probably still asleep.

'It's hard to sleep,' Ravenna said. 'I have such strange dreams.'

'Dreams of what?'

'Perdition's Shore. Your brother before he died, calling out for us to kill him and be avenged for everything he'd done.' She paused. 'It's odd, I haven't dreamt about that night for nearly three years, but I think about it all the time.'

She'd never mentioned it, never reminded anyone that Orosius had become almost human again before he died. Or that he had given me his seal, and entrusted me with telling Palatine she was now Empress.

'It's hard to forget. Sometimes it feels as though that was the last real thing that happened, and everything since has just been a long, horrible dream. Something that the ship has done to us while we're lying there, still asleep in one of those great echoing rooms.'

'Do you still want to go back?' I asked. 'To *Aeon*?'

'You know I do.'

There was another series of dull thuds, then silence. The hum of the reactor changed tune very slightly, dropped in tone as the engines were cut. A gantry, then, or they'd have left the engines on to help keep station.

I swung out of bed and fumbled for my tunic, pulling it on over my head without being sure whether it was the right way round. I didn't want to be at any disadvantage when Ukmadorian came for us.

I followed her out of my little side cabin and tried not to collide with the furniture. It was a little lighter in here, and I managed to find one of the chairs and sit down, unable to make out more than vague shapes. What time was it? I could have been asleep for only a couple of hours, or all night.

It was a half-life Sagantha had condemned us to by interceding two days ago, reasoning with Ukmadorian when we hadn't expected him to. We'd seen nothing of any of them since, and now heavens knew who they'd met on the other manta. I only hoped it wasn't more of Ukmadorian's reactionary friends.

I had no idea who was on the Council now. Sagantha, presumably, but how many others had been caught in the purges or had publicly defected in order to save their skins? Was it really the leadership of what forces the heresy had left, or was Ukmadorian merely deluding himself?

Long before I'd expected to, I heard the sound of footsteps and subdued voices from the corridor outside. I made myself sit back in the chair and closed my eyes so I wouldn't be dazzled by the light.

I opened my eyes again a second or two later, as light flooded into the room from the dimmed panels in the corridor, to see three figures in the doorway.

Tekla stood between two men; I glanced warily at them, they were both Thetians dressed in the same nondescript black.

'What is it?' I asked, trying not to look concerned.

'Your trial is about to begin.'

'Trial?' Ravenna repeated. 'On whose authority are we to be tried?'

'Your bravado is meaningless – and pointless. It is not for you to question us, as though you yourself had some authority. When in fact the only person you have any authority over is Cathan, and that's just because he's too weak to stand up to you.'

My heart sank. Wherever we were, this place was also run by friends of Ukmadorian, more rigid old fossils too absorbed in their own past to see their mistake. I'd hoped we might have ended up somewhere where people understood that the only thing that mattered was fighting the Domain.

'If you resist, I'll have you treated as violent and dangerous,' Tekla said, in a bland tone of voice. 'As it is, you will be blindfolded. It's normal procedure.'

'What procedure?' Ravenna started to say, and then tailed off. We had precious little left but our dignity, and neither of us wanted to sacrifice that to no purpose. But as I stood there and let one of the guards tie a strip of black cloth over my eyes, I felt more than a twinge of apprehension.

The blindfold was painfully tight and almost complete, and I was led out of the room in total blackness. At first, I knew where we were as we walked down the corridor and uneasily down the steps into the well. I heard one or two voices, and then felt a breath of cool outside air on my face.

'Hatch,' the man leading me said, a moment later, and I stepped through the hatch and into the connecting gantry, managing not to trip over in the process. There was a faint breeze here, and the air became cooler and damper as we approached the other end.

Once we were inside the undersea harbour, wherever it was, I lost all sense of direction. There was a set of spiral stairs leading up – two flights, I thought – and then we went through some doors and down again, into a larger space that was stone, and cold enough to make me feel uncomfortable in the thin tunic. It was very damp, too, and after a moment I realised I could hear surf.

I was still desperately asking myself why the Council were doing this, why what we'd done was such a threat to them. I was beginning to feel like a prisoner of the Domain, and these were people I'd expected to support us.

We were taken into another room, and I heard the sound of a door clanging shut behind us. I swallowed hard, thinking how metallic the sound had been, but didn't have time to think what that might mean before we were pushed through a second door and into a place where all sound was deadened. Hands pulled my sandals off, and I felt fingers at the back of my head removing my blindfold, but there was only light for a brief second before the door closed behind me.

'Ravenna?' I said, tentatively, waiting for my eyes to adjust to the little light there was; it seeped in round the edges of wherever they had brought us. I reached out in front of me, felt metal bars and then cloth beyond them. The floor underfoot was wet and chilly, and I wished they hadn't taken my sandals. The cuts and abrasions I'd sustained in the forest were only half-healed despite Engare's ministrations. What was the point of all this? I had the uncomfortable feeling there was more to it than simply Tekla's unpleasantness.

'Yes, I'm here, although I don't have any more idea of what's going on than you do.' Ravenna's voice sounded oddly dulled, soaked up as it was by the cloth that surrounded us.

We were in a cage of some kind, inexplicably covered in black cloth. I strained to hear anything from outside, to gain a clue about where we were, but there was only the faint, distant sound of surf – not very strong surf, either. I touched the wall behind me: it was slightly damp stone. We were probably at sea level – but where was this place? We could be anywhere within two days' sail of Qalathar, but it seemed impossible that the Domain could have missed a heretic fortress this close. The locals would surely have betrayed its existence.

I felt a sudden stab of fear, wondered if we'd been handed over to the Domain after all. It was a ludicrous thought, but as time dragged on, I became more and more worried.

In the end, I mentioned my fears to Ravenna, but she wasn't any more sure about it than I was. What if Tekla and Ukmadorian had already apostasised, and everything they'd said had been a lie? No, they couldn't have set up anything so elaborate just to catch us, especially on such short notice. They couldn't have known we'd head for the south coast, even though Tekla had somehow been able to find us. It was no coincidence; he must have been following us, or known where to find us. Yet we ourselves hadn't known where we were. How could anyone else – unless whoever had been controlling that storm . . .

It gradually grew warmer, but also more stuffy. There was no way for air to circulate in here, and I found myself wishing for the cold of the corridor again. Or the sea, so tantalisingly close.

What were they up to? Tekla had said it was time for our trial, but what kind of trial was this? I hadn't believed Ukmadorian, thought he was just blustering as always, but that didn't seem so likely now.

I pressed the cloth, wondering if I could push it away and let more air in, but it seemed to be secured at the bottom. It wasn't a very big space we were in – probably a third person could just have squeezed in beside us.

I ran my hands along all the bars near me, wondering if any of them had a break in them for a door, but all I felt was that they were old, knobbly and with patches of rust here and there.

Time still seemed to drag on; I couldn't hear anything from outside except the faint sound of the surf, and it became stuffier and stuffier. We tried standing as far apart as possible, moving from side to side to get some air flowing, but nothing seemed to work.

Finally a door opened, although not the one behind us. There were footsteps in front of us – several pairs of feet, slow and measured. Everything was muffled. A moment later, I heard the unmistakable sound of several people sitting down.

The seconds ticked by, and then at last a man's voice rang out in a sonorous chant that went on and on.

'In the name of the Most Holy Gods and Goddesses of the Eight Elements, Thetis, Lady of Water, Hyperias, Lord of Earth, Althana, Lady of Wind, Ranthas, Lord of Fire, Tenebra, Lady of the Shadows, Phaeton, Lord of Light, Ethani of the Spirits and Chronos the Master of Years, may we speak with Thy voices and dispense Thy most holy justice. As our forefathers before us, we gather here for the practice of that law which has been handed down, that we may restore Thy lost brightness to the world and work for the day when all of Thy children may live and worship openly.'

There was a pause, and a moment later the same voice

began again, speaking now rather than chanting, although I couldn't understand most of what was said.

'I declare the Twenty-Second Proceeding of the Forty-Third Court of the Ring of Eight now begun. We shall follow the procedures as laid down by the founders of this court, and in the absence of Eight, let Six preside. The proceedings shall be secret and not subject to the law of Archipelago, Domain or Empire. Let the prisoners be shown.'

There was a rustle of cloth, and suddenly the curtains parted in the centre and light streamed in, dazzling both of us. By the time I opened my eyes again, squinting in the harsh glare of aether light that seemed to be focused exclusively on us, the cloth around us – although not above us – was gone.

For a few moments I couldn't see anything at all; I could only hear that voice again, coming from somewhere to the left. We weren't in a large room, I could tell that, although it had quite a high ceiling.

What did they mean, *not subject to the law of Archipelago, Domain or Empire*? What court was this? I couldn't believe the Council had abrogated so much power to itself – and that we were to be the ones to suffer. It was becoming painfully obvious how wrong I'd been to underestimate Ukmadorian.

And what did they mean by the Ring of Eight and those cryptic numbers?

'The prisoners Cathan Tauro and Ravenna Ulfhada, former mages of the Element Shadow,' the man announced. 'Neither has been consecrated to any position of authority which overrules this court's. They are therefore fully subject to all censures, verdicts and sentences passed by the Ring of Eight. In the absence of a crowned Pharaoh or Hierarch, there is no higher authority. The decision of five of the Eight will be final.'

As my eyes adjusted, I could make out faint forms

behind the light, but they all seemed to be wearing hooded robes, and I couldn't see any of their faces. Who were they?

'They are accused of blasphemy, apostasy and treason. As they have incriminated themselves, their guilt is beyond question. This court will consider only the magnitude of the offence and the suitable punishment.'

'What right have you to do this?' Ravenna demanded. 'The only laws we've broken are the Domain's.'

'Silence,' said one of the figures directly in front of us, speaking for the first time. His voice sounded familiar, but I couldn't place him. 'You have been told this court is beyond the jurisdiction of any law except its own.'

'Because you've decided it is!' She was angry, but it was an anger fuelled by worry as much as simple temper. I was more and more uneasy as every second went past. This wasn't a bad dream, or some pretence of the Council's. There were no windows in the room, but black drapes on the walls that looked as if they'd been there for ever. This room had been built for this purpose – but who by?

'You have no choice but to listen and obey,' the man said.

Ravenna opened her mouth to say something else, but before she could speak her face contorted and her knees gave way. She fell forward against the bars, and I found myself frozen, unable to help. Tekla again, curse him.

I knew this was what they did in Inquisition courts. I remembered descriptions from people who'd got off lightly – that is, sentenced to years of penance rather than death at the stake. Those who'd been willing to talk about it had mentioned mind-mages used to impose order, hooded judges, even the cage we were in.

This wasn't an Inquisition court, though. Why would the heretics model themselves on it? They used methods that weren't exactly praiseworthy, but they hated everything the Inquisition stood for – its secret trials, lack of justice, non-adherence to the principles of Thetian and its

236

derivative Archipelagan law. Surely this wasn't a heretic court – but in that case, what was it?

'Only mild interrogation has been applied to Cathan so far,' said Tekla, in the respectful voice of a court official. I must have missed something that had been said. 'Ravenna was thoroughly questioned some time ago by another officer of the Ring.'

'Is this officer present?'

'Yes.'

'Then let him produce his evidence.'

The man who stepped forward was dressed in black and hooded like all the rest, but when he began speaking Ravenna gave an agonised scream.

I stared at him for a moment, unable to believe who I was hearing, and then despair washed over me like a wave, crushing me completely. My legs were suddenly too weak to support me, but I managed to kneel of my own accord, staring down at the floor in absolute misery.

We might as well have surrendered to them above the lake, rather than endure that flight through the forest to freedom and then straight back into Memnon's hands.

'He's working for the Domain!' I shouted, but they silenced me as they'd silenced Ravenna, with a bursting pain inside my head. I screwed my eyes shut as if that would make it any better, but then I found images forming in my mind, images of what had happened to Ravenna in Tehama more than a year ago.

I saw her covering the last few yards of a cliff road coming towards me, a slender figure wrapped in a heavy cloak. It was cold, bitingly cold, and the air was painfully thin. She was gasping for breath and leaning on a man in functional black clothes.

I was seeing this through Memnon's eyes; after a moment he moved down to greet her, helped her the last few yards to the top of the pass. Towering mountains surrounded them, snow-capped peaks devoid of any life whatsoever. Below him, the way he'd come, there was only a layer of cloud – a broken carpet that was just thick enough to obscure any view of Qalathar, miles below. I had just time to notice that, and the other cloud layer above Memnon.

Ravenna stopped over the lip, just out of the wind, and I got my first look at the scene before him: a grey lake half-hidden by mist further along its length, surrounded by dark green forests that spilled up the mountains on all sides. Rainforest, I realised after a moment – those weren't pine trees or even cedars. How rainforest could thrive up here when it seemed to be so cold I had no idea, but it was a strange sight, with that still, misty water lying there.

Memnon and the men and women with him accompanied her down through the forest, back into the humid warmth they'd left to greet her. The road was very old, worn around the edges and not in good condition, but there didn't seem to be any wheeled traffic.

The scene abruptly changed, a disorienting feeling that left me dazed for a few seconds before I could take in the next one, in a huge circular hall with giant ochre pillars and a domed roof. A group of men and women emerged from the far side to greet Ravenna, and I saw the pleasure on her face as she embraced Drances, several of the others, and finally a much older woman who looked very like Ravenna. An aunt, even her grandmother? She didn't look old enough for that – perhaps in her late fifties, the age Ravenna's parents would have been now had they lived. An aunt, then.

'Welcome back, little crow,' Drances said affectionately, and Ravenna didn't seem to take it as an insult at all.

'The College of Tribunes welcomes you,' said another woman. 'You must be exhausted, but I hope you'll join me for dinner.'

A minute or two later, most of the people had left, and Drances swept Ravenna, Memnon, the aunt and one or two others out of the hall.

Again a scene change, less uncomfortable this time because I was getting used to it.

This time the same group was sitting around a table in a beautifully decorated room which didn't seem to be lit either by flamewood or aether. The walls were decorated with paintings that were neither Qalathari nor Thetian, but another style altogether, more naturalistic than what I'd seen of Qalathari art only very different in its emphasis from the Thetian.

The aunt raised a rock crystal goblet in a toast. 'Welcome home, Raimunda. It's been too long.'

Sitting opposite her, looking rested and in better shape this time, Ravenna looked so happy that I felt a terrible pang, thinking of where we were now. It was amazing how relaxed she was – she'd left here when she was seven, or was it thirteen? I couldn't imagine how strange it must be to go home after so long.

'It was so lucky we found you,' Drances said finally. There were four or five guests including him and his son. 'Memnon tells me the Inquisitors had captured you – what were you doing in Thetia anyway?'

'Learning,' Ravenna said. 'There was an oceanographer there who'd been famous once, but the Domain outlawed her.'

'Oceanography?' said Drances's wife, a tall and slightly distant woman who'd said little so far. 'Why oceanography? It can't be much use against the Domain.'

Ravenna hesitated, bit her lip – a gesture I knew very well. She was thinking. 'Not on its own. But Salderis – the oceanographer we learnt with – was different.'

'Salderis?' Drances said sharply, his eyebrows raised. 'The one who wrote that book about the storms?'

Ravenna nodded. 'Yes. That was forty years ago. We were the only people she'd ever taught.'

'She was the one who died that night, wasn't she?'

239

Memnon said. Ravenna looked round at him to answer the question but, as she did, Memnon caught the expression on his father's face. As if a cloud had suddenly covered the sun and then gone away again. When Drances next spoke I thought his tone was slightly more forced.

Why had she trusted them? There was no indication of why Memnon had been working for the Domain, and his presence here and now in the courtroom and in the dream being replayed in my mind, made it clear he was playing a double game — but to what effect I had no idea. I wondered what explanation he'd given Ravenna.

Memnon watched as Ravenna told them some of what she'd learnt, but he kept glancing over at his father. Drances sounded politely interested, as if his interest was in what Ravenna was doing rather than in that particular subject he knew nothing about. By contrast, Memnon sounded genuinely curious when he asked questions.

There were more scene changes — Ravenna walking with Memnon on a terrace, looking out over the still-misty lake; inside again, talking to him and some people whose names I didn't catch. There was another man there in the next scene, who seemed to be the nearest the Tehamans had to an oceanographer, someone Ravenna didn't know but Memnon had introduced her to.

I saw Memnon exchange wary glances with another man. He must have been an informant of some kind, sent by Drances as a back up to Memnon.

How had it gone wrong? Drances didn't like the idea of the storms, although I couldn't tell why. Ravenna didn't seem to have realised that all was not well, while she was talking to her other new acquaintances about the storms.

Another scene formed in my mind: Drances had summoned Memnon to give evidence before the College of Tribunes in secret session.

A whisper of horror went round the chamber when Memnon finished. Some of the Tribunes were shaking their heads and pursing their lips and muttering to their neighbours.

'You can't play about with storms.'

'Look what happened when . . .'

'I remember my father telling me . . .'

'This is most disturbing,' said a Tribune, speaking up so that all could hear him. He was a bear-like man with a worried expression on his face. 'Taking an academic interest as Salderis did is bad enough, but we have no idea of the consequences should this be actually used.'

'It would be a formidable weapon, Lausus,' said the woman who'd greeted Ravenna in the Council's name earlier on.

'It was,' the bear-like Lausus said. 'Our Tuonetar allies used it in the war against the Thetians. Look at the damage they did. We mustn't let this happen. She must be stopped before she spreads this evil any further.'

There were nods of agreement.

'We know,' Drances said, 'just how much the War cost everyone. Few others have any idea of it; their history has been too distorted by the Domain and the Thetians. Ravenna has been led astray by this man's ideas, and now they think they can use the storms against the Domain without altering the climate.'

'Salderis didn't think so,' Lausus said. 'Not if I read her book right.'

'So what do we do?' the woman asked. 'I agree with what's been said. It could be a devastating weapon – devastating to everybody. It's not something you can use specifically against your enemies.'

'I believe they genuinely want to understand it,' Memnon said. 'They know how to use the storms already, but they wanted to understand how the atmosphere functions before they tried anything more.'

Drances shook his head. 'It just allows them to do more damage with less effort.'

241

'We need proof of what they intend, though,' another man said. 'And we need to decide what to do with Ravenna. She's Orethura's granddaughter; we can't just remove her. I'm not happy with punishing her anyway, but in the circumstances I agree it needs to be done. We just have to strip her of her reputation and position and expose her as a danger – publicly.'

'We could get her to give a demonstration,' Memnon suggested.

'Are you mad?' Lausus roared, half-rising from his seat. 'You'd invite her to work her terror on us?'

Memnon shook his head. 'Not at all. She'll prepare it, and then before she begins we can expose her in view of everyone.'

'It'll be a terrible blow to her aunt,' one of the others, a much older woman said. 'Ravenna is her only family, and she dotes on the girl. Having her come back after so long just to be taken away again like that might kill her.'

'We'll do what we can for Beroe,' Drances said, 'but Tehama comes first. Ravenna doesn't seem to realise how much more vulnerable we are to climate changes up here.'

'Let her begin her demonstration, then,' said Lausus. 'Then we can be ready to arrest her.'

'And afterwards?' the older woman said.

'We interrogate her,' said the younger woman. 'Properly. Find out everything we can about this confederate of hers. After that, we can decide. Perhaps we can leave her alive, that would kinder on Beroe.'

'I'm not sure that's such a good idea,' Lausus said. 'I don't like leaving loose ends. Think of how many deaths she could still cause. This may be the only chance to stop this dreadful scheme before it gains further support.'

'Agreed? Shall we vote?'

The vote was unanimous. The scene changed again. I knew what was coming, but, caught inside Memnon's images of the past, I couldn't look away.

CHAPTER XVI

They were outside again now, I couldn't tell how much later. Under a dark, threatening sky, Ravenna stood with Memnon and a few others on the summit of a watchtower above the city, looking down on to its tiled roofs and the lake beyond. The wind had stirred the grey water up into whitecaps, and from the distance I could hear the ominous rumble of thunder. A small crowd waited at the top of the city, clothes flapping in the wind.

Ravenna looked down worriedly, then around at her companions. Their faces were unreadable, although I caught worried looks from some of them every now and then. Memnon was watching Ravenna carefully as she glanced up at the sky, then began drawing on her power.

Memnon waited only a few seconds, then stepped in. He grabbed her arm and dragged her round to face him.

'This is too dangerous,' he said. 'We'll not share our allies' fate.'

She began to protest, then looked more closely at Memnon. I saw the sudden realisation, her awful wrench as she realised Memnon had betrayed her.

The mind-mage glanced beyond her, over the parapet to where the crowd had parted to let a detachment of men with jaguars through.

For a moment she hesitated, them one of the jaguars growled, giving the hunters' presence away. Before Memnon could react, Ravenna elbowed him in the stomach, sending him sprawling against the parapet.

Seeing the scene through Memnon's eyes, I missed the next few seconds. It took Memnon a while to recover his breath, then he rushed downstairs and joined the other hunters. The jaguars were already ahead of him, crashing through the undergrowth. It didn't take long for them to bring her down, and Memnon reached her just after the first huntsman, his father a moment or two behind. One of the jaguars had pinned her with its paws, while the other had its jaws clasped around her heel. Blood from a wound covered her lower leg.

'What a disappointment,' Drances said.

Then the scene shifted once more, later from the looks of it. Drances was wearing different clothes, and the wound on Ravenna's foot had begun to heal. This was another scene I remembered; she was chained to the stone table while Memnon set about probing her mind.

It was painful to watch, her mind trying to hold its own and retain its privacy as the mind-mage ruthlessly burrowed through it for any information he could find. I heard Drances say that it was proving far more difficult than they had expected, but bit by bit, no longer master of her own body or mind, she was made to give up her secrets.

Only after four days, exhausting for both captive and interrogator, did Memnon manage to force the location of *Aeon* out of her, satisfying his father at last. The two left her semi-conscious on the table and walked upstairs to inform the other Tribunes.

'What do we do?' the older woman asked. 'Her friends know where it is, so does this Cathan.'

'They're not the only ones,' Drances said. 'Others may even be capable of going on without them.'

'Could the Domain help us?' Lausus said.

'They're the only ones who can. We could try to find all of these people and deal with them, but it would take too long. The Domain has more resources, much as I dislike asking them for assistance. We have no obligation to remain aligned with them indefinitely, of course.'

'We could give Ravenna to them,' the other woman suggested. 'They might kill her, but our hands would be clean. They can do what they like with her. She nearly destroyed us all; does she deserve anything better?'

The voting was again unanimous.

The images faded out and I found myself back in the courtroom, my head aching as if someone had been thumping it continuously with hammers. Still huddled miserably in a corner of the cage, my head reeling from what had happened to Ravenna in Tehama, I didn't even look up when the hooded man in the centre spoke again.

'Thank you for your testimony, Memnon. Could I now request the interrogation of the other prisoner in similar fashion?'

'It will take too long,' Tekla objected.

'We need to know what other damage has been done.'

They meant me. They wanted to rape my mind as they had Ravenna's.

'Show us his memories of what the storm did to his home city of Lepidor,' Ukmadorian said, speaking for the first time. 'It would be enlightening, if the accounts I've heard are true, and demonstrate just how much damage they are capable of.'

'Please,' Ravenna said in a strangled voice, pulling herself half upright. 'Let us tell you. I wouldn't inflict that on anyone.'

'Your opinions count for nothing in this court,' the man presiding said.

'No.' It was one of the others, another familiar voice. 'All we require is a confession. If Cathan's account isn't sufficient, we can apply certain procedures to make him more tractable.'

'We have always used mind-mages to extract confessions.' *Always?* For how long?

'I agree,' Tekla said, unexpectedly. 'Cathan has too much elemental blood. He's capable of killing the mind-mage involved even if he isn't trying to do so. It's too dangerous, and other methods will do just as well.'

245

'Very well. Prisoner, you will answer every question you are asked. If you refuse, you will be tortured until your answer is to our satisfaction.'

Unlike the Inquisition, they didn't bother with oblique terms like *put to the question*. How could we ever have been on their side? Were these the people who had taught me at the Citadel, who'd taught friends at other Citadels? The heretics whose shining realm had been destroyed by the savagery of the Crusade?

'Cathan, give them what they want,' Ravenna said. 'Trust me.'

The questions began. They were relentless, phrased to prevent me wriggling out of them in any way – and I knew what would happen if I tried. And knowing that at the end of this I had nothing to hope for, because I would either end up dead or in Domain hands again, I couldn't even summon up the anger to try and turn on them. With two mind-mages, I wasn't sure I could have managed.

They made me describe what had happened when I unleashed the storm on Lepidor, the effects Salderis had predicted of various storms, and even recited passages from the History describing what the Tuonetar had done to create the storms in the first place.

They'd already decided I was guilty, but they wanted to know who else was involved, who else might understand. I told them the truth: that while others might have known of our plans, of the *Aeon*'s location, only the two of us could control the storms or had been taught by Salderis.

'You are trying to protect others,' the questioner said ominously.

'I'm not!'

'We don't believe you. You are refusing to answer. Tell me their names now and you will be spared.'

'There aren't any others!' I repeated.

'Only by exposing them can you help yourself,' the man said insistently.

'We're the only ones. I was made a penitent the night Salderis died, I had no opportunity to teach anyone else.'

'You will have had plenty of chances to infect others,' he said. 'As we have given you the chance to reveal their names. You have not, so we will have to turn to less pleasant ways.'

'There are no others. I've told you that. Salderis never taught anyone else, we're the only ones.'

Why? Why were they pressing me on this? Why were they so ready to use torture, just so they could find more of their own side to hunt down?

As the silence dragged on, I found myself asking the familiar question of why this kept happening to me. I'd fallen into people's hands so many times; even finding *Aeon* had made no difference.

I knew I had to stay alive. I'd made a promise to Salderis before she died. Elements, what did that have to do with it? I wanted so badly to live, and be free from all this. To have the chance to be a research oceanographer somewhere, perhaps in Thetia, and spend my life doing the science I loved. With Ravenna, of course, but only if that was what she wanted to do.

I sat on the cold floor of the gloomy courtroom, dreading what was to come and praying for a miracle. No miracle came. I heard only the sound of the door behind me opening. I tried to resist, but the guards pulled me out of the cage with pathetic ease and dragged me through the next room, a honeycomb-shaped cell, through more doors and then back into the courtroom, depositing me in the centre of the floor.

Away from the dazzle of the aether lights, I could see everything more clearly: the hooded judges behind their raised benches, the black draperies – and the insignia on the cloth above the central judge's seat.

A black olive tree against a golden sun was emblazoned on it, with the scales of justice beneath. The insignia of

Lord Orethura and Ravenna's family. I shook my head, trying to clear it. I must be mistaken.

There was a bang behind me and I looked round to see two more of the Council's men bringing a frame into the room. I could see the cogs and the pulleys on it, and guessed it was probably a rack. As they moved it into place the two men holding me dragged me over and pushed me down on to it, one holding me while the other began tying my feet.

'Traitors!' Ravenna shouted. Tekla, standing just in front of me, turned to her with a contemptuous gesture, but after a moment I saw his supercilious expression disappear, to be replaced by a look of panic.

'Guards!' he shouted. The man tying me down paused, and I was able to twist round, see Ravenna hurl a *thing* of pure Shadow at him. It was too hastily constructed to be called a proper spell, it was more raw energy, but it engulfed the man, and I heard a frenzied scream as it hid him from sight.

Before she could attack Tekla, the door behind her opened and two more guards rushed in. One delivered a savage punch to her stomach while the other dragged her across the cage, hurling her into the bars where I'd been until a moment or two before. There was a sickening sound, then she slumped to the floor.

It was bad enough when they hurt me, but I couldn't bear them attacking her.

I finally found the anger I needed. A tide of pent-up fury at everything I'd endured, at Tekla's contempt and his arrogance. Without using any magic, I twisted round and pushed the other man off balance, sending him crashing into the panels below where the judges were sitting.

'*How dare you?*' I shouted. Tekla turned, caught off-guard again, but the sight of his face was all I needed. I felt as if an aether surge had gone through me, only instead of jarring every nerve in my body and leaving me in agony, it had simply charged me with demonic energy.

I didn't think about it. I didn't even need to form the void in my mind that was supposed to be vital to construct proper magic. I stepped forward, touched Tekla's arm and let go, unleashing the raw power straight into him. His face contorted and he collapsed to the ground, screaming as I remembered screaming when my brother did the same to me.

I heard a step behind me. I spun round and sucked all the water out of the air around Tekla, compressed it and sent it hurtling at Memnon's chest. The Tehaman was thrown backwards even more violently than Ravenna and the guard had been.

I heard terrified shouts from the benches ten or twelve feet above me, ignored them for a second and fashioned more globes of water, shattering every single one of the lights.

It made no difference to me, except that the world became grey instead of dim, but for the rest of them the lights had gone out. I was surrounded by Shadow.

They were monsters. They had arranged this, set themselves up as judges over us. Their time was past.

Being in the utter darkness was as good as being underwater, as if I was immersed in an ocean of pure liquid Shadow. With each wave of my fingers I created whirlpools and eddies, currents and streams, and sent them flying at the panicked judges as they tried to escape, suffocating them, dragging them down, drowning them in darkness. They screamed, but only when all of them had been engulfed did I turn round to deal with the guards who'd attacked Ravenna.

One of them was already lying on the floor of the cage, felled by Ravenna. She looked dangerously pale and in pain. I reached out, poured the Shadow into her as if giving her a drink, and watched as she looked around, gave me a faint smile and sent black vengeance after the second guard.

The room was a babel of screams, and I thought of Tekla in the oceanographic library in Ral Tumar where he'd forced me to kneel and beg him not to betray Ravenna to the Inquisitors. I remembered the cave below the cliffs and my brother's confessions as he died. Again I lashed out, sending more energy against him until he couldn't even scream for trying to gasp in breath.

Then, as if hit by an aether surge, Tekla went limp. I stared at him, unable to take in what had happened. I'd done no more to him than my brother did to me – but Tekla was dead.

I looked round, taking in the grey wreckage of the courtroom. Ravenna stepped unsteadily out of the twisted bars of the cage. No-one else was moving. It was very dark and cold.

'It's gloomy in here,' I said inanely, still feeling an incredible sense of elation. 'Enough of Shadow. *Light!*'

For a second, just a second, the room flared with bright sunlight as if a lightning flash had illuminated it, but then it was gone and my shadowsight was still working.

Using her shadowsight as I was, Ravenna stepped over the comatose form of the guard to stand in front of me. She had a strange expression on her face.

I noticed the rack again for the first time and wondered if that was why she looked so puzzled. I waved my hand. Shadows rushed in, and there was another crash.

A pile of splinters and frayed ropes lay on the floor.

Still not satisfied, I looked up, saw the swirling eddies and currents of Shadow milling over the unmoving judges. I brought them together, sucking them all towards three or four points in the space of the room, until they were whirling faster and faster around those points.

Then I sent them crashing through the door, hunting, seeking more Council people to devour. They would pay, and then the Domain would pay.

As Tekla had already paid.

I looked down at his body and saw a faint blue glow surrounding it. What did that mean? I drew in Shadow, creating a strange greyness in the air around me as the shadows were stretched thin. No light replaced them, which left an eerie, rippling effect.

Tekla's still corpse glowed, and after a while the glow began to change and broaden. Then, as briefly as the illusion of light, his features melted into those of my brother. The blue glow shrank in on itself and disappeared.

There was silence for a moment, broken only by a crashing sound from somewhere beyond the courtroom. My whirlpools were hunting, driven by the parts of my mind still unoccupied by the carnage in here.

'That was the part of him that was still the Emperor,' Ravenna said. 'Perhaps that was the strange thing about him, why I always felt uneasy. His soul was never entirely his own.' She stared at me for a moment. 'Cathan, how did you do that?'

I shook my head, feeling the elation drain away, to leave a feeling of satisfaction and fulfilment. I was purged of the anger that had been stored up inside me.

'I don't know,' I said after a moment. I could see her almost normally now, as if the two of us were standing with white aether lights shining on us. One hand was pressed to her side, where her ribs had hit the bars of the cage, but she looked no more in need of help than I was.

'You shouldn't have been able to,' she said quietly. 'No human should.'

'It was no more than my brother could do.'

'The power, the amount you had, makes sense; you've finally realised how you can use it. But the light, what you just did, it worries me.'

'Why should it? We're free of them.'

Free of them in an explosion of power that I'd never expected. I'd thought I could use my anger to neutralise Tekla's and Memnon's powers until I could take care of them with normal magic. But not once in that whole time had I used any of the techniques we'd been taught.

'You shouldn't have been able to do that, it's not really part of your elements, so you must have been going very deep. Please don't do that again.'

'I won't.' I smiled at her, still feeling as if I could have taken on everyone I knew in a race and beaten them all by a mile.

How long did this strange power last? I stared into the darkness for a minute and willed another whirlpool to form. I saw the distortion; after a moment I banished it. There was no change yet.

'Shall we find some real light?' she suggested, after a brief silence.

We walked out of the courtroom without a second glance, stopping only to collect our sandals from the cell behind the cage. It was fine going barefoot on a beach, or in a forest, or indoors, but not on this cold, uneven stone.

With no idea where we were going, we navigated by shadowsight until we came up a flight of stairs to a window and I could use my normal sight again. We found ourselves looking out at a grey, overcast bay surrounded by cliffs with headlands so close at its entrance they were almost touching.

We got a better look from a higher window, in a corridor where a woman in Council colours lay unconscious against a door. I'd never seen her before and had no idea who she was. She would live, I supposed, as would the others I'd sent the whirlpools after.

We were in a fortress in almost the exact centre of the beach, opposite the headlands. I could just see towering cliffs up to one side, but they were lost in low cloud. There was a strange roar from somewhere, too loud for it to be the gentle surf in the protected waters of the bay.

'I want to know who ran this place,' said Ravenna, looking into a room that must have been a torture chamber once, although it didn't seem to have been used for many years. 'What is this Ring of Eight?'

She was angry now, with a hard, bitter anger that didn't surprise me in the circumstances.

I wasn't sure whether it was a huge building or had been designed by somebody with a labyrinthine mind. It seemed to go on for ever. We stopped at a window on the landward side, but the only view was of a few hundred yards of tropical forest and then a sheer cliff rising straight into the clouds.

'It's a strange place to build a fortress,' she said musingly. 'There doesn't seem to be any strategic point . . .' She stopped. 'I wonder. Can we find some more windows?'

Eventually we found the one she wanted, and I stared in amazement at a sheet of white water falling down the cliffs into the sea with a thunderous roar, creating a cauldron of spume and spray that drenched everything for dozens of yards around it.

'Kavatang Falls,' she said, unable to take her eyes off it. 'We're in Kavatang Bay, on the west coast of Tehama. The sea out there is the end of Perdition's Shore.'

'How do you know? Have you been here before?'

'No. I was told about it in Tehama. There was a city here before the War, but it was destroyed by the Thetians when they came to seal off Tehama. If only they'd done a better job, I would never have been born.'

'They betrayed you,' I began, but she cut me off.

'And if I'd never been born, none of this would have happened. It's blindingly obvious that my grandfather wouldn't have been any worse off if he'd had no children, and for all the good I've done him and his cause, I might as well never have existed. Everyone would have been much happier anyway.'

'No, not everyone. I wouldn't have been happier. Nor would Palatine, Persea, Laeas – or my parents.'

She gave a faint smile. 'Thank you for saying that,

Cathan, but you'd have found someone else to love. We're cut off from the heresy now, as well as from the Tehamans, the Domain – everyone really.'

'Do you think Palatine will reject us because of what's happened? Or Marshal Tanais? He hates the Tehamans.'

'Where are they? Do they know what's going on here?' The fire that seemed to have died down flared up again. 'Cathan, I always thought this fortress was my grandfather's, that he used it to hide people from the Domain. Only an expert pilot can get through the entrance, so it's safe enough – but what have the Council been using it for? What was that court of theirs? There must be a clue somewhere in the building.'

We set off again, through doors splintered by the whirlpools. It was strangely empty now, and we didn't see anyone. Neither of us heard any movement, or voices, or any other evidence that there were people here. I was beginning to feel uneasy about having left Memnon and Ukmadorian in the courtroom. They might be able to organise a counter-attack, and I wasn't sure whether I'd be able to deal with that so easily.

'Should we try and find a ship?' I suggested, as we passed what I thought was the entrance to the undersea harbour.

'Later,' she said, distracted. 'If a ship leaves, we'll hear, and you should be able to stop it in the bay.'

We came to an iron-banded door, at the end of an upper corridor. There had been guards in front of it; a sword still lay here and there were traces of blood on the floor, but no sign of the men themselves.

There was an aether lock on the door, but it was the work of a moment to destroy it. Beyond the door was a staircase. We went cautiously up it and found ourselves in a set of light, airy rooms at the very top of the building.

We were in a circular tower, and one of the rooms took up a large part of it, not quite a semicircle. A door stood open, but there was no-one inside. Only a desk, some chairs and rugs. We went up to the desk, and Ravenna started riffling through its wooden compartments.

It was hard to tell whose the room had been. There were two portraits on the walls – both, I realised a moment later, of men I'd seen before.

On the side closest to the desk, a benevolent Lord Orethura smiled down at us, dressed in long blue robes. He had a tolerant, slightly amused expression on his swarthy face, and grey hair only added to the look of wisdom and kindness. I'd seen other portraits, some less formal, but they were all much the same.

Ravenna stopped and followed my gaze, came round to stand beside me.

'You see how hard it is to feel worthy of him?' she said, resting one hand on my shoulder. 'People revere him because he did so much for them, and all I've ever done is to let them down.'

'He had seventy years to accomplish everything,' I reminded her gently. 'You've only had twenty-five.'

'And when I'm seventy there won't be an Archipelago left. Not if the Domain has its way.'

Alciana had said the same thing after Sarhaddon's speech in Tandaris four and a half years ago. A Crusade would be the end for the Archipelago, she'd predicted, and it seemed that all the brightness of Orethura's time had been lost for ever.

It was only then that I turned my attention to the other portrait. I moved over so I could see it properly, without the light making the man in it almost invisible.

He was a burly man with greying black hair in the uniform of a Qalathari legate. If Orethura was the image of a wise and benevolent ruler, the other man reminded me of Admiral Charidemus who I'd seen briefly in Ral Tumar. The image of a professional naval officer, although this man had been a marine commander.

'Who is he?' I asked Ravenna, but there was a stricken look on her face.

'Oh no, please!' she said. 'Not after all this . . . no.'

'Did you have the dream too?' I asked, my throat very tight.

She nodded. 'Yes – you did as well?' But she didn't seem to expect an answer.

'Who is he?'

'His name was Phirias. He was my grandfather's military adviser. He managed to survive the Crusade and was made Viceroy. I met him when I was eight. He was very kind to me.'

I remembered the dream from the fort, our shared dream. The legate ordering the deaths of the prisoners, an advance – an advance that must have been the Crusader troops thirty years ago.

The legate had been an Archipelagan. This Archipelagan.

I felt the last of my elation draining away, and my joy at escaping the trial and the rack fled out of the circle of windows as it had never been.

The best-loved of the Viceroys, Orethura's commander. Neither of us could fail to make the connection: he had been part of this mysterious Ring of Eight. Whatever exactly it was, it stretched to the heart of the heresy and the old Archipelago, the golden past we'd been told about.

How far had it gone? And who else was part of it?

Hamilcar Barca to Oltan Canadrath,
Greetings,

I am writing to you in my rooms in a rather faded part of
the city, one of many districts which seem to have lost
most of their population since they were rebuilt after the
sack. I expect my designated courier to appear any
minute, but I must keep him waiting while I write this. I
never intended to stay so long here, but I have found
myself delaying my stay for a day at a time, always
postponing it so I could investigate one more faction or
make contact with one more faction; I know it is
indiscreet, but my stay here has provided more intelligence than we could otherwise have gleaned in ten years.

I shall be extending my stay here for yet another week
or so, principally because I have a feeling that something
important is going on here, something we cannot afford to
miss. Call it business instinct based on a few apparently
unrelated facts and pieces of information I have managed
to glean. Many of my contacts here are not people of
whom Eshar would approve, and I know I am being
carefully watched. Still, I will see what I can uncover
without alerting the Emperor's hunters.

The failure of my mission is all the more frustrating
now I see that Selerian is such a huge market, and what an
incredible appetite for luxury its people have, even now
after years under Eshar. They do not consider fine living,
comfort and tortuous political intrigue to be a sign of
decadence, but rather that they have lifted themselves to a
level where they can enjoy what life has to offer. Their
extravagance can go too far, but who is to say austerity and
asceticism are any better? Religious dreamers and hair-
shirt fanatics we can well do without. I see little difference

from Taneth except that we are more hypocritical about it.

The Emperor's continuing requisitions, while pleasing the military, are hitting the clans and trade in general quite hard – he is not making himself any friends by it. A few more years of these conditions and he may run into some problems.

I find it heartening that people here have no more love for Reglath Eshar than we do, but we must remember that Selerian Alastre to all intents and purposes *is* Thetia, and that this city was a republican city-state with a turbulent population long before the Empire. Its people – and I do not mean simply the clans, because the Emperor's suspicion of me seems to raise my status with the ordinary citizens who will gladly talk to me – are well aware of that. Respect for the Tar'Conanturs does not run all that deep in this city, and a surprising number of people seem to revere the memory of the republican leader Reinhardt Canteni, Palatine's father.

My courier has arrived, so I will have to finish here and give him time to make his allotted leaving slot. I will undoubtedly send you further reports in due course, and I suggest that some reinforcement of our agents here might be no bad thing. If you do not feel it beneath your dignity, we may be able to make a healthy profit with some well-chosen smuggling operations.

Peace and good business,
Hamilcar

CHAPTER XVII

'I think we've found what we were looking for,' Ravenna said after a moment, still staring at the portrait of Legate Phirias. The papers she'd been riffling through lay in disarray on the desk, forgotten now. 'I just wanted to believe that this was just Ukmadorian being vindictive, that it didn't go any further than him and his colleagues. But it does.'

Her hand slipped off my shoulder and she walked back to the desk, giving one of the pieces of paper a desultory flick with her finger.

'Shouldn't we be going?' I said. I hoped the manta was still here.

'I suppose so. If we stayed longer, we might be able to find out who's in charge of this.'

'What if Ukmadorian comes round again and orders the whole place searched for us? We'd be trapped.'

She nodded. We made our way down the stairs and retraced our steps. It was easy to find the harbour: there was a direct route from the upper rooms to it. A long spiral staircase led down to a small anteroom and then to a large, glass-walled room under the sea that gave access to the gantry.

There was no manta. Only a corpse, one of the Council guards, slumped against the inner door in a pool of blood. Someone had driven a dagger into his eye. Who else would be killing Council guards? I looked away again, not wanting to acknowledge it was there. The whirlwinds had been meant to stun, not to kill, and I hadn't even intended to kill Tekla.

'There may be other prisoners,' Ravenna said as we

went up the other staircase, back into the main body of the fortress. 'Why should we be the only ones?'

We hadn't looked earlier on, when we'd taken the most direct route out of the courtroom without stopping to see what lay behind the iron doors. So now we went back, going down through a broken outer door into the cellars and tunnels surrounding the courtroom. The courtroom itself was separated from the rest of the prisons by a sequence of gates. The first of the gates we came to was broken open, and beyond it was a larger room with four cells – cages, rather – off it, all unoccupied.

I stopped, listening for any signs of life, but there were still none. Where was everyone? Where were the rest of the Council guards?

It was only later that I learnt what had happened. Ukmadorian and one of the other judges had only been dazed, and within a minute or two after we'd left the courtroom, they were back on their feet. Having left his colleague to wake up the other judges, Ukmadorian assembled whatever Council guards he could find conscious and went to secure the prisoners. He had been afraid that we'd release them and take over the fortress with their help.

There were prisoners, but they were left locked deep inside the fortress, while the remaining Council members took the manta and all the searays they could find. They moved into the bay to deny us any chance of escape by water when we were wandering aimlessly about the upper storeys.

We found a great many cells, none occupied, although some had perhaps been used quite recently if the bedding and the jugs of stagnant water were anything to go by.

'It seems that the prisoners had more sense than we did,' said Ravenna finally. 'Shouldn't your magic have had the same effect on them as on the Council people?'

We went into one room which had metal bars on the

260

walls. A brazier still glowed faintly next to an overturned rack of metal instruments; easy enough to tell what their grim purpose was.

We kept on searching, hoping to find some prisoners. Nothing, and no-one, until I suddenly heard a faint tapping sound. 'Can you hear that?'

Ravenna nodded. We stood still for a moment, keeping our eyes on the corridor ahead.

There was a rhythm to the tapping, I realised after a moment. Long, short–short, long, short–short–short . . . It reminded me of a song, although I couldn't pin it down.

Someone was trying to get our attention – or was it a trap? I listened hard and moved a little way along the corridor to the next intersection. No, the sound was definitely less distinct here.

'Try down there,' Ravenna said, pointing into a side corridor. I didn't think we'd been down it before, but the architecture was all the same, vaulted brick with a stone floor and laid out confusingly.

I followed her. She was right, the sound was coming from down here.

'Careful, it could be a trap,' Ravenna said as we came to an unopened door. There was a grille in it, but peering through I could only see a small room much the same as any of the other cells.

Even with shadowsight I couldn't detect anything out of the ordinary, so I went in cautiously, backing myself against the wall.

I needn't have worried. Only one person was in the cell, a young man secured to a metal frame by wires that cut deeply into his flesh. His olive skin was covered by dried and half-dried blood. A foul smell lingered in the air, reminding me uncomfortably of the Inquisition's pyres.

He looked up at us, and even though a metal gag had been fastened in his mouth, covering much of his face, I could tell he was Thetian.

'Who is he?' said Ravenna hesitantly. 'Not that it matters.'

Unsure whether to use magic or not, I realised after a moment there was nothing else in the cell to free him with, and it would take far too long to unfasten all the wires.

'This will hurt,' I said in Thetian, 'but probably not as much as what they've already done to you.'

'Let me,' Ravenna said. 'If you do it, I'll have to stop him falling forward once he's released, and I'm not sure I could after being thrown around that cage. Anyway, your magic doesn't seem to work on a small scale.'

So I stood about a foot away from the prisoner while she covered him with a net of Shadow drawn from a dark neighbouring cell. For a moment it had no effect, then the man's eyes bulged as the wires turned black and the net disappeared. It was a minute or two before the tracery she'd woven around him was entirely gone, then the wires shivered and crumbled and he fell forward. The grate moved slightly with him, and I realised that was how he'd made the knocking sound, by leaning his weight against it to make it bang against the wall.

The sudden impact of his weight almost knocked me off my feet, but I managed to step back and get my balance before lowering him gently to the floor. Blood began seeping from the channels in his flesh where the wires had bitten deep.

I rolled him on to his back, not sure what I should do. The gag was easily removed, but when he tried to say anything he only managed a croak. There was a stricken expression on his face.

'There's some water here,' Ravenna said, picking up a rough earthenware jug that was propped up on the floor. She swirled it around and sniffed at it. 'It seems all right.'

She gave it to him in small sips, as we'd been taught at the Citadel. He looked painfully thin, which meant he was probably half-starved.

It was a few minutes before he was able to speak, but neither of us was prepared for what he said.

'I wasn't strong enough,' he whispered. 'I failed You, O Lord.'

Ravenna looked at me, her sympathetic expression vanishing.

'He's Domain. A fanatic.'

The man looked up at her, and said brokenly, 'When they began, I welcomed what they were doing. I would suffer for the Faith, and I would join Ranthas in Paradise. I wasn't strong enough. So much pain. And now I've been rescued by heretics, wielders of evil magic, my soul will be lost.'

'That *evil magic* was the only way we could cut you down, but I'm not sure you deserved it.' She looked disgusted. 'He's a would-be martyr.'

'Why is it every time we find an injured man, you want to kill him?'

'If this man were alive and free, he'd be killing people whether they were injured or not. Which order are you?' she demanded.

Looking dreadfully ashamed, the man whispered, 'Venatic. I wanted to have Sarhaddon's strength, his courage . . .'

'His treachery, his deceit,' Ravenna finished. 'Another of Sarhaddon's admirers, that's all we need. You deserved all of this,' she added sharply, speaking to the man.

'Did we deserve it?' I said quietly. 'Either of us? What they were going to do to me was nothing beside this, and there's probably worse we haven't seen.'

'We were on the Council's side. Did we ever send anyone to the stake?'

None of us had realised, when we'd first encountered Sarhaddon's order four years ago, that the word *Venatic* had two meanings. It meant *pure of heart* in Tanethan, but it also meant *hunter* in Old High Thetian. The second was far more appropriate, and I'd heard them called Hounds of Ranthas many times.

'You said yourself we couldn't leave him like that. What if all the Council people really have gone? Would you have left him to starve to death?'

"Are you leaving?' the Venatic said.

'Yes,' said Ravenna.

'Kill me before you go. Then I will be free of this body, and I will have died as a martyr. Otherwise I will be unworthy.'

Four years ago I'd tried to save Orosius as well, when he'd been dying on the bridge of his flagship, killed by Sarhaddon's treachery. Ravenna hadn't wanted him to live then, not surprisingly after what he'd done to her, but in his last minutes Orosius's madness had disappeared and I'd seen the man he might have been.

I closed my eyes for a moment, remembering. The chaos of *Valdur*'s bridge, with its twisted metal and steam from broken vents. The flagship had finally come to rest nine miles below the surface, leaking and mortally wounded like its Emperor. Orosius had been trapped under the wreckage of the bridge surrounded by officers who had died at their posts.

'Please kill me before you go,' Orosius pleaded. *'I'm sure you can grant me that favour, brother, even if she won't.'*

I shook my head mutely, not sure why.

'Why? Why after everything I did to you can neither of you kill me? Cathan, I don't deserve to live, I'm a monster, you said it yourself. Mother said it, everyone says it. They all know what I did.'

'Life is a greater curse than death, say those who know not how to live.'

'Cathan, no!' Ravenna said urgently. *'Remember who you are, who he is.'*

I shook my head slightly, trying to clear the image from mind. This wasn't my brother, but the similarities were so eerie. Even the man's Thetian face reminded me of him, although the features were different. He might have some Archipelagan blood, I thought distractedly.

But this time I didn't need to intervene, because with those last words the man had said exactly the wrong thing. For a moment Ravenna seemed to be torn between leaving him to the mercy of the Council and the Ring of Eight or helping him, and thus preventing him attaining the martyrdom he seemed to want so badly. In the end, for whatever reason, the second option won out.

'You're already unworthy,' she said ruthlessly. 'You wanted us to cut you down, didn't you.'

She held his gaze for a moment, and eventually he nodded.

'Your Order expects absolute dedication to the Faith. Your life doesn't matter, you're expected to put the cause of the Faith above it. You've broken your vows. Even worse, you called us with your tapping, hoping we'd come and help you.'

She stared at him until he nodded his head miserably. He looked as though he was on the verge of tears.

'We'll let you choose. Either we leave you here where the Council will find you and begin the torture again, the pain getting worse and worse until they let you die, or we can take you with us. Two heretic mages.'

I tried to interrupt, but she held up a hand to silence me. 'No, Cathan, we're giving him a choice.'

'Not the choice he wants.'

'He's not in a position to ask. I'm sure by now you understand why I have no sympathy for anyone in Domain robes, Inquisitor, Venatic or otherwise.' She turned back to the prisoner, ignoring his slowly bleeding wounds. 'How long did you hang there?'

'I don't know. For ever. Please, kill me.'

'No. Come with us, or stay to be put back on there again.'

265

There was a long drawn-out silence.

'Ranthas means me to be spared,' he whispered finally.

'I don't think so,' Ravenna said. 'You've broken the vows you made to him. Shall we leave you here?

She was being brutal, but I couldn't think of any way to intervene. She was right; it was his choice.

He closed his eyes, his lips moving in what perhaps was a silent prayer, but after a moment he shook his head again.

'Ranthas, why didn't You give me strength when I begged for it?'

'Because He isn't listening.' Her expression was vengeful. 'He doesn't care. And because His powers are all illusions.'

She scooped up some dust from the floor and held it out in her palm where he could see, and I saw her face go tight with concentration. For long moments she said nothing at all, and then there was a surge of magic. Just for a second, orange flames flickered over the dust. The prisoner's eyes widened in shock.

It was my turn to be stunned. What she'd just done was impossible, it violated everything Ukmadorian had taught us.

Ravenna gave me a smile that was half mischievous and half superior. The first I'd seen since we arrived here.

'I'll explain later,' she said maddeningly, before turning back to the prisoner.

'Have you decided yet?'

'You must be emissaries of Ranthas,' the man said, clinging on to his one hope. 'Only a true believer could do that. You are testing my faith.'

'You haven't been chosen for any higher purpose. Now we don't have any longer, so you can come or stay. Die with the wires twisted in your flesh, or live to smell the palm trees and swim in the sea again.'

I could tell from his expression that she'd hit a nerve there. She was being hideously unfair, but then I could understand it. I had far more sympathy for her than him, and I only wanted to let him live because of what I'd nearly been through, and because I still regretted Orosius's death.

'I will come,' he said finally.

We had no particular idea where we were going, except we knew we had to get away from the fortress. It soon became apparent that the man was in no condition to walk a long distance, weakened by torture and, I suspected, fasting and asceticism before his capture. I supported him most of the way along the corridor, because Ravenna didn't look in very good condition. If my rudimentary medical training was anything to go by, she'd broken at least one rib.

We needed to find some form of boat, but I doubted whether a surface ship could survive the crushing waves at the entrance to the bay. Surely there would be searays here, to maintain communication with the outside world – and for the fortress commanders to evacuate by in time of emergency.

We should have checked the harbour when we first escaped. Now, hampered by the crippled Venatic, we didn't have many options. And I was reluctant to split up. One of us would have to stay with the man, making us both more vulnerable.

Unsure where else to go, we went back down to the harbour.

I searched every part of it, looking for a searay bay, but when I eventually found one it was empty, and the floor was still wet. I wondered if the rays were lurking out of sight in the bay, regrouping for an attack.

'You have no way to get out. I'm a burden to you, so deliver me up to Ranthas's grace,' our unwilling comrade said. I still had no idea what his name was, and decided to ask him rather than state the obvious.

'My name is Amadeo.'

'No, your real name,' said Ravenna. She was assuming that, like most of his fellow, he had taken another name when he joined the order.

'I have no other name,' he insisted. 'That is the name I was given by my superiors, and it's the only one I have.'

I was still wondering what to do next when, to my astonishment, I saw a searay appear out of the murk, gliding gently in towards its berth.

'They're coming back,' she said. 'Can you deal with them?'

'Move away from the door. I'll wait until they come out.'

We propped Amadeo up against a wall, Ravenna went over and pulled the dagger from the dead guard's eye. She wiped it on the carpet with an expression of distaste, and inspected it.

'This isn't the sort of thing a guard would usually carry. It's more like a high official's dagger, ornamental or belonging to someone very rich.' She studied it for a moment, held it up to the light. 'Cambressian Admiralty.'

Might that mean Sagantha had been here, had even killed a Council guard?

I felt a glimmer of hope, but it was soon buried by apprehension as the lone searay vanished from sight inside the berth. There was a muffled clang, probably the bay doors closing behind the ray, and then a second later what sounded like an echo – only we wouldn't hear an echo from a chamber full of water.

Amadeo, slumped against one wall, looked anxiously up the stairway.

How long would it be until the water drained from the bay? We might not have much time.

I strained to hear anything more from above us, but couldn't. Time seemed be stretching out – was the bay being emptied one drop at a time? It was an age before the mechanical lock on the door to the bay snapped open, indicating that the last of the water was gone. Bays and gantries worked on much less complex technology than mantas. That might be an advantage.

Ravenna watched through the small window set into the door while I kept a wary eye on the stairs.

'It is Sagantha!' she cried. 'He's gesturing for us to come in. Is he for us or against us?'

'On our side,' I said fervently, praying that I was right.

'Quick,' Sagantha said, as Ravenna opened the door. 'We don't have much time. They'll realise where I've gone in a moment and try to blockade the entrance. Who's this?' he added, as I helped Amadeo into the bay and slammed the door shut behind us. The lock wouldn't work unless there was water in here.

Ravenna gave Amadeo a sour look. 'A would-be martyr who didn't have the courage to die as he'd promised. We can drop him off somewhere remote, but Cathan didn't want to leave him to the mercies of the Council.'

'I wouldn't leave anyone to their mercies,' he said curtly. 'Not even you, as you can see. Bring him inside, we'll see to him later.'

As we pushed him into the ray and I clambered in after him, I heard shouts from the corridor and the sound of running feet. The Council had discovered what we were up to.

Sagantha reached down and grabbed the back of my tunic, more or less pitching me headfirst into the ray. I landed with a painful thump on the carpet and just managed to scramble out of his way as he closed the hatch. The noise from outside was abruptly cut off, shielded by the ray's thick skin.

'Give me a hand,' he said, pulling me to my feet again. 'Not you, Ravenna, Cathan's more useful at the moment. Secure yourself and whoever this is, we'll have to do some creative navigating.'

The uncanny parallels to the night of Orosius's death struck me again as I sat down in the co-pilot's seat, remembering the flight from *Valdur*. Once again we had to escape and navigate through Perdition's Shore – to where? Where could we find a refuge now? Even if not all the heretics were Ring of Eight, they still owed loyalty to the Council, and the Council seemed to be controlled by its most vicious members.

Sagantha activated the aether control that would open the bay hatch, providing the mechanism hadn't been damaged by the Council people. Were they still in the room or had they retreated? The inner door would be locked now.

A moment later the outer hatch lifted, and water cascaded in, lifting the searay off the floor. There was no way they could stop us now, at least not from inside the fortress.

Only when the bay was full was it safe to fire the engines and creep out into the lagoon, veering left to keep away from the gantry. The water was shallow here, I reckoned it had to be dredged quite frequently to give the proper depth.

'Strap in,' Sagantha ordered. I fumbled for the straps, but hadn't managed to fasten them all when he sent the searay's nose forward, arrowing down towards the bottom of the lagoon. I hung on doggedly until we levelled out, skimming through the mud of the sea bottom. It would be mud here, not sand, given that the Tehaman lake emptied into it. I hadn't thought of that; it would give good cover.

'Aether sensors are distorted by fresh water,' Sagantha said, keeping the craft as low as he could. There was the occasional dull thud as we banged against something hard, but he seemed to be expecting that. 'They're built to operate in the sea, and the fresh water stream here should give us an advantage. If we can find it. Look on the display for a blurred area.'

He turned the searay gradually to starboard as I sank my hands into the aether pads and scanned the bay using the sensors. The mud didn't help, and there wasn't much point trying to detect a fuzzy patch against water. I needed rocks, a background – somewhere off to the right.

There. Were those rocks? I couldn't tell – yes, they were, but the image of them wasn't quite clear, as if – using human senses again – I'd been looking at them through tears. I pointed it out to Sagantha, and navigated him backwards and into the stream. It didn't have clearly defined edges, it was just the only fast-flowing current in the bay. This would be a fascinating place for oceanographic study, I thought as we began moving along with the stream again, with this mix of fresh and salt water and the effect of the falls. Even the biologists would have a field day with creatures swept down from the lake on the plateau. Was the water warmer or colder up there than the open ocean? Hard to guess.

I didn't have time to wonder. A moment later the sensors gave a warning flash, and I saw the dim forms of four searays and a full-sized manta lurking by the entrance to the bay.

CHAPTER XVIII

'They know we're here,' Sagantha said, his attention riveted to the controls. 'The question is whether they can pinpoint us. If not, they'll be firing into the dark. Be ready with the weapons systems.'

He'd slowed our speed and we were creeping along the bottom of the bay towards the waiting flotilla of Council craft above and ahead of us. Did he really mean to do this, I wondered? Go against the Council for our sake? I didn't want to trust him any more than I ever had, but I had no choice. With thirty years' naval experience behind him, he stood more chance of breaking through to open water than I did.

'Wouldn't it make more sense to use magic?' I asked.

'No. There are more mind-mages on the *Meridian*. They can't influence you from here, but they can deflect your magic, possibly even turn it straight back at you. We're going to do this the practical way. Just follow my orders, and don't fire at anything unless I tell you to, no matter how tempting it is.'

They were less than half a mile away now, indeterminate shapes moving into positions across the deep gash that marked the opening of the bay. Two of the searays were diving, spiralling down to block the very bottom of the gully. Our sensors were no better off, but we had five targets outlined against the seawater and the rocks, while they were looking for one in the murk. *Meridian* seemed to be heading out to sea, perhaps to find waters where they could manoeuvre more effectively.

'This ray doesn't have torpedoes,' Sagantha said after a moment. 'Just twin pulse cannon, standard naval issue of about twenty years ago. We can't really do much against them directly. When I give the order, I want you to fire an arc into the mud about a hundred cubits in front of those two at the bottom.'

Still linked with the searay's sensors, I kept my hands on the pads, seeing what the ship itself saw through the aether imaging system. The cannon were mounted below our feet, fixed as always in the direction we were heading.

Sagantha brought the ray sharply to port.

'We're leaving the stream,' I said, feeling even less safe now we were out of the protection of the fresh water.

'I know.'

As he spoke, points of brightness flared from the searays guarding the upper level, and pulses of indistinct orange fire raced through the water towards us. Searay weaponry was, due to size and reactor limitations, smaller than that mounted in full-size mantas, which meant a reduced range. We were still too far away, but the pulses left trails of steam that immediately began drifting and clouded the sensors.

'Now!' Sagantha ordered.

I fired as he'd instructed, shots from our pulse cannon slamming into the mud and boiling it. Sagantha brought the ray round so that a curtain of steam and mud across the entrance blocked off the sensors entirely.

'Keep on firing, I'm taking us down again.'

I was firing directly into our path, and after a second or so the sensors were completely swamped as we moved into the clouds stirred up from the bottom.

There was answering fire now, although I couldn't see which searay it was coming from. We were only a quarter of a mile or so from the entrance, I guessed, although I couldn't make out much detail. Sagantha seemed to be increasing speed as much as possible, although it was capped at a lower level as long as I kept on firing.

'Cease fire.'

I obeyed, and the cloud immediately started to dissipate; I could even work out the shapes of the lowest two searays again. One hovered in the entrance, while the other was sweeping back and forward in an attempt to gain a better view.

More shots, this time too close for comfort, and the bottom off to port was engulfed by murky billows. I gave a moment's thought to the oceanographic treasure trove whose creatures we were killing off, but at the moment our survival was all that mattered.

'The rays near the surface have a better view of what's going on,' Sagantha said. 'The mud doesn't reach them, and so they can make out roughly where we are. The two at the bottom don't count now. Be ready to fire again when I tell you, at the rock this time.'

The upper pair of rays seemed indeed to have realised what we were doing, and the streams of pulses were getting uncomfortably close. We had shields, of a kind: an aether shell around the ray could absorb a limited amount of energy, but after a while it would be saturated. Like most searays, it had the smallest reactor it was possible to build – five feet around, due to the heat shielding – and thus a very limited aether capacity.

Sagantha brought the nose up suddenly, and I was thrown back in my seat, my hands almost jerked out of the aether pads. For a moment I felt dislocated, half-in and half-out of the controls, at the very moment he told me to fire again.

I pushed my hands deeper, and let fly with the cannon again, although I wasn't quite sure why we were firing at the rock. I was aiming near the top of a pinnacle separated by a narrow space – ten feet or so at that point – from the actual headland. We were moving wide now, circling round to come at the entrance from a steeper angle, and the shots from the searays were following us.

Then there was a series of jolts, heavy impacts on the

274

roof. The lights flickered; they'd hit us at last.

'Steady,' Sagantha warned. 'Keep firing until I give the word.'

Successive hits were taking their toll on the pinnacle, less than a hundred yards in front. The opposing fire suddenly broke off. We were too close to the rock; they'd have to circle.

'Another ray coming up from below,' I said, noticing a vague shape curving round just outside the entrance. They'd be in a perfect position to fire as we came over – or through? – the rock pinnacle. But it was still there.

'Now,' came the command. Sagantha's voice was still steady – unlike the ray, which canted sharply over even as he spoke. I slid over to one side of my chair, only held in by the straps, as we cut abruptly to port and shot through the narrow central channel with a dozen yards to spare.

Sagantha was driving the searay at its fastest speed now, and we cleared the channel in a few seconds. The sensors cleared perceptibly, and I saw ahead of us the shelving, twisted landscape of Perdition's Shore, falling away into the abyss of the open ocean.

And barring the way, a beautiful, sleek shape in half-profile against the silvery grey surface, was the *Meridian*. She was a mile or so away, turning towards us with a lethal grace, preparing to bring her full armament to bear on us. Unlike the rays, she could cover more than just one arc of fire – and she was a purpose-built Thetian warship.

'Now?' I said, waiting for the command.

Sagantha gave me a curious smile. 'We can neither outfight nor outrun an Imperial warship in something as weak as this. If you're willing to accept some damage, though, we can deal with the *Meridian*.'

'How much damage?'

'Enough to take the shields down, perhaps more. I don't have time to explain, you'll have to trust me.'

'That doesn't sound like a good idea,' Ravenna called.

'Sagantha, trusting anyone is a bad idea, and trusting you is even worse.'

'Use your magic as a last resort, if it comes to it. We have to move quickly.'

'Go on then,' I said warily. 'Only, why are you helping us? As everyone keeps saying, we're the eternal losers. I can't see why you'd bother – unless of course you're leading us into a trap.'

'Do you have so little faith in my abilities?' Sagantha accelerated the craft again, heading out to port, almost in the opposite direction from *Meridian*'s current heading. It would only gain us a few more seconds, and I wondered what the point of that would be.

'Shouldn't we be able to outrun them in this?' Ravenna asked.

'For a while, but we don't have the power to maintain this kind of speed for long. Especially not in Perdition's Shore.'

'That should work for us,' I pointed out. 'They may be bigger, but I can navigate through Perdition's Shore and they can't.'

'Not as well, perhaps,' he conceded. 'But they can keep up long enough to overtake and deal with us.'

The *Meridian* was completing its turn now, still bearing round to follow us. They were out of range for the moment, but the manta had a warship's armament, which would include several weapons more destructive than anything on the searays, maybe even pressure charges that could crush us. And, I thought, as a temperature warning light flashed in front of me, a reactor built at the optimum size, more than twice the circumference of ours and much less likely to overheat.

For someone brought up by the ignorant Halettites, Eshar had embraced Thetian technology enthusiastically and made sure his Navy was well-equipped.

'How long can we keep ahead of them?' I asked

Sagantha, as he adjusted course to keep a safe distance away from the rock to starboard. The cliffs were relatively straight and sheer here, but ahead I could see the beginnings of Perdition's Shore proper – jagged outcrops, sunken islands, caves – all perfect for a smaller craft.

'At full speed, not very long – perhaps two or three hours.'

'Let's press on. Unless you've a very good reason not to.'

'The longer we wait, the less likely my plan is to succeed.'

'Explain, first,' Ravenna said firmly.

'Who's in charge here?'

'I know you're the expert, but I want to hear this plan before we try it.'

He was too involved with piloting the searay to turn round and look at her. For a moment he didn't say anything.

I detected what he was doing a second before it happened, but by then it was too late. The ray suddenly slewed round to port, and a massive surge blotted out my view of everything. I fell back in the chair as a sensation hideously like fire surged up my arms, over my whole body, then subsided to a burning sensation like pins and needles. It was pain like being stabbed with a thousand little thorns at once.

There was a sharp crack and a whine from somewhere aft, loud and high enough to be painful. The hum of the engine abruptly dropped in tone; we were slowing down.

I stared at Sagantha for a moment, unable to move, as he moved a lever and a metal barrier slid into place over the cabin door, sealing us off from Ravenna in the cabin behind. After a moment, it started to glow faintly as he surrounded it with a double aether shield.

'We have to be ready for anything,' he said calmly, pulling out two of the magic-restraining bracelets I knew so well and slipping them on to my wrists, then securing my arms to the chair. 'It's better this way. Otherwise you'll cause too much trouble.'

Then he opened the communications link.

'Sagantha to *Meridian*. I've secured them, but I had to overload the reactor to do it. It'll be a few more minutes before I can move. Come and pick us up. Send the other searays back in; they picked up one prisoner and we don't know whether any others could be loose in there.'

A moment later someone replied, 'As you wish, sir.'

'Why?' I mouthed, overwhelmed with the bitterness of being betrayed again.

'It isn't what you think it is,' he said, with a faint smile. 'And you didn't think I'd really have come back without being allowed to? Now, I have some housekeeping to do.'

Deprived of the aether sensors, unable to see anything but darkness outside the windows, I could only wait in helpless frustration while he sat waiting, absorbed in whatever it was he was doing to the ship. I was so stupid not to have seen it coming, to have trusted him at all . . . I could probably have overwhelmed *Meridian* with a pressure wave, pushing them away from us.

It wasn't long before I saw a faint lightening outside, the watery glare of the *Meridian*'s underside lights as she manoeuvred into position above us.

'Bay open, sir. Can you make it in?' Presumably they'd released one of their escape rays to make room.

'Stand by,' Sagantha said.

A moment later there was an ominous groan and the shields over the door wavered. What had he done with Ravenna, I wondered? Aether shields would absorb magic energy as well as pulse energy, so was that all that stopped her from breaking through the door – or had he done something else?

The groan rose louder and louder, then subsided.

'We've got a small problem here,' Sagantha said. 'The

overload caused a little more damage than I thought. Reactor temperature is rising. Engineer's advice?'

There was a momentary pause, then another voice came on.

'Sir?'

Sagantha explained the problem again as we hung below *Meridian*'s belly. I could move again, although only slightly, and the pain was beginning to subside. The same surge from a full-sized manta would have killed me, so I'd been lucky.

'I'd shut down if I were you, and we'll pull you in manually. Better that than flood the reactor.'

'Fine. Shutting down.'

For a moment there was a long silence, then another groan, louder this time. What was going on? My grasp of aether engineering was sketchy at best, but Sagantha and the engineer must both have known what they were talking about.

'Temperature's rising,' Sagantha noted, a moment later. 'I'll flood her.'

There was an explosive thump aft, and the searay tilted a little, the tail falling below the level of the nose.

That shouldn't be happening.

'We're moving away,' *Meridian*'s engineer reported, as bubbles streamed past the window. I saw the edge of the manta's open bay coming into view, moving into line with the searay's horns.

'Emergency,' Sagantha said, for no apparent reason. 'We're . . .'

And then, with no warning at all, he fired the pulse cannon directly into the interior of the unshielded *Meridian*. I had no time to take in the streams of orange fire, because we were barely ten yards away – only the gouts of flame which blossomed inside the manta. He kept on firing, and I heard a dreadful grinding sound in the water as the communications link went dead.

The impact of the shots had pushed the manta away from us and, as he fired, Sagantha activated the small set of thrusters on the searay that gave us a reverse capability. We were moving overhead faster now.

'Close your eyes,' Sagantha said. 'Now.'

Even through closed eyelids, the world went painfully bright; had they been open, the fireball of *Meridian*'s destruction would have been blinding at such short distance.

He brought the nose down and accelerated. The shock wave hit us, physically pushing the ray deeper. Aether crackled through the panel, and the weird, artificial noise of the warning siren sounded painfully loud in my ears.

The whole craft shook, and the angle of dive became ever steeper until I was almost hanging out of my chair.

'You can open your eyes again now,' Sagantha said after a moment, as we moved faster and faster, our angle no less extreme.

All I could see was the black water and the tense-faced man sitting next to me, a man who had just destroyed his own ship and subordinates. Several warning lights were blinking red in front of me.

'We're trailing debris,' Sagantha said tersely. It felt as though the engines had cut out now, and we were being carried deeper and deeper simply by the searay's momentum. 'Shields are down, the explosion must have scorched the skin. I can't feel whole sections of it. There's no time to repair now.'

We must have glided a few hundred yards further before coming to rest, gently, in what Sagantha described as a safe place. Risking contact with the aether again, I saw what he meant – we were on the bottom, half-hidden behind some rock and camouflaged against the bottom sediment.

'Now we lie low,' he said, shutting the sensors down, the engines – everything except some small lights that wouldn't be picked up by aether. He leaned over and removed the bracelets and fastenings from my arms.

'Why did you bother?' I asked, shifting position and rubbing my arms, as if that would get rid of the prickly feeling of aether contamination. It wouldn't do any permanent damage, just leave me feeling brittle and uncomfortable for a few hours.

'The closer to the truth a lie is, the more convincing it will be. I said you were both secure – that was true and they could tell it was.'

'What did you do to Ravenna?' I asked as he deactivated the aether shield over the door and twisted round to lever the metal barrier out of the way.

'The same. Aether surge, shields to keep her in.'

I jumped out of my seat and moved back to where Ravenna sat slumped in her chair next to Amadeo, who seemed only half conscious.

'I'm fine,' she lied, but her eyes were looking beyond me, to Sagantha. 'Why?' she said, loosening her straps and wincing as she moved. 'Why did you do that?'

Sagantha left the bridge and came to stand in the doorway, a trim but exhausted-looking figure in his naval fatigues. 'One day I'll tell you,' he said grimly. 'When we've survived this.'

He halted, paused to turn the lights in the cabin down to a minimum, dark enough that I could hardly make out their faces. 'The searays will come looking for survivors and wreckage, but they shouldn't find us here. An hour or two and we can be gone.'

'Are we in any state to go?' I asked him.

'We'll have to wait to find out. We should get a little way, but how far depends on whether the skin is dead or only damaged.'

Ravenna stood up, steadying herself on the arm of the chair. '*One day I'll tell you* isn't good enough. Those were your allies, your subordinates, on the *Meridian*. They

281

trusted you, and unlike me they never suspected for a moment you'd betray them.'

'You should be more consistent, Ravenna. Those were your enemies I just killed, for your sake.'

'And what would you think of me if I sacrificed the Archipelago to help Thetia.'

'It was for the Archipelago. The Archipelago and you.'

Neither of them moved. 'Easy words. I can't believe them.'

'You've come a long way from when I first knew you,' Sagantha said. 'Not happily, either. But there are still things you can't understand.'

'Like why no-one can be trusted?' she interrupted. 'No, they can't. I've never met someone who could keep a promise they made. No-one at all.'

Including me, I knew. Which I wouldn't be allowed to forget.

'I am your Regent, Ravenna. The only lawfully appointed ruler of the Archipelago until you're crowned. That doesn't count for much, but I work in your interests. Not the Elemental Council's, and not the Ring of Eight. Neither of them had the authority to depose you.'

'My interests, because it suits you.'

'How does it suit me more to be stuck on a damaged searay with the two of you and a Domain fanatic rather than on the bridge of *Meridian* with the full backing of the Council?'

'I can't trust you,' she repeated. 'You betrayed them, you could just as easily betray me.'

'But I never have. What did you think the judges would do to you? Tell you not to do it again and keep a tighter rein on you than before? If you thought that, then you've learnt nothing. They'd already held a conclave, decided in advance that you were more of a liability than an asset, and that they'd find someone else to be Pharaoh. Not enough people know otherwise. They wouldn't even have bothered with a formal execution, you just wouldn't have left that cage alive.'

Would they really have done that? Surely not, he was simply trying to justify himself.

'You look sceptical. Did they have any qualms about burrowing through your mind, Ravenna? Can you seriously imagine they weren't about to use the rack on Cathan? That court and all its procedures came straight from the Inquisition. And afterwards, they would have regrouped and dealt with you. Was I supposed to stand by and let them? Would you rather I had?'

'You didn't want to leave me to them,' Amadeo said weakly, 'and I am your enemy. This man seems to be a friend. Why shouldn't you trust him?'

'What would a priest know of friendship?' said Sagantha, turning to look at the wounded priest in the chair. Ravenna had wrapped a spare blanket from the searay's emergency stores around him, but he still looked very pale and weak.

'I only need the friendship of Ranthas,' Amadeo said. 'He would not have sent you if I had not been chosen for some purpose. That is why He wouldn't give me the strength to die at their hands.'

'Surprising how quickly it's changed,' Ravenna said scornfully. 'I thought it was your weakness. Are you going to pass that off as the will of Ranthas, because you're too much of a coward even to admit you're one?'

'I am His servant,' Amadeo said, with a touch of defiance. 'It was His will that you came. All of you.'

I was still dazed by what had happened and the carnage I'd wreaked. I stared down at my palms as if expecting to see some trace of what had happened, blood or residue of the magic, but there was only the dry, cracked feeling left by the aether.

'You condemn us for our methods, yet you use them yourselves. Can you really draw such a distinction after what's happened, after what you've seen today?' Amadeo stared first at me, then Ravenna. 'What of all the people I heard screaming while I was waiting for my turn? All the people who must have been tortured in there over the years? Who is responsible for that? I don't think you know your own past as well as you believe.'

'He who controls the past commands the future,' Ravenna said. 'Everyone knows that. The Domain best of all.'

'It's a lesson your own people took to heart. Did you listen to Sarhaddon when he gave his orations in Tandaris? I was there for all of them, and it was through him that I came to see Ranthas's truth.'

'You were there?' I said, wondering if I'd seen him – but why should I have noticed one face in that crowd, the face of a man I wouldn't meet for another four years.

'You know what I'm talking about,' Amadeo said. 'You remember what Sarhaddon said. How could anyone forget?'

'Not all of us admire him.' I searched the man's face, trying to find – what? I wasn't sure. I only saw what I expected to see, the dedication and the shadow of Sarhaddon's fanaticism, his gift to this unknown Thetian. 'But then, you never saw him betray someone who trusted him. You weren't there when he killed my brother off this shore four years ago.'

'A godless and evil man your brother must have been, then.' Amadeo met my gaze without flinching.

'Godless and evil, perhaps. Did you think he was? You know who I'm talking about. You know perfectly well who I am.'

'It was Ranthas's will,' Amadeo said. 'He brought Sarhaddon to us to show the lies of the heresy for what they are. And He has shown you that today, as well. He has destroyed them in His flames, working through us. You gave me what you knew was an unfair choice when you found me. Now I ask you a fair question.

284

'Can either of you say truthfully that the men you saw weren't the leaders of the heresy, that they were only a fraction of it? Sagantha must know who the Ring's leader is. How have your false gods helped you? Your leadership is intolerant and corrupt, everything they claim we are. How can you believe anything they've told you?'

Amadeo turned his head slightly, and his eyes reflected the aether light shining dimly over Sagantha's head.

'Think of all the people who've taught you, who showed you the horrors of what our Crusaders did thirty years ago. They were there, but have they ever told you the truth? Have they ever told you what it was the Crusaders brought to an end? The terror, the tyranny – that was what we destroyed. Do you have any idea what the Archipelago was like thirty years ago?'

'Was it worse?' she demanded. 'We were our own masters, we had our cities, our past, everything that you took away in the first Crusade.'

'We broke the tyranny,' he began, but Ravenna cut him off.

'Liar!' she almost shouted. 'You destroy everything you touch, and you try to taint everything we believe in!' She advanced on him, her left hand pointing at his face, and for a moment I thought she would have attacked him.

She stopped a foot or two away, a peculiar expression on her face.

'Ravenna, I suggest you sit down,' Sagantha said. He still hadn't moved. 'You've broken at least one rib, and you'll only do more damage if you go on.' She looked sick for a moment, and the admiral moved smoothly to steady her, gently but firmly pushing her back down into a chair. 'Stay there while I find the medical equipment. This is not the time for arguments. Amadeo, if you say anything more I'll simply send you to sleep for a very long time.'

Ravenna didn't protest, just sat there with her eyes closed. Amadeo said nothing. A faint smile flitted across his face.

PART FOUR:
THE SHARDS OF EDEN

CHAPTER XIX

The buzzing of cicadas filled the early evening air as we made our way up the hill along a winding avenue of cypress trees. The stones of the road were reassuringly old and Archipelagan, deeply worn except on the insides of switchbacks, where it looked as if some unknown force had preserved the road in mint condition. To either side, oleanders and the occasional dwarf palm rustled in the breeze.

I stared upwards, wondering how much further we had to go. The houses perched on the landward cliffs seemed very far away still, no larger than when I'd last looked a few minutes ago. Ilthys seemed to be nothing but hills and cliffs, it was even more bumpy than Qalathar. But where the island we'd fled from a week ago had been huge and cloud-enshrouded, Ilthys was a chain of emeralds across a tropical sea.

We'd seen the city from above as we came over the ridge half an hour or so ago. A jumbled array of white houses and blue domes on its outcrop above the sea, Ilthys looked the same as when I'd last seen it four years ago. New walls surrounded the Governor's Palace, the Temple seemed to have grown a little, but there were no ziggurats, no ugly Halettite-built barracks to break up the patchwork of houses and trees, balconies with flowers spilling down from them.

'Your friend Ithien was Governor here, wasn't he?' Sagantha said. 'A republican.'

'Yes. Did you ever meet him?' We hadn't stopped, but kept on walking into the valley below the city. An aqueduct bridged the gap over to one side, a graceful series of arches bringing water from the springs on the side of the mountain, but the road more or less followed the lie of the land.

'I did, at a reception in Ral Tumar when he was just an attaché. He seemed like a typical Thetian, too arrogant for his own good.'

'Are we really all that bad?'

'When did you start thinking of yourself as one?'

'I spent three years in Thetia. Even if it was only in a castle full of Polinskarn academics.'

'Being Thetian is a state of mind,' Sagantha quoted; I didn't remember who had said or written that. His next words weren't derived from any Thetian poet, though. 'Halettites think they're God's chosen people, but they're never sure. Thetians *know* they are. They like to remind you they were living in cities with running water when the rest of the world hadn't got round to building huts yet. That's as may be, but only the Thetians could overlook the Tuonetar and the Tehamans.'

His tone was more bitter and dismissive than the words might have suggested. I could understand it. The Thetians had abandoned the Archipelago to its fate in the Crusade.

Now, as we approached the single landward gate of Ilthys, I was thinking about Ithien and the city he'd ruled, somewhere I hadn't expected to see again. We were approaching the gate now. The houses on either side had slightly thicker walls, and someone had recently added on a gatehouse above the gate itself that didn't look at all like a house. There were four soldiers on guard, more than I'd expected.

But the Thetian marines on duty only asked us the most cursory questions and searched us for weapons before letting us through. The road led up a little more before it reached normal street level, a fairly wide road flanked by whitewashed houses that went towards the agora, always the centre of an Archipelagan or Thetian town.

I knew Ilthys perhaps better than any other Archipelagan town from the two weeks I'd spent here on that unfortunate journey to Tandaris. The old streets of Ilthys with their plants and fountains were a relic of a time before the Domain, and as we walked slowly along, it seemed little had changed from my last visit. Clematis and tropical creepers still grew up the walls, forming arches over the entrances to tiny courtyards. We went through a little square I remembered, with a group of old ladies sitting on a stone bench talking while a cat chased a leaf across the stones. Those women had probably been there last time I came; some things were timeless.

'Khalia's house is on the far seaward edge, isn't it?' Sagantha said. The agora was ahead, and I caught a brief glimpse of the temple facade. 'I'm not quite sure what the best way is. Try turning right.' Giuliana, Khalia's apprentice, had given us directions, but they were vague; the girl had studied with Khalia in Thetia, and had only visited Ilthys once.

Neither of us wanted to go past the Temple, so we skirted the edge of the agora, making our way down a narrow road made even narrower by the amphorae stacked along one side, propped against the wall.

We managed to avoid the Temple, but it was only when we'd walked on for several minutes that I realised we'd have to go past the Governor's Palace. We should have gone round the other side.

However, no-one gave us a second glance as we walked briskly through another large square past the palace, now rather out of proportion because its walls had been raised and a small watchtower added above the gate. There were marines standing around, but they had no interest in stopping passers-by, and in a city of well over twenty thousand there was no way for them to recognise us as outsiders.

It was a peculiar mentality I'd managed to acquire from somewhere, this ever-present feeling of being too striking and noticeable. I still couldn't walk past a Sacrus or an Inquisitor without feeling distinctly uneasy, as if I bore a mark of heresy.

The sun was touching the horizon by the time we reached the seaward edge of town; it would be dark in a few minutes, and the flamewood lanterns that illuminated the streets had already been lit. Ilthys was the most Thetian place outside Thetia itself, and possessed every amenity the Thetians had ever come up with, from the lighting to a substantial opera house and an open-air theatre.

'It's off a courtyard just along here, she told me.' Sagantha stared along the right-hand side of the street. 'Is that an opening? No, it isn't. You know, Engare has no sense of direction either. He's a very good healer, but give him a map and he doesn't know up and down. Maybe it goes with the profession.'

'Was Engare on *Meridian* when you destroyed her?' I asked. Sagantha was talking about him in the present tense.

'No, thankfully. He's one of the few Council officers I could stand. He was still in the fortress, looking after the prisoners.'

We walked on a little way, past houses whose lights were just coming on. Cooking smells came wafting out of a taverna with black and white woodwork, up a flight of steps with a wooden sign informing customers that it possessed a sea terrace.

Just beyond the restaurant the road bent sharply to the left, but we headed off down a small passageway into a long, thin whitewashed courtyard with a couple of oleander bushes growing in the centre. A group of children were playing with carved wooden horses by the fountain.

'Who do you want?' one of them demanded, staring over at us. The others looked up.

'Khalia Mezzarro,' Sagantha said. 'The Thetian healer.'

'Is she expecting you?' one of the girls said. 'She doesn't like being disturbed.'

292

'We've a message for her, from an old friend. Where can we find her?'

The children were still conferring noisily when half of a double door was pushed open in front of us and light flooded into the courtyard. A woman in tailored shirt and trousers, her silver hair cut elegantly short, said, 'Who are you?'

'Are you Khalia Mezzarro? We were sent here by an apprentice of yours, Giuliana Barrati. It's a private matter.'

The woman paused for a moment. 'I am Khalia.'

'How can we be sure of that?'

'You can't. You'll have to take my word for it. How is Giuliana? Is she enjoying her exile on the Ilahi Islands among all the fishermen?'

'No,' Sagantha said. 'She's the only healer on the island since the Domain arrested all the others, and she's having a hard time coping.'

'She'll manage,' Khalia said. 'It's her own fault for volunteering. I told her a war-zone wouldn't be pretty. Come inside.'

She led us into the main hallway, where two older children were talking to each other, hanging on the banisters. She sent them packing with a warning not to damage the woodwork and led us up the stairs.

The building was a maze of staircases and small passages, but it was a noisy, lively place, full of people, and I remembered with a pang of homesickness my own House in Lepidor. It had been bigger than this, since my father was clan President, but I'd grown up in a large House with dozens of people, rather in the Archipelagan manner, and some things didn't change.

Her room was one floor up. It was spacious and looked out over the sea to the south-east. From the smell of cooking, much stronger than it had been in the hallway, we were close to the restaurant.

It was dim when we came in, but once she'd turned the

lanterns on, I realised the apartment was bigger than I'd thought, with two rooms separated by an archway, and a door off to one side. It was sparsely but elegantly decorated in a Thetian style.

'So. Tell me your names, before I go any further.' She stopped, stared at me for a moment. 'Say *Selerian*,' she ordered, in exactly the tone she'd have used if I was a patient, telling me to roll up my sleeve so she could examine a wound.

Suddenly unsure, I complied and added that my name was Cathan.

'What is it?' Sagantha demanded.

'Nothing in particular,' the healer said, with a slight shrug. She stepped back a few paces across a sumptuous green rug, tilted her head to one side slightly, the way Ravenna sometimes did. 'What is the message you've brought me?'

'It's not, strictly speaking, a message,' Sagantha said smoothly. 'We have two injured friends who need to remain inconspicuous. Both of them have been through some fairly unpleasant experiences. Giuliana was the only healer we could find in Qalathar, and she was being watched by the Domain, so she couldn't treat them properly.'

She gave us both a keen stare. 'Where are they? In the town?'

'No. We had to leave them in a ray about fifteen miles from here. They couldn't have walked that far.'

'In that case, it will be difficult to bring them where I can attend to them. You look surprised, gentlemen, that I've agreed. I am . . . was a professional healer – but a court healer. Let me remind you that before I taught at the university in Selerian Alastre I worked for several notables, always for a hefty fee.'

'So you'll charge us?' Sagantha said warily. 'It could take us some time to find the money.'

'It'll take some time, but it's a story I want, not money,' Khalia said. 'I still look after the rich and famous here in Ilthys – this Governor, the past Governor, the occasional priest, rich merchants – as you can probably see, I do quite well for myself. It's not a bad retirement, and I keep on with my teaching. So I have no need of money from you. On the other hand, you have stories to tell, and one of you has a story I very much want to hear.'

I looked at Sagantha, wondering what he made of this. He'd grown a beard to make his features less clear-cut and recognisable, but it made his expressions even harder to read – not that I'd had much luck before.

'I don't think we have any choice, not the way Ravenna is,' he said to me.

I couldn't but agree; my nerves had worn ragged trying to cope with her. She was a terrible invalid, refusing even to admit that her broken ribs hampered her mobility at all, and she had flatly refused to let us treat her as though she was incapacitated in any way. At least she'd finally admitted she needed to see a healer. I was worried about her and had been ever since Engare's examination. If the internal injuries had been that severe, who knew what else might be wrong?

Khalia became even more brisk and businesslike, questioning us closely about both patients, their age, condition, what we thought the injuries were, what had caused them. She wrote rapidly on a wax tablet as we answered, moving closer to one of the lanterns to get a better light.

'As for the man, if it's been nearly two weeks since he was first tortured, there shouldn't be anything life-threatening – if his injuries were going to turn septic, they'd have done so already. It'll be a case of cleaning him up, I expect. The woman will certainly need rest and monitoring, which means, gentlemen, that you'll have to bring her here.'

'We can't come into port in the searay,' Sagantha said.

'We stole it from an Imperial warship and it's rather noticeable.'

'You let these little nuggets slip very skilfully,' Khalia commented. 'Is there anything else I should know?'

'Some people here may know our faces.'

'Of course they do,' she said dryly. 'The only sensible reason for growing a beard is if you're trying to hide something. Now, there's no way we can do anything until morning. The gates are closed at dusk. There's no need for it, not on this island, but the new Governor insists.'

'What about the night fishing fleet?'

'They'll not help you. Not unless you're Ithien Eirillia in disguise. They have this absurd loyalty to the man. Perhaps it's because he's such a charmer, or then again it could simply be some favours he did them while he was here. In any case, they head out to the south-east, and you must be lying to the west. No, it's the day fishermen we'll need, and I have some contacts among them.'

'Enough to get away with carrying someone into town on a stretcher?' Sagantha said with polite disbelief. 'That's hard to believe.'

'On a stretcher?' I said, wondering whether Sagantha had lost his mind. 'You want her to be carried into town on a stretcher? How long have you known her?'

'She'll do what I tell her to do,' said Khalia firmly

'I hope so,' I said. 'She'll be worried; we weren't planning to be this long.'

'It's too risky to try slipping out now. If you were caught, they'd trace you back here, which would make life difficult for me.'

Could we leave them until tomorrow? I wasn't worried about Amadeo escaping, but what if something else went wrong? Something we couldn't have predicted? Such as another malfunction on the heavily damaged searay, already strained from crossing two thousand miles of ocean after the battle with *Meridian*.

'There's no choice,' Khalia said. 'I'll find you a guest room for tonight, and you can enjoy the hospitality of my House. After that, you'll have to pay for your accommodation. Times are hard, and trade is bad enough for people to need all the money they can earn. I'm sure one of you has a fair amount of money at your disposal.'

'I'd pay for anything that remotely resembles a bed at the moment,' Sagantha said, with a weariness that was perhaps exaggerated. The damage sustained in the battle had meant there were only beds for Amadeo and Ravenna, and Sagantha and I had slept on the seats or the floor ever since leaving Kavatang.

We ate supper with her rather than the House as a whole, the first properly cooked meal I'd had after two weeks on survival rations in the searay. Khalia had expensive tastes in wine, and obviously enough income to support them. As was traditional in Thetia, she brought out the blue wine at the end of a meal, poured two glasses and one half-glass and handed the latter to me. I stared at her for a moment. Was she being deliberately rude?

'If you drink any more than that, you'll be out until morning,' she said, motioning us over to sit down on the cushioned divan in her main room. 'It's not etiquette, but I know how strong this blue wine is.'

'And how do you know he can't take drink?' Sagantha said. 'Just how notable were these patients of yours?'

'I leave you to guess. Now, Cathan, while I must confess to being interested in who this man is that he feels obliged to conceal his face behind an overgrown clothes-brush, I want to hear your story.'

'Why are you so interested?'

Khalia gave me a cool look. 'I'm a healer, or a physician as the apprentices prefer to call themselves now. I've spent my life looking after the illnesses of Thetia's elite. I know all the secrets of their gossip for the last thirty years, because people find it hard to hide things from their doctor. I know, but I don't tell.

'Since I was born a Thetian, I had the chance to be a healer rather than simply a midwife, which is all women are allowed to be on most of the barbaric continents. I haven't actually delivered very many children; the court has its own fashionable midwives, and I was never one of them. I didn't want to be.

'So I very well remember the few children I've delivered. Better than my adult patients in many cases. I only helped when there was no-one else, or when a special friend asked me to.

'Twenty-six years ago, one of my greatest friends went into labour on a night when everything, but everything, went wrong. The Palace was in chaos, there were guards everywhere, and His Imperial Majesty was flapping about like a trapped seagull, as indecisive as ever. It would have been a perfectly normal birth, except that one of the midwives had poisoned the mother.'

'Poisoned?' Sagantha said, with disbelief. 'But the oath . . .'

'The Domain can absolve people from obeying any oath,' Khalia said. 'This is the Thetian court we're talking about, where everything is for sale at a price. As it was, one of the other midwives had the sense to summon me and I was able to administer an antidote. The child was born safely, and as soon as the news got out, in marched a phalanx of women from one of the Domain's nursing orders with instructions from the Prime himself to look after the newly delivered mother. Only I knew something they didn't.

'I was suspicious about why they'd come, and when they threw me out of the chamber, I went straight to the Chancellor. The shifty old fox found me a piece of paper with the Emperor's signature on it, forged an Imperial decree and accompanied me back to the chamber. We brought a few soldiers with us, a detachment of female marines from the Empress's guard and a dozen or so Ninth Legionaries, and they had the chamber cleared in a few seconds.

'I didn't know which midwives to trust, so I had to deliver the second child myself, surrounded by armed marines and with the palace chaplain pounding on the door, calling down curses on all of us. By the time I'd finished, the mother had slipped into unconsciousness but the child was fine. The mother was my responsibility, so I gave the child to one of the marines and told her to find Chancellor Baethelen.

'I presume you know what happened. Baethelen waved the Imperial warrant at the marines and told them they had to get the child to safety. There was some fighting in the corridors, but he got away and vanished, the younger child with him. I never saw Baethelen again, nor the younger child.' She looked directly at me. 'Until today.'

I'd known from early on in her account exactly who she was talking about, but she'd studiously avoided mentioning some of the names. Baethelen was ancient history now, but my mother wasn't.

Had this woman really delivered me and saved my mother's life on that chaotic night in Selerian Alastre a quarter of a century ago? The Domain had intended to spirit me away as they had done my uncle Aetius. They had brought him up in Haleth, where he had risen from royal companion to general, until an opportunity presented itself and he became Emperor Aetius.

'Now do you see why I want to hear your story?' Khalia said, in a slightly gentler tone. 'Your mother survived, but she never knew you, and your brother turned into a monster. Did you ever meet him?'

I nodded. 'Yes. You've agreed to heal some of the injuries he inflicted.'

'I won't have to tell your mother about that when I write to her. She already knows.'

'You write to my mother?' I couldn't keep the amazement out of my voice.

'Every month. That's why I want to hear your story, so that I can pass it on to her. Also, you appear to be perfectly rational and human. Unlike your brother.'

I didn't feel very rational at that moment. Not after what had happened in the courtroom. But if this woman really was in contact with my mother, Aurelia, if she was still alive and had rejoined her people as Palatine suspected . . .

'Now. I've already given you half a story, so you owe me more. I know all about Orosius's life. Now I want to hear your story, Carausius.'

So that was my birth name. I'd always wondered what it was. It couldn't be Cathan, since that name, given to me by Baethelen, didn't end in *us* or *tine*. Did I feel any sense of pleasure at this revelation? No, the name meant little to me. I had never wanted to be a Tar'Conantur, and I was perfectly happy with my own name.

'I'm Cathan,' I said, meeting her gaze.

She nodded. 'I can understand that. Go on.'

It was strange and rather awkward, trying to recount my life in an hour or two in the company of the slippery admiral and the poised Thetian healer who belonged to another age. The events of that night, Selerian Alastre itself, were as distant from me now as the surface of one of the moons. The detail she'd inadvertently revealed, that someone had tried to kill Aurelia the night I was born, was no more than I'd expected. The Domain did things like that.

So did the Council, I thought, skipping over my time in the Citadel as best I could, trying to forget how happy I'd been there, and how easily I'd believed everything Ukmadorian and his fellows told me. Their history had been as one-sided as that of the Domain, and I'd been too gullible, as everyone else had. Maybe it was just that they caught us all when we were still idealistic enough to be ready to believe without question and had given us something to devote our energies to.

I didn't like telling my own story, and it came out flat, hesitant and rushed. I told her nothing that the Domain, and Sarhaddon in particular, didn't already know about me, and left out a lot more. She must have known how uncomfortable I felt, but she made me keep on.

Some things were hard to explain without telling her who Ravenna was, which I wasn't going to do. Sarhaddon knew that, but few others did, and I felt it would only complicate the issue if she knew.

Khalia was intrigued by the idea of the storms, but after Memnon's deception in Tehama, I revealed as little as I could. No more than the idea, because that was what the Domain and their Tehaman allies were so afraid of. Letting some other people know would only hinder their efforts to silence me.

It was late by the time I'd finished, and the faint noises of shouting and laughter from the corridor had long since died down. Most members of the House would be in bed now – as I wished I were. I wouldn't normally have had any problems with the walk, but after so much enforced inactivity in the searay I was out of shape.

'You've been the luckiest of your family,' Khalia said, finally. 'When you have a title, you lose control over some of your own destiny. The higher the title, the more you lose, until as Emperor you discover there's nothing left. Your father found it very stifling; he should never have been Emperor. It destroyed your brother. The Tar'Conanturs at least recognised how hard it was to bear, especially since they had to put up with arranged marriages, unlike the rest of Thetia. The heirs were free to choose anyone they wanted, as long as he or she was an Exile – they had no time for the usual inbreeding.'

'Royalty tend to do that, don't they?' said Sagantha with a trace of contempt.

'Nobility too. Preserving the royal blood is one thing, but you'd have thought someone would realise eventually that it just leads to idiocy. Although the Exiles bring their own problems. Most Exile women can only give birth once, nobody knows why, and that's why all their children are twins. Your grandmother, Cathan, was one of the exceptions, but you can see why the family keeps so nearly going extinct.'

'Isn't that the best place for them?' Sagantha said. 'Present company excepted.'

'No,' she said firmly. 'But you have more than the freedom to marry who you want, Cathan. You've also had the opportunity to do more or less what you wanted in life.'

'Rather less than more,' I said.

'Don't complain. No-one's succeeded in pushing you into accepting a crown you've never wanted. A lot of forceful people have tried, after all. I applaud anyone who can stand up to Ithien, Mauriz and Palatine all at once. And Palatine was such a forceful young lady when I knew her. I left Palace practice just after Marshal Tanais started teaching her. He wanted her to go into the military, as I recall, but she got her own way even with him.'

I was surprised at that; I didn't know Tanais had had any plans for her, although from what I knew of the Marshal I should probably have expected it.

'Tanais is back again,' Sagantha said, apropos of nothing in particular. 'I heard a few months ago.'

'Officially?' Khalia said.

'No.'

'I didn't think so. I would have heard. I still have correspondents at court, although I haven't made as many friends among the military as I should have done. They and the Domain are running the show now, and the priesthood are so dreary. Individuals can be interesting, but all the non-Thetian ones were scandalised to find a woman in

302

such a position. How absurd they are.' She shook her head, suddenly less cheerful. 'The new Emperor brought all his barbaric attitudes with him, and there are hardly any women left at court. He even disbanded the Empress's guard, said he couldn't abide women in armour and since there was no Empress to protect, they were unnecessary.'

For a retired healer, she seemed very well connected – but then she must have been almost a courtier in her own right, and one who wielded quite a lot of influence.

She set aside her goblet and stood up. 'You've paid your price. I've already sent someone off to organise what we'll need, so I advise you gentlemen to get some sleep. The fishermen leave early in the morning, and it's not going to be smooth sailing, not by anyone's reckoning.'

CHAPTER XX

Gulls shrieked overhead as the fishing dhow tacked in towards the south coast of Ilthys, the carved eyes on its bows staring out over the green water to the mountains and forests of the island. From my vantage point by the bowsprit, out of the crew's way, I could see down through the clear water to the seabed, deceptively close.

Only the odd patch of clear sand broke up the seagrass meadows that covered the gentle swell of the seabed here, perhaps twenty or thirty feet down. Sometimes I could make out larger fish like a young white-tipped shark cruising for a meal, but anything smaller was staying sensibly hidden among the waving fronds of the seagrass. This was quite short here, but closer in we'd hidden the ray behind a giant seagrass stand, more than tall enough to swallow a man.

Over to starboard I could see another dhow, its faded sails gleaming white in the brilliant sunshine, making its way along the shore in leisurely sweeps, occasionally hauling-to while they pulled a man in. These were rich fishing areas, but most of the valuable prey had to be hunted individually on the sea bottom or trapped in coves, and the effort was too much for most crews. Once in a while they would come out here when things were going well, to spend a day hunting the elusive but more valuable fish that the grass beds harboured. Most of the time, it wasn't worth the bother. Sagantha had paid a substantial amount to make the trip worth this crew's while – I didn't want to ask where he'd got the money from; I suspected it had been removed from Ring of Eight coffers, or perhaps he had a credit note on one of the Tanethan Houses that operated in the city.

'We'll be going quite close to that other boat. *Hummingbird*, I think she's called.' Sagantha remarked, crossing the deck to join me with a fishing crossbow in his hands. He was wearing a fisherman's tunic and rope sandals, a far cry from his naval or viceregal finery, but he had the physical shape to pass for a proper fisherman, and he knew what he was doing; his mother's family had been fishermen somewhere among the southern islands.

'Too close?'

'Hard to say. We can't poach their prey, but we should be all right as long as they keep their distance. It's only if they decide to pick exactly the same bay as us that we have to worry, and there's no reason why they should. They're doing open-water fishing at the moment, and what we've come for is quite different.'

He inspected the crossbow critically, adjusting the mechanism that would shoot the thin, barbed spear several yards underwater. The float line was neatly coiled behind it, secured in exactly the position it was supposed to be; Sagantha had obviously remembered his childhood skills. They were one-shot weapons, too cumbersome to reload during a hunt, and it took a skilled man to catch anything with them.

'Could they find the ray?' I said anxiously.

Sagantha shook his head confidently. 'Only if they were looking for it. The only problem is that the *Hummingbird*'s captain is apparently fairly devout, and therefore less ready to get involved in anything that might harm the Domain. If it all goes wrong, we'll have to persuade him that this has nothing to do with them, that it's some Imperial intrigue. Ilthys has always been caught up in one plot or another, simply because of where it is.'

I kept my eyes fixed on the *Hummingbird* as it weaved its way across the open water, heading roughly in our direction. I could see the bottle-shaped bay where we'd left the searay, an opening between two rocky headlands about a mile in front of us. It meant another tack, with the wind from such an inconvenient quarter.

Most of the small crew of *Whitewake* were crouched on the deck by the mainmast, preparing the crossbows and nets that would be used to block escape routes for their prey. I gave what help I could, but I was more of a liability than an asset.

I glanced over at the cliffs again when we tacked, bearing round for the final approach to the bay and the green forests beyond it. This was what passed for a wild coast on Ilthys, although I could see several whitewashed villages nestled a little way inland, surrounded by patches of lighter vegetation from gardens and orchards. The soil was very good on the slopes of the mountain, apparently, but not many had settled there because of the forest.

Hummingbird had turned away now, and I gave a sigh of relief. They were too far out to make it to the bay before us, and apparently once we reached it, we'd be undisturbed. They would not poach.

Jagged rocks showed above the sea like broken teeth as we passed the entrance to the bay, sailing over more seagrass beds.

'This is fine!' the captain shouted, 'Drop anchor.'

It was only when the dhow had come to a rest that he walked over to us.

'Where is your ray?' he said, sweeping his hand over the green water. He was a small, voluble man, thin and clean-shaven, looking more like a small-time merchant than a fisherman. 'Which side?'

'Over there,' Sagantha said, pointing to the left, where dark seagrass beds surrounded more evil rocks; it was a corner of the inlet that no sailing ship would ever venture into.

'You've got sense,' the captain said. 'But you'll have a long way to swim. This is as close as we'll get.'

'We'll bring her out, if you can have a bosun's chair rigged.'

The captain nodded. 'Good hunting.'

Some of the crew were already busy by the port rail, preparing two of their number for the first hunt. Ropes creaked as they winched a floating platform over the side and held it to the ship, long enough for the men to climb over, taking crossbows and long, slightly curved knives.

This was still a fishing expedition, so we had to wait our turn until three of the dhow's four rafts had been readied. My hair was just long enough to be a nuisance, and I'd have it cut as soon as there was the time, but for now I tied it back with a tattered length of cloth. I helped Sagantha down with the equipment and then followed him down the rope ladder on to the swaying raft. It was more than big enough for the two of us now, but it would be a lot smaller with a substantial fish or a shark on it.

Dark stains marred the wet wood, no doubt blood from previous visits, but at least the crew had cleaned them off.

It was hard work paddling the raft away from the ship, slowly making our way towards the rocks ahead. It was a quarter of a mile or so away, and we didn't have a helpful current to make things easier. There were other problems, too; we soon discovered that the raft had a tendency to veer to the left because of a warped timber on its underside, and so one of us had to paddle faster simply to keep it in a straight line.

I heard shouts behind us, an answering call, and looked round to see three or four men clustered in the bows of the anchored dhow. The second raft floated empty a hundred yards or so inshore; the men on it must have caught sight of something.

The seagrass beds were much closer here, and I could make out brightly coloured smaller fish darting between the leaves, flitting away from the intrusion of my paddle whenever I took a stroke. Nothing larger yet, although there would be sharks in the bay somewhere. The question was how big they were, and whether they were considered edible. If we saw one, we should go after it, but there were other fish, easier to handle, that were more common. Less highly prized by the Thetian gourmets who dominated Ilthysian society, but thicker on the ground.

We were close enough now but the raft's list was becoming even more of a problem. It wasn't in any danger of sinking, but it could easily get lodged on a rock just below the surface.

'Seagrass dropping away on this side,' Sagantha said. 'This is where we brought her in. We might as well stay here, it'll give us enough room to get the ray out.'

Ravenna and Amadeo would have detected our presence long ago, and become worried about discovery. It was time to reassure them. I grabbed the end of the raft's mooring line and dived into the water, pushing myself downwards until I found a rock to secure it to. Then I looked around in the gloom, orienting myself over the gently waving seagrass beds, and kicked out towards the ray.

It was a pleasure, as always, being in the water again, especially here where the sea was blissfully warm and everything was in vivid colours. I kept fairly close to the surface, because although this type of seagrass wasn't dangerous, there were occasionally nasty surprises lurking in its roots.

There was a huge, tall patch ahead, stretching along more or less parallel to the cliff face behind, a patch that shielded the ray. I veered round to one side, heading for a slightly less dense area, and swam through it, feeling the fronds brushing against my skin.

The ray was still there on the other side, settled neatly where we'd left it on a patch of open sand. For a second I saw Ravenna's worried face in the cabin windows, then a relieved look as she smiled and gestured with her hands.

She'd have to bring the ray up before I could board.

I moved out of the way again, keeping my distance while she brought the ray slowly up to the surface, then I swam over and waited for her to open the hatch.

'Are you with the fishing boat?' she asked urgently, pointing over to where the dhow lay anchored.

'We hired it for the day,' I said, pulling myself up on to the wing. 'Sagantha wants to take it as close as we can and then the two of you can disembark.'

'We'll be visible from the villages, though.'

'Not for long. If you'd rather go back on the raft, you're welcome to.'

Sagantha appeared beside me, brushing wet hair out of his eyes.

'What about the ray?' Ravenna said to him. 'I forgot to ask you when you left – if we're all going back to Ilthys, we'll have to leave it on the surface.'

Sagantha pulled himself up on to the wing. 'One of us will have to stay with it. I was planning to take a trip out to some of the other islands; I have several old contacts there.'

'And if you get delayed, or discovered?'

'I won't,' he said shortly. 'And you might gain a few more allies. It's a pity we had to come here; I know far more people in the south. In any case, there are enough ships coming and going from Ilthys that you can escape without difficulty. At the moment you're in no condition to be doing any escaping.'

She said, 'You found the healer, then. Is she any good?'

'Yes. She has old connections with the court, but she's trustworthy. Now, if you'll let me into the cabin, we'll return to the ship. Cathan, go back to the raft and signal that we're coming. They'll be sending more men out to take our place, so you'll have to swim back.'

I didn't have any problem with that, so I let go of the wing and swam back through the seagrass. I went more slowly now, enjoying being underwater and taking a more roundabout route, closer to the rocks. There was a different kind of seaweed growing around them, a vivid blue-tinged green plant like kelp. It looked familiar, but I couldn't think where I'd seen it before.

I had enough time to investigate, so I swam over to it. It didn't look poisonous, and there was something in the shape of the leaves that rang a bell. It was much more luxuriant than anything I could remember, and these were only little specimens, presumably.

I pulled off a leaf and rubbed it between my fingers. There was no particular reason I should have recognised this particular plant, and I wasn't even a biologist, but for some reason it intrigued me.

It must have been the sudden change in pressure that alerted me. I let go of the plant's trunk and pulled my legs up, letting myself head to the surface. Something rushed past underneath me, catching the skin on the top of my feet and scraping it off. I barely had time to register before it had come round and was twisting for another attack.

Then my head broke water, and for a moment I lost sight of it. The rocks were still several feet away.

I pushed my head back under, looking around wildly for the sleek grey shape as I kicked towards the rocks.

There it was! Gods, that didn't belong here! It was a monster, a juvenile leviathan with wicked jaws and a long, flexible neck. It was too long to turn quickly, but it was coming round as fast as it could, one small eye fixed on me. I reached the first of the rocks, grabbed the nearest and cursed as something sharp cut into my hand. I shifted my hand, pulled myself up as soon as I found a sharp edge and hung for a moment, half out of the water. There seemed to be no flat surfaces anywhere, and I could see the leviathan's wave as it arrowed in towards me.

Leviathans didn't attack people! They were carnivores, but they fed on smaller fish and carrion. Their mouths weren't anywhere near big enough to eat something my size, although it had more than enough teeth to kill me if it bit the right place. What was wrong with this one?

But it was attacking me. I gritted my teeth and hauled myself out of the water, clambering over and around the nearest rock only just in time. I cut my leg and my arm as I did, only slightly but enough to bleed, and fell backwards as the leviathan reached the rock. Its small, streamlined head lifted out of the water for a moment, eyes fixed on me. There was barely a foot of water over the rocks here, and another channel a few feet away.

It would follow the scent of blood. I had to get out of the water.

Unless I could attract the attention of one of the hunting packs. I waved my arms and shouted as long as I dared, but no-one seemed to notice. The leviathan was moving round the rocks, looking for an opening to get through them.

The shore was more than a dozen yards away still, and it looked as if there was another patch of open water at the far end. If I could lure the creature into the shallows, strand it even momentarily, I might be able to get away.

I kept on moving over the rocks. Most of them were covered in seaweed, and slippery. I looked back every few seconds to see where it was. If only I'd been on some deserted shore in the middle of nowhere! To use magic here would bring the Domain searchers down on me within hours.

I came abruptly to a deeper stretch of water where the rocks shelved away from each other, and looked back to realise I'd lost track of the leviathan. Where was it?

It couldn't be close behind me, because I'd been out of the water, and it couldn't be to my right because the rocks there were three or four feet above the surface. Where else? I couldn't cross this until I knew . . . Perhaps it had been forced to go round?

Something tugged violently at my ankles, and I felt myself slipping on the treacherous seaweed, sliding into the water. I reached out too late to save myself and felt the water closing over my head.

I had to close my eyes for a second, forcing myself to stay underwater. This was like an underwater ditch, open at both ends. I couldn't see anything against the rocks, was it a dead end?

Then I looked the other way, and froze as I saw a reptilian bulk five or six yards away and a narrow head with its eyes fixed on me. Its mouth was slightly open, revealing thin, pointed teeth like stilettos.

It stared at me for a moment, its head swaying from side to side like a snake's. It was akin to having a staring contest with a human; I'd never seen such depths in a sea creature's eyes before.

Something prickled down my back, but I didn't move, hoping that I could keep the creature from striking long enough to think of something. It was too close for me to get out of the water again; I stood a better chance if it couldn't snap at my limbs, because my body was too big. Was there anything I could use as a weapon? Driftwood, loose rocks? I searched desperately but couldn't see anything, only seaweed and sand. More of the seaweed I'd been looking at when it attacked me.

Could I somehow entangle it in the seaweed for long enough to make my escape? No, there was hardly enough of it, and I wouldn't have time.

I already didn't have time. It was just waiting for an opening, a movement, anything that would give it an easy target to strike at.

I was still thinking when its flippers suddenly surged into movement and it lunged forward. Blindly I did the only thing I could think of and pushed myself up again, over the line of its attack.

Searing pain engulfed my ankle; I hadn't been fast

enough. I jerked my leg forward in desperation and reached downwards, searching for the creature's neck. It was too big to fit through the channel, so it had to move slowly, backing water. Its skin was incredibly abrasive and scraped my arms as I clung on to the base of its neck, but I was safe for a moment; it wasn't flexible enough to reach me here with those wicked teeth.

I saw a cloud of my own blood in the water as the creature moved backwards again. It was only a second or two before it was out in open water once more, curving round to one side, almost in a circle. It twisted its neck as far as it would go, trying to snap at me, but failed; all its thrashings did was scrape more skin off my arms.

I saw the shapes of other fish in the water, thin silvery shapes which for a second looked like bloodfish. Then they darted away again and I felt a twinge of relief. Bloodfish would come, though, given enough time, and I had no way to deal with those. Small and vicious, they could tear a wounded creature apart in minutes. I'd be a sitting duck for them.

The leviathan straightened out and headed towards the rocks again, its two pairs of flippers beating alternately up and down with a slow, deliberate rhythm now. It twisted over, veering round and straightening its neck so its head was level with its body.

I realised almost too late what it was trying to do and only just let go of its neck in time to push myself away from it and the rocks, narrowly missing a blow from the rear flippers.

As it began circling over the seagrass beds I started to clamber up the side of the rocks, but either the brief fight had drained my energy completely or it took far more effort than it should have done. Suddenly it was like trying to swim through treacle, and I felt the same odd sensation I had a few minutes ago, as if an insect was crawling over my back.

Then, without any warning, I saw a shadow over the seagrass beds and a crossbow bolt slicing through the water towards the leviathan as though in slow motion. At the last moment the creature dived out of the way. To my huge relief, it headed off into the open water rather than back towards me again.

The fisherman swam into view for a moment – or was it a woman? I was at the wrong angle to see, still too dazed from what had happened, but I realised a moment later that it was a woman, wearing a strange kind of helmet which half-covered her face. Presumably a protection against bites, although it didn't seem much use to protect just the head.

She carefully hung the crossbow at her belt, treading water as she did, and gestured for me to surface. It didn't seem difficult now, and a moment later I emerged into the sunlight trying to ignore the stinging pain in my leg.

The chase had taken me a little closer to the dhow, still anchored where I'd left it, although one of the platforms was alongside and the carcass of a substantial fish was being hoisted up on to the deck.

'Can you swim the distance?' she asked.

'Of course. What about bloodfish, though?'

She grimaced, looked around. 'We'll have to risk it. Otherwise we'd have to wait until they've finished with that platform.'

'Mine must be somewhere round.'

'No, they went back. You seem curiously unarmed for a fisherman.'

I stared at her for a moment.

'You aren't from the *Whitewake*.'

She shook her head as we started out towards the dhow. 'I'm not. I chased a shark round the headland, didn't realise your ship was in the bay until I was right on top of you.'

She said nothing more until we reached the side of the dhow and I hauled myself up a rope ladder, wrinkling my nose at the smell of fish guts and blood. It was a shark they'd caught, and it had been hung on hooks from the rigging for the poisonous blood to drain away.

The captain came over as soon as I clambered over the gunwale.

'What happened to you? And who is this? Was she on the ray?'

'I got lost,' the woman said coldly. 'He was being attacked by a leviathan. I suggest that in future you make sure your disguises are more convincing.'

'Which ship are you from?' the captain asked suspiciously.

'*Manatee*. She's anchored in the next bay.'

'I know her, but I've never seen you before.'

As he spoke, I heard a shout from the bow and looked over my shoulder. The ray was just breaking water a few feet away from the dhow's starboard side, out of view of the open sea – but not of the woman in the helmet.

'That's an interesting fish,' she observed. 'Do you catch a lot of those?'

The captain's face went grim, and he motioned to his men. Two of them came over, hands resting on the hilts of their knives. 'Who are you?' he demanded. 'If you are on *Manatee*'s crew, you're a spy for someone.'

'And why should you be worried about spies? Because you're smuggling, engaging in illicit operations without permission?' she said.

The men glanced uneasily at one another, and a third came over to join them with a huge fish-hook in his hands.

'If I've got permission, it isn't exactly an illicit operation, is it?' the captain said. All eyes were fixed on the little group now. 'You expect me to ask the Governor's permission for everything I do?'

'A good start,' she said.

She seemed very confident. I moved back a little, looked out at the open sea in case there were any ships coming, and then down into the water beneath the *Silverwing*'s side.

For a moment I wasn't sure whether I was just seeing waving seagrass or moving figures, but then someone swam round the edge of a patch of sand and I realised they were men, all converging on the boat.

'We've got company, Captain!' I shouted. I noticed a look of chagrin on the woman's face, but didn't have time to think about it now. 'Repel boarders!'

One of the men rushed to the side, drew his knife. 'He's right! Lots of them.'

'Everyone get to a weapon!' the captain ordered. 'Grab her, we can use a hostage.'

But the woman was too quick for him, brushed aside the bosun with contemptuous ease and darted across to the side, drawing her own knife as she did. 'There are too many of us for you to fend off, Captain.'

'The hell you're going to take my ship,' he said, drawing his own knife and advancing on her. One of the others pushed a knife into my hand as his comrades hurriedly grabbed the fishing crossbows.

I counted at least eight men on this side, maybe more, and I couldn't see how many there were on the other side. Only seven of the boat's crew were on deck at the moment; another four were still out on the rafts, while Sagantha and Ravenna must still be inside the searay. We were severely outnumbered.

'Stay back, or we shoot!' the bosun shouted as the first of the divers broke water just under the *Whitewake*'s side.

The man backed off. He was wearing a helmet like the woman's and carried a bow slung across his back, of all things.

'Surrender in the name of the Governor,' he called. 'You won't be harmed.'

'What kind of fool do you take me for? Everyone knows how deep the Governor's prisons go.'

But the man didn't answer. The reply came from the stern, where three figures had just hauled themselves over the after rail and now stood looking down. Two wore the royal blue of the Imperial Navy, and had arrows already set to their bows, trained on the captain. The middle one was wearing what seemed to be armour of some kind, although how he had swum in it, I didn't know. He wore a helmet too, but there was something familiar about him.

'And no-one better than the Governor himself,' he said, crossing his arms and staring coolly down at the man in the waist, who had suddenly gone pale. 'I warned you not to cross the line again, but you refused to listen. Whoever else thinks they rule these islands, they're wrong. I do, and I will have an explanation, *now*.'

CHAPTER XXI

For a second the captain stood silently, looking fearfully up at the armoured figure who had just appeared out of the bay. The boarders took advantage of the pause to scramble up the sides, but by the time the first of them clambered over the gunwale I had already walked over to stand in front of the captain.

'He's on Pharaoh's business, Ithien. And mine. Is this any way to treat old friends?'

The former Governor of Ilthys waved to his men to lower their weapons and strode forward round the wheel, jumping down to the main deck instead of using the steps.

'You made it! What in Thetis's name happened?' he said exuberantly, then paused. 'You look older even than you did by the lake.'

'It'll take a while to tell you.' I could barely suppress an urge to jump around the deck for sheer elation.

He pulled off his helmet and handed it to one of the boarders – another woman, which didn't surprise me. It was a moment later that I recognised her, realised who she was.

'Palatine!' I said, hardly believing it was her. She looked a little older, but the face, the hair, oddly light for a Thetian, the expression – none of those had changed.

We embraced tightly, the last members of our family left alive, and old friends. Thetis, it was wonderful to see her. Ithien had done what he'd promised, even though he probably hadn't intended it to be so soon.

'Well met, in any case,' he said, with a broad smile. 'Forgive us for the intrusion.'

'Why did you come?' I asked, still reeling from the

surprise of seeing Palatine again.

'I discovered someone had hired this ship for the day. There was no way to know it was you.' He shook his head, looked around. 'Gods, Cathan, we thought we'd never see you again.'

'You nearly didn't.' I didn't want to let the elation go. 'Can I tell you later?'

'Of course. You'll dine in state tonight.'

One of the men nearby raised an eyebrow. 'He's still living in the old days.'

'Stop being so prosaic,' Ithien said. 'You always have to point out the flaws in everything.'

'Someone has to do it. Are we going to do anything about the searay, by the way?'

'There are injured on it,' I said. 'We were taking them back to the city for help.'

'We have a healer of sorts,' he began, but I cut him off.

'I don't want a healer of sorts.'

'Oh, I suppose that means you found Khalia.' Ithien nodded. 'She'll help them if anyone can, but she refuses to co-operate with me. She says she's beyond all this, but evidently she isn't.'

'Healing the injured isn't quite the same as rebellion.'

'She did more than enough plotting in her time. Don't let that pleasant exterior of hers deceive you, she's as cunning and ruthless as they come.' He turned to the man who'd spoken a moment ago. 'Cadmos, we need to get them to Khalia – how many injured did you say, Cathan?'

'Two. They can walk, but not far. Certainly not up the hill into Ilthys. Khalia said she needs to keep them where she can see them.'

Ithien asked me to explain what Khalia had proposed, then shook his head when I'd finished. 'Too risky. She should have got in touch with me.'

'And how was she supposed to do that in time for this morning?' I demanded. 'You'd have had to confirm it and make arrangements, and by that time another day would have gone.'

'I can move faster than you think. How else did I manage to get here so quickly? No, I have a better idea. They'll arrive as if sent for treatment by a family on one of the further islands. The Governor has no real way to check, and the Avarch likes to think he knows everything that's going on, but really he doesn't. How could he, with thirty or so Sacri and three Inquisitors? He doesn't need any more. Ilthys is the most peaceful and obedient province in all the Archipelago.'

He said the last words very lightly, meaning them to sound contrived. Without knowing that much, I couldn't believe that the Domain could really be unaware of the existence of groups as organised and well-trained as Ithien's. Well, Ithien's now, but I guessed they had been Cadmos's until recently. Only the Domain would never tolerate them if it knew about them.

'It sounds like a good idea, but you'll have to talk the plan over with the others,' I said.

'You're a good republican,' he said, the smile much fainter this time, then turned away before I had time to answer. 'Cadmos. Get that searay . . .'

'Perhaps it's better if I tell them,' I said, interrupting. 'You've alarmed enough people.'

There was a trace of surprise on his face when he turned back to me, but I walked over to the bow without waiting for him to answer and jumped back into the water again. Sagantha had submerged the searay again. He had pointed it towards the entrance of the bay, ready to flee if necessary. Only when I'd swum round and given him the thumbs-up did he bring the craft to the surface.

I pulled myself up on to the wing even before the hatch had opened. One or two of Ithien's people were watching warily from the rail, but he and his lieutenant were out of sight, presumably dealing with the arrangements for transporting Ravenna and Amadeo.

'What's going on?' Sagantha asked as soon as he'd opened the hatch. 'Who are these people?'

'Allies,' I said. 'Thetians, of course. Who else would be attacking from underwater? They're republicans, maybe some Ilthysian heretics. And Palatine.'

'Not Council, though?'

'Not that I know of. And in any case, they couldn't have heard about us. No-one could have got here from Kavatang any faster than we did. They claim to have a better way to get Ravenna and Amadeo into Khalia's house.'

'Do they?' he said. 'I think we should talk about it.'

There were still ropes swung over the side, so it was the work of a moment to leave Ravenna in charge of the searay again and climb back aboard the *Whitewake*. Ithien was still deep in discussion with Cadmos and Palatine, and only looked up when we came over to him.

It was a strange moment, the meeting of those two men, and it wasn't at all as a historian might have imagined it. Both were still wet, Sagantha wearing a fisherman's tunic and Ithien that peculiar underwater armour.

'Ithien Eirillia – Sagantha Karao,' was all I said.

They couldn't help but look each other up and down; both knew the other's reputation, both were used to wielding power even if their commands had shrunk. Ithien was fractionally taller than me and considerably shorter than Sagantha, but height was of no consequence here.

'How very appropriate,' said Ithien after a moment, 'that I meet the master of disguises looking like the Old Man of the Sea. You should have been a Thetian.'

Sagantha returned his questioning stare. 'You're Thetian enough for both of us. And as for master of disguises – weren't you working for the Emperor when last I heard of you?'

'Loyalties change, as you know. Sometimes we even

have to do things we don't like. It doesn't matter so much what the world thinks of us if we know what we think of ourselves.'

Ithien looked more amused than hostile. I couldn't read Sagantha's expression.

'A philosopher as well,' he said after a moment.

'Not really. A republican. Everything else is secondary.'

Palatine nodded her agreement.

'You've had the luxury of being idealistic,' said Sagantha. 'Some of us were too busy dealing with the Inquisition.'

'We're all dealing with the Inquisition,' Ithien said quietly. 'Them and their puppet of an Emperor. He's no different from any of his ancestors, but none of them had the power of the Domain behind them. At least they were interested in more than destruction. *Ranthas's anointed Emperor*, indeed.'

'He's built up Thetia's power more than anyone since the fourth Aetius,' Sagantha replied. The mood seemed to have changed with Ithien's last words. 'Surely that's enough reason to support him.'

'Support an Empire founded in blood? The Empire was built on law, not conquest, and it should go back to being that way. Nothing can change while the Domain rules.'

'Then it seems we have a common interest.' Sagantha gave him an even look. 'Her Majesty can't regain her throne while Midian rules the Archipelago.' He glanced away, up at the forested hills of Ilthys rearing above the bay, up into a dazzling blue sky. No-one said anything for a moment.

'Can you see why I changed sides?' Ithien said, walking past Sagantha and ducking around the main yard. He stood staring at the same vista for a moment. 'It never gets any less painful, looking at these hills and knowing that they could end up as charred cinders. If I'd tried to resist, they might have been. As it is, Ilthys can't be safe until there can be no more question of burnings or atrocities. Nowhere can be, not even Thetia.'

'Yet it's Ilthys you worry about, not Thetia.'

'I haven't spent more than a few months in Thetia since the Assembly appointed me Governor six years ago. Since Orosius died I've been on business for the new Emperor, betraying my friends in an effort to keep Ilthys free of their taint. Now I've abandoned the pretence of loyalty, who knows what will happen?' He turned back again.

'Why did you?' I asked. 'What was so important about the dam?'

'The dam doesn't exist any more,' Ithien said, but there was no joy in his voice. 'The warning lamps were depth charges, they blew the centre out of it. The Domain won't be able to colonise the mountain areas for another twenty years. That was why we went, but the other reason was that I was in danger, all of you were in danger. There were far more secrets than any of us realised, and they wanted to kill you all at the end to protect those secrets. Amonis was beginning to see through my double act, and he had an agenda of his own that I still don't understand.'

'You sacrificed an Imperial career for a dam and a group of prisoners?' Sagantha asked.

Ithien looked at me rather than Sagantha when he replied. 'Not ordinary prisoners. Oceanographers, underwater architects and masons. Skilled people.'

'Rather than marines, naval officers, people who can fight?' Sagantha was scornful.

'Look what the people who can fight have done,' I reminded him mildly. 'They work only by terror, there aren't any other weapons they can use.'

'I prefer not to discuss this,' Ithien said. 'Sevasteos was killed by one of the Sacri on the manta. He was a good friend, the only man in Eshar's court I ever liked. Now, we should deal with pressing business.'

Ithien made a small sign with his hand, and his men

herded the crew towards the back as the three of us walked over to stand in the forepeak.

'Cathan is right,' he said to Sagantha. 'There'll be more time to discuss this later, but we can't win this one by force alone. You've been Admiral, Suffete, Viceroy. You know as well as anyone that this isn't a question of tactics or strategy. I think all of us have come separately to the same conclusion. Palatine and I did, Cathan and Ravenna realised it long before the rest of us.'

'The numbers are against us,' Sagantha said, with a brief nod. 'Forget heroic ballads, we're not living in Ethelos's poems. We realised that thirty years ago.'

'And look what came of it,' I said. 'The Ring of Eight, their dungeons and their torture chambers. It must have gone wrong fairly quickly.'

'It was never right,' Sagantha said abruptly, then said to Ithien, 'You're saying there are other ways?'

'You know there are. They're more difficult, that's all. More subtle, but less costly.'

'More interesting,' said Sagantha. He paused, then said, 'We shouldn't underestimate the Domain. The Halettites may be unsophisticated barbarians, but the priests know all about deviousness and trickery.'

'And how much do they know about science?' I asked both of them. 'If there's one thing they all agree on, it's that they'd prefer to do without oceanographers at all.'

'They think they can,' Sagantha said. 'Ask Amadeo, I'm told most of the information came from him. I may have used some fairly unpleasant methods to get information from people, but never on the scale of my esteemed colleagues.'

'I think we have a lot to discuss,' Ithien said. 'I think it should wait – Cathan said you have injured people. We need to get them to the city.'

We listened while Ithien sketched out what he intended to do, which I had to admit made more sense than our original plan. He had more resources to draw on than Khalia, and probably more contacts across the city. Sagantha looked doubtful at first, but I'd told him before what had happened at the dam. Ithien was no less trustworthy than Sagantha, perhaps more so, in fact.

In the end, Palatine convinced him, and he returned to the searay to pilot it round the point. Ravenna and Amadeo were to go to Ilthys on Ithien's ship as two people from the out islands who'd been in accidents and needed better help than the apprentice healers out there would give.

'What have you been doing?' I asked Palatine, as we seemed to be the only people left with no tasks. 'I've heard stories of you, but nothing concrete.'

'Fighting,' she said, with a trace of sadness. 'Nothing interesting, nothing that I'd have chosen to do in a better world. Nothing that makes any difference, really. Hiding, eating bad food and killing people in mosquito-size raids. Doing what I can to hurt the Domain, even though it isn't very much. Trying to keep just the idea of a republic alive, capturing the occasional supply ship. And an Imperial manta once, for the Council.'

Meridian, no doubt. She must have seen something in my face.

'What is it?'

'The Council . . . I'll tell you later.'

Green eyes held mine for a moment. 'Ravenna? Or both of you?'

'All of us.' I felt a sudden bitterness swelling up, swamping my good mood. 'They lied to us all, made us believe what they wanted just as effectively as Etlae converted Sarhaddon. He was right, you know.'

Before you call me a fanatic again, Cathan, look at yourself.

'I think you should tell me what's happened,' Palatine said. 'It's eating you up, and if it's about the Council, it concerns all of us.'

I shook my head. 'Later. No point in spoiling this. And if it's any consolation, Ithien and your republic are the only reason I'm here instead of back in the dust of Qalathar where the Domain thinks I belong.'

'No,' she said, and this time smiled faintly. 'You belong in the depths of their deepest hell. I should take that as a compliment.'

I didn't get a chance to reply properly, because Ithien had finished interrogating the captain and came over to join us. Most of his marines had swum back to the other ship now, and only a few waited by the rail, keeping a watchful eye on the crew of the *Whitewake* as they resumed their fishing.

'How did you get here so quickly?' I asked, squinting up into the sky. It was still barely noon, and I wasn't sure how he could have made it from the out islands in the morning when we'd only secured the ship yesterday evening.

'People keep me informed,' he said evasively. 'The restrictions are quite light here, there's been very little trouble. I suspect that will change when they hear of my desertion. It was one of the Emperor's conditions when he accepted me into Imperial service, that I never come back here.'

'Do they follow you rather than the Pharaoh?' I asked carefully.

'Heavens, yes. Ilthys is virtually a Thetian city anyway, if bigger than many of ours. Their President was a friend of mine; Cadmos was his tribune of marines, several of the others are Ilthysian born. The Pharaoh is gone now, Cathan. Only you know if she's still alive, but people don't believe in her any more.'

'What do they believe in, then? The Assembly with all its quarrels?'

Ithien shook his head. 'They believe in anyone who can stop them being arrested. It's better now than it was, there hasn't been much trouble in the central islands, and so the Inquisitors have got lax.' He paused for a moment. 'Oddly enough, in a lot of places it seems to be the Navy they look to. The Navy is powerful, and the Emperor won't tolerate anything that gets in its way. If you're under the Navy's protection, you have to do something serious before the Inquisitors can get at you. The Navy still works by Thetian law, and only the Emperor or the General Staff can order a military case transferred to the Inquisition.'

Eshar looked after his own, all right. The Navy had welcomed him with open arms, and he'd made a point of proving how right they'd been.

'It's strange,' Ithien said, a moment later, his eyes following a pair of birds soaring over the eastern shore of the bay, 'how far away it all feels now. You've never been to Selerian Alastre, you have no idea what it's like, how it feels to be in the centre of the world. Much as I loathe Eshar, he's changed the place, brought it to life again. By sucking the blood of the Archipelago, for the most part.'

'Would you have been able to do the same?'

'I don't know. It would be painful to admit otherwise, but then none of us want to think that this was the only way to produce change. Why should it have to be through so much death?'

It was a rhetorical question, because all of us knew the answer. After a moment Ithien looked back at me, and then down at the crew standing in the waist of the boat. 'It's time we were going,' he said. 'You should probably stay here, otherwise somebody at the harbour might start wondering why two crewmen from this boat ended up on a different one.'

'There must be people on shore who've seen all this.'

'I doubt anyone's watching. Only Palatine would assume there were spies in every house, but then she's like that.'

'She's not the only one,' Palatine said.

'Don't delay too long,' I said.

'I won't,' Ithien promised. 'We'll be in Ilthys before you, so I'm afraid you've got a day of fishing ahead . . .' He stopped and looked at my legs and hands. 'On second thoughts, you're useless on this boat, you can't possibly go fishing with open wounds. You pick up injuries more easily than anyone else I've met. What on earth happened?'

I explained as we walked back down to join his men, and he looked sceptical until the woman who'd rescued me came to corroborate it.

'Must be weak in the head, if he thought you were worth eating,' Ithien said. 'We Thetians are a stringy lot, not much meat on us. Feed it a Merchant Lord instead, they'd be much more to its liking.'

'Too big for it,' I said lightly, thinking of Hamilcar, not a small man, who'd probably grown a true Tanethan beard by now, one that reached halfway to his waist. He was certainly too bulky for any leviathan to handle.

'Yes, but if he was counting his money, it could eat most of him before he noticed.' Such a familiar comment, but a light-hearted one considering how rapacious a few of the Merchant Houses had been. The old grudges were still there – greedy Tanethans, decadent Thetians, slow-witted Huasans, but many of them had proved double-edged taunts, as the Thetians had set out to prove how wrong people had been.

Ithien strolled over to the *Whitewake*'s captain again, an assured figure in his half-dry armour. 'Thank you for your hospitality, Captain, and should you inform me next time you take unusual passengers, I'll make it well worth your while. As for boarding you – well, that was a precaution. My people will send you over a couple of fish before we go; we caught them while we were waiting for you. I hope they'll be worth the inconvenience. Good day.'

He made an abrupt gesture to his men and walked over

to the side, diving gracefully back into the crystal water; his armour was hardly heavy enough to weigh him down. As his remaining marines followed suit, I realised I was meant to go too, and I was only too glad to be back in the water again. The marines surrounded me as we swam away from the ship. I'd still be giving off the scent of blood and although I could protect myself with magic if all else failed, I'd rather not.

In the event, the swim round the headland to Ithien's ship was without problems, although I didn't feel as comfortable in the water as I had a few hours earlier.

Ithien's ship was a vessel very similar to the *Whitewake*, a single-masted fishing vessel with rakish lines and a huge lateen sail. It was anchored just beyond the point, inside a shallow stretch of water hemmed in by reefs which was almost an artificial bay, if not as sheltered.

Almost as soon as I'd pulled myself up the rope and on to the deck, I heard someone shout my name – my assumed name – and swung round, to see a delighted-looking Vespasia hand a coiled rope to a sailor and rush across to greet me.

There were four or five others there that I'd known from the dam, including Oailos, who seemed slightly detached, less forthright than he'd been as our unofficial leader at the dam. He probably didn't like playing second fiddle to the unreliable Ithien. All of them wanted to know what had happened, but I had at least as much to ask them. They were here, so there must have been a manta in the inlet, a manta they'd sailed out through the section of Perdition's Shore where *Valdur* and *Peleus* had been lost.

'Good navigation,' said Vespasia, when I asked. She looked more like the woman I'd known at the Retreat, less the gaunt scarecrow of the Desert. Which was hardly a surprise, given her changed circumstances.

'Raise anchor!' Ithien shouted from aft, assuming command the instant he reached the deck. 'We've lingered here·long enough, so we need to make good speed for Ilthys if we're to get back home before dark.'

Being somewhat superfluous to requirements, I found a perch by the mast where I could keep out of the crew's way as they bent on sail and headed out to sea, clearing the reefs for a quicker and less dangerous passage back to the capital. The ship that had shadowed us earlier this morning was a sail in the distance, just visible in the entrance to another small bay further along the coast. Ithien released Palatine from her duties, and I sat and talked to her and Vespasia for most of the journey back.

We tacked round the mole into the harbour of Ilthys in early afternoon, the sleepiest part of the day. There was no activity among the night fleet ships and merchantmen anchored in the harbour, and the only people on the quays were a pair of longshoremen dozing under a faded awning.

I was almost the first to go ashore, sent ahead with one of the marines to warn Khalia that we were coming, and to tell her of the change of plans. We didn't pass anyone else as we walked briskly between the warehouses; it was only as we went by the undersea harbour that a group of dock workers came out of a building, talking in low, serious voices.

'There may be news,' the marine said. 'Slow down, we'll walk up the hill with them and see if it's anything important.'

We reached the gates of the undersea harbour at almost exactly the same time as the dockers emerged, and the marine gave them a friendly nod.

'You an out islander?' one of the dockers said, without any particular hostility. He'd been drinking something from a gourd, and he handed it to his companion and wiped his lips before he spoke.

The marine nodded. He must have been a fisherman at some point, because the way of speaking came naturally to him. I didn't say anything; my accent wasn't particularly unusual, but it wasn't Ilthysian.

'Came over with some injured. Waste of a good day's fishing, but one of them's my cousin, he's in quite a bad way.'

'Bad luck. What happened?'

'Some fool of a contractor repaired a split balcony, used cheap pins instead of proper ones. My cousin wouldn't be here if he hadn't landed in a rose bush, but it cut him up quite badly.'

'Have you taken them to court?' the docker asked. 'Make the bastards pay. My neighbours had a floor collapse on them, it killed their youngest. Bad business, but they got the contractor into a Navy prison. Hope he likes it there.'

'Go to the military court if your judge isn't harsh enough.' said one of his companions, a shorter man with – unusually – a beard. His eyes lit up. 'Have you heard the news?'

'What news?'

The docker's face took on the self-important look of someone telling momentous news. 'We were talking to the crew of *Alchemist*, just in from Qalathar. Disaster, war, everything! A dam burst in the north, caused a small tidal wave on some of the islands. And the priests found a heretic fortress on Qalathar itself! Right under their noses. There's uproar in the temples. But that's not the whole of it.' He paused for dramatic effect, knowing we were hanging on his every word. 'The Thetian Grand Fleet has arrived in Tandaris. Thirty, forty ships, half the Navy sent to Qalathar to keep order and show everyone who's in charge. They say there hasn't been such a force anywhere in the world since the Crusade, everyone reckons Eshar has some special plan for the island.'

CHAPTER XXII

Within a few days, we had plenty of other things to worry about. An impromptu conference in Khalia's house had brought few results, except an increased tension between Ithien and Sagantha. No-one had any firm ideas why the Grand Fleet had been deployed, and after arguing for hours, we made our way back to our lodgings.

As we skirted through the streets well away from the Temple, we met a group of men – masons, from the guild badge one of them wore – walking home from a bar. It was too narrow a street to walk past on the other side.

One of them recognised Ithien almost instantly, despite the gloom and the cosmetic alterations to his face and hair, which were more useful in the daytime anyway.

'Lord Governor,' he said, stopping his friends with a sharp hand gesture. 'Is that you?'

'I think you're mistaking me,' said Ithien calmly, but I heard Sagantha's intake of breath.

'No, I'm not. You're back. There's rumours that you've defected.'

'There are. Some of them may be true.'

'We won't give you away,' said a man with a neatly groomed moustache. 'My son got into a bar brawl with some Ranthas soldiers, they shipped him off to Qalathar for it.'

'Don't tell people I'm here,' Ithien warned him. 'You're the ones who will suffer.'

'We've suffered enough anyway,' said the first man. 'You were a foreign Governor, but we didn't mind you. You didn't interfere and you got us money from the Assembly. That's what a Governor's supposed to do.'

One of the others whispered something.

'Best not to stand and talk,' the mason said. 'We're here if we're needed. 'Night.'

They went on their way. Sagantha looked accusingly at Ithien.

'There was nothing I could do,' the former Governor said. 'I know them. They won't betray me, but that's the least of our problems now. By tomorrow evening the news will be all around the city, and then there'll be trouble.'

He was right. The news of his return was all over the city within two days – at least, it was two days later that someone mentioned it to Vespasia and me as we loaded supplies for his men in the out islands into the hold of the schooner *Manatee*.

Rumours were rife, as always, and I'd heard several third and fourth-hand sightings of Ithien, complete with mysterious circumstances and promises of help.

The Domain already knew he'd defected: a courier manta had arrived yesterday and disgorged a priest who had demanded to be taken straight to the Governor. Ithien's successor was a naval officer, Fleet Admiral Vanari. He'd commanded the Emperor's vanguard against the Cambressians at Poralos Atoll, had been promoted and received a Governorship for his part in the victory.

Now he was closeted with the Inquisitor, I heard, which was bad news. Ilthys's Avarch was away in the Holy City, and the resident Venatic was seriously ill: with those two out of the way, the Inquisitor held even more power than usual.

I couldn't help but feel nervous, even though none of us had had any contact with Khalia since we brought Ravenna there. The members of that House had too much to lose by informing, but we still weren't safe.

'They don't have the resources to search the whole city,' Vespasia said reassuringly as we clattered down the gangplank to collect more crates of fruit. A makeshift awning had been erected over the crates to shield them from the afternoon sun, but it was only a delaying measure. Fruit didn't have an enormously long lifetime even in the coldest part of a manta, so most of it would need to be preserved.

I glanced out at the flat blue expanse of ocean beyond the harbour mouth, wondering if more mantas were coming with Imperial troops to impose order. The news couldn't have reached Selerian Alastre yet, not if it had only now arrived from Qalathar. It was another three or four days to the capital from here. We had a while before the Emperor could act.

'Do they need to?' We took one side of the crate each and heaved it back on to the *Manatee*. She was far more graceful a ship than her name might indicate, although little different from any other fishing schooner across the islands.

'How else are they going to find him among fifty thousand people?'

'He's probably shot straight to the top of our beloved Emperor's most wanted list,' I said, climbing down into the hold so she could heave it down to me. My voice echoed in the half-empty space. 'Which will put a lot of pressure on the people here to find him, now that these rumours have started.'

'Still, they can't do all that much with only a hundred or so troops.'

They could always call for reinforcements, I thought as I took the crate from her and braced myself to take its whole weight. There would be more people to help us once the last deliveries had arrived, but for now we were on our own.

It was late afternoon, and the harbour had livened up somewhat after the heat of the day. *Manatee* was in the fishing harbour, tied up alongside a quay at the edge of the night fishing fleet, but we could see across into the commercial side of the harbour where two or three galleons were being loaded and unloaded, and a number of smaller coasters were tied up.

Not to mention the four frigates further out in the bay, the core of Vanari's surface fleet lying at anchor. Three had sails furled and showed little sign of activity, but the fourth was just preparing to go out on patrol, and there were men scurrying along her yards.

It was easy to forget that there were more men on one of those frigates than three or four mantas, given how much labour they needed to deal with the sails. Vanari had over a thousand men in his surface fleet. More than enough for his purpose.

We stared out at the frigates for a moment, resting between moving two crates. They were such beautiful ships, with their royal blue sides and towering masts, but I knew from experience how fragile they were in storms. They belonged to a different age from the mantas.

'Those ships – we use them locally now, but people sailed halfway around the world in them all those centuries ago, before there were any mantas. Can you imagine, it must have taken a few days just to sail across Thetia, and the Commonwealth . . .'

'Months and months from one side to the other, relying on wind and currents.' She nodded. 'Impossible to keep control of anything over that distance, I suppose. Fine if you were sailing along a coastline with supply stations, but you'd have to cross so much empty ocean. You certainly couldn't have got to the continents in them.'

'People must have gone, one way or the other, since most of the world was inhabited.'

'Maybe it was the Tuonetar. I remember reading that they already had arkships when we first developed mantas. They had the whole of Thure, though, with all those metals and forests. It's not as hot as it is down here, and the ice-cap must have been much smaller for them to build cities up there.'

'Heavens only know how anyone could have lived here

before the storms, let alone build empires.' It was merely hot now, rather than blazing – a wonderful heat that had been rare when I was growing up in Oceanus; heat that I'd become accustomed to after so many years in the Archipelago.

'Maybe we have something to thank the Tuonetar for.' She went over to collect the gourd of water we'd stored in the coolest place we could find, came back and offered it to me. I drank gratefully and handed it back to her.

'I'd rather not have to thank them for anything,' I said.

It was a moment before she finished drinking and replied. 'What did Salderis say about the climate before the War?'

'Not very much. She concentrated on the storms and how they'd evolved, how they worked. I don't think she was really as interested in the climate itself. She touches on the subject in the conclusion to her book, but it's mostly negative.'

'*Ghosts of Paradise*. Even if it was hotter than this, the climate can't have been all that bad. Not for Thetia to achieve what it did. Just imagine; no real winter, sun all year round.' She paused. 'Maybe it wasn't that much hotter in the tropics. The worst of the storms are further north and south, after all.'

'There's still the Commonwealth. Qalathar's too hot as it is.'

'You don't need to tell me, not after the dam.' There was a faraway look in her eyes for a moment. 'Give me Thetia any day. I suppose the only difference would be that you'd have to take a longer siesta. The Tuonetar got a raw deal from their storms, didn't they? Thure turns into a frozen wasteland that no-one can live in, Thetia merely gets a little cooler and more bearable. Fairly ironic.'

'They must have been desperate.'

'Or didn't know what they were doing. It's perfectly possible; Salderis seems to have been the first one to work it out. It's easy with hindsight, we can look back and see what a bad idea it was.'

I perched on the gunwale, tired of standing up, and Vespasia sat down on the coiled anchor chain. This was taking a longer break than we were entitled to, but we had been working solidly most of the afternoon, and there weren't many crates left.

'The Tuonetar were supposed to have been winning the War. The attack on Aran Cthun was a huge gamble – the Thetians knew they were losing.'

'I don't know that much about the history. From my point of view – and you've told me a fair amount of what Salderis taught you – the Tuonetar made a staggering mistake. Bad for them, good for the Thetians and the Domain, so-so for everyone else. They were mages, they used magic where we use machinery. Why should they have any more understanding of the climate or the oceans than your average mage?'

'Still, it doesn't make much strategic sense.'

'I thought you weren't the expert on that. Who knows what they were thinking? It gives us more of a chance, in a way, because the Domain are like them. The Tuonetar didn't have science, the Domain can't stand it. Both of them use armies and magic without stopping to wonder if there's another way.'

'Do we know so much more about the planet? Can we predict all the consequences?'

'You worry too much.' She smiled. 'Leave the Viceroys and the Governors of the world to take care of those. They know what you can do, and they know that Salderis taught you, but even so, do they pay much attention? They're still thinking in the same terms as always, leaving us oceanographers to get on with our insignificant work. We have ways to fight back that they've never dreamed of.'

'Do I count as an oceanographer?' I asked, but she didn't notice that I hadn't been entirely serious.

'Of course you do. Ask any of us from the dam. You

337

studied under Salderis – you more or less gave up your title for this. You know as well as any of us now how it feels to be trodden on all the time.' She held my gaze for a moment. 'From what Sagantha says, the Elemental Council still exists. What do you think our chances are if they win? They hate us almost as much as the Domain.'

'Only because of what I've done.'

'You sullied their idea of magic by looking at it the way any oceanographer would. No-one's ever done that, because there have never been oceanographer mages before, and they distrust all of us for it. How do they know what's next? Might we come up with a way to dispense with the magic? They don't know. Nor do we, it has to be said. It sounds unlikely, but it worries them.'

'In any case, if the Council somehow managed to win despite everything, what would change? Four religions instead of one and no Crusaders, but they're already using the Domain's methods. They've decided that what you came up with is heresy. They'd treat the Guild as the Domain has.'

It was a bleak prospect, for me and for the Guild.

'What Ravenna and I can do involves magic.'

'Yes, it does, but you've actually thought about how to apply it. And there are one or two other things we've thought of that don't involve magic at all. Little things, but our ideas all the same.'

'If I have to use the storms and things go wrong . . .'

'Then we all pay the price. That's not really what I'm saying. You don't expect theories to spring into being fully-formed. You just begin with the principle that despised oceanographers, mechanics or technicians as they call us, can actually accomplish something on our own.'

I was beginning to see what she meant, but it was still dangerous ground. 'It gives the Domain the excuse it would need to suppress the Guild completely.'

'Where would they be then? Would the fishing fleets go

out, would anyone know what conditions at sea were like? They can't do that.'

For all her experiences as a penitent, Vespasia still seemed hopelessly optimistic. Not that it was such a bad thing, but it could get us all into trouble.

'Polinskarn never dreamed that anyone could do without their libraries. Many of them have gone now, the rest have been purged. Who'd have thought the Domain would assassinate an Emperor?'

We'd spent too long doing nothing, so we reluctantly stood up and went back to moving the crates, talking when we had the opportunity to. It was an odd conversation, punctuated by periods of silence as we concentrated on shifting the cargo or recovered our breath.

'Do we have any choice?' Vespasia said a little later, as I manoeuvred a pile of crates as far back as possible into a crevice of the hold. We were under strict instructions to leave a substantial area of the hold empty for the remaining supplies.

'Choice in what?'

'Acting on our own initiative. Doing what you originally proposed.' She bent down to tighten a strap holding one of the first crates in place.

'The storms are a last resort.'

'And according to you, Salderis told you not to use them almost in the same breath as saying that they'd get worse as the centuries went on, and so the Domain's power would increase.'

Neither of us said anything for a moment or two as we levered the last crate we'd brought down on to the top of a stack. It was precarious, and would fall off unless we tied it down safely. Vespasia wormed her way in behind the stack with a length of rope to secure it to a ring in the bulkhead.

'And at the same time she warned me that using storms as a weapon could speed the cycle up,' I said. 'There's not much I can really do.'

'Without the Domain – damn this bolt, it's broken – we might have enough latitude to work out a way to stop the storm cycle. There is a way, only we don't have the power at present. She thought in terms of magic, since that was how the storms had been created. What if instead we used mages to channel the power from reactors? Who's to say we even need mages for that?'

She was even more of a heretic than Ravenna. Although, come to think of it, there were one or two things Ravenna had said that suggested she might be coming to the same conclusion.

'It's too much of a risk.'

There was a pause as she fumbled with the broken bolt. 'I've done it.' She emerged from behind the stack. 'Why are you so timid all of a sudden? You're the one who's got us this far, with a little help from Salderis. If you could get hold of that ship – of *Aeon*, I mean, the two of you might be able to do more damage to the Domain in a few hours than all the heretics could in two hundred years. There are a lot of people out there who'd welcome that.'

'And then curse us all when what I do to the climate makes Worldsend look like Paradise.' I would go back to *Aeon*, at least, because I doubted that the Council could have reached or even moved it by now – but I had no idea what I'd actually do once I was there. Until I stood in the room Carausius had called the Hall of the World and saw Aquasilva in its entirety, could at last apply what Salderis had taught me to the planet itself, there would be no way to be certain.

'Or you have virtually no effect on the climate, and people realise that the Domain isn't all-powerful any more, that it can't actually protect itself from you.'

'Whatever I do, they'll suffer too, and we'll end up being as hated as they are now simply for the damage we've caused.'

'Why are you coming up with worst-case scenarios all the time?' she demanded, climbing back up the ladder. She went on with her harangue once we were both on deck. 'You could deal them a colossal blow . . .'

I interrupted, her, glancing around to check that there was still nobody within earshot. The night crews were all asleep, though, and the rest of Ithien's men hadn't come back. 'You're looking at this too much from an oceanographer's point of view. If I was fighting the Thetians, the Cambressians, any nation, it would be easy enough. But I can't hurt the Domain without hurting those around them, because wherever the Domain are, there are also Archipelagans.'

'I didn't want to suggest this,' Vespasia said after a moment, 'but Ravenna already has, when I talked to her for a few minutes the other night. There is a place that stands for the Domain and nowhere else . . .'

She trailed off deliberately, waiting for me to say it.

'The Holy City,' I finished, staring at her. 'Only Ravenna would think of destroying the Holy City!'

'Not only Ravenna. All of us.'

'All of you? Who exactly?'

'All of us from the dam, everyone who spent those years as slaves. Everyone you know who's suffered because of the Domain. Sagantha and the others aren't thinking in those terms. We could shatter the Domain in a few hours.'

I closed my eyes, still feeling the heat of the sun and the slight, gentle motion of the *Manatee*. What she was talking about seemed unreal on this balmy day, as remote as the snows of northern Oceanus must seem to a woman who'd spent her life in Thetia and the central Archipelago.

I wasn't really sure why I was arguing with her. It wasn't really a single reason, more an aggregation of little ones that seemed to slip away when I tried to dissect them. After what the Domain had done to us, I could think of no better justice than to do what Ravenna and Vespasia had proposed.

Even the thought of it gave me a curious kind of exultation, the idea that we could, perhaps, unmake the Domain in a single day and show the world how wrong it had been. I doubted there would ever be a better chance, or two more people with the combined ability to do it.

The best path to take is always the one that involves the least bloodshed. This wasn't it — or was it? How many more would die at the Domain's hands if we sat by and did nothing?

It wasn't a matter of simple arithmetic. One had to take account of the lives that would be lost, the vendettas and grudges it would create in the Domain survivors, even bereft of leadership. Nothing was ever so simple.

Yet . . . yet I remembered the wild pleasure of revenge, standing in the wreckage of the courtroom, how satisfying it had been. And how little I had suffered for it since.

I opened my eyes again, to see Vespasia looking worriedly at me, and shook my head.

'No. We can't even think of the damage that would do.'

'Is it up to you?' she demanded as we walked down to collect another crate. She stood over it glaring at me. 'How many are there who would jump at the chance to be in your position, who wouldn't hesitate for a moment?'

'Is that such a good thing? You sound like Ravenna.'

She ignored me. 'The two of you are the only ones with this kind of power, the only ones in a position to strike back. We can help you, but in the end we can't do it ourselves. And we can't stand by and let you refuse to act.'

'I'll decide this for myself,' I said, crouching to grasp one side of the crate.

'There's nothing to decide. Think about what Salderis said for a moment. If you use the storms as weapons, the climate may deteriorate faster. Why?'

I was on easier ground here. 'We're interfering with

342

something we still don't understand properly. Who knows what effect that will have?'

'If now you still can't say you understand it, how long will it be? Decades? Centuries?'

'How well do we understand the oceans now? The Guild has been here for two hundred years, but we can't say we know all there is to know.'

'Wait for two hundred years, and the storms will be so severe that to weaken the Domain's power would cause ten times as much destruction. If we acted now, we'd have a chance to find protection that doesn't depend on the good-will of legions of murderous priests and their tame fanatics.'

She bent down to lift the next crate, and neither of us said anything until we'd hauled it up the hatchway and stowed it in the hold.

'And the storms themselves,' she went on. 'If you use them as a weapon, all you're doing is drawing on the power and the fabric of an existing storm. None of us are pretending you can create a storm out of nothing. The storms are a source and a vessel of power that you can concentrate on one particular place. You're not actually changing the weather systems.'

'Do we know that for sure?'

Would Salderis have mentioned it if it wasn't important? I know she'd been trying to persuade me to take that wretched throne, but she'd always said it was dangerous to interfere with the weather pattern.

I refused to say anything more for several more loads, until we'd dragged the last up and packed it in the hold. I wasn't particularly tired, but it was hard work using muscles that I hadn't used since the canal.

'Is that the reason you think I'm objecting?' I asked, sinking down with my back against the far gunwale, facing the gangplank and in the shade of the deck awning covering the hold. 'Because of the climatic damage?'

'That's the main one. Isn't it?'

I shook my head. 'It would accumulate far too much bitterness, the Crusade would be nothing by comparison.'

'As opposed to the bitterness that has already built up? The Crusade was thirty years ago, but we're still feeling the effects. And what about all the people singled out, dragged off to the stake or to penance? Does anyone know how many penitents there are? We grew up away from all this, we haven't had to live through it. It was peaceful for us before we were dragged into this, but when you remember how wonderful it was, it's easy to ignore that the Archipelago wasn't the same. They didn't have the peace that we enjoyed.'

A single memory floated into my mind as she said that, the last time I could really pretend everything had been normal. That evening in Courtières' palace with his son and the Cambressians had been six years ago, but felt like another millennium. A time when I'd been nothing more than the Escount of Lepidor, and had known next to nothing about heresy or the Archipelago, and when Sarhaddon had been a friend instead of an implacable enemy.

I would have given my soul at that moment, just to be in a Lepidor again where none of this had ever happened, and I couldn't be blamed.

'Horrible, isn't it?' Vespasia said, mistaking the stricken expression on my face.

'And if I do what you're asking, nothing will really change. This time it'd be the Continentals out to avenge what we did to them.'

'And if they're too frightened of the damage we can do to them?'

'Then we'll have begun a tyranny as bad as any the Domain could impose, based on sheer terror, and as time went on we'd use the storms to crush smaller and smaller uprisings. We'd have become ten times as powerful as any Emperor in history.' I stared her in the face for a moment. 'Don't you see, Vespasia? This isn't about the science. It's the monster we'd create. In a way, Ukmadorian was right, but his methods are wrong.'

'Then what are we supposed to do?' she asked, sounding angry now. 'The one thing we got out of that meeting the other day was to realise that we can't really win by conventional means. Whatever happens, there'll be more bloodshed.'

'But if we destroy one tyranny to replace it with another, all the blood will have been for nothing.' I stood up again, drank some more water and went over to lean on the rail. I saw figures moving over by the harbourmaster's office and narrowed my eyes to see what was going on.

There were two figures in red standing by the wooden board on which the harbour notices were pinned up.

Sacri.

As I watched, one of them reached up with a gloved hand to tear down the notices that were there. He simply ripped them off and let the light breeze whip them away. Then the other held up a sheet of paper against the centre of the board, and the first hammered it in.

It only took a moment or two, then the Sacri set off for the town again, still veiled despite the heat.

Vespasia and I looked at each other for a moment.

'A decree from the Avarch or the Governor,' she said, our argument forgotten.

I nodded. 'Stay with the ship. We need someone on watch. I'll go over, see what it says.'

I left before she could protest, walked as briskly as I dared without seeming too eager to the office. Three or four men were already standing around the notice, and several more were on their way.

It was nailed to the board at eye level, and there were two heavy seals at the bottom, of both the Avarch and the Governor.

My apprehension growing, I moved as close as I could and began reading.

Hamilcar Barca to Oltan Canadrath,

ENCRYPTED

I have encrypted this because I have to warn you of what is about to happen, but even if the letter is intercepted it must not be read. There is a plot against the Emperor's life, to be carried out when he arrives here on an inspection tour in two days' time. There are dissident clansmen involved, but they are not in a position to be doing something this big on their own. I suspect a larger moving force, but have no positive leads as yet.

I am not helping the attempt, even though I sympathise; it is more important that the Imperial military do not see a Tanethan connection, as that could generate a serious backlash, possibly even an alliance with the Halettites against us.

The plot is, as far as I can tell, as likely to succeed as any, so we may be looking at a serious setback for the Domain. I hope this warning will allow you to capitalise on the news when it does come, prepare some confusion for House Foryth and its allies.

I will leave for Qalathar as soon as I hear what happened, and hopefully arrive there in advance of the official couriers. My *Aegeta* is shaping up well, and has demonstrated a good turn of speed up to now; I have every confidence in her ability to outrun hostile vessels even if fully laden.

In urgency,
Hamilcar Barca

CHAPTER XXIII

'What tact and restraint,' the harbourmaster remarked, scanning down through the decree. He exchanged glances with one or two of the other men. 'They don't do things by halves.'

I craned over the shoulder of the cargomaster, who obligingly moved slightly to the right to let me see better.

'Won't affect you so much in the out islands,' he said. 'If you are an out islander.'

This was Ilthys, so no-one commented on my obviously Thetian features. They were only half Archipelagan here anyway.

I turned my attention back to the decree, automatically filtering out most of the stilted wording I was so used to in order to get to the gist of it.

It has been made known to us by His Imperial Highness . . . firstly, that the traitor and heretic Ithien Cerolis Eirillia . . . all holdings, assets and property seized by our court.

Eshar had taken to using the royal plural again, I noticed. It wasn't something the Thetian Emperors had always bothered with.

Furthermore that . . . the aforesaid traitor and heretic is by decree of Courts Secular and Courts Religious condemned to death – they didn't seem to do anything else these days – *must be handed over to our officers or those of our holy Domain universal for execution.*

It was a tenet of Thetian law and the Imperial Peace that no-one except Imperial officers had the authority to take life. Eshar hadn't changed that, it suited his autocratic nature too well. He'd just added 'and the Domain.'

It is our belief that the said traitor is in hiding in the territory of Ilthys . . . unless he shall be handed over to the representatives of powers secular or religious within four days . . . a reward of one thousand corons to be paid . . . to prevent the taint of heresy from spreading within this territory of Ilthys . . . penance to be done for this disobedience against the laws of Ranthas . . . two hundred citizens shall do penance for the good of the city. Should these conditions still remain unfulfilled, then by the authority of our holy Domain universal Interdict shall be placed on the city, that it shall be sundered from the blessed fire of Ranthas . . . so it shall be done.

Admiral Vanari, Imperial Navy; Interim Avarch Abisamar, Ordo Inquisitori.

Abisamar. I remembered Abisamar, and not with any affection either. He had been the Avarch whose hunt for Qalathari heretics had crippled Mauriz's *Lodestar* and brought us to Ilthys. A typical, bigoted Halettite, definitely not an ascetic, but one who had displayed a dangerous and unusual knowledge of how the Archipelago worked.

That wasn't good news, and none of the rapidly growing crowd around me seemed to think so either.

'Who do they think they are?' the cargomaster demanded. 'Chasing after shadows. Rumours are all they've got to go on.'

'They don't need facts, my dear fellow,' said the harbourmaster, a thin, fussy man whose attention to detail had nearly driven the *Manatee*'s captain mad. 'Most irritating, whatever happens there'll be trouble.'

'Trouble for all of us,' said one of the dockers I recognised from the other day, cargomaster at the undersea harbour. His words sparked off an argument among the shipmen and I slipped away, walked back along to the *Manatee* and told Vespasia what the notice had said.

She glanced up at the town, a jumble of houses and colonnades on the clifftop. 'Oailos thought that coming here would do more harm than good, and I'm beginning to think he was right. Now, when we leave, Ilthys will suffer.'

'We could make it obvious that Ithien's left.'

'Bad idea. They'd chase us instead.'

I looked away from the city and saw a handcart emerge from between two warehouses, followed by two more. There were three or four men and women accompanying them, and they began threading their way towards us.

'All done?' Palatine called as she approached, running ahead of the others.

I nodded. 'We left as much space as we could.'

'Give us a hand with this lot, then we're ready to go. You heard about the proclamation, of course?'

'Two Sacri just nailed it up on the harbourmaster's board.'

'We passed them coming down and guessed that was what they were up to.' She ran up the gangplank to join us on deck. 'There'll be trouble. People in the city aren't happy. Some of them aren't pleased that he's come back, others – well, they're mutinous, I suppose. Similar things happened in one or two other places, and the city always comes off badly.'

'Are they really that fond of Ithien?' Vespasia asked.

'It's not Ithien so much,' one of the men said. 'A lot of people have already been shipped off as penitents, and after each purge is over someone's realised that a fair number of the people who've gone couldn't be heretics. It's not as bad them taking genuine heretics, not if it stops a Crusade, but so many – something's wrong.'

'I'd be happier if the lot of them vanished under the waves,' said the *Manatee*'s captain, coming up the gangplank again. 'Let's get this on board.'

It took less than an hour with seven people helping, and by the time we'd finished the remainder of the *Manatee*'s crew had appeared with smaller but more valuable items – including a small cache of flamewood one had managed to procure. From what his friends said about it, I got the distinct impression he was the crew's wheeler-dealer.

'Better hide that,' the captain said. 'See if we've got a watertight container, and stow it in the bilge. If we're caught with that, there'll be hell to pay.' He turned to Vespasia and me. 'You're not coming with us, are you?'

'No. We're needed here for the time being.' I avoided mentioning Ithien's name.

'He'd be a lot better off away from here, but he won't listen.' The captain was being circumspect too, a good precaution given the reward offered. 'I'll probably see you in a few days. Many thanks for your help.'

We said goodbye and left them to cast off; by the time we reached the road up into the town, *Manatee* was already under tow and heading out past the frigates.

We heard the shouting before we came in through the gates, a muffled roar from somewhere further in the city. The two Thetian guards were nowhere to be seen, and the streets were oddly deserted.

'Trouble,' Vespasia said. 'We need to steer clear of it.'

The sound was coming from the agora ahead, louder and clearer now. One or two people ran past us just as the noise swelled and died again.

'A riot?' There was a bend in the street ahead, so I couldn't see into the agora or hear anything clearly.

'Sounds like it,' she said. 'We don't want to get caught up in it, although I assume it's not a religious riot. It's been a few months since the last purge. This must be to do with Ithien.'

Both of us were curious to find out what was happening, but caution won out and we took a side-street to cut off the agora. This was one of the poorer parts of the city, and the paintwork was shabby and old, the paving irregular and dusted with the occasional scatter of debris. We passed a dyers' workshop, the drain outside it stained dark by years of waste materials. Every so often, as we crossed a street leading inwards, the noise of the crowd was louder again for a few seconds.

'Empty, isn't it?' said Vespasia in a hushed voice as we went through a passageway underneath a house. 'We should have visited the oceanographers here while no-one was looking.'

'And why would you want to do that?' said a sharp voice from one side. I stopped abruptly, looking into the shadows of a doorway from where the voice had come. An apartment building, from the looks of it, with the door open and an old woman sitting on a chair just inside, working on something I couldn't see because of the gloom. 'Two fine young people, loyal supporters of the old Governor of course. Why aren't you shouting like everyone else?'

Her voice took on a nasal pitch as she shuffled round. 'Maybe you've got other things to do. Maybe you're oceanographers, come here to work your black arts on our city and wreck our fisheries.'

We started walking on again, but her voice followed us, rising in tone as we went. 'Heretics! Oceanographers!'

Another voice answered, a man's this time, and I quickened my pace. Vespasia didn't need any encouragement to catch up.

'They went that way!' I heard the old woman say. We headed into the next side street as more voices sounded behind us, footsteps. This was something I'd never expected, but as I looked ahead I realised we were heading straight towards the agora.

'Foreign oceanographers!' someone else shouted behind us, and we started running, dodging the missing paving stones and the empty crates stacked up on one side.

We turned a corner and almost ran into a solid wall of people, their backs turned to us, and the sound hit me like a wave. Even from here I could see that the agora was crowded with people, a sea of them unbroken except by the trees, and caught a glimpse of the firmly shut temple gates.

'Into the crowd,' Vespasia said.

'No!' I caught her by the arm before she could move any further. 'If we're taken for spies in that, they'll rip us apart.'

'ITHIEN!' the crowd roared, the first time I'd heard anything, and then they started chanting, something that sounded like *No more penance*.

I'd never seen or even heard of anything like this since the purges began – why in peaceful Ilthys, of all places? What had driven them to this? I would have expected to see it in Qalathar, or the more volatile far south, but not so close to Thetia. It wasn't even as if Ilthys had suffered beyond endurance, because compared to Sianor and Beraetha it hadn't suffered at all.

I didn't think that was what mattered to the people of Ilthys, but at that moment our pursuers caught up with us, and we had other things to worry about.

'Oceanographers, are you? Come to wreck our fishing fleet again?' said the ringleader, a smallish man with dirty, floppy hair, flanked now by two big men.

'No,' I said evenly, able for once to disguise my concern. My heart was thumping against my chest, but I was more afraid of the mob in the square than these men.

'Of course you'd say that.'

More men were coming now, forming a smaller mob separated from the main one only by us. One or two of the people at the back of the agora crowd were turning round now, and they seemed to be friends of the lot who'd cornered us.

'What do we do with oceanographers?' the small man asked, looking round. There were ugly expressions on one or two faces. 'The Domain obviously doesn't have its eye on them, not if they're wandering around like this.'

'Their masters can't protect them now,' said another man, leering at Vespasia. 'How about we have some fun first?'

'I don't need anyone to protect me,' I said, staring him in the face. 'Why don't you go and deal with the right people for a change?'

It was the wrong thing to say, and there was a murmur from the crowd, some of them started moving closer. I saw a mild scuffle to one side, one man elbow another out of the way and push his way to the front.

'They're not spies!' he shouted, as the small man motioned his thugs forward. 'Stop!'

I felt a surge of relief as I recognised Oailos, followed by the moustachioed mason from the other night.

'We caught them creeping through the backstreets!' shrilled the old woman from somewhere behind.

'I saw them with the Governor!' said Oailos. 'The *real* Governor, not this tight-fisted stooge they've put in charge now. They're his friends!'

The mood changed, and the small man looked uncertain.

'Are you sure? You can't trust oceanographers.'

'Positive. You don't think I'd forget her face? They're Thetians, friends of the Governor from the old days.'

Thankfully his comment had been addressed to Vespasia, and I was glad Ravenna hadn't been here. She lost her temper at exactly the wrong moments sometimes.

I risked saying something. 'He wanted something done down at the harbour, we'd been working down there. Didn't want to get caught up in the agora in case they started arresting people.'

'Are you sure you saw them?'

The mason nodded. 'Absolutely. The Governor wouldn't be hanging around with spies. Unless they were his, in which case they're friends.'

There were nods of agreement, and I thought I heard disappointed muttering from the old woman. It was hard to understand this loyalty. I couldn't see how an aristo-cratic Thetian with all his arrogance had managed to win over Ilthys so completely. Even down to the artisans and inhabitants of the poorer areas, it seemed.

'Have you seen the decree?' the mason asked.

I nodded. 'Is that what the riot's about?'

'Of course. Bastards want to start shipping everybody off again. Just because Ithien couldn't stand that thug of an Emperor any more. Who knows what the Domain makes them do in Qalathar?'

'They build more ziggurats, dig canals through the forest so that Halettite farmers can make a living there,' Vespasia said.

'I heard they burn people when they don't work hard enough,' said the old woman, screeching to make herself heard. She evidently didn't want to be left out of what was going on, even if she'd been denied her witch-hunt. 'Just in the street, like that. Do they? You must have seen it.'

'You've lived through it,' the mason said. 'Which is more than we have. Oailos here — you remember him, don't you?'

There were nods of agreement.

'You were shipped off as a heretic,' the small man said. 'Otherwise the Inquisition would have arrested your whole guild.'

'I was shipped off because Badoas denounced me,' Oailos said. 'Had I ever done anything to any of you? Did you know I didn't worship Ranthas?'

There were uncertain nods.

'Don't you remember what happened?' the other mason demanded. He must have been an old friend of Oailos. 'When the temple was damaged, and they made us repair it for nothing? Two months without pay because it was the work of God, and so we all had to starve while we rebuilt their temple.'

'I remember,' shouted the old woman, eager to retake the limelight. She pushed herself through the crowd in two seconds flat. 'You told them you weren't going to

354

work for nothing any more, the whole guild went on strike until that little worm Badoas denounced you as a heretic and got himself made guildmaster.'

'Then we had to work another month, while Badoas got to line his pockets,' the moustachioed mason said.

'Five of us denounced and shipped off as penitents because we wouldn't do their dirty work for them,' Oailos said. 'How is that divine justice? How is that saving us from the Crusade they hang over our heads?'

People had turned from the back of the crowd to look now and I saw, like a ripple of light, the shift in focus as people turned to see what their neighbours were looking at, and the square turned to look at Oailos.

To his credit, he went on, even when at a motion from the small man the thugs lifted Oailos up so the crowd could see. No doubt he was glad that Oailos had stolen his limelight, he didn't seem the sort of person who wanted to be prominent in that way.

'They come here, they take our children and our money, they arrest people and torture them into confessing. Every month we have to breathe in the stench of smoke as they roast more of us alive!' Oailos had lifted his voice, was roaring out at the now-silent crowd, but I doubted that many of them could hear or even see him.

It didn't matter. In a way, that was better, given that he was out of sight of the Temple and thus had a chance of remaining anonymous.

'Do you feel lucky, people of Ilthys? Do you feel special? NO? Well, you'd better, because you're still here. You aren't breaking your backs doing penance for the Domain, cutting down forests and building canals so they can settle their own farmers on our islands. We have to bow and scrape to the priests and their lackeys, give everything we have to fund their butchery, watch while they burn our relatives, but we're lucky.'

He was better as a speaker than I'd expected, but as I

watched, one of the other men whispered that he had been vice-master of the masons' guild, and so wasn't exactly a novice in public speaking.

'There's never enough food. Why? Is it because the oceanographers have betrayed us? There were oceanographers I met doing lifetime penances for nothing at all! We've been told that they destroyed our fishing fleet, that they are all heretics out to destroy the Archipelago. Or could it be, could it just possibly be, that the Domain wants us to think that?'

There was an angry roar. He was on shaky ground here, given the hatred of oceanographers that the Domain had managed to instil in the people of Ilthys.

'Why should they? Why after two hundred years should they do anything other than measure the currents for us, tell our fishermen where the fish will be and when it's safe to go out? Why should they want to destroy the cities they were born in, lived and died in? Do you remember when we lost five ships in a whirlpool nobody had predicted? Do you remember Phassili and his ship? The Domain burned Phassili's sister because they said she'd lied about the current and killed her own brother! Do you think she would have done that?'

There was another roar, but more subdued this time.

'Let me tell you a story the Domain's kept from us all this time. It's about a city in Oceanus, about half the size of Ilthys. It was a rich city, and the Domain wanted it so they could make weapons for a Crusade. Five years ago the Domain were already planning a Crusade, so they wanted this city for themselves. They wanted to take it over and burn its leaders at the stake.'

I stared up at him, wondering how he knew this. He was embellishing, but I could see why. I just hoped he wasn't going to bring me into this. If this came up again, who knew what revenge the Domain might decide to take on Lepidor?

'They were defeated,' Oailos shouted, 'by a few oceanographers and a motley assortment of marines! They were humiliated, driven out! And who exactly were the priests who survived this? I can tell you their names. They were Midian and Sarhaddon! Our mighty Exarch, with his murdering soldiers he claims are invincible, was humbled by a few oceanographers. That's why he hates them, that's why he and his crony Sarhaddon want to destroy them!'

This time there was silence.

'And some of those oceanographers were friends of our Governor, Ithien. Our real Governor, not our esteemed admiral, who can't get dressed in the morning until that fat butcher Abisamar tells him what to wear. The Domain want to arrest Ithien because he shows them up as the dictators they are. If that ignorant Halettite peasant Abisamar decides someone is guilty, then no-one can stop him. We all know his favourite activities – burning, torturing, raping the women he's made his concubines.'

There was a roar from the crowd, which had moved out until it surrounded me completely, and I was pressed in on all sides by people craning to look up at Oailos as he shouted defiance at the Temple and its blind arch, a building where Abisamar had intended to try Mauriz on a trumped-up charge until Ithien intervened.

'So they'll tell us that if we refuse to obey them, if we don't keep on as their slaves, they'll treat us the same way and turn our city – our city, our clan, our home – into a barren wasteland and ship us all off to Qalathar. You all know what happened in Sianor and Beraetha. That will happen here if we don't bow our heads and turn the other cheek, until one morning we wake up and, like the esteemed admiral, we can't put our clothes on until they've told us what to wear.'

He shook his fist at the Temple, and I felt the crowd do the same, people all around me raising their hands until I did too, staring at the blank face of the Temple with a

357

loathing only deepened by the memories that were still very vivid in my head. It was like being carried along on the crest of the wave.

Someone started chanting – *Butchers* – and the shout was quickly taken up. The man who'd whispered to them started shouting, and again I had to join in. The noise was deafening, and the smell of so many people packed into the space was fairly unpleasant, but I screamed rage at the Temple with all the rest of them.

There was no response. No-one stirred behind the high walls that shielded its front – they hadn't been there when I came last time – and there were no signs of life from it, no cracks of thunder or detachment of Sacri.

'We are beneath their notice, Ilthys!' Oailos shouted, hardly audible at first. 'We are beneath their notice, because to them we're only raw materials, despised heretics and subjects who provide the blood for their grand designs! Where will they destroy next? Ilthys? How many of us will pay with our lives?'

The crowd shifted, and I was swept a little away from Oailos and from Vespasia, into the edge of a group of apprentices and merchants' sons, children of the wealthier parts of Ilthysian society from the look of them.

'Now they're asking us to hand over the Governor. The real Governor, not Abisamar's puppet. What has he done wrong? They don't bother to tell us, because it doesn't matter. They don't need excuses, they don't need trials. They come with the word of Ranthas! What is the word of Ranthas? There is only one word, and so they're all his faithful servants. The word of Ranthas is KILL!'

We shouted again at that, hurling our rage at the Temple like one vast, mindless animal, as if we could shatter it and bring down the walls simply by the power of our voices.

'Are we going to let them have our Governor? They took our President, our consuls, the guildmasters who dared to stand up to them. They took anyone they thought might cause them trouble, but they left all of us! So they're wrong. Will we let them arrest Ithien?'

'NO!' we screamed. My throat was hoarse already, but I shouted all the same, as the crowd followed Oailos's lead.

There was an ear-splitting crack, and I flinched.

Then a sudden wave of magical heat, and all at once the fifteen or so trees across the square burst into flame. A bright, scorching flame that consumed their leaves within seconds and burnt the crowd below. For a second the shouts went on, and then they became screams. I felt a sudden wave of pressure from one side as the apprentices were pushed into me, and I half fell against the man on my other side, only just retaining my balance.

There was a look of apprehension on the apprentices' faces as they stumbled to their feet, the relentless pressure of the crowd bearing down on us. Abruptly the people on one side moved away and I almost fell, caught myself just in time and started running, pursued by the vast, half-blind mass of people, as the flames leapt up from the trees.

I cannoned into someone else, pushed past them as I heard the pounding of hundreds if not thousands of running feet behind me. I was too short of breath to scream, but I could hear shrieks coming from further back into the square.

I looked frantically around for Vespasia, but there was no-one I recognised, and no time to stop. I kept on, sprinting into the side-street I had come down and blindly running on.

I'd barely taken one turn before I tripped over a loose paving stone, fell painfully on to the edge of a step. Someone kicked me in the side and sprawled over me as I rolled desperately out of the way. There were more people behind me, an endless tide of them.

I felt a hand grab me as I flattened myself against the wall. Someone dragged me up the steps and into an open doorway, where I slumped down against one wall and rubbed my knee. It was another apartment block like the one the old lady had been in; the paint was peeling off inside and there was hardly any light in the dark hallway.

I looked up to see who had rescued me, but he'd already stepped over me again and was dragging someone else into the safety of the doorway.

'Lucky you fell so close to me,' said my rescuer. 'Stay here until it's over.'

I recognised him, although it took me a moment to remember the dockers who'd told us the news of the new campaign. He'd been one of them, but I didn't see why he'd rescued me.

He hauled one or two more people out of the crowd as the stampede went on, and I realised that, for whatever reasons, he was helping everybody he could. There were six or seven people in the hall by the time the rush died down, and some of them seemed to know him.

I sat there in a daze in the hall as screams and shouting filled the air outside, until the chaos had died down and the street was quiet again.

'Best be going,' he said, hauling me to my feet. 'You live near here?'

'Yes.' I remembered taking a right turn, so I was almost at the edge of the artisan's quarter. 'I had a friend there.'

'Don't try looking for her,' he said. 'Go back to where you were staying, you could wander the streets for ever searching for each other.'

'Why did you help me?'

'You'd have died otherwise. You could have been my brother, my cousin, anyone. Good luck.'

I thanked him, walked slowly out of the door and looked around the street. There were one or two people still lying there, but none of them was alone. Most of the people fleeing this way had come from this quarter, and the casualties could well be friends or neighbours.

Further on, as I came into a wider street that I recognised, there were knots of people moving seemingly randomly and more bodies lying around. It was horrible – people crushed and mangled by the stampede, who only a few minutes before had been law-abiding citizens of Ilthys. One or two of them were pitifully small, but all of those I saw were being helped by someone.

I passed someone cradling a blackened arm to his chest, crying out for water until he saw a fountain, ran over and jumped into the pool. From somewhere I could still hear screaming.

Why? Why had they done this? Didn't they think simply dispersing the mob was enough – did they have to kill and maim people in the process? It would be Abisamar's doing, I knew it. Admiral Vanari, whatever his faults, couldn't and wouldn't have ordered this, It was an Inquisitor's malice, the punishment of Ranthas on Ilthys.

A woman screamed behind me, very close, and I looked round to see a detachment of red-cloaked figures coming down the street, occasionally stopping to grab a man or woman. Those they'd taken were being rounded up into a column under the supervision of two more Sacri, their swords held ready. It didn't seem to be everybody, just whoever they felt like seizing.

They took the woman who'd screamed and marched on down the street. I started moving away, as inconspicuously as possible, heard an enraged shriek from the woman, sharply cut off by the sound of a blow.

'Tie her,' I heard the leader say. 'She resisted arrest, she may be a heretic.'

I slipped into a side passage as their attention was distracted, watched them pass and wondered if anyone would ever see those hostages again.

CHAPTER XXIV

The news had flashed around the city like wildfire. We heard the shouting in the street and went outside to find a large number of people out there, with three or four people running along and shouting. Maybe it was just the shock of the news and the people gathered together like that, but there was an oppressive, sultry feel to the air.

The landlady had hurried down the steps to confer with her neighbour, and when we asked what happened, confided that Ithien been captured.

One of her friends seemed unable to believe it, said it was a vicious lie put about by the Domain, but then a man from across the street came over and said he'd spoken to someone who had seen it with his own eyes, had seen the Governor walk up to the gates of the Temple.

I felt as if I'd been winded, but this time it was Palatine who needed assistance. She closed her eyes and for a moment I thought she'd faint. She didn't, but she went very pale.

Sagantha had gone to ferret out every tiny piece of information he could in his usual efficient way, and the landlady and her friends had retreated into a little huddle.

Palatine sat down heavily on the edge of a stone fountain bowl below the house's steps, crushing a few tendrils of the oleander growing by the wall.

'How could he?' she said, shutting her eyes for a moment. 'What happened to him?'

I didn't say anything, since that was a question she could answer as well as me. In a way, it was the ultimate expression of his loyalty to Ilthys – but why? Why couldn't he have seen that we all needed him? There were some people who might have been more use as martyrs than alive, but Ithien wasn't one of them.

He'd been so alive, so joyful, when we met again in the bay, almost the Ithien I remembered, and back on home turf in his beloved Ilthys. That had been five days ago.

Now he was in the hands of the Domain.

'It's so stupid,' Palatine said. 'They'll torture him, make him tell them who his associates are. The Pharaoh, the Viceroy, the only two members of Eshar's family that he hasn't killed off yet. What an intelligent thing to do.'

He still didn't know that Ravenna was the Pharaoh, but that hardly made anything better.

She pressed her fists against her face as the sudden anger turned back to despair. She was crying now, something I'd never expected to see. It was painful to watch. I moved to comfort her but she waved me off without saying anything.

'You bastards!' she whispered, staring into the blue tropical sky, dotted today with fluffy white clouds. 'Wasn't it enough to kill Mauriz and Telesta, and Aelin, and Rhaisamel, and Diego, and Giova, and all the others? Why do you have to take him as well?'

The easiest path to take is always the one that involves the least bloodshed. Khalia's words rang suddenly in my head. Did that mean there was an easier way for the Domain to take, I wondered, or did that only apply to people with a few scruples?

Maybe it was just Khalia's idealism, or some lesser-known clause of the Isenic Oath that the Great Library physicians took. If there was a path that involved less bloodshed, I couldn't see it appealing to the butcher Prime and his blood-soaked fanatics.

They would torture and kill Ithien, who'd twice saved me from the Domain. What would any more of us dying accomplish? It was time that the Domain repaid me, and with the lives they deserved so little.

I could destroy the Temple, bring it down on their head – but that would kill too many innocent people inside. I'd discovered at Kavatang just how difficult it was for anyone to resist me when I used my magic properly. If none of those Council mages, Tehaman mind-mages or others had been able to stop me, there wouldn't be anyone in this small provincial Temple who could manage it. Especially if I had a chance to deal with Abisamar.

'Don't worry, Palatine,' I said and noticed, almost in passing, that my voice sounded different.

Someone called out further down the streets, and I heard a chorus of angry yells, people shouting Ithien's name.

Palatine looked up at me, her pain suddenly mixed with concern.

'It's too dangerous,' she said flatly.

'Not any more.'

There were more shouts, taken up by people nearby. The street was crowded now, and it was beginning to feel uncomfortably like the mob from yesterday morning. Who knew what the Domain would try this time?

Unless there was no-one left to try anything. Their mage wouldn't stand a chance, and once the mage was gone . . .

There was already someone standing on the steps brandishing a fighting stave, and a moment later he was joined by someone wielding a wicked-looking metal tool that looked like an instrument of torture.

'Another mob,' said Sagantha, suddenly appearing. 'Now we have problems.'

'We'll have more problems in a moment,' I said, as I dived into the crowd. People were already starting to move towards the centre, and more weapons were appearing as they grabbed whatever they could from their houses. One or two people even came out carrying antiquated fishing crossbows, older and bulkier versions of the ones we'd used on *Whitewake*.

'To the Temple!' someone shouted.

'Cathan, you fool!' I heard Sagantha shout, then he was out of earshot.

I was carried along by the mob again. This time it was advancing rather than retreating, but its anger was greater than its terror had been the previous time. We were running now, splitting up to charge down the narrower streets towards the back of the Temple. There was some organisation at work: a group of men who'd been in the street emerged from a furniture workshop as I came past, carrying a substantial-looking piece of timber that could double as a battering ram. The Temple might be protected, but I wasn't sure it could stand up to this kind of assault.

Nor could the crowd stand up to the mage, and Abisamar would probably order the hostages killed the moment he heard there was more trouble.

I shouted Ithien's name as I ran on, surrounded by a group of men whose features were distorted with fury – as were mine. More people joined us, coming out of houses clutching whatever weapons they could find. Thetis, there were even more of them than there had been yesterday. If the mage used fire this time, the deaths could be in the thousands.

I rounded a corner and saw the side wall of the Temple with the faint glow of its aether shield, just visible against a shadowed corner of the main building. There were Sacri on the walls – I could just make out their helmets as they crouched behind the parapet.

Already the street below the Temple was full, and the men with the ram were threading their way through the crowds to one of the back gates. There was a massive roar from over to the right, where people were gathering in the agora.

'Here, stones!' someone hissed, and I turned to see a

woman with her arms full of smooth, rounded stones. 'Take one!'

I took one, wondering whether it would be any use, and within a few seconds they were all gone.

A figure appeared on the Temple's turret, just visible from where I was standing. I could feel the magic crackling around him and recognised the bulky figure of Abisamar. A moment later, there was another ear-splitting crack, but this time all that happened was that the Avarch's amplified voice boomed out across the crowd.

'People of Ilthys!' he roared. 'You are heretics and traitors! Do not try to match you puny weapons against the might of the Domain, for all will perish in Ranthas's furnace! Only hell awaits you now. You will be cast into the fiery pit and burn in agony for all eternity, consumed by the flames but never dying through all the ages of the world!

'You have taken up arms against the holy Domain universal! You have screamed defiance at the emissaries of Ranthas on Aquasilva! You will be punished in this world and the next, and I hereby pronounce the sentence of the Inquisition!' He went on, his voice more measured now, inexorably pronouncing the sentence.

'This city of Ilthys is cast out of the grace of Ranthas. Its inhabitants are condemned to the fires of hell, excluded from all the rites and the chance of redemption through holy Ranthas. It shall have no fire whatsoever, no heat, no light save that of the sun.

'Look up into the sky. Can you see the clouds? Can you feel the heat in the air? A storm is coming, a storm that carries with it the wrath of Ranthas upon you all! As He in His mercy provides you with protection, so in His wrath He shall bring down the anger of his subject elements upon you all, and his servants *will not protect you*!

'You shall be left naked to the mercy of the winds and the waves, your ships shall be dashed against the quays, your fish traps shall be broken in pieces. You shall freeze to death in your houses, living on uncooked food, your children shiver in the night without warmth. There shall be no fire at all, no forms of heat at all save what the sun gives you. We shall see how long you survive.'

There was another crack, seemingly for effect, and the sky briefly flashed as if with lightning. There was less blue than there had been a few minutes ago. We hadn't had a storm since I'd been here, it was about time.

Or was it?

'You were warned!' Abisamar bellowed. 'You were warned of the consequences of disobedience, and you have left it too long. In your arrogance you believed that you had a voice! You do not. The will of Ranthas is absolute! There is no bargaining, there is no halfway! You are loyal servants of Ranthas or you are His enemies, and you have chosen to be His enemies. You will pay the price of heresy, of apostasy, as henceforth it will be paid across the world – at the mercy of His wrath!'

This was the Archipelago – no-one would freeze to death. But a city of twenty thousand people without fire, without heat of any kind, couldn't cope for long. Too many industries depended on it, there were too many people for them all to live off fruit, and slowly the island would begin to starve. Had they applied it to the whole island? I remembered how we'd evaded a smaller-scale Interdict on Sagantha's palace in Tandaris – the rest of the city had still had heat and light, and we'd managed to rig up a new aether connection.

Ilthys had no such luxury.

'Since we wouldn't want to give anyone our protection who didn't deserve it,' Abisamar said, more quietly but with his voice still amplified enough to be audible at the back of the crowd, 'we won't keep the hostages inside the Temple. They'll be in the outer gardens, and if any of them are still alive afterwards you'll be welcome to come and get them.'

He stepped back, and after a moment was out of sight. The Temple walls were deserted again except for the crouching Sacri.

I heard people shriek and hurl abuse; the noise came from the crowd in a vast groan. Thousands of faces lifted to the sky as the sun went in again, behind a cloud that was beginning to take on a threatening grey colour. We had another hour before the storm began, I reckoned, but it would build fast and strengthen. Three or four hours before the worst of it hit, I estimated, and it might last for several days. They intended to kill the hostages under cover of the storm, a final blow to Ilthys, that those who survived would find all of their missing friends and relatives dead.

It was monstrous, and the promised terror had taken the heart out of the mob. People looked uncertain, afraid, kept glancing up at the sky. I wasn't sure how many understood what Abisamar was saying, whether they thought it was simply a matter of facing this storm without the shield, rather than the truth – that storm after storm would come, wearing the city's defences down with no way for the Ilthysians for fight back. Or almost no way, at least. If only I could get to Ravenna, we might have a chance.

'Kill the bastards!' shouted the woman who'd been handing out stones. 'They'll leave our people out in the storm to die.'

People gave her uncertain glances now, though. 'What about our homes?' someone else said. 'All the fires gone, and with this storm coming too.'

'Just because none of your family were taken, you don't care!'

'Stop arguing!' said a tall man who cupped his hands and shouted, 'To the gardens! Ram the door! Rescue the hostages!'

The mob surged forwards, and some people began throwing stones at the battlements. The aether shield robbed them of their momentum, and most fell uselessly just inside. After a moment or two they were thrown back, and this time they did hit people. There was a panicked surge away from the walls, although not strong enough to cause another stampede. No-one threw any more stones.

The crowd was beginning to move towards the gardens. I moved to one side and stood in the shadow of a doorway. I closed my eyes, drawing on my rage at Ithien's imminent death and Abisamar's speech. It was the work of a moment, then I looked around for something, anything, to draw power from. Water – there was water, further on. I saw a fountain, just metres from the wall.

It was difficult to work from this far away, and I couldn't see the fountain clearly through the crowd, but I drew the water out of the bowl. I heard amazed cries from the people nearby. I compressed it more and more, then flung it at a point about halfway up the wall. A network of cracks spread outwards, but the wall held.

I heard shouts of alarm and rage from inside, and a moment later the mage appeared on the battlements accompanied by two or three acolytes holding burning brands. The mage pointed down the street at me, but this time it was easier. The air had become close and humid, there was plenty of water in it.

Thetis, it was so easy! I felt the same incredible energy running through me as I remembered from the court-room, the same sensation of being able to do anything I wanted.

I fixed my eyes on the fire-mage, and drew the moisture in a steadily closing sphere even as he was drawing on the power of the torches, and closed it around him like a mousetrap swinging shut.

The torches flickered for a second, then went out. The mage fell back, not dead but stunned at least, and there was a roar from the crowd. The men came forward with a battering ram, and began to batter the cracked places on

369

the wall. It was child's play to summon more impacts on that spot. I felt the crowd move as people backed away, leaving space for the wall to crumble.

After two or three more impacts, I didn't need to help them any more. The parapet wobbled and the rammers ran back, then there was a wild cheer as with a thunderous crash the wall of the Temple fell inwards into the outer courtyard, leaving a gaping breach in the wall.

I watched as the crowd surged in through the gap in a vast human wave, more and more people pouring through until the street began to empty. The priests didn't have a chance now, with so many people inside the Temple walls, and I only hoped they'd find Ithien in time.

I looked up again. I didn't think there was anything we could do against it – but if there was, Ravenna would surely know. We'd never planned to be on the receiving end of a storm, even a natural one.

I slipped into a side-street and started making my way through a maze of small lanes with white-painted walls on either side. With a feeling of unreality, I noticed baskets of flowers hanging from brackets, and glanced into half-hidden courtyards as I went past. There was no-one in sight, although at one point I heard voices from behind a wall, where some people were desperately trying to get things down into their cellar.

Our lodgings were quite a long way from Khalia's house, and it seemed to take forever to get there. The magic was still a fierce glow inside me, giving me more than enough strength to run, but several times I took wrong turns, and once I ended up very close to the agora and heard the sounds of the destruction of the Temple. Across and a little up from the agora, in a hidden square at the back, the Governor's Palace had its own shield. It stood with gates defiantly barred against the outside. Admiral Vanari had every intention of sitting out the fury, then. Good luck to him.

No-one stopped to ask me what was going on. They were too worried about the approaching storm. The sky was almost entirely grey now, and the wind from the sea was stronger than it had been a few minutes ago.

At last I came out into the wide, curving street with Khalia's house, although it took me a minute to realise how far along I was. I must have taken another wrong turning, since I was further up than I'd intended. I sprinted the last distance along the street, half-skidded into Khalia's courtyard and banged on the door.

It was one of her relatives who opened it. I muttered an apology and brushed past her to run upstairs. I hammered on Khalia's door, cursing the delay while she came over and unlocked it.

'You . . . What is it?'

'Storm,' I said, gasping for breath. I wasn't in as good shape as I'd imagined, and it was only the magic that was keeping me going. 'I need to ask Ravenna, she might know if there's anything we can do.'

'Why do you need her? You're a Tar'Conantur, you should be able to protect us on your own.' She obviously didn't know everything about my family, then.

'No time to explain, we work together. Please, where is she? It doesn't matter what condition she's in. You live here, if you want to keep on living then please help!'

I was almost incoherent by the end of that sentence, mixing up words and having to say them again, but Khalia realised I wouldn't be in this state without a good reason. She led me − frustratingly slowly − up another flight of steps, along a corridor and into a small blue-painted room with a bed and one or two other pieces of furniture. A flamewood lamp cast a reassuringly warm glow.

Ravenna was sitting at the desk writing, and I could tell from her expression that she wasn't in a good mood. She could feel the power being used, and I wondered why she hadn't just rushed out anyway.

'There's an emergency,' said Khalia briskly. 'Cathan needs your help.'

I explained what had happened at the Temple, and she only needed to look out of the window to see how serious the oncoming storm was.

'It isn't this storm that will matter,' Ravenna said, one hand briefly massaging her side. 'Things will get worse and worse.'

'I know.' There wasn't anything we could do about it, though.

Or was there? I closed my eyes, thinking as hard as I could, trying to remember what it was that nagged at the edge of my mind.

'Do we know how an Interdict works?' Ravenna said after a moment, before I'd had a chance to recall. The thought vanished, and I cursed silently.

I shook my head. 'Who knows? We couldn't do it with Water or Air, could we?' I tried to imagine how such a thing would work, but there didn't seem to be an obvious solution. Short of evaporating it all, how could you rid an entire city of its water? And prevent more falling from the sky, or bubbling up from the ground?

Evaporating. Steam. There was that thought again.

'Or Shadow,' she said, musingly. 'Or Light, or Earth. Certainly not Spirit.'

As for Time, no-one even knew why there was a god of Time in the first place, because he'd never had any followers and there was no such thing as time-magic.

'Cathan, this may sound a little academic, and I'm not sure this is the time for discussions,' Ravenna said, 'but haven't you noticed some problems with the way our magic works?'

I stared at her for a moment, wondering whether I shouldn't be with the others in the square, in case something had gone wrong and the prisoners were still being held.

'Please,' she said, as I wavered. 'Give me a minute or two to explain this, I might be able to help us.'

'I can't stay,' I said. 'Ithien, Vespasia . . .'

She looked uneasy for a second, but stood up and collected her storm-cloak.

'I'm coming with you then. Don't even try to argue.'

I did, but to no effect, and Khalia had no more success when we met her at the bottom. We walked through the courtyard and out into the streets, past row upon row of dark houses, not a light or a warm colour to be seen.

'What problems?' I asked, feeling a little guilty that I hadn't wanted to listen, had almost forced her to come out with me and explain.

'Steam,' she said, mirroring my own thought of a minute or two before. 'You heat water with fire, and it turns into steam. What element is it then?'

'Both,' I said, remembering endless dull lessons at the Citadel, Ukmadorian teaching us in great detail the limits of our provinces of magic, beyond which the power strayed over into another element's realm. There were crossovers, substances or areas which were mingling of two or more elements, and we'd had to learn lists of them.

Never rely on crossover substances, Ukmadorian had warned. *The power to be gained from them is severely reduced by their mingling with another element.*

'It's not such a good example now because there isn't really any around,' she said, her voice partly muffled by the hood.

'Example of what, though?'

'Of how the order of things breaks down,' she said. 'Read the *Book of Ranthas*, or any explanation of the nature of magic. Each element is separate, ruled by its own god or goddess. We know that, everybody on the planet knows that. So why are there grey areas? Steam, mud. Flamewood lamps, for heaven's sake – fire and light together. People forget there's supposed to be an element Light. No-one worships Phaeton because all his followers sided with the Domain two hundred years ago.'

I still didn't see what she was getting at. This was higher theology, the province of men who had spent their lives pondering the questions of which element steam fell into, or where fire hid before it was coaxed from wood. I'd never had much time for theology, although Ravenna had often seemed more interested.

I thought I heard a splash behind us, looked round to see whether someone was following us. No – only someone pouring water out into a drain. There were few people about, even in this broad a street.

We turned into a narrow road leading in towards the agora, full of drips from overhanging balconies.

'But how does this help us with the Interdict?'

'Patience! Now, think,' she instructed. 'We can both use two elements, for different reasons. That's most unusual. Ukmadorian told us it was more proof that the Domain were wrong in insisting that there could only be one god, because we belong to the provinces of two.'

I wondered what Sarhaddon would have said to that. He could probably run rings around Ukmadorian's powerful but blinkered intellect. If I remembered rightly, Sarhaddon felt that there was only one true god, that the others were merely elemental spirits.

'Sorry if I'm taking my time, but it's better if I explain – are we going in the right direction, by the way?'

I checked at the next side street, but I was sure we were going the right way. Again, I had the feeling of someone following me, but when I turned my head and peered around the hood there was no sign of anyone. I was getting paranoid.

'Go on,' I said, but my mind was more on Ithien and Vespasia than on her – unfair, I knew, but I didn't see how this was helping.

'Why can we use two elements? Tell me,' she

demanded. 'I have to be sure you're listening.'

'You're turning into a teacher,' I accused.

'I'm not having an easy time of it.'

Was this her revenge for these days of inactivity with no-one to talk to?

'We've been taught them both.'

'Not quite. *I* was taught them both, you're part elemental, so you didn't have to learn.'

They hadn't liked the idea of us learning two elements' magic, not at all. I hadn't particularly wanted to, given that the techniques for each were so different and it would have meant learning a whole new type of magic.

'And you were very young when you started,' I said.

'Exactly. I had the time. In any case, I couldn't learn more than two.'

'Ravenna, what is this about?' I demanded, as we reached a small square with a tiny fountain in the middle. A café was just being closed up against the storm – and because he couldn't serve hot food or coffee any more, I supposed. 'Is there any point to this?'

She stopped, grabbed my arm before I could walk on, and swung me round to face her.

'Yes there is,' she said, suddenly furious, 'but you're too caught up with your own problems to listen!' She glanced around, eyes suddenly narrowed, then left me behind and darted over to the street we'd just come from.

There was a cry, and a moment later she pulled a man in a shabby red cloak out of it. Amadeo? What was he doing here?

'Spying on us, no doubt,' Ravenna said, pulling him over to join us. He was bigger than either of us, but even with Ravenna in a weakened state, he lacked the physical training we both had.

'You were working your evil magic,' Amadeo said defiantly. 'I followed you to see if I could prevent you.'

'Still the same old tune,' Ravenna said contemptuously.

A thought struck me. 'The city is under Interdict, Amadeo,' I said. 'Do you know how an Interdict works?'

He stared at me for a moment.

'Of course,' he said. 'Ranthas is the embodiment of Fire. It is His gift, and His mages can prevent anyone else from using Fire without His permission.'

Straight from the Catechism, but I'd forgotten it. 'So no fire will be able to light anywhere in the city?' I asked, stating the obvious.

'Or on the island,' he said, regaining some of his confidence. 'Do not think you can thwart His purposes so easily.'

I stopped Ravenna before she could lash out at him. 'If the fire-mage is dead, will the Interdict be lifted?'

'No,' said Amadeo, with a cold smile. 'Only a fire-mage may call fire on the island, and only a fire-mage may lift the Interdict. Your heretic powers are no use now.'

Ravenna stared at me for a moment. 'No fire-mage would lift the ban unless the Domain allowed it,' she said.

'The Domain will not allow it to be lifted until all heretics have been hunted down.'

'We saved your life,' said Ravenna. 'You were too cowardly to face death, so you decided we must be agents of Ranthas.'

'You were. He did not intend me to die.'

'No, he wanted you to see something,' Ravenna said. She dragged him over to the café, where the disconsolate owner was just taking the last of his tables indoors.

'Excuse me,' she said, 'May I ask you a rather odd favour?'

'We're closed,' he said, 'but I've still got cold drinks. Cold drinks are all there'll be now.'

'We'll buy drinks,' she said, 'but do you have a sheet of paper?'

The man looked bemused, led us inside the café and poured each of us a spiced fruit juice. I paid for them, since neither of the others had any money.

'You want paper?' the man asked doubtfully.

'If they want a piece of paper, then get them one,' said his wife, a small dapper woman, emerging through the bead curtain behind the bar.

The man found a sheet of paper, and Ravenna crumpled it up, laid it on her outstretched palm as the couple looked on curiously. Amadeo stood off to one side with a contemptuous expression.

'I apologise in advance if nothing happens,' she said to all of us. 'I'm just testing a theory.'

There was a silence broken only by the hissing of the rain outside. She closed her eyes, and I felt the unmistakable tingle of magic. It grew stronger and stronger, her expression more and more intense, but nothing seemed to be happening.

Then, without warning, the sheet of paper burst into flame.

CHAPTER XXV

I saw Ravenna's instinctive reaction as a look of pain crossed her face. For a moment or two she held the burning paper there, then she threw it on to the polished wooden surface of the bar and watched until it was consumed and only a pile of ash remained. She pressed her hand against the wet fabric of her tunic.

'Are you Domain?' the café-owner asked, backing away nervously.

'No,' she said. 'I'm not.'

The contempt on Amadeo's face had vanished, replaced by a curious mixture of scorn and disbelief, as if he wanted to ridicule what she'd just done but couldn't bring himself to.

I stared at her, then at the ash. That time in Amadeo's cell she'd done this, but I'd forgotten all about it. But she'd created fire.

'You've burnt your hand,' said the woman quietly a moment later, then went behind the curtain again and came back with a wet cloth. Ravenna accepted it gratefully, squeezing it against her palm.

It was an anticlimax, after the astonishing moment when the paper had burst into flames. Flames that had been created by a mage of Shadow, of the element the Domain most reviled.

'That's impossible,' Amadeo said weakly.

'No it isn't,' the café-owner said brusquely. 'You've seen it.'

'Fire is the embodiment of Ranthas from which all life comes,' Amadeo repeated. The café-owner gave him a look of disgust.

'I know, he's a priest,' Ravenna said. 'We rescued him to use as a hostage.'

Neither of us wanted to be thought of as Domain, so almost without thinking I drew on a tiny bit of my water-magic and transferred the water from her sodden tunic into the cloth she was holding against her hand.

'Do you have a torch or two?' Ravenna asked the café-owner.

We left a moment or two later, after Ravenna had lit the fire in his hearth. No matter how he tried, the tinder-box refused to produce a spark. Ravenna had defied the Interdict, but it was still in place. Lifting it was something else again.

Amadeo followed us along more alleys and into the agora, not saying another word. We both ignored him.

There were quite a few people in the agora, and from the look of it they had begun looting the Temple, no longer the home of Ranthas but a devastated building that had housed the butcher Abisamar. I doubted any of the priests had survived the mob, but there would be troops inside the Governor's Palace, and I wondered why there was no sign of them. Vanari should surely have come to the priests' rescue by now. Maybe he simply didn't have enough men.

I couldn't see anyone I recognised, but there was no reason for them to be out in the rain. If Ithien had survived, he'd be under cover somewhere in the Temple, not out there in the howling wind under black and angry clouds.

The gates to the Temple, set inside a huge blind arch on its façade, had been ripped from their hinges and thrown on to the beds of the small ornamental garden just in front. There was no-one on guard, only people staggering out under loads of cloth from the Temple's walls and altars.

The echoing antechamber with its red walls had been stripped bare of anything valuable, and it looked as though people had even tried to prise up the tiles from the floor in one area. I wondered who'd had the authority to stop them.

'Listen,' said Ravenna. 'In the hall.' She gestured through a narrow doorway to one side. 'Voices.'

Four years ago we'd come out this way after Ithien had rescued us from Abisamar's trial, when we had emerged into the street to the delighted surprise of the Thetian consuls when they discovered that Palatine was still alive.

Now, as we came into the hall, I knew straight away that this was a more sombre occasion. A group of people were gathered around someone lying on the dais, and I knew with an awful wrench who it had to be.

'Cathan,' Oailos said, looking up as we came in. He must have seen my expression. 'Don't worry. He'll live.'

Vespasia was there, looking shaken but otherwise unharmed – so were Sagantha and Palatine, and several of the others from the dam.

Ithien was unconscious, lying on a pile of cloaks and what looked like an altar cloth, and the arm of his tunic was stained with blood. There was a bruise on his cheekbone that would take a while to fade.

'What happened?' I asked.

'They wanted to save him for a public execution,' Oailos said. 'Some of my guild got inside and attacked the Sacri, distracted them while he could get away. Good friends to me.'

'I'm sorry.'

He nodded. 'The Domain will pay for them,' Oailos said, an ugly look on his face. He turned to one of the men from the dam, another Ilthysian. 'Call the guildmasters together. We have the Thetian puppet Governor to deal with still.'

But the messenger had barely gone when I heard a commotion from the entrance hall, and the puppet Governor himself appeared, in naval uniform with an escort of armoured marines. There were two other men with him, one a Thetian official and the other . . . the other was Hamilcar Barca.

To my surprise, Admiral Vanari didn't march straight in and order us all arrested. A short but well-built man in his late forties, he looked around the room for a moment, motioned to his troops to stay put.

'I don't know what to make of this,' he said finally. 'Rebellion, heresy, treason, sacrilege, I could spend all day listing the crimes that have been committed.'

'Where do you want to start?' Oailos demanded.

'No,' said Sagantha, in a voice that brooked no argument. 'Ithien asked us not to shed any more blood, we will respect that.'

'I don't think this Thetian lackey counts,' said Oailos. 'Who are you to tell us what to do, in any case? You're not Ilthysian.'

'You heard what Ithien wanted,' Sagantha said. 'We hold the cards at the moment, Admiral, as I'm sure you realise.'

'Not for long,' Vanari said. 'The Emperor won't tolerate this, nor will the Exarch. Ilthys will be attacked as soon as they hear about it.'

'And what of your own part in this? You failed to protect the Temple or save the Avarch. I don't think your career is going to flourish after this fiasco.'

'I was supposed to restore order against a mob and a heretic mage with fewer than a hundred troops. Yes, I have failed,' the admiral admitted. 'Unless I can restore order now.'

'Little chance of that,' Oailos said. 'We rule the city now.'

'We?'

'The guilds. Our own officials, until Ithien recovers.'

'You will rule for two or three weeks, until the Emperor arrives with his fleet. The ships left in Thetia are more than enough to deal with this insurrection,' Vanari said. 'If you surrender now, he won't have to besiege the town, and I may be able to secure a trial for you under Thetian law rather than Domain. This cannot go unpunished, you must realise that.'

'He's right,' Ravenna said. 'There's no way we can hold the city.'

'So we should just give ourselves up?' Oailos demanded. 'You know what will happen. You're a mage, for Thetis's sake, it'll be even worse for you. Or maybe you mean to slip away and cause trouble somewhere else.'

'I am implicated in this as much as any of you,' she said. 'The Domain have been hunting me for seven years, I have just as much to lose.' Twenty-four years would be more accurate, but evidently she didn't want to make that widely known.

'On a more practical level,' Sagantha said, addressing the Thetian admiral again, 'you have a crisis on your hands. No fires, no heat. In three weeks there may not be enough people left in Ilthys for the Emperor to punish.'

'You exaggerate, but I see the problem,' the Admiral said. '*Domine* Abisamar neglected to exclude my palace from the Interdict, so I am in as bad a position as any of you.'

'Or not, as the case may be,' Ravenna said. She took the café-owner's torch out from under her cloak.

Would she be able to do it in here? I didn't know, but as she closed her eyes and I felt the tingle of magic, I willed her to be able to do it. Please, Ranthas.

As before, there was an uncertain pause. Then the tiniest flame flickered on the oil, spread until the torch was ablaze, lighting up the grey hall with a welcome glow.

'As you can see,' she said, to everyone this time, 'the Domain doesn't have as much power as it thinks.'

'You're inside the Temple,' someone pointed out.

'She made fire in a house across the agora,' Amadeo

said, an unnoticed figure in the corner. 'She has the gift of fire-magic.'

There was a sudden profound silence.

Oailos looked at her suspiciously. 'You claimed to be a heretic,' he said finally.

'I am,' she said. 'Don't you see? The Domain claims that only the *righteous* can use fire-magic.'

All eyes were on her then, and it took a moment to sink in.

'Do these boundaries mean anything?' she said into the quiet. 'How can their god be the only one, when a mage of Shadow can call fire in a temple of Ranthas?'

I looked round, taking in the expressions of utter astonishment on people's faces. Only a few looked anything other than stunned. The two admirals – Sagantha and Vanari – both looked grey and ten years older, although I suspected for different reasons. Oailos's pugnacious expression had disappeared, replaced with outright awe. Amadeo seemed to be in the middle of a religious revelation – which was fair enough, in a way.

It was Palatine who finally broke the silence.

'Take all the wood,' she said. 'Everything that will burn, and pile it in the middle of the square. Pour oil on it, make a fire that they'll be able to see in Tandaris.'

'Give them a hand,' said Vanari to his men, a moment later.

In the end we all helped, taking the benches and chairs from the hall, the few, plain vestments that remained inside the Temple, and the fuel for the dead sanctuary fire in the Temple, including a few flamewood branches. People saw what we were doing and helped without being asked. A crowd had begun to gather, wondering what was going on. Hoping.

People poured oil over it as Palatine had suggested, trying to make it just sufficient to make the ancient wood burn and not be put out by the light rain.

We left a wide circle around it, and by the time Ravenna stepped forward people had come from all over the city, the third such crowd in as many days. This time there were no priests left to wreak vengeance, only the charred trees around the agora as a reminder of what had happened.

It took a little longer this time, and for a moment I thought she would fail, that somehow those first two times had been exceptions. But then a spark flared, flames began dancing over the oil, spreading round until the whole pile was ablaze and orange flames were leaping up, defying the rain.

'What Ranthas gives, He may never take away!' Ravenna shouted after a moment.

It would be known as the Miracle of Ilthys, that fire, bringing life back where the Domain had tried to take it away. People came forward with torches, sticks of wood, anything they could manage to take from the fire and relight the fires in their own homes and the town furnaces under the Temple.

Within an hour, the lights of Ilthys had come back on, challenging the storm to throw at them whatever it could, It had taken perhaps an hour for the Interdict to be broken, an hour to defy and overcome the greatest weapon the Domain could call on.

We stood there in the rain even once the storm itself had hit, and we'd placed a protection over the fire. Ilthys could warm itself against the storms as it had done for two centuries.

Even as people relit the fires in their homes, though, they brought more fuel to keep the beacon in the square going. The charred trees had been too badly burned ever to give fruit again, so they were cut down one by one and fed on to the fire. New trees would soon be brought from plantations further inland, and in time they would grow to match the old ones.

As I stood there watching the flames, I felt a tap on my shoulder. It was Palatine, with Hamilcar standing a little behind her. She drew all of us a little away from the Ilthysians.

'I can't say how glad I am to see you all again,' Hamilcar said gravely. His beard looked a little bedraggled in the rain, and he had a faded military storm-cloak on over his finery. 'The Count, your father, still asks me if I have news of you, Cathan. We haven't heard anything for more than a year.' I'd managed to get a few letters a year off to him from the Retreat, but nothing from Qalathar.

'The Domain's too busy sending decrees back and forth for anyone else to get a word in edgeways,' I said.

Before anyone could start asking more questions, Hamilcar raised a hand. 'We can talk later, there's a lot to catch up on. I have to tell you something which Sagantha, for his own reasons, seems not to have let on.'

Palatine looked accusingly at him.

'I defected from the Council three weeks ago,' Sagantha said levelly. 'What have you heard?'

'Heard?' Hamilcar said. 'I know.' He looked round at the rest of us. 'There's no longer an Emperor. Reglath Eshar has been assassinated.'

PART FIVE:
THE CLOUDS OF WAR

CHAPTER XXVI

A warm gust of moisture-laden air heavy with the scent of subtropical vegetation greeted me as I waded the last few feet through the surf. The sand underfoot was white, very pale and bleached under the brilliant summer stars, with a crescent moon just strong enough to sketch the shadows of palm trees on the beach.

There was only one person waiting for me under the edge of the forest, an indistinct figure in a tunic and light cloak.

It felt too warm for a cloak, although it was hours after sunset, and not even the chill of the gentle breeze blowing off the trees was uncomfortable. The island and its fellows apparently existed in a climate of their own, a tiny outpost of Thetia several thousand miles from its heart.

I heard splashes behind me as Palatine joined me on the sand, the only noise beside the plashing of wavelets and the haunting calls of night birds in the forest.

'Only two of you?' the figure asked, coming out of the shadows. It was a woman, not much older than I was, with a classically Thetian face, her hair bound back in a braid. It wasn't a servant's tunic she was wearing, and I wondered who she was, that she'd been sent to escort us.

'Only two,' I confirmed.

She stared at me for a moment, her eyes hidden in shadow. 'I didn't expect you to look so much like him,' she said finally. Mine was, after all, a family in which some of the dead inspired more fear and respect than many of the living.

'My brother is dead,' I said. 'He can have nothing to do with this.'

'You're mistaken there. Anyway, enough of this. Follow me.'

The forest had seemed unbroken at first glance, but as we reached the top of the beach I saw that was only an illusion; a curving path where the undergrowth had been cleared ran back into the trees. The canopy overhead was so thick that only faint dapplings of moonlight shone through, but my night vision was more than good enough to follow her along the earth track.

We never left the sound of the waves behind, although the buzzing of cicadas and other insects was almost as loud. The path ran parallel to the shoreline and slightly upwards.

Our destination was much closer than I'd imagined, an unassuming single-storey house of white stone surrounded by a terrace, just high enough above the water to escape the battering of storm waves. A flight of steps led down to a small quay in the lagoon below it, but from up here I could see the water wasn't deep enough for us to have come ashore anywhere nearby.

'How many people know about this place?' I asked, as we left the forest, walking through a stand of shrub palms no taller than I was.

'There are thousands of such houses across the Archipelago,' our guide said, without turning round. She moved with the fluid grace which I'd come to associate with trained fighters of one form or another, although I thought she lacked the hard edge that such people usually had. 'Every clan has them, on nameless islands like this one. It would take decades just to search every one of our islands, even without including our allies' or other clans' territory. I admit, this one is special. Larger than most.'

She sounded very confident, but I had little faith in the value of remote safe havens any more. There was no place so secret or so out of the way that it couldn't be found, given time, and four years ago we'd found a similarly hidden place in a single day.

Welcoming yellow light blazed from the house windows, but I wasn't taken into the house. Instead, the woman told Palatine to wait and led me up some steps and along a colonnade to a wide, open terrace on the seaward side, looking over the lagoon. Torches flickered in metal sconces underneath a wooden framework covered in plants and flowers, but the windows were shuttered and there was no other artificial light.

I saw only one person, staring out over the wall, across the still waters to the sandbar and the black sea beyond, lit by a glittering panorama of stars. Her hair was a deep copper, made more vivid by the torchlight.

She turned as I approached, and I caught my breath as I saw her face. Heavens, but she looked so young, was my first thought.

'Cathan,' she said a moment later, her eyes flickering over me.

I stood still for a moment, hardly able to believe who this was. She spread her arms wide, took a step towards me, and I moved forward to embrace her.

'Mother.'

We stood there for a second as my brain whirled round and round, still trying to come to grips with the idea that this was real, that this was a person of flesh and blood I was embracing.

After a moment we stepped back a little, neither of us sure what to say. I had a foster-mother in Lepidor, a woman who'd brought me up with as much love as if I had been her own child. It had been four years since I'd seen her.

But this astonishingly ageless woman with her coppery hair had given birth to me and lost me again, without ever seeing me.

Aurelia Tel-Mandra, Empress of Thetia. My mother.

'It isn't often,' she said finally, 'that Thetis takes a child away from you and then gives him back.'

Suddenly feeling very awkward, I didn't know what to reply. I'd often wondered about her, had asked Palatine more than once for her memories of her, but until chance had brought me to a meeting with Khalia, I'd never expected to meet her.

What did I say to the mother I hadn't seen since I was less than an hour old?

The breeze ruffled my hair briefly, tugged at the long blue tunic she was wearing. I looked over at the empty space to my right, as if I could see the ghost who stood there in spirit, the man who should have been here.

'He wanted me to tell you he was sorry,' I said at last. 'That he loved you, and that he was sorry, sorry for everything.'

'He said that?' she asked.

'Before he died, he changed back. He kept rambling about being ill, calling out for you. I tried to save him, but it was too late.'

'Why? Why, after what he must have done to you?'

'I thought I could give him a second chance. Neither of us ever escaped the Domain, but they'd destroyed him and I was still myself.'

'And are you still?'

'I hope so.'

I saw a tear trickle down her face, but even as it did she smiled. 'I have mourned what he was. I will have time to remember him again. Thank you for telling me. I'm glad that you met.'

I wavered for a second, uncertain what she meant. She knew it couldn't have been a pleasant encounter – but I had the feeling she was talking about the Orosius I'd glimpsed in those last few nightmare minutes on *Valdur*'s bridge.

'I'm sorry I never came to find you before,' I said, wondering how I could be so awkward. This surely wasn't the way it should be.

'I doubt you could have done. I'm not welcome in Thetia, I keep myself hidden out here. But you aren't here simply to see me, are you? There's something else.'

I nodded, desperately guilty that it had only been need and expedience that drove me here at last. I had no excuses.

'The Emperor's been assassinated.'

'Your uncle Aetius,' she said carefully. 'Are you sure of this? You're not just going on rumours.'

'As sure as anyone can be. Hamilcar's seen the body.'

'This is your uncle, yet you don't show any regret.'

'He isn't worth it.'

'You might have said Orosius wasn't, before he died.'

'If Eshar had survived, all of us would be ashes in the end. I wouldn't have plotted to kill him, but I wouldn't have saved him. Even if there had been a chance.'

He had executed her closest friend Aelin Salassa, purged Thetia of many its brightest minds. She had more to hate him for than I did, if anything.

'So you are coming back as Emperor,' she said.

I shook my head.

We had gathered in a sumptuous room belonging to the dyers, richest of all the Ilthysian guilds because of the extent of the trade. Three tall windows overlooked the rain-swept agora, and the walls were hung with bolts of cloth in brilliant scarlet. It was where the masters of all the guilds regularly met, and I could tell from the carved chairs and the oval wavewood table that they hadn't spared any expense.

We didn't sit round the table, because it wasn't that kind of meeting, and only two of the guildmasters were there – the host and Oailos, who'd been promoted by the acclamation of his fellows at the expense of the treacherous Badoas.

As soon as the doors had closed behind the last servant,

Ithien turned to Hamilcar. They'd only met a few minutes earlier; Ithien had been initially suspicious, but the rest of us had been able to vouch for the Tanethan. Hamilcar was an old friend, my Lepidor family's contract partner and a man who'd been selling weapons to the Elemental Council for four years. None of us had ever suspected what the weapons were being used for.

'Can you be sure of this?' Ithien demanded. He was sitting on a couch, propped up and with his bandaged arm resting on cushions. The rest of us were sitting on chairs from round the table, or on the divans below the windows. 'Tell us how.'

Hamilcar told us about his stay in Mare Alastre, his gradual penetration of the groups who took shelter there, and then what he'd seen of the Emperor's last hours. 'I was told he'd been poisoned. I assumed it was a latent poison that built up over time.'

He looked round at us. 'It isn't. I made some enquiries with Khalia here. It's only activated when it comes into contact with another herb, *voltella*.'

'No-one eats *voltella*,' Oailos pointed out. 'It's bitter.'

'It has medicinal uses,' Khalia said. 'On its own.'

'Ah, but as you would know if you still worshipped Ranthas,' Hamilcar went on, 'it has other uses. The Domain make incense out of it which is burnt all the time in the inner sanctuaries of temples, where only rulers and high-ranking priests may go.'

'And Eshar is devout,' Khalia finished. I could tell she wasn't happy. 'Every Ranthasday he goes to the sanctuary to worship. He'd breathe in the incense and it would react with the poison already in his system. A few minutes and he'd be dead, as if he'd fallen asleep. In the right circumstances, it might look like natural causes, perhaps a heart attack.'

Hamilcar nodded. 'He died in the temple sanctuary in Mare Alastre six days ago. Dozens of people saw them carrying the body down, but there hasn't been any announcement. The two most senior admirals, Charidemus and Alexios, are in the Archipelago; the rest of the General Staff are holding off any decision until they get back.'

'Do we know who was behind it?' Oailos asked.

Hamilcar nodded. 'The Thetians claim not to know, they're looking for people to blame, but I spent enough time there to know who did it.'

'The Elemental Council,' Ravenna said. 'Sagantha, perhaps you can explain?'

He'd known this was coming, ever since Hamilcar mentioned his complicity earlier. I waited to see how he'd wriggle out of it.

'The Council has been discussing it for years,' he explained. 'He's the Domain's perfect Emperor, so killing him could do them a lot of harm. Tekla was very much in favour of it, he wanted to avenge Orosius's death. So we sent him away and told him to see whether it could be done.'

'Tekla himself has been dead for three weeks,' she pointed out.

'He was organising it, I didn't say he was commissioned to carry out the assassination.'

'Organising it,' Ithien said. 'That's different from merely investigating the possibility. You authorised it, didn't you?'

'It didn't come before the Council before I defected,' Sagantha insisted.

He was deliberately concealing something, I could tell. Hardly surprising, but we couldn't afford to know any less than the truth, not now.

'It didn't come before the Council,' I said. 'What about the Ring of Eight, though? Surely they would have been in control.'

Neither of the Ilthysians knew what the Ring of Eight was, so I described what little I knew of it, not sparing any of the grim details.

Hamilcar, I discovered, had had no idea either, and looked disturbed when I mentioned the fortress at Kavatang and the secret trial. In some ways we were all equally to blame, because most of us had helped to set up the sale of weapons which Hamilcar and his ally Lord Canadrath had kept going. There had to be huge stockpiles of weapons somewhere in heretic-controlled territory, probably down at the Citadels.

'Of course the Ring will have known about it,' Sagantha said. 'Tekla had told them it was possible, and so they may have decided to take action on their own.'

I finally realised what he'd been struggling to hide from us all along. I remembered the images the Council had shown us of the Crusade and the fall of Vararu. The Elemental Council had offered Orethura their help – help they weren't obliged to give – and he had turned them down.

'The Ring of Eight is separate from the Council, isn't it?' I said, watching his expression carefully.

I hoped that had trapped him, and would force him either to admit that the Council had been responsible for the Ring's brutality – or that the Ring had a very different and far more sinister origin. I waited.

'They work together,' he said.

Ithien pounced. 'So they're separate. In which case, where do the Ring's members come from? Who founded it? If they're behind the Emperor's death, we need to know.'

There was silence for a moment, only punctuated by the sound of rain on the window-panes. I didn't want to say anything, because what came next was bound to hurt Ravenna and I didn't want to be the one to strike the blow.

'The Archipelago.' It was Ravenna who spoke, not Sagantha, and that was entirely unexpected. 'My grandfather and his Tehaman allies.'

396

There was a deep sadness in her voice as she spoke, but I couldn't pick up a trace of the despair I'd expected. She clung to his memory, though, and it was hard to believe she'd admit what I had suspected all along. I'd never wanted to mention it to her.

'Your grandfather?' Palatine said.

'Yes. Who else could it have been?'

There was no answer, because all those of us who knew enough to judge had already come to that conclusion. Including the man who'd been both on the Council and, presumably, heavily embroiled in the Ring of Eight. Sagantha must have been involved. There simply wasn't enough time for the Council to have authorised the assassination *after* the debacle at Kavatang and sent a message.

'The Navy will avenge the Emperor if they can,' Ithien remarked pointedly.

'If they can,' said Sagantha. 'There's a chance the Council will seize control of the Navy.'

'How much of a chance?' Palatine asked.

Sagantha looked unsure. Eventually, he shrugged. 'There were a number of plans – I wasn't convinced most of them were workable, but combined with news of the Emperor's death, in that particular set of circumstances . . .'

We fell silent again. Everyone knew what the biggest question of all was, but no-one wanted to be the first to bring it up.

'We should go to Thetia,' Ithien said emphatically. 'There'll be a power vacuum, no-one knowing what's happening. We'll never get another chance like this.'

'A chance to do what, Ithien?' said Khalia. 'Found a republic?'

'Of course. What else? The Emperor is dead, and there's no obvious successor. Thetia will be ours for the taking.' His eyes were shining, and his enthusiasm was infectious. 'Think of it. There's no question about it: we have a chance to take control of Thetia and once we're in charge, we can push the Domain out of the Archipelago! There's no way they can stand up to the Navy, no way they can even launch a Crusade when Thetia is there to protect the Archipelago.'

'We can reconvene the Assembly in Selerian Alastre, let the Presidents have a say again. None of them like the Domain and they'll be only too ready to help.'

'A republic,' Palatine said, almost dreamily. 'After all these years.'

Predictably, it was Sagantha who burst the bubble.

'Found a republic?' he said slowly. 'The Assembly is a dinosaur that can't even agree what day of the week it is. You expect it to suddenly sit up, come to a consensus and rule a country that's been through two Emperors and a purge in less than four years? You expect the Navy to follow the Assembly?' His tone was scornful, his words harsh but realistic.

'The Navy is loyal to Thetia, and the Assembly is Thetia,' Ithien insisted.

'The Navy was loyal to Reglath Eshar,' Hamilcar said. 'They followed him out of devotion, because he's done more for them than anyone else in two hundred years.'

'And now he's dead . . .'

'Now he's dead, whoever they support will succeed,' said Sagantha. He was standing up again; I'd noticed he always preferred to move around while he was talking. Perhaps it gave him a kind of advantage.

The two Ilthysians, Oailos and the Guildmaster, were out of their depth now; it would have been discourteous to leave them out, but I didn't think the dyer in particular had had any idea of the status of the other people in the room with him. He would get more shocks in a minute or two, if I read the trend of the conversation right.

'He's right,' said Khalia. 'Even though he knows less about Thetian politics than the rest of you. Ithien, you're dreaming. The Navy will never follow the Assembly, not the way things are now.'

'So we have four more centuries of Tar'Conantur rule?' Ithien demanded, looking fit to explode. 'You'd rather have another Valdur, another Orosius, another Eshar?'

'In a word, yes,' Khalia said. 'The Emperors gave Thetia stability and coherent leadership. I remember the night Perseus died, when there was a clear heir but he was only three. It was so unexpected, there was absolute chaos for more than a week as everybody tried to take control of the Regency Council.

'And all through that the Assembly sat and debated how many clans should be represented on the Council. In the end, it was three because three of the leaders decided to ignore the Assembly and take matters into their own hands. *That* is how the Assembly works, gentlemen, and to expect it to take control after a far stronger Emperor has been assassinated is a ludicrous idea.'

I had never expected her to take such a central role, but she understood more of Thetian politics than any of us, including Ithien. You couldn't be healer to the Thetian court for so long without understanding how it worked.

'Well, what about a stopgap?' Palatine said. 'Someone who can restore order, bring the Navy into line and then step down when the Assembly is strong enough. Marshal Tanais, for example.'

'Tanais would be an excellent choice,' I said, 'but we have no idea where he is. What are the chances of us tracking him down in the next two or three days?'

We were taking it for granted that we had little time to lose, if anything was going to happen we'd have to be in Thetia by the time Eshar's death was announced. People had already been sent to collect Ithien's manta, and the Domain courier had been captured and made ready for sea. Hamilcar had offered us the use of his *Aegeta* as well, although she was only a merchantman. It would take time to get them ready, which was why we had the luxury of sitting around here for an hour or two.

'It's a better idea,' Sagantha said.

'But what's to stop someone simply seizing power?' said Ithien. 'Admiral Charidemus would be able to hold things together, but he'd make a bid for the throne the moment he found out Eshar was dead.'

'Would he really?' Vespasia said. 'After all these centuries, people think the Imperial family is special, that it *belongs* in power and no-one else can fill the gap.'

'They haven't been particularly lucky recently,' commented Khalia. 'However, we have two people here who are members of the family.'

Including one who had been named Empress by Orosius before he died. I'd never told her, and I'd thrown the dolphin pendant Orosius had given me into the darkness of *Aeon*. Deliberately.

Ravenna, Sagantha, Hamilcar and Vespasia all looked at Palatine. Ithien, Khalia and Oailos, ignoring Palatine, turned their attention to me. I felt a curious thrill run through me at the idea that anyone at all would look to me now.

'No,' Palatine and I said together, then fell silent. I seized the opportunity to go on, knowing with an absolute certainty that I could never do what they asked of me, that if I allowed myself to become the puppet even of friends I would lead myself and Thetia to disaster.

'I can't help you,' I said firmly, as I tried to decide what was the best line of argument. 'No-one knows I exist, and, besides, I look too like Orosius. Some people might even think I was Orosius. The Navy hated him, you have to remember that.'

It wasn't the most pressing reason, but it was far more convincing than the obvious truth: that I was not Imperial calibre. I was too weak, too indecisive, too inexperienced.

But the mention of Orosius worked as the truth might

400

not have done, because it was something concrete, and a reason everyone knew was sound.

Those few words were all it took, I thought, as the others nodded and turned their attention to Palatine, to disbar me from an Imperial crown for ever. It was absurd enough to think that we could be discussing it so seriously in this room, and there was an air of unreality about the whole thing.

'People know you,' Sagantha said to her. 'They respected you, they respected your father. You have the ability.'

His words hung in the air for a moment as we all stared at the brown-haired woman who sat there in a worn green tunic, looking back at each of us in turn, perhaps wondering what was driving each of us to pick on her.

She shook her head. 'No.'

What she said next shook me more than Ravenna's admission of her grandfather's guilt, and in a way the fact that she even said it supported my own decision more strongly than any argument could have done.

'I would not be an interim ruler,' she said quietly. 'I would take power and I would use it, better than Orosius or Eshar have done. And I would not give it up, never in a thousand years. Even if I'm a Canteni, I have Tar'Conantur blood. We don't share power, we use it. You cannot give the throne to one of us and expect us to relinquish it, because we never will.'

I moved forward, perching on the edge of the cushioned chair. Every word beat on me like a hammer. To hear Palatine, the icon of the republicans, almost the embodiment of freedom for thousands, say those words . . .

All of us knew they were true. All of us knew that she'd grasped what so many failed to see in a lifetime.

All of us knew she could have kept it to herself.

'It's ironic,' Khalia said into the profound quiet, 'that

401

the only Tar'Conanturs who should be allowed to rule are those who realise that they must never do so.'

I knew exactly what she meant. But was she trying to influence the others?

'I thought you approved of them,' Ithien said.

'I'm a monarchist,' Khalia admitted. 'I believe in the family, because they have the talent to rule the Empire. But none of them that I know of has ever realised what power does to them, and here we have two in the same room who seem well aware of its consequences.'

'The last two,' Sagantha said. 'Who else is there? Will we sit by and watch the power struggle? Leave the Archipelago to the mercies of whoever ends up in charge? Because once the Navy realises there are no more Tar'Conanturs, or no more available, one of the High Command, probably Charidemus, will make a bid for the throne, and I doubt he'd encounter any serious opposition.'

'Like your people,' Oailos said. 'The Cambressians, I mean. You'd have the admirals ruling it. It's not as bad as Eshar, but do you think they'd bother to protect the Archipelago?'

No more Tar'Conanturs. A thalassocracy, Thetia run by the admirals. Oailos was right, it wouldn't save the Archipelago. Nor would a republic, which would only hasten the admirals' determination to take power. Yet there was no-one else. Palatine's mother was a recluse . . .

There was one more person.

'Aurelia,' said Palatine, again at the same instant as me. One or two people smiled, and the tension relaxed slightly.

'Are you sure she isn't your twin?' Vespasia said.

'I wish she had been,' I replied.

But the others had already moved on, the brief second of humour forgotten.

'Aurelia,' Sagantha repeated. 'The Empress Dowager. She isn't a Tar'Conantur.'

'I don't think that would matter in her case,' Hamilcar

said. 'She was respected, people will recognise her, she's associated with the family and the throne.'

'Can you have someone on the throne who isn't royal?' Oailos asked dubiously. 'I mean, she was married to the Emperor, but she isn't a member of the Imperial family.'

Ever since I'd discovered who I was, I'd been profoundly glad that the Tar'Conanturs had always been terrified of inbreeding. So terrified, that apparently in Thetia you weren't even allowed to marry your second cousin, let alone your first.

'She's royal,' Palatine said, some of her enthusiasm coming back. 'It may not be immediately obvious, but the Imperial line goes through the Exiles.'

Ravenna looked puzzled. 'But it's the Thetians who . . .'

'Yes, it is,' Palatine said. 'Thetians reckon descent through their mothers, except the Tar'Conanturs. You can only be Tar'Conantur if one of your parents is an Exile. At least theoretically; in practice it hasn't always worked out so neatly. The royal twins always had to marry Exiles, it was part of a treaty we made with them centuries ago. You inherit the name and the claim to the throne only through an Exile. In any other family, I'd have taken my mother's clan or name — Tar'Conantur — but since she wasn't an Exile, I couldn't. It's complicated, but in fact Aurelia has a much better claim to the throne than I do.'

'It's a most irregular system,' Sagantha commented. 'Why can't you do things like everyone else?'

'I assume she's still alive, if you're all considering her,' Hamilcar said, 'but how do we get hold of her? She could be as hard to find as Tanais.'

'She isn't,' Khalia said, 'and I know where you can find her.'

We stood there in silence for a moment, alone on the terrace against the canopy of stars. I heard faint voices from inside the house.

'No, I'm not coming back as Emperor,' I said. My carefully thought out words deserted me then; having stayed in my head up till now, they fled when I needed them most. 'I'm here to ask you to take my place.'

'For whose sake?'

'For everyone's sake.' And for mine most of all, I added inwardly.

CHAPTER XXVII

'So what is your plan?' Aurelia asked.

The others – all of those from the meeting in Ilthys, except the two guildmasters – stood around the edge of the terrace, and I could sense their faint air of impatience. They hadn't been needed to persuade her, as we thought they might have been, and everybody was acutely conscious of how much we still had to do.

'We go back to Thetia, claim the throne,' Ithien said promptly.

'No,' Palatine said. 'Think about it. We're relying on the Navy, first and foremost. Whatever else we think is important, it's the Navy that matters. And it's scattered all over the world with only about twenty ships in Thetia at the moment.'

'You can't seize the Thetian crown from outside Thetia,' Ithien objected.

'Yes, you can,' said Hamilcar. 'Charidemus has five mantas in Tandaris – but also there is the entire Grand Fleet, thirty or so mantas under another admiral; his name is Alexios. Two of the four most senior admirals, the bulk of the fleet. You can't do anything without securing their loyalty. And there's always the danger of that fleet falling into Council hands. No, once we hold the Grand Fleet, it's effectively over. The rest of the Navy is scattered, won't be able to stop us without starting a civil war.'

'So we need to reach Tandaris as soon as possible.'

'Within two days,' Sagantha said. 'That's the shortest time any Council ship could possibly make it there with news of the assassination and put whatever plans they have into effect.'

'They have plans?' Khalia asked.

Sagantha nodded. 'Several, and the last I heard, it hadn't been decided which one would be implemented. What I'm sure of is that they've been assembling ships and men. They'll try to seize the fleet, there's no doubt of that, but I'm not yet sure how.'

'Your mantas will never be able to make it in time,' Aurelia said. 'We have to get there before anyone else can take control of that fleet.'

'The courier might,' Hamilcar said. 'At the very least it'll be there only a few hours late.'

'What good will that do us?' Ithien asked. The courier was tiny, hardly bigger than a searay and with space only for two crew and four passengers. 'Aurelia will arrive in the city without any support, no marines at all – it's madness.'

'I could go with her,' Hamilcar said. 'I've made a lot of contacts and I can find enough people to tide us through for a few hours or a day.'

'You're a Tanethan, why would they trust you?'

'Because they know I hate Eshar as much as they do. I've been selling weapons to the Archipelago for years, remember, I can make direct contact with Canadrath's people.'

'How much protection do we need to give?' Ravenna asked.

'A lot,' said Hamilcar. He'd discarded his heavy Tanethan robes for a long Thetian-style tunic that was still soaked at the bottom from wading through the surf. He looked curiously out of place in it.

'Even if I assume the throne,' said Aurelia, 'it isn't over yet.'

'No. The Domain will fight tooth and nail to stop us. They drove Her Majesty out in the first place and they know it could mean disaster for them if she comes back.'

'That's the idea,' Palatine said. 'Might they try to set up a Council instead?'

The others looked doubtful.

'The Navy won't support anything that looks as though it'll be divisive,' Sagantha said. 'Their own High Command would be acceptable, and I suspect they'd have no problems with Her Majesty. But there are bound to be people who want to impose their own agenda.'

'The Domain has a number of Sacri in Tandaris,' said Hamilcar. 'Not only that, but Sarhaddon sailed from Taneth a little under a month ago with more Venatics and a decree from the Prime. He'll have stopped at Ral Tumar, but he was going to bypass Ilthys for once and head straight for Tandaris – he could be there any day now.'

'It could be too dangerous,' Ithien began, but Aurelia cut him off.

'It may be, but that's up to you. I shall go in the courier. We don't have time to waste in argument, every minute we sit here brings Sarhaddon closer. Hamilcar, Ithien, you will come with me. The rest of you follow and bring as much support as you can. If we're to take on the Domain, there'll be sympathisers who don't have any particular loyalty to the Council – Thetian expatriates in the islands, for instance.'

It was extraordinary how quickly she'd accepted, slipping into her role just as we'd hoped. Why? What had possessed her to leave her exile behind so suddenly and throw herself back into the thick of Thetian politics? Reinhardt, Orosius, Aelin, most of her friends and family had died violently at the Domain's hands, and Eshar – who was, after all, her brother-in-law – had just been assassinated. I could only guess what was driving her.

The last lights flickered out in the house. The dark-haired attendant emerged carrying a canvas bag and began to extinguish the lights on the terrace.

'May I have some paper?' Hamilcar asked.

He wrote a hurried note to the captain of his ship explaining what was happening and leaving Sagantha in charge.

'We should move, gentlemen,' Aurelia said, motioning for us to go first.

I followed the path back through the trees to the beach, saw the two searays and the courier floating out beyond the surf line. The courier's captain had brought her in close to a rocky outcrop where the water was quite deep, saving those who would be travelling on it a long swim out into the lagoon.

The others began wading out into the surf, heading for the searays, but I hung back until Aurelia and her attendant emerged.

'I don't know whether this is for the best,' she said, pausing as Ithien and Hamilcar started walking along the beach towards the rocks, 'but your coming to find me makes it worthwhile. I shall see you again in Tandaris.'

I embraced my mother once more. Then she set off after the others, her robe dragging slightly in the white sand.

She was so assured, so calm. I wondered if I'd inherited anything from her at all, whether I had some of her qualities instead of the Tar'Conantur ones I so obviously lacked.

I realised, with an odd feeling of regret, that if we succeeded, we'd have taken one more step towards the extinction of my family. That wasn't something I should mind, not after everything that had happened.

Palatine was gesticulating from one of the searays, and I realised I was holding them up. I ran out into the water, enjoying the feel of the waves breaking over my legs, and swam the last distance through the shallows to clamber up into the searay.

It set off almost immediately, giving me hardly enough time for a last look at that astonishing sky before we dived.

'The engineer is going to love us,' Palatine commented. 'Twelve hundred miles in three days.'

Aurelia and Hamilcar would be on their own in

Tandaris for a day or two. I could only hope that we got to them before the Domain did.

And simply needing to arrive ahead of them wasn't our only worry.

Vespasia had insisted on showing us around the stolen manta the moment we boarded. I wasn't very happy to discover her name was *Crusade*. When we'd boarded there had been crewmen hastily putting cloth hangings on the walls. I could see why they were willing to take the risk of fire. The flame sigil of the Domain had been emblazoned on every panel, and there was what looked like a small shrine just aft of the well. I glanced up – it was only a two-decker, despite its larger than usual size, and I wondered where the extra space had gone.

The bridge was no better – that flame sigil was everywhere.

'So far, it just seems like a standard manta with the usual objectionable decoration, although it has a much thicker hull,' Vespasia said, taking us back out of the bridge and along one of the curving side corridors to the engine room. Here I could see some differences, not least that it was a double-reactor ship, more expensive to run but more powerful and able to carry more weapons.

And there were a lot of those, I noticed. Plans of the ship had been engraved into a glass-covered metal plate on the wall, with details of where the conduits ran and where the armaments were.

'It's overgunned,' Sagantha said critically, then paused, pointed at the lower decks, where the cargo bay would have been. 'What's that?'

'That's why you're here.' Vespasia led us downstairs, past the searay bays, to where the cargo hold would normally have taken up most of the space. Instead, the corridor forked and branched into two as it did on the upper deck, and there was another room ahead.

409

'Holy Ranthas,' Sagantha said a moment later.

I stared at the room's contents, taking in the twin small flamewood reactors positioned either side of a huge piece of machinery. Part of it was an aether generator, I could see, but there was far too much bulk there for it to be simply that.

'What is it?' Sagantha demanded. 'Tell us.'

'Do you know the technique the priests use for destroying enemy ships? The one they invented a few months before Orosius died?'

'Boiling the water, you mean?'

Vespasia nodded, and then I finally understood. I remembered the terrible damage inflicted on a fleeing Qalathari ship and the *Lodestar* by Abisamar's mages. The same magic had destroyed the *Valdur*, boiling the water underneath the ship to create a pressure fist of bubbles and expanding water that in most cases turned the victim over on its back, wrecking the interior and killing most of the occupants.

Including Mauriz, Telesta, my brother, and two Qalatharis who'd helped us in the attempt to rescue Ravenna. Not to mention the *Valdur*'s hundreds-strong crew.

'This is a mechanical weapon that will do the same thing. It uses a lot of power, a lot of flamewood, but unlike a mage, it can be used again after a few minutes of cooling down.' She swallowed, looked down at the deck uneasily. 'At our best guess, it could probably take out two or three mantas at normal battle-line separation.'

'How many of these are there?' Sagantha demanded. 'Where do they come from – surely we'd have heard of them being built?'

'We think there are two,' she said. 'Five years ago, the Domain helped pay for a new deep-sea research vessel to be converted out of an old war manta – *Missionary*. We're not sure why, but we think they wanted to search for *Aeon*.

At the same time they started building, in a Thetian yard, another manta that would have a much thicker hull and could withstand far higher pressures.

'The weapon was Clan Polinskarn's idea, an attempt to build a weapon for the clans that would even the odds against the Emperor. They called in as many shipwrights as they could find, stole or copied the designs for the thick-hulled manta, and grew another deep hull which they took to a research yard in south-eastern Thetia, a library outpost called the Retreat, to outfit.

'Somehow the Domain found out about it, and they swooped on the shipyard just as the manta was undergoing sea trials, under the pretext of purging the Retreat for banned books. They shipped everyone off to do penance in the most miserable places they could think of, and finished the manta for themselves.

'This is the one that was built at the Retreat, but as far as we know the deep-research manta, *Theocracy,* has also been armed. They have the plans. I'm not sure why they took this one down to Qalathar, but there's still another one and the possibility of building more.'

'Is it a weapon anybody can use?' Sagantha asked.

'No. It has some kind of a key which can only be unlocked by a fire-mage, but it doesn't have to be a very competent fire-mage, and the Domain has plenty of those to spare.'

There was a shocked silence. I stared at the weapon, silently thanking Vespasia for finding out what had happened at the Retreat and explaining why the Inquisitors had come and inflicted all this misery on us. This weapon, this ship was the reason I'd spent more than a year as a penitent. It hadn't had anything to do with the banned books.

I found some words floating in my heads, a fragment of an otherwise half-remembered conversation.

The worst one is a Sacrus called Lachazzar. He believes that the Domain should use its powers to enforce religion far more strictly. In effect, he wants the Domain to rule the world. Perhaps Sarhaddon had been exaggerating, but he'd said more than once that Lachazzar had always believed in a secular supremacy as well as a spiritual one.

This ship and its sisters gave him the tool, the Archipelago the excuse he had dreamed of for so long. I could see where it would go – first a few Domain mantas equipped with them, then Thetian ships with Sacri and fire-mages on board, then entire fleets. The Emperor would co-operate, be glad of his newfound power without ever considering what it would do to his successors. Others would realise, but too late. Even the General Staff would be powerless to do anything, because by then their Navy would belong to the Domain.

And then the Domain would have a control of the seas that no-one else, including the Thetians, had ever really possessed, because the weapons were useless without fire-mages. The political power that Sarhaddon and his Venatics wielded was only a first step, because Lachazzar was not a subtle man, he would want something more effective, more concrete, and so eventually there would be no need for the Venatics to stand beside each ruler.

Finally Sagantha took a deep breath, breaking into my bleak projection. 'I can't even begin to think of what a fleet of these could do,' he said, echoing my own thoughts. Now he'd seen it, he would come to the same conclusion soon enough. 'Thank you, Vespasia.'

None of us were comfortable on *Crusade*, but necessity and safety had compelled us to travel on her rather than the better appointed and less creepy *Aegeta*. Hamilcar's ship was new, and fast, but lightly armed and armoured for all that. There was always the possibility, however small, that we could encounter *Theocracy* in between here and Tandaris, a prospect none of us wanted to think about it.

When we joined Sagantha in the map room the next morning, we'd left the island far behind and were deep in the open ocean northwest of Tandaris, tracing a long arc north of Tehama towards the manta channels between the Ilahi Islands.

Sagantha brought the map of Qalathar up on the aether table. It was astonishingly detailed, made up of the data from thousands of individual surveys. I'd seen it before, and this wasn't even the best of the maps made with this technique. Thetia, not Qalathar, had been the Guild's highest priority when they developed the new scanning technology.

'We're here,' he said, pointing to a yellow pinprick that seemed a painfully long way from anywhere. A moment later, a white indicator appeared over Tandaris, as if the city was lit up by a single sunbeam breaking through the clouds.

He traced our intended course, running parallel to the line of Qalathar itself until we reached the northern edge, then through the Aetian Channel and almost due south across the Inland Sea to Tandaris itself.

'This is the place that matters,' Sagantha said, pointing at the deep-water channel, one of the few safe routes into the Inland Sea and the easiest way to reach Tandaris. 'If there's going to be a problem, I expect to meet it there.'

'What kind of problem?' Khalia asked.

'A blockade, if someone hostile is in control of the city. Possibly an ambush. Or an encounter with anyone else who is trying to reach the city from the north. Sarhaddon, for example, He'll probably have come through the Jayan Gap, like anyone else coming from the east, but he could have had plenty of time to send ships to the other entrances. There are only three safe channels.'

'We aren't going to arrive at the same time as him, though.'

Palatine and Sagantha both looked uncertain. The odds

413

were stacked against it, but it was a possibility none of us could ignore. Especially given the damage that the fire-weapons might do in relatively shallow waters.

'The channel is too narrow and too shallow to use the fire-weapon,' Sagantha said. 'It could cause a tsunami and do severe damage to the coastline.'

'The Domain won't care about that,' said Ravenna. 'If they have *Theocracy*, they'll use her and to hell with anyone who might get swamped.'

'As far as they're concerned, we all belong in hell anyway,' Palatine said. 'No-one has any idea where *Theocracy* is stationed, I take it? No? Well, she was built as a deep-ocean research ship, so she shouldn't be in the Inland Sea, but I haven't heard of much deep-ocean research going on since the Domain decided the Guild was full of heretics.'

Did they need *Theocracy*, though? 'If they get there before us, they might persuade the Navy to blockade the channel.'

Khalia didn't think much of that. 'We're dealing in speculation at the moment. What we need to be thinking about is shaving an hour or two off our time.'

'We're more likely to be adding some hours on,' Palatine said. 'The people we have here aren't going to make much difference to the outcome. Where could we find some marines? Any extra manpower, really.'

It was a matter of bodies to put between the Empress and the Domain, when it came down to it. Two Emperors had been assassinated in four years; the Domain wouldn't baulk at a third assassination.

Vespasia stared at the map. 'The clans on the Ilahi Islands are an independent-minded lot. They were Thetian colonists from the southern cities hundreds of years ago, put in place by Carausius to guard Tehama. They aren't too sympathetic to the Tehamans, unless a lot has changed.'

414

'We don't need many people.' Palatine paused, calculating figures in her head. 'We might be able to get a hundred marines out of those clans, perhaps a manta if we're lucky.'

'But we'd have to talk to them, to persuade them to give us their troops,' Khalia said. 'That won't be so easy. Would you lend a detachment of marines to a strange Tanethan ship which appeared out of nowhere and claimed to be following the Empress?'

'We'd be able to do it.'

'Yes, you might, but you'd lose two or three hours at each capital, not to mention having to divert to reach them in the first place.'

'I might be able to convince Clan Jaya to help us,' Vespasia said. 'My uncle married a Tethil woman, so he's one of them now. He was living in the capital when last I heard, I'm sure he'd speak for us. There's a Polinskarn consulate in Jaya, and the only oceanographic station left in Qalathar – if Polinskarn and the Guild won't help us, nobody will.'

Sagantha looked thoughtful, 'It's out of our way again, but it might be a better proposition,' he said musingly. 'No marines, only a few Coast Watchers, who probably can't use anything more than fighting sticks, and some oceanographers who are bound to help us if they haven't all been arrested . . . Sorry, Vespasia.'

'I know,' she said. I knew some of her family had been oceanographers, and with the purges it was all too likely that some of them had been arrested and shipped off. 'They'll help us, you can count on it.'

They would be fools not to. It would be a gamble, but even I, with little political acumen, could tell that Jaya stood to gain hugely if we were successful.

'It seems a sound idea,' Palatine said. 'At least some people willing to fight, a few oceanographers . . . Perhaps we could send *Aegeta* to Jaya on the way.'

But Sagantha vetoed that idea, not wanting to split up the force we had. The Jayans would be doubly suspicious if a ship full of Tanethans turned up asking for their help in a conspiracy to seize the throne.

He was nothing if not thorough, and we spent another couple of hours in the chart room studying the aether maps of Tandaris, reminding ourselves of the city Sagantha and Ravenna knew well, but Palatine and I had only spent a few months in over that winter four years ago.

In a way, the planning was beneficial. It kept our minds off the waiting, the interminable hours while *Crusade* and *Aegeta* winged their way through the offshore gloom towards Qalathar. Going to the bridge to check on our progress became almost a neurosis, and Sagantha grew so tired of us that he cleared everyone out and displayed our position in the map room. It was pointless, I knew, but what else was there to do?

I was not the only one who felt that way, but there seemed very little for me to do in all this – Palatine and Sagantha had plans to make, Vespasia would have to convince the oceanographers to help, while Khalia knew people in the city who might be of help, and would almost inevitably be called on as a healer.

Only Ravenna and I had no clearly defined task. There was nothing for us to do. We might conceivably need to use magic if things went badly wrong, but all of us were hoping it wouldn't come to that. Both of us felt useless, and both of us knew it was a feeling we shared.

'You're feeling as aimless as I am,' she said when we met in the well, moving aside to let one of the sailors go past; two of the officers were conferring by the entrance to the bridge.

I nodded, surprised that she'd brought it up.

'They don't really need us, do they?'

'Not really,' she said. 'We've played our part, this has nothing to do with Storm. Not much to do with either of us.'

416

But even as we headed upstairs, Sagantha came out of the bridge and called us down again.

'We have company,' was all he said.

CHAPTER XXVIII

The other ship stayed at the very limit of our sensors, occasionally slipping out of sight but always returning. She never responded to hails, never made an attempt to come any closer, and we couldn't tell anything other than that she was a manta, and evidently pursuing us. The Council, because no recognised power would bother to skulk around, and no pirate would attack what seemed to be a Domain warship.

Hours dragged on, the unknown ship matching our speed but never catching up, permanently a few miles behind. It wasn't easy, that long chase, and nerves frayed on the bridge. Sagantha grew more and more abrupt and snappy, while Palatine as his first officer had to squash mutinous murmuring from some of the crewmen, who seemed to know more about his trickiness than any of us had realised. One of them had passed round a story about how profligate with lives he'd been in the Cambressian Navy, one I hadn't heard. It didn't paint him in a flattering light.

The second day out from the island, Sagantha decided to part company with *Aegeta*, as her reactors began to show signs of stress. We'd tried a few manoeuvres, attempts to confuse the pursuer, but none had been successful, so we decided that she'd be more use elsewhere. Vespasia transferred to her, and we watched as she veered off to port, heading for Jaya after all in the hope that we'd find some help there. I wished them a silent good luck, knowing that once they were out of contact with us, they'd have a better chance.

It was hard to relax in this situation, half a mile beneath the ocean surface in an absolutely unchanging world for hour after hour, and I knew I wasn't the best of company either. I was too worried about the courier and *Aegeta*, different ghastly scenarios playing themselves over in my mind. Having little to do made it worse, even though I was able to escape the tense atmosphere in the command area. Khalia wisely kept out of the way, except when she drew on the supplies from Ilthys and made coffee for everyone on the ship.

It went without saying that I didn't sleep well those nights, especially not the last before we expected to arrive. It was all the more frustrating since we'd arrive in Tandaris shortly before sunset the next day and might be up most of the night.

I hadn't expected the dreams, though. They seemed to begin almost the moment I lay down in my small room on the upper deck. A monastic cell in all but name, it was fitted with bunks for two Sacri section leaders – their men were expected to sleep in a dormitory on the main deck. I'd covered up the flame on the wall with a piece of cloth, but when I closed my eyes, it still seemed to be there.

I dreamt of the Citadel, and of the images of the Crusade that the Council had shown us. They were all mixed up as dreams always are, fragments of one time intruding into another – but only ever the worst fragments.

And somehow the Tehaman jaguars were there as well, stalking me through the night-time canopy of the island's forest. No matter how loud I shouted, no-one came – even when I found the others sitting around a campfire, they all ignored me. All except Ukmadorian in his grey cloak, who turned round and said, *You're not one of us, we can't help you.* Beside him, Persea and Laeas nodded grimly, then turned away.

But, as they had in the forest, after a while the dreams changed, became less disjointed, until I realised that these events had happened, they weren't constructs of my own mind.

I was in a stone-walled room, windowless and damp. There were four other men in there, one of them stripped and tied down on a metal frame — a rack, I realised after a moment. His skin was very dark, not black like a Mons Ferratan's, but exceptionally swarthy; his features seemed a mixture of Thetian and Archipelagan.

'You lie,' said one of the other men. Legate Phirias, I realized a moment later as he turned slightly towards me. 'You aren't from the Archipelago, are you?'

'I come from the south,' croaked the man on the rack.

'There is nothing to the south,' said Phirias harshly. 'Only the Desolation.'

'Beyond . . .'

'You expect us to believe this? You sailed across the Desolation on a catamaran? I think not. Lieutenant, I want this man to tell us who sent him. Get the information out of him any way you can.'

It was the same lieutenant, the one I'd recognised. This was a scene from the fort.

'Sir, all the other sailors say the same thing,' said the lieutenant. 'Perhaps he's telling the truth.'

Phirias turned a withering glare on his subordinate. 'Next you'll be telling me he's the Emperor's illegitimate son. We haven't made him hurt enough. I'll be back in two hours, see that he's ready to talk by then.' The legate turned on his heels and strode out of the cell. I heard a scream from the distance.

The lieutenant turned towards me, and for the first time I saw his face with stunned dismay. He was thirty years younger, but the features were unmistakable.

'*Illuminatus*, would you be able to work on him?'

'His mind is too strong,' I heard myself saying.

The young Sagantha Karao nodded. 'As I thought. Interrogator, continue your work.'

The interrogator turned the rack's wheel again as Sagantha stood by, asking the same question over and over again. The man cried out at the third turn, screamed at the fourth, but his answer was always the same.

'I think some new approaches are needed,' Sagantha said eventually. His face was set. 'It is unfortunate for you that you continue to resist my friend here; it would make your life much easier.'

The prisoner shook his head.

'I thought not. In that case, we should continue. Interrogator, try something new.'

There was no escape from the dream, no way to pull out of it until Phirias returned to the same answer and the scene faded.

Then I saw him again, this time in a green uniform instead of a black one, standing on the bridge of a manta. Cambressian, without a doubt.

'Heretic ships approaching, sir,' said a young officer by the aether tank. He was several years younger than Sagantha but wore the same rank insignia. 'I make it four war-mantas, the last one must be a transport.'

A tall man with silver hair sat beside the ship's captain, watching the scene. A junior admiral from the stars on his uniform, and the orders he gave a moment later on the fleet command net.

'They won't be properly trained. *Oryx* and *Eye of Amon* assume V formation around us. *Zenobia* and *Cicada* head out to port and come round, concentrate your fire on the last ship in their line of battle. Don't let the transport escape.'

It was only a few moments before the two forces engaged. Sagantha was comm officer, co-ordinating the actions of the other ships. I watched the three central Cambressian ships bear down on the enemy and open fire, pulse cannons and torpedoes blazing. The enemy returned fire vigorously, and the flagship was hit, once, twice.

An enemy torpedo struck near the bridge and an aether conduit burst, showering sparks over the weapons officer.

'Lieutenant Karao, move to weapons,' the captain ordered, as a healer's assistant carried the injured officer away. Sagantha obeyed, and the flagship directed its fire on the enemy ship responsible – Archipelagan, from its horn colours. A few minutes later a torpedo detonated near its engine vent.

The remaining enemy ships were already turning away, having destroyed the smaller *Cicada* at some point, but before I could discover what had happened, the images were gone.

I lashed out, catching the bedclothes, and felt myself teetering over the edge of the bed. I hit the floor with a thump, banging my head painfully. For a moment I lay there, feeling as if I'd been roasted, then I dragged at the bedclothes, tearing them away from me so I could cool down. Why was it so hot?

Somehow I anticipated the knock on the door as I lay there, head reeling and trying to cool off. I knew who it would be. Ravenna had a tunic on, but she was barefoot and her hair hadn't recovered from being slept on. As she turned on the tiny flamewood lamp that was the room's only illumination, I could see she hadn't slept well either.

'Same dream?' she said, shutting the door behind her.

'Sagantha?' I asked, rubbing my head.

'I hoped it was just me, but that was only wishful thinking.'

'Whose eyes were we seeing it through?' I asked.

'Memnon wasn't born thirty years ago. Probably Drances. He's a mind-mage too, though not as good as Memnon.'

Neither of us said anything for a second. She sat down beside me on the bed, since there was little room to stand.

'Somehow I could never imagine him being involved with that,' she said. 'I know he isn't to be trusted, and he'll always put his own interests first, but . . . torturing people,

Cathan. We claim to hate everything the Domain stands for, and yet we use their methods.'

'Neither of us have,' I said, but I only sounded weak.

'But all these years we've been trying to overthrow the Domain, fighting for a group of people who are every bit as backward-looking, as rigid and as cruel as they are. We *believed* what they taught us at the Citadel. Cathan, we actually thought that it was as black and white as they showed us. We've believed it this time. We only found out it wasn't so because the Tehamans have been interfering with our minds, not because we were intelligent enough to see through their lies.'

'Why would the Tehamans show us this?' I asked. 'It doesn't help them.'

'They're showing us what Sagantha is like, what he's done.' She stared at the wall, as if she could see into the next room. 'They're showing us that we aren't any better. We trust him, and he was on the Council for twenty years, in the Ring of Eight – it's almost an accident that he's ended up helping us instead of them.'

Something else we could never be certain of. 'We're sure he *is* on our side?'

'Yes,' she said firmly. 'He saved us at Kavatang. That wasn't the time to trick us, they had us at their mercy. There was no point letting us get away, and they certainly wouldn't have sacrificed a manta like *Meridian*.'

'It doesn't make sense from his point of view either.'

'Cathan, stop it. Drances is putting these thoughts in your head. Has Sagantha ever actually deceived you, betrayed you?' I noticed she didn't say *us*.

'You're the one who matters to him. Or at least he claims you are.'

She leant back on the bed, resting her head against the wall. 'I've trusted very few people, and almost all of them have betrayed my trust at some point. Even you and Palatine. I don't blame you for it, but you did. Sagantha I never trusted, not from the moment I first became his ward, and you know I ran away because he was talking about arranging a marriage. But the oddest thing is that he's never broken a promise he made.'

'Perhaps because he doesn't make many.'

'No, but the ones he makes he keeps. At least to me, and that's all I can afford to worry about at the moment.'

'It's not much to go on.' She'd never forgotten my revealing her identity when I'd promised not to, even though it had been a necessity and among friends. My guilt was still there, waiting to come to the surface whenever she mentioned it.

'What more is there? He's never given me his word and broken it, he's never treated me as a commodity, he's never imprisoned me in the middle of nowhere.'

Ravenna wasn't given to generalisations, and I knew who was responsible for each of those.

'He didn't speak up for us at the trial,' I said, feeling more awake now. And bitter, bitter and guilty.

'Right now, he's probably the only person who can get us to Tandaris in time. Like Hamilcar, we can rely on him because we know where his interests lie.'

'Is that the way you think of everybody?'

'It's the way Hamilcar thinks of everybody. He's done fairly well for himself.'

I shook my head. 'I don't agree. Yes, he's a Tanethan and a Merchant Lord, but he doesn't work that way. Why else would he have helped us in Lepidor?'

'I knew you'd bring that up.'

'So is that all we are to you? People who happen to share your aims?' I went on, persisting even though it was bound to be a touchy subject, and would rebound on me in a minute or two.

The look she gave me indicated she was fully awake now, even if her appearance and her hair suggested otherwise.

'You've asked me that before,' she said evenly.

'It's an impression you give.' I wasn't going to back down. Not yet, at any rate, because I'd lost every one of these arguments.

'To pretend that's all you are would be a lie,' she said softly. 'I'm as human as anybody, I just don't trust people. I can't afford to.'

'And in a few days' time, when your years of hiding are over and Aurelia makes you Pharaoh with the Navy's support, what then?'

'I'll be Pharaoh. Monarchs can't really trust anyone.'

'It's a lonely existence.'

'I know. I've always known it will be. I'm used to it.' Anyone else might have sounded self-pitying, but Ravenna didn't. She was only stating a fact. 'You turned away from your inheritance; you had the chance to make that decision, and you made it the right way. So did Palatine. But if you'd been the only possible choice, if you hadn't had your mother or Tanais to fall back on, you'd have done nothing but harm.'

Because Thetia needed its ruler at the moment, was the unspoken addition. As did the Archipelago. And while my mother could take my place in Thetia, there was no-one to take Ravenna's even if she'd wanted to give it up. Presently I said:

'You may find that's not the case. Can you think of anyone who ruled well without trusting anyone, any close friends? Even Eshar had his military cronies.'

'Don't try to turn this into a history lesson.' She paused, closed her eyes for a second.

I felt a stab of despair in my chest.

'I will be taking the crown,' she said at last, ' in order to rebuild the Archipelago. To undo all the damage the Domain has caused, to make it into a state that can stand up on its own without the help of the Empire.

'Nothing would please me more than to have you with

me, to have your help, but I suspect there is very little that would make you more miserable. If you'd accepted the throne, a state marriage would have been perfect. For me. You would have been incredibly unhappy.'

I started to say something, but she pressed a finger to my lips.

'You have the perception and the intelligence to know that you wouldn't make a ruler, not because you're bad at it but because it's a life you'd hate. It would wear you out too quickly, and so would being my consort.'

Our gazes met, and I saw pain very clearly written on her face. I wanted to tell her she was wrong, that there were ways round it, but she didn't let me.

'Please hear me out. You'll say that it won't, because you don't want to believe me. I didn't want to say this now. I wanted to leave it until we had time, until there was nothing else to worry about, but for once I can't.

'I love you, Cathan.' She closed her eyes, whispered it again. 'I love you. I want to spend the rest of my life in your company. In an ideal world, I would have done.' She bit her lip as she looked at me again. 'This isn't an ideal world. You know what you want to do with your life, and you'll be able to. I don't believe for a moment it's anything as small as Salderis told you. I have my own duty, and it's poles apart from you.'

She took her finger away as she finished speaking, reached down for my hand and squeezed it. I didn't know what to say. I was desperate for this not to happen, but a small voice in my head was telling me that she knew me only too well.

'If I married you, you wouldn't be just a citizen any more. You'd be part of the court, part of its politics. I love you too much to let that happen.'

'Is my world really that small?' I said finally, hardly able to breathe.

'Our worlds aren't the same. Salderis thought you were

one of the most brilliant oceanographers she'd ever taught, but for her it was more important that you were a Tar'Conantur. It isn't any more. The world has more than enough princes and emperors, but not nearly enough scientists.'

I'd had no idea Salderis had said that, but it didn't matter. I'd been in love with Ravenna – or loved her, which wasn't the same thing – for five years. Our paths had always lain together, but then . . . how could I sacrifice this for a dream which so many people had told me was below my abilities? I wasn't so sure any more that I would be happy merely as an oceanographer.

'You'll never be *merely* anything,' she said, reading my mind yet again. Her hand tightened on mine. 'You have your own future, and I *will not* let you sacrifice it for me.'

'Is that my choice or yours?'

'Yours, of course. But mine as well. I can see I shouldn't have brought this up.'

I interrupted her. 'Better that you have.'

'Not really. I just couldn't go on and let you think that . . .'

'That everything would be fine, and one day we might end up married to each other.'

She nodded. 'I suppose so. Something like that, in any case. It didn't matter until now, because the chances of either of us having a life free from the Domain was almost nothing. I doubt mine will ever be, not with two hundred years of their mistakes to try and put right, not to mention my own family's.'

'There are plenty of people to help you.'

'If only I trust them. Yes, I know.'

Neither of us said anything for a long moment, which as the seconds dragged by became endless, sitting side by side in that tiny room. *Oh Thetis, why?*

'We were a good partnership,' I said finally, lost for words.

'Yes, we were.'

But that was all either of us could say, because nothing would have been adequate. We hugged each other fiercely, neither wanting nor able to let go.

Finally, reluctantly, we drew apart.

'If I stay here any longer, I'll change my mind,' Ravenna said at last. 'I should never have had to do this.' She stood up, paused for a second and kissed me very quickly before leaving. I heard her footsteps outside and the sound of her door closing, five cubits and a thousand miles away.

And as the first of the morning watch woke from their dream-tampered sleep two decks below, I sat there on the side of the bed and whispered *Goodbye*.

CHAPTER XXIX

Had I not lived through the next few hours in a kind of numb emptiness, had Ravenna not chosen that night to be open for once in her life, I might have noticed the trouble in time. I had no idea how long I spent lying on my bed, staring up into the darkness and utterly unable to sleep.

But I was too wrapped up in myself, too apathetic and depressed to care very much what was going on around me. Almost as I had been before the invasion of Lepidor four years ago, and for the same reason – but now, however bad her timing was, she hadn't done it out of anger or hatred.

Or was it? She'd only ever said *I love you* once before, the night she'd drugged me and escaped from Ilthys. Almost as if she'd been softening the blow both times.

And, I told myself, I should have known this was coming. I'd felt the gulf between us since that night in Ilthys, or maybe even before. Trust wasn't the only barrier we'd never crossed, only the most important.

After a while, introspection gave way to simple despair, the dreams and Sagantha's treachery forgotten. There was nothing I could tell myself to relieve the pain, nothing really to cushion the blow.

Eventually I must have slept, because I dreamed again. I stood alone in a vast domed room, its glass sides held by ribs that arched up to meet far above my head. Brilliant sunshine flooded down on to a marble floor patterned like a whirlpool, its centre on the point where I was standing.

'Where am I?' I said.

'You promised you'd bring Ravenna here,' said a familiar voice. I turned round, saw my brother standing

429

there in his white cloak and tunic, seemingly unaffected by the incredible heat. 'Now you never will.'

I looked around, trying to get my bearings, but the hall was so vast I could only see ocean in all directions. I tried to move towards the edge, but it was as if I was walking on the spot, could never break away from the centre of the whirlpool.

'Where is this?'

'It's the holiest place in the world,' Orosius said. 'The Hall of Deep Time in Sanction.'

Part of me wanted to say that Sanction had been lost, but here I was. I remembered promising Ravenna that we'd watch the sunset one day from this place, as Hierarchs had done for generations until the usurpation. It was a ritual of a kind, but one whose origins were lost. Nothing I'd read had told me why it was so important.

'The sun is sinking.' Orosius pointed up, and I shielded my eyes from the glare. It was later in the day than I imagined, perhaps mid-afternoon. 'You don't have forever.'

'I'm not Hierarch.'

'You are. I made you Hierarch before I died. I left you my medallion; what have you done with it?'

My hands flew to my chest, but there was no dolphin medallion there. 'It isn't here.'

His expression changed, became darker. 'You've lost it, haven't you?'

'No. I left it in Thetia.'

'You're lying.' He reached inside his tunic and lifted the medallion out, a carved dolphin leaping over a huge flawed sapphire. 'You left it behind, you never bothered to search for it. Another broken promise. No wonder she doesn't want you, you're as untrustworthy as any priest.'

'That's not true!' I protested. 'She loves me.'

The grey eyes bored into me. 'No, she doesn't. She lied as often as you broke your promises. You never really knew what she thought about you, did you?'

I heard her voice echo round the hall, suddenly saw her sitting on a wall above some water with a man in black. 'Cathan's kind enough, but he's a doormat. In the end, he'll always do what people tell him, because he's weak-minded. It gets on my nerves.'

'He takes after his father,' said the man. Memnon. 'You can't really blame him, though, weakness runs in the family. It's not as if you're going back to him.'

'I suppose not,' she said, looking up at him. She touched his arm and smiled. 'We've time enough to worry about the lowlanders later.'

They moved closer together, and I tore my head away, unable to watch. It was twice as bad for knowing that he'd betrayed and tortured her.

The scene faded again, and there was only Orosius.

'I don't think you've lost as much as you imagine,' he said offhandedly. 'She certainly hasn't lost anything at all. She doesn't have time for the little people, even though she's as unimportant as you are.'

The little people. How contemptuous he'd been of us all, confident that he could brush us aside with a flick of his hand. As he had done, because we'd been at his mercy when a far greater person than he was had brushed him aside in turn.

'You're one of the little people too,' I said, putting as much venom into my tone as I could. 'We survived you, but you didn't survive Sarhaddon. You're dead, people only remember a demented and pathetic man. Hardly a fitting epitaph.'

Even as I was speaking in the dream, I felt dizzy. A moment later the hall had gone, and I was being led up to the stake in the square in Lepidor, held at the point of the sword while the Sacri tied me to it. But this time there was no-one bound beside or below me, I would die alone. I looked around, saw Ravenna standing by Etlae. All the others were standing around the square, not a single one about to share my fate.

On a gibbet on the far side of the square, the bodies of the marine tribune and his men hung, swaying slightly in the wind. They'd been our rescuers. I tried slipping into the void that would isolate me from the pain, but to my horror I couldn't. I struggled, but the ropes were too tight for me to even move.

'You won't escape.' Orosius had gone, it was Sarhaddon who stood at the foot of the pile of wood, a flickering torch in one hand. 'He didn't survive me, and nor will you. Not this time.'

I stared into the orange flames, feeling the heat even from here. Why couldn't I slip into the void? What was wrong? I tried to wrench myself away from the stake, not believing that this could happen, but I was helpless.

'Please,' I said desperately. 'Please don't.'

'You had your chance to change something, you were too much of a coward to take it. History has no time for mediocrities, she burns them out of her memory. Only fire can do that for her, and you signed your own death warrant.'

He threw over a sheet of papyrus with official writing, a notice of execution with my own signature at the bottom beside an Oceanographic Guild seal. It landed by my feet, lay there on the faggots. Suddenly the pile grew higher, and I was covered up to the knees with pieces of paper and papyrus, log-books and official decrees, letters and even wooden racks used to hold water test samples.

'What are these?' I asked, almost sick with panic. This couldn't be happening! Why were none of them trying to rescue me?

'Every record of your existence,' Sarhaddon said, the wind brushing his robes against the lowest level of the pile. 'Everything that has your name on it, everything that proves you ever lived. It all has to go with you,

432

otherwise the world won't be purified.'

'Why are none of the others with me?' I asked. 'You condemned them all as well.'

Sarhaddon shook his cowled head. 'I condemn no-one. Only you and Ranthas have the power to bring you here. All of them have done things that will be remembered. Sagantha, Palatine, Etlae, Lord Barca, Ravenna – they all helped to change the world, whether for better or worse. You don't deserve a place in their company.'

As he spoke, someone stepped out of the crowd to a lectern in the open space, a grave woman dressed in black with flashes of gold at her collar. But Telesta hadn't been there, I thought wildly.

The crowd bowed their heads, including Sarhaddon and Etlae.

'The pages of history only have room for those who deserve inclusion. We remember the best and the worst, the brightest successes and the darkest failures. They will all be remembered in the annals of time, and there is no room beside them for those who have not shone, who have kept their eyes on the earth and failed to listen to the call of the stars urging them onwards.

'We give thanks that this day we purify the strands of time by erasing all records of one such, that we are here to see justice done and the ways of Time observed. May you all walk through the arches of bright eternity from now until the stars grow old, and may each one of you shine as a beacon out of the darkness of the past. In the name of Chronos, Lord of Time and History, we give thanks.'

She stepped back again and the assembled crowd looked at me expectantly. Dread had engulfed me, and I couldn't breathe.

'So be it,' Sarhaddon said solemnly, and he lifted the torch and threw it down on to the pile of papers. Flames licked over them, spreading around and upwards as the crowd watched.

'Help!' I pleaded, but there was no sympathy on the faces of the people nearest, not even on Ravenna's or Palatine's.

Then the flames moved towards me, and I felt the heat on my legs, tried to move away but couldn't because of the ropes. They reached my feet and I began to scream.

'This lies ahead of you still,' said Sarhaddon as excruciating agony swept over me. I could hardly hear his voice. 'I will see you in Tandaris . . .'

Something banged close by, and the image vanished. I sat upright, feeling literally as if I'd been roasted alive.

'What is it?' It was Palatine, fully dressed and wearing a corselet of Thetian scale armour. She was outlined against the light of the corridor for a moment.

'A nightmare,' I said, looking around to reassure myself this was real, there were no flames. Instinctively I reached down towards the end of the bed, but my legs were no hotter than the rest of me. This room was stifling; the ventilation on *Crusade* seemed to be minimal.

'You poor thing,' Palatine said. 'Wait.'

She was back a moment later with a glass of cool water, which I drank gratefully.

'What's the time?' I said when I'd gathered enough wits to speak. 'Why the armour?'

'We've got some serious problems,' she said. 'Trouble among the crew.'

'Trouble,' I echoed stupidly. 'What kind of trouble?'

'They want us to deal with the other ship, to turn round and use the fire-weapon on her.'

'That doesn't make sense, why would they . . .?'

'Why would they what?'

'Didn't Ravenna tell you about the Tehamans, the dreams?'

'No. She's still asleep as well, I don't know what's wrong with you both.'

I remembered with an awful wrench what had

434

happened in the night, and my few moments of blessed amnesia were gone. Loneliness came crashing down on me again. I didn't mention that, though, only the dreams we'd had.

I told her what I was willing to tell, the nightmares from last night and our flight from the dam, with the Tehamans the only common factor.

'Tehaman mind-mages,' she said. 'Yes, you're right. They've been working on you and Ravenna, but why would they try and convince the crew to turn round and attack them? They don't know about the fire-weapon, do they? Not even all of the crew did.'

Crusade's crew were a mixture, some people from the dam and some Ilthysians Oailos had recruited. For them, anyone who opposed the Domain was an ally, and they wouldn't believe us if we told them about the Tehamans and their mind-mages. Most of them had no idea the Tehamans existed.

'Are they in control?' I asked. I needed a wash, but I wasn't sure I had time.

'No. Not yet. There's a lot of muttering, but they're all still at their stations. I think Amadeo's causing some of the trouble and maybe Oailos as well.'

That was my fault. We should have left Amadeo in Ilthys, but since Ravenna's very public demonstration of how hollow the Domain's claims were, he'd changed, seemed to have had a revelation of some kind. I'd hoped that by the time we reached Tandaris he'd be ready to spread news of what had happened, to undermine the Domain's credibility with more effectiveness than anyone else, given his past and the oratorical training he'd have received as a Venatic.

I grabbed a towel and some fresh clothes, rinsed myself in icy cold water to wake myself up, and dressed while I was still half wet. It wasn't pleasant, but the shock would help wake me up. Palatine had banged on Ravenna's door

– none of them had locks, of course, because Sacri officers couldn't be allowed to keep their superiors out – and she emerged red-eyed. Ravenna didn't seem to have slept since she left my room, and there were dark shadows under her eyes. She pushed past Palatine and into the washroom before either of us could say a word.

'I'll ask later,' said Palatine, as the Thetian who'd saved me from the leviathan – Zaria, her name was – came along the corridor. She was wearing another of the scale corselets, and carrying two more. Palatine made me put one of them on. I disliked armour and hadn't worn it for years, but this was hardly heavier than a winter coat and felt like a silk shirt.

'You can't buy this for all the gold in Taneth,' Palatine said. 'It's wonderful stuff.'

She made Ravenna put the other suit on, then hustled us back down the passageway. It was strange to see the two of them in armour, and Ravenna looked ill at ease. No wonder, given that we might have to protect ourselves against fellow penitents from the dam. I hoped this was an exaggeration.

'We'll be at battle stations in an hour or two,' Palatine said as we came down the stairs into the well.

'Has the other ship gained on us?' I asked.

'No change. But Sagantha wanted us to be ready in case it does come to a battle. We can't afford to have anyone seriously injured in some skirmish this far out from the city.'

Sagantha was on the bridge when we arrived, looking as if he'd got at least some sleep in one of the small cabins to either side of the bridge. He was wearing a white naval uniform – Thetian, I thought – with admiral's stars.

'There you are,' he said, when we came in. 'You took your time.'

'One moment,' Palatine said, gesturing at the cabin. They went in and Sagantha, after giving instructions that he wasn't to be disturbed, closed the door behind him.

Would Sagantha decide to do something drastic? With Vespasia gone, I was the only one of us who knew Oailos at all well. I might be able to find out what was going on, whether this was indeed some evil plan of the Tehamans.

I slipped out of the bridge and went back into the main dormitory, which was serving as the crew's mess, to find them. Only the two day-watches were sleeping in here; the night-watch had been given cabins of their own so they could get some rest during the day. Not that a watch was huge in any case; a normal manta had twelve in a watch, we'd only been able to manage nine.

'Cathan,' Oailos said when I came in, gesturing me over to where he was sitting on a bunk. He was talking to Amadeo, the last combination I'd have expected. Amadeo was a Venatic, after all, and we'd brought him along on sufferance to prevent him causing mischief in Ilthys while we were away. He didn't seem to have minded, though, and had hardly said anything since that moment in the café in Ilthys.

'You don't look happy,' said Amadeo immediately. He was, rather incongruously, wearing a fairly shabby guildsman's robe, the kind they wore for meetings or official occasions.

'I didn't sleep well,' I said shortly. There was no way he was going to know what had happened.

'I didn't either,' said Oailos. 'Nightmares.'

'The work of our enemies,' Amadeo said.

'Since when were they *our* enemies?' I asked. He was unsettling, and I had no idea what to make of him.

'We're all in this together,' Oailos said. 'It's not as if that ship's going to be selective when it attacks us.'

'It hasn't attacked us so far,' I pointed out.

'It has, though,' Amadeo insisted. 'It attacks our minds. We have a weapon that can destroy it with a single shot. The people on that ship are trying to stop us getting to

Tandaris, and it's clear that all of you consider them as enemies.'

'They're not naval, are they?' said Oailos, looking up at me. He was turning a piece of carved stone over and over in his hands.

'No.'

'They're not Domain, either,' Amadeo said. 'No Domain ship would have behaved this way.'

'It doesn't matter,' Oailos said. 'If they were, we'd have had just as much reason to destroy them. I was on the bridge yesterday, and I heard all about Kavatang. I don't have any more time for that bunch of arrogant bastards than you do. I was proud to follow the old gods, and not least because I thought their priests were better. But they lie as much as anyone.'

Another man sitting nearby nodded assent. He was Sciapho, an oceanographer who'd been with us at the dam.

'Whoever the Council really are, they're no better than the Domain,' he said bitterly. 'I helped them pass messages, spent two years as a slave for it, and all they're interested in is keeping their own cosy little circles of power and squabbling between each other.'

'They'll hate what happened in Ilthys just as much as the Domain,' Amadeo said.

'You're no longer part of the Domain?' I asked. 'Where's your admiration for Sarhaddon gone? Your devotion to Ranthas?'

Amadeo smiled. 'I believe in Ranthas as strongly as I ever did. But the Domain's approach is the wrong one. Fire isn't the only element, it is not different from all the others. Why else would Ravenna be able to use its power?'

'You sound like Sarhaddon,' I said, not concealing my hostility. I was in no mood for a priest's sermonising; why were the others listening to him?

'I could never equal his eloquence. I'm saying that

Ravenna has taught us to look beyond what the Domain is saying, and what the Council taught you. This is a message from Ranthas himself telling us that we've gone down the wrong path.' There was an urgent edge to his voice suddenly, and I saw some of the others look round.

'You believed what the Council taught you,' Amadeo said, looking at me now.

I nodded. 'Yes.' It was only the truth, after all. I wasn't really concentrating; the hollow emptiness inside me was too strong.

'They lied to you. Like the Domain, they rewrote history, they forced you to accept their own version of events.'

'And like the Domain, when you came up with a new idea, they squashed it,' Sciapho said. 'Such as the storms.'

'How does this help us?' Amadeo demanded, pressing on before I could reply. 'I was as bad as any of them, worse maybe. My Order exists to purge the Archipelago of heresy, and it seems the Council and their minions treat people who disagree with them no better than the Domain. We should put an end to both of them.'

'We should certainly put an end to that ship behind us,' Oailos said. 'They have mind-mages of their own, why else would some of us suddenly have nightmares? They don't deserve our mercy.'

I wondered how they'd discovered about the nightmares. I would have thought that only a few people had had them, and it wasn't the sort of thing that would usually be discussed.

'We know the damage they do, so why wait?' Amadeo said. 'Why can't we just turn around and put a stop to their trickery for ever, deprive the Council of some of its power?'

This time all of the ten or so people in there murmured or nodded agreement.

'We should suggest it,' said Oailos firmly. He stood up.

439

'Sagantha may be captain, but this isn't a naval ship and he doesn't have the right to ignore us. A few minutes' work and we can put them out of the reckoning, and out of our minds .'

'Begin the work of fighting back,' Amadeo said. 'A good idea.'

So much for attempting to defuse the situation. My mere presence had set them off, and for once it hadn't even been anything that I had said.

What could I do now? I knew there were Tehamans on board that manta, maybe Memnon and Drances, but there would probably be other people I knew on it, more who would die if we used the fire-weapon.

They took me along with them to the bridge, not aggressive or hostile, simply determined to have their way.

'Rock shelf ahead, sir,' the helmsman reported as we came in. 'Two miles down.'

Sagantha frowned. 'Earlier than I expected,' he said. 'We've made better time than I thought. In an hour or so we should be in more interesting waters, and then it'll be time to deal with our mind-warping friends out there.'

'Captain?' Oailos said.

Sagantha looked round, frowning as he saw virtually the entire off-duty watch crowding on to the bridge. 'What is it?'

'What are we waiting for?' Oailos demanded. 'Use the fire-weapon, stop them interfering with our minds.'

'Why are you so eager to use the Domain's weapon? This isn't a Domain ship.'

'It's an enemy. What do we have to lose?' Oailos insisted. 'Or are you afraid you'll kill some of your friends if you use it?'

'We don't want to use that weapon,' Sagantha said. 'I can put them out of action when we're closer inshore, without relying on it. It's never been test-fired, we have no idea how much damage it will do.' He'd been the one in favour of it earlier on.

'We can destroy the ship without losing a single man,' Sciapho said. 'If we engage, there'll be casualties.'

'He's right,' Palatine said. 'Wouldn't it be better to cripple her now? Set off the fire-weapon a little way beneath her, enough to damage but not kill everyone?'

'Why not destroy her?' Oailos demanded.

'Because we build up more resentment,' Khalia said from behind us. 'Render them helpless, come back later and capture them rather than kill them.'

'It's an idea,' Sagantha said. 'It would lose us time, but then . . .' He paused, apparently pondering. 'Cathan, Ravenna, would one of you be so kind as to arm the fire-weapon?'

'Only to cripple?' Ravenna said.

'Only to cripple,' he assured her.

Would he keep his word, I wondered, as Ravenna went over to the weapon's console – it had one all to itself, in front of a chair below the captain's. There was a covering over the aether panel, like a piece of metal sealed in place. That, I presumed, was the safeguard; only fire-magic could break through it.

She held her hand over it as members of the bridge crew craned round to watch. I felt the tingle of magic, strong enough to be felt on the other ship, and a moment later a flame seemed to jump from her hand to the panel.

I will see you in Tandaris.

She plunged her hand through the flames and into the panel. Palatine moved over to push her sleeve up and keep it out of the flames that now ringed the panel.

'Turn us through a full circle,' Sagantha ordered the helmsman. 'As tight as you can make it, and leave our bow pointing slightly down.'

As tight as possible still meant a large arc, and every reserve thruster cut in as *Crusade* began her turn, banking hard around to port. The deck tilted, a little at first and then more and more as we came round at a steeper angle. I hurriedly sat down in the nearest chair and strapped myself in, while Palatine supported Ravenna so she could keep her hand out of the flames. Polinskarn wouldn't have designed it with such a mechanism, so there should be a way round it.

Sagantha sank his hand into his own aether pads, waited until we were pointing almost directly at the Council battle cruiser.

'Now,' he said. There was a deep, sonorous vibration and the entire ship shook once, then twice.

I could see it through the windows, a red flare in the water and a stream of bubbles suddenly materialising, vanishing again into the gloom. In the aether tank, a red line lanced out from *Crusade* with astonishing speed to a point about three hundred yards below the battle cruiser and very slightly in front.

Then I saw the familiar white-hot flare in the water, bright enough that I could see the glow through the windows, and a cloud of bubbles spread outwards, engulfing the battle cruiser. We continued to turn, still heeling round at the same angle.

Ravenna pulled her hand out of the panel; the flames closed in again and disappeared. There was a thump from somewhere behind us, and more angry shouts from the well. Ithien's marines stood braced against the wall with drawn swords.

When the cloud of bubbles finally began to clear, I saw the other manta slowing, turning crazily round to one side with bubbles of her own rising from an engine vent where superheated flamewood was escaping from the reactor.

'One less problem to deal with,' Sagantha said, looking satisfied. 'They know what we can do now, but they can hardly reply. It's an effective weapon, isn't it?'

We returned to our original course, but less than five

minutes after the weapon had been fired, four more mantas appeared at extreme range. They were waiting between us and the entrance to the deep-water channel.

They must be Imperial Navy. No-one else had a squadron that size in Imperial waters, and I sighed in relief.

'Steer for them,' Sagantha said, but just then the comm buzzed into life, and a familiar voice came over the system. In the aether tank, the image of the leading manta flashed to indicate where the signal was coming from.

'This is Captain Kauanhameha of the Archipelagan battle cruiser *Shadowstar*. Surrender in the name of the Pharaoh.'

CHAPTER XXX

'Destroy them,' Oailos said. 'They're here to destroy us.'

The bridge was silent for a second as we stared at the new images in the aether tank. How many ships did they have? We'd seen two battle cruisers so far, even mistaken one for *Shadowstar* when it wasn't. Battle cruisers were incredibly expensive and jealously guarded by the Navies that built them – so how come the Council had this many?

'I know who they are,' Ravenna snapped, turning on him. 'And that captain is my friend. Sagantha, turn on the comm.'

'Better for them to think we're Domain,' Sagantha said.

'No. I can hope that not everyone on those ships is Ring of Eight.'

It might be a forlorn hope, though.

'Turn on the comm,' Ravenna repeated. 'I'll not fight without having tried this. And see if we can send to the other ships as well.'

After a moment, Sagantha reluctantly obeyed.

Ravenna took a deep breath, went to stand closer so the receiver could transmit her voice clearly.

'This is not a Domain ship,' she said. 'I am Ravenna Ulfhada, granddaughter of Lord Orethura and Pharaoh of Qalathar. We are Archipelagans.'

There was a pause, and the voice that answered wasn't the same.

'You,' said Ukmadorian, and I could hear the venom in his voice. 'You have been deposed. You are nothing! I will see you destroyed!'

'Ukmadorian, we are fighting the Domain as well,' she said. I could see how much of an effort it was for her to

444

keep calm. 'We only stand to lose by destroying each other.'

'There is no *each other*.' The other mantas began to move towards us, forming up into a claw formation that would allow them to concentrate their firepower on us. 'Your foul arts will not help you now. We will destroy you and liberate the Archipelago!'

'You bring death to all of us,' she replied. 'The Navy will crush you.'

'The Navy will soon be ours,' Ukmadorian said, the hate obvious in his voice. 'They cannot do anything. And nor can you.'

'How dare they threaten her?' Amadeo whispered. The Ilthysians looked angry. Oailos clenched his fists.

'She is Pharaoh,' Sciapho said wonderingly. 'She is Pharaoh, yet they betray her? They aren't worthy to live! We should wipe them off the face of the waters.'

His words were loud enough to be heard by Ukmadorian, who laughed contemptuously.

'Four against one?' he said. 'Your mage can't work so close in. Shout in vain, there is no-one to hear you. I'm done with you.' There was a final click as the commlink closed.

'Battle stations!' Oailos shouted.

Sagantha had practised battle drills on the way down, so there was only a moment's hesitation as men rushed to consoles and weapons stations. Khalia sighed and headed back to the sickbay. She'd be needed soon enough.

'How long does the weapon take to charge?' Sagantha asked. 'Vespasia said it needed a few minutes between shots. Oailos, send an engineer down there.'

'This isn't looking encouraging,' Palatine said, watching the other ships advance. 'Battle plan, sir?'

Sagantha only took a moment to think. 'Helm, twenty degrees to port, bring her down a quarter of a mile.' He sank his hands into the panels and a moment later a soft, almost inaudible purring sound indicated that the aether shields were up.

I tried to use magic, but couldn't. There had to be mind-mages on *Shadowstar* as well, and as long as we were within a few miles, they'd be able to blank out my magic and Ravenna's. I could escape their control easily enough, but the curbs on my magic were another matter.

'We can't help,' Ravenna said a moment later, having tried the same thing. All we could do was sit by in helpless frustration. I cursed, sick of the Tehamans and their interference, sick of what the Council was trying to do.

'We should have killed every last mind-mage on that other ship,' Oailos said. 'Let's see if we can deal with the ones here as well.'

I could feel the anger of the others on the bridge, all except the calmly professional Sagantha. They at least could man weapons stations and hit back at the enemy, but what use were we? Would it be the same all the way?

If there was to be a way. *Crusade* was heavily armoured and overgunned, but one against four was a grim outlook. A creeping fear replaced the emptiness, the realisation that none of this might matter in the end.

I'd only been in two naval engagements before, once under attack by *Shadowstar* and once on board her, fighting off the pirates that had attacked Hamilcar. Both times the battle cruiser's armament had dealt with the enemy in short order.

I could remember the faces of the crew in that second fight, every single one of the people on the bridge and all of the others who'd been shipmates with us. I'd never dreamed that I would go into battle against them a second time.

Another memory came to the surface with an awful wrench; my first meeting with Ravenna after the brief battle between *Pakle* and *Shadowstar*. I recalled the terror of actually being confronted with people who might have been pirates, out to kill every single one of us. Then the chilling meeting with Ukmadorian, Ravenna, and Prime Etlae.

Ukmadorian and Etlae had wanted me out of the way, and for years afterwards I'd believed that meant taking me to the Citadel there and then. But now, knowing what both Etlae and Ukmadorian were really like, it was hard to believe that.

So Ravenna had saved my life back then. Oh, Thetis, why had it come to this? Why was she seeing everything in such a grim light?

I shouldn't be thinking about this now.

Palatine, knowing as well as anyone how frustrating it was to be left out, found stations for both of us. It was out of sympathy rather than any particular need for my services, but concentrating on anything, even something as mundane as the shield controls, was enough. And it meant someone more experienced could be moved to man one of the major weapons stations. I had no desire to do that myself.

The tank showed us to be on a converging course with the four Council ships, now properly deployed into their claw. They'd started off to starboard, so we had a few more minutes yet, but the strait was still a few miles away, we didn't have enough of a lead to stay ahead of them until then.

'We'll have to hold them off,' Sagantha said. 'Fire when you can. We'll see if we can't cripple one of them in the first engagement. I want to get into the Inland Sea.'

We could easily have spiralled down towards and below the bedrock, too deep for them to follow, but that would make us several hours later at Tandaris. If the Elemental Council were there in force, we didn't have that time.

Unless Aurelia, Hamilcar and Ithien were all still in favour with the Council. Ukmadorian didn't know Ithien, had no idea that the others were involved, while Ithien and

Hamilcar were both aware what troubles we'd had with the Council. Why would the heretic leaders suspect them of collusion with us, when they had no reason to? They should be safe for the time being.

No. It wouldn't work, because the only channels straight into the Inland Sea were the Aetian Islands one we were heading for and the more dangerous one to the west that went through Perdition's Shore.

Sagantha and Palatine had probably thought of it, but if they hadn't . . . it was worth mentioning. People were used to not being able to navigate Perdition's Shore, but I was one of the few people alive who could.

'What about the western channel?' I suggested.

They both looked thoughtful, and Palatine estimated it would probably add another four hours to the journey, more than any of us were comfortable with. On the other hand, we could be sure of arriving in one piece. There was a danger that they'd blockade the deep-water passages in the Inland Sea, but despite its overall shallowness, there were too many places for a manta to slip through for that to be effective.

Shadowstar had fired its first torpedoes at extreme range, and the pursuit showed no sign of letting up. It was a pity that they were too close for us to use the fire-weapon, really, but the shockwave would do almost as much damage to us at this distance; I was told the Domain had lost a manta to the side-effects of their own weapon at one point. Good riddance.

'Begin a turn to port, steep descent,' Sagantha ordered the helmsman. 'As sharp a turn as you can make it, we'll see if we can't go underneath them.'

Oailos and Amadeo both looked up.

'Aren't we engaging?' Oailos asked.

'No,' Sagantha said, and explained what I'd proposed.

'We have thicker armour and more weapons,' said Amadeo stubbornly. 'Why are we fleeing from them?'

'If you want to live to pass on these new ideas of yours, then do what I say,' said Sagantha with faint irritation in his voice. 'We can't take on four Council warships on our own.'

'Maybe Ravenna should try talking to them again,' Sciapho suggested. 'At least some of their crews might be willing to help us.'

We turned sharply round and began to double back, driving downwards. We were already a few hundred yards deeper than the four Council mantas, and they were now coming almost exactly at us – just at the wrong depth.

The rear two broke off the chase and turned steeply round, heading back to try and intercept us. They'd expected us to try and blast our way through them, then, not turn and escape.

I hurriedly belted myself into my chair as we drove downwards at a steeper and steeper angle. We'd left *Shadowstar* and her companion behind, and the other two ships would have a struggle to catch up.

What had they been doing here? Presumably whoever was on the now-crippled battle cruiser had alerted Ukmadorian's squadron using mind-magic, which was a disturbing prospect.

'Could we make a dash for it now?' Palatine said. Unbelievably, we'd left the first two floundering behind and above us, trying desperately to come round and engage. 'Charge through the rear ships?'

Sagantha paused. 'No. *Shadowstar* would reach us before we made the channel. Keep on with the original plan. Helm, keep our speed as high as you can.'

'She won't like it,' Oailos said. 'Not if we go too deep, and the reactors are already failing.'

'Can we hook up the weapon reactor to the engines?' Palatine said.

Sagantha looked questioningly at the only engineer left on the bridge, who shrugged. 'I'll give it a try,' he said. 'I can't guarantee it will work.'

'That takes away our best weapon,' Amadeo began, but Sagantha silenced him.

'Running on three reactors, we won't *need* the weapon.' That might be because the engines would have exploded due to the pressure on them, but it would take a while for that to happen, if it was going to.

Then I saw *Shadowstar* and her first consort break off and veer over to port, now heading for the Aetian Islands channel.

'They'll come round through the Inland Sea and try to cut us off,' Sagantha said. 'Leave the gap wide open for anybody else trying to get in. Keep our descent steady.'

The other two stayed doggedly on our tail as we headed further and further into the abyss. We were unlikely to have time to get so deep that they'd lose us, but both were ordinary war mantas and would have trouble operating below six or seven miles. Sagantha identified one of our pursuers as the other Shadow manta, *Rhadamanthys*, from a notch on the trailing edge of its wing. Its companion must belong to another of the Citadels, but we had no idea which.

'Cathan, are there any mind-mages on those ships?' Sagantha asked.

I tried, and a moment later felt my magic blocked – but not as strongly as before.

'One.'

'Can you tell which ship?'

That was something Ravenna would be better at, and after a few moments she managed – heavens only knew how – to pinpoint him on *Rhadamanthys*.

'We'll engage them once we're at depth,' Sagantha ordered. 'No need to destroy them, crippling their engines will do. We won't use the fire-weapon; have a full spread of torpedoes ready, target *Rhadamanthys*.'

'If we fire at the other one, I may have a chance to win *Rhadamanthys* over,' Ravenna said hesitantly. 'We don't know who's on it, and they wouldn't have heard me earlier.'

'Enemies,' said Oailos intolerantly. 'If they're on that ship, they believe Ukmadorian's lies and they aren't going to listen.'

'I have to give them a chance,' Ravenna insisted. 'I believed the Council for twenty-five years, and I should have been able to see through them.'

'Wait till they're out of range of the others,' Sagantha suggested.

So we waited, held in our chairs only by the straps. Even though the third reactor hadn't yet been connected, we were beginning to leave both our pursuers behind. The distance between us would only get greater with depth, but I wasn't sure that we'd lose them altogether in time to slip through Perdition's Shore unobserved.

The descent was a painfully long process, and maybe half an hour passed before we passed below six miles, running parallel to the bedrock. We'd have to come up again within an hour or two, but at this depth the heavily armoured *Crusade* had the advantage.

'They're levelling off above us,' the helm reported.

'Just at the limit of their range,' said Sagantha. 'At least one of their captains has a brain in his head. Ravenna, go ahead.'

'This is Pharaoh Ravenna,' she said, when the link had been opened. We were directing it at both ships, just in case. 'Do any of you remember me?'

'You are an apostate,' said a harsh voice a moment later.

Was there no end to the people involved in this? But then, Chlamas had been on the Elemental Council when he taught us at the Citadel, and I shouldn't have been surprised. Cold though he was, he'd taught Ravenna most of her Shadow-magic, and I could see her distress.

'I was as loyal as anyone,' she said. 'I still was, until you put me on trial for having a thought of my own.'

451

'You would have destroyed us all.'

'Do you think I would? Do any of you think that's what Cathan and Palatine and I wanted to do? We're on our way to Tandaris to try and save the Archipelago from the Domain. The same as you, or have the Council convinced you all that a woman and a handful of her friends are more danger to you than the Domain?' She was talking to *Rhadamanthys*'s bridge crew now, probably a far more receptive audience than Chlamas or its captain.

'We will have time enough to deal with the Domain,' Chlamas said, echoing Ukmadorian's words earlier. They were surprisingly confident, and that was worrying. They might have ten or twelve ships at most, certainly not enough to defeat the Grand Fleet, even without taking into account the Navy's superior training and equipment.

And what good would that do, in any case? The Grand Fleet was only half of the peacetime Navy, and even a defeat wouldn't be a battle of annihilation. No, they had to have something else on their side. *The Navy will soon be ours*, Ukmadorian had said. What did he mean by that?

'Tell, when did you join the Inquisition, Chlamas? What did they offer you? Did the rest of the Council join as well? I'm waiting to hear.'

I could hear the fury in Chlamas's voice, his reply angry enough to be almost incoherent. Ravenna held her ground.

'It's a brilliant way for the Inquisition to take care of all its opposition, and kill the Pharaoh they've been trying to find all this time. The Council spends its time hunting its own people, and meanwhile the Domain can do what it likes. Marvellous.'

There was a click and the link was broken.

'It was worth a try,' she said sadly.

Sagantha's face was bleak, but, as ever, I couldn't tell whether it was a mask or not. He'd learnt to conceal his emotions well over the last thirty years.

'Any progress on linking up the reactor?' Sagantha asked, but there wasn't.

'Keep on,' he ordered. 'Helm, hard round to port and twenty degrees up. All weapons stations, fire at target B as soon as you're in range.'

The Council mantas would have time to react, since we weren't using the fire-weapons, and for once they were quick off the mark. We'd hardly done a quarter of the turn before the two began separating and curving out to come at us from both sides like pincers.

I sank my hands into the aether pads, closed my eyes so I saw with the ship's senses, rather than my own. *Crusade*'s equipment was brand new and very expensive, so the feeling of actually being in the aether tank, seeing everything, was even more intense than usual.

'Full speed ahead!' Sagantha ordered suddenly, before we'd finished the turn. *Crusade* was moving out and behind at an angle now, ready to meet the second ship head-on instead of presenting our starboard wing to her. The forward armament had the longest range, so the manoeuvre made more sense.

As if we'd passed through an invisible barrier, all the forward weapons opened up at once, and streaks of orange pulse fire sped through the water towards the other ship, followed by a spread of torpedoes. They were marked by our sensors, but would be almost impossible for the other ship to see at this depth. Of course, the same went for anything they fired at us, but it was a moment before their cannons opened up. By then there were already eight torpedoes in the water, and the pulse fire was being absorbed by their shields.

I felt the jolt as the first of their fire hit us, again absorbed by our shields acting as an outer skin of pure energy. I transferred some of the excess forward, since we were still out of *Rhadamanthys*'s range.

We continued heading directly for the second ship, and

after a moment or two the first torpedoes reached their target. Two sped uselessly past the wings, and there were bright ripples in the shields, flares of yellow and white as the effect of the explosions was dissipated.

'More torpedoes.' I heard Sagantha say, just as the first of their salvo reached us.

I jerked, not expecting the sensation like a small aether shock, as each one of them hit the shields. I was feeling the ship's own reaction, which I should have expected. It was much more intense at this position.

But the shield held without any signs of weakening, while further pulse fire and the second spread of torpedoes took their toll on the second ship. One glanced on the wing and exploded above their weaker aft shields, two more impacted without their effect being properly dissipated.

We were closing now, holding on a collision course. *Crusade* began to veer upwards, bringing some of the side and belly weapons into play. Line after line of tracer fire slammed into the other ship's shields until the ripples from each impact joined to form a single wave.

As we swept over them, the amount of energy being poured into the shields reached critical point and they collapsed, leaving the other manta helpless as our gunners continued their fire. I saw it shake under each impact, the gout of flame as one of our after-gunners managed to hit an engine vent.

I felt more stabs of pain, and realised that *Rhadamanthys* had opened fire on our weakened after-shields. I'd been too engrossed in defending us against the second ship and hadn't reinforced them. Thetis, what an idiot I was.

Thankfully, *Crusade's* thick armour had prevented any damage by the time I'd put it right, and our gunners were firing into *Rhadamanthys*. More torpedoes, this time at very close range, slammed into her armour. Sagantha was being quite profligate with them; we didn't have an endless supply.

We veered round again in an effort to stay within range of *Rhadamanthys*, now passing directly over her crippled colleague. Her fire was severely off-target, but ours was little better. There were almost no trained crew with us, so it was hardly a surprise.

'Hold your fire,' Sagantha ordered. 'Helm, close the range.'

Glad to be free of the aether shocks for a few minutes, I watched us closing in on *Rhadamanthys*, now attempting to turn round. I felt another tingle, and wondered where the fire was coming from.

Only for a second. Then something seemed to form around us like a black cloud, and all our sensors went black. I was blind, and I heard a curse from Sagantha. The mind-mage had relaxed his control for a second for Chlamas's benefit, but by the time I tried to draw on my own magic again the block was back up. We were still riding blind, and heading for a collision with the other ship.

Sagantha cursed. 'Twenty to port, up a hundred yards.' We'd been going round in circles to port since the beginning of the engagement. If only I could deal with that wretched mind-mage.

But even that manoeuvre didn't bring us out of the cloud of shadow, it seemed to be everywhere. Why hadn't I thought of something so obvious? Chlamas had used it a hundred times in night exercises at the Citadel, and there was far more shadow to draw on down here. Yet – surely, not enough to blanket this whole area?

The cliff face was only five or six miles away, so we couldn't simply strike off in a straight line.

'Are you sure you can't use your own magic?' Sagantha demanded. Ravenna answered for both of us as *Crusade* floundered on around its turn.

'Weapons stations, fire off some bursts,' Sagantha ordered. 'See if that disperses it.' But that was no better; it seemed to be impervious to anything except magic. Heavens only knew where he got the power to keep it up for so long.

But what if he'd anchored it to the hull? He couldn't have done, the shields would stop it.

Unless it was dependent on the shields.

More jolts, this time from pulse fire. They were moving across the hull too quickly for me to tell where they'd come from.

I found the control and deactivated the shields. The whole bridge shook as pulse fire slammed directly into the armour, but I could see again.

'Cathan, bring the shields up!' Sagantha ordered. The impacts were jarring, almost as painful as the aether shocks of the shield, and it was a relief when the shields were up again.

'We have eyes,' Palatine said. 'Fire!'

The gunners didn't need any urging, and they let rip into *Rhadamanthys* at close range, four or five tracer streams finding their marks on the other vessel's hull as it raced past us. More torpedoes against our shields; I was beginning to feel slightly sick. Heavens only knew what it was like in a fleet engagement; presumably shield duty was rotated.

Rhadamanthys moved out of range, and it took us a few minutes to swing round and back again, ready to engage her. Her companion was dead in the water, adrift and powerless as the battle raged around.

'Let's finish her off,' said Sagantha coldly, and Oailos voiced agreement. One of *Rhadamanthys*'s engine vents, always the most vulnerable parts, was damaged, and she was venting something into the water. This pass might well be fatal for her.

Then the comm crackled, and the shock of hearing the voice hailing us was worse than anything the aether had done.

'This is Second Officer Laeas Tigrana of *Rhadamanthys*.

Ravenna, for Thetis's sake cease fire!' His voice was distorted, but I could hear shrieks in the background.

'It's a trick,' Oailos said. 'Keep on.'

'No,' Ravenna said. 'Cease fire. Now.'

I could only hear their voices, not see their expressions.

'They want time to manoeuvre,' Amadeo said.

'Laeas is a friend,' I said. 'Trust him.'

Ravenna activated the comm. and spoke to Laeas. 'Is the mind-mage still alive?'

'Yes . . . just about. He's unconscious.' He paused. 'The captain and first are dead, I'm not in much better shape. We won't survive another pass.'

'And Chlamas?'

'Chlamas . . . won't be troubling you. I'm sorry for this, Ravenna. And Cathan and Palatine, if you can hear me. I really am.'

Ravenna said nothing for a moment.

'We can't afford to wait,' she said. 'Will you survive?'

'We can make it to Jaya,' Laeas said after a moment. 'At least, most of us can. Some won't live that long, and *Sea Spirit*'s engines are gone.'

'We'll send a rescue out when we're safely in Tandaris,' she said.

There was a very long silence on the end of the line, and I thought I heard some whispered conversation.

'You'll have problems,' Laeas said. 'I don't know what the Council's planning, but there are at least twelve of our ships in the Inland Sea. They know which way you'll be heading, and they've brought every mage and mind-mage in the Archipelago. Ukmadorian's sworn to destroy all of you.'

'Thank you,' Ravenna said. 'I'm sorry we can't stay and help.'

'I understand,' said Laeas. 'Good luck.'

By then the helmsman was already bringing us around, and we sped away into the darkness leaving *Rhadamanthys* and *Sea Spirit* to take their chances. There was nothing else we could do.

I slipped out of the aether pads and looked round, massaging my fingers to cushion the effects of the shocks.

'Well done,' Palatine said, but there was little joy in her voice. 'Sagantha, how many ships does the Council have?'

'A month ago, nineteen.'

I heard indrawn breaths from people.

'*Nineteen?*' Ravenna said quietly.

Huasa, smallest and least important of the continents, had sixteen mantas in its Navy, none of them battle cruisers. Taneth and Cambress had sixty mantas each, Thetia eighty.

Nineteen didn't sound that much, but we'd believed all these years that the Council was nothing, its forces unable to stand up to even a few ships.

'Why?' Ravenna demanded, walking over to stand in front of his chair. '*Why didn't you tell me?*' she shouted.

Oailos was about to say something, but I shook my head, gestured for him to stay quiet. For now. All eyes were on the two figures in the middle of the bridge, the admiral and the Pharaoh.

'It wasn't time for you to know.'

'When was the time?' she said, a ragged edge to her voice. 'All those years I believed what they told me, and I believed what you told me. We didn't have the ships, we couldn't do anything.'

'Those ships wouldn't have won us a war,' Sagantha said.

'It looks like they're going to now. How can you claim you have my best interests at heart? How can you dare to say you're loyal to me?'

'I am,' said Sagantha. 'I always have been. Too loyal to let you throw away your chances chasing shadows.'

'I can decide that for myself,' she said. 'Am I never allowed to grow up and decide for myself? When I'm

458

seventy, will you still be telling me *a few more years?*'

'If we'd let you use that fleet to regain control, the Domain would have declared a Crusade,' he said evenly, a calm figure in his captain's chair. 'You would have been Pharaoh of a wasteland.'

'That's not a good enough reason. That was my decision to make. I knew that being Pharaoh was all about living as a pawn of everyone else, of everyone who claimed they had my interests at heart. I didn't realise it would go on like that for the rest of my life! Fine, Admiral Karao. You want to control me, you want to tell the Archipelago what it does? You can!

'I'll let you, because it's the only decision I'll ever be allowed to make. From this moment forward, I am no longer Pharaoh. I am no longer anything. I'll join Cathan in the obscurity he was clever enough to want. As of now, *you* are Pharaoh of the Archipelago. And may Thetis have mercy on your soul.'

As she stormed out, all eyes were on Sagantha. It was a moment before he spoke.

'Cathan, go down to the searay bays and make sure she doesn't do something stupid. Helm, continue on course for Perdition's Shore.'

There had been no sign of her when I returned to the bridge to help navigate us through the Shore, and I didn't see any more of her until we met *Shadowstar* and four more Council mantas in the shallow waters of the Inland Sea.

CHAPTER XXXI

I remember much of that battle only as a blur, a sequence of events to the accompaniment of noise and pain and fire, from which only a few moments stand out clearly.

Back at the shield controls, I almost immediately sank into a kind of pained half-life, trying to keep the shields up as countless impacts battered them. We had little room to manoeuvre, and not even tactical evasions could keep much of the fire off as we pressed on.

I have no clear recollection of those first minutes, of the second and last firing of the fire-weapon that destroyed two of the Council mantas and damaged a third, or the movements of any of the survivors

Sagantha didn't try to escape. He simply charged through their battle line, absorbing the crippling fire from their first salvo to barrel through into the open waters beyond. The Council mantas were quicker this time and turned fast enough to stay on our tail and swoop in from the sides to make passes.

Even with *Crusade*'s armour and weapons, three against one was a tall order, and we were further hampered by the knowledge that there were other Council ships out there, no doubt already heading this way. Out in the open sea, with time to spare, we might have defeated them completely.

I remember very clearly one of the most horrible moments, when the damaged ship, its engines crippled by a well-placed torpedo, opened fire on us as we swung round to avoid fire from *Shadowstar*. Amadeo had pushed one of the Ilthysians off a weapons station and poured a torrent of fire into the crippled manta, urged on by Oailos and the others. We would have been powerless to stop them.

We were only a few hundred yards away when it exploded, the fireball bright enough that we saw the water lighten in front of the windows. After that there was no question of quarter.

Then, as *Crusade* began to feel the pummelling even through the shield, things inside started to fall apart. The aether conduits lasted a surprisingly long time before they ruptured, but other systems began disintegrating, and a buckled vent caused a fire in one of the side cabins.

There was the most appalling noise all the way through pounding on the hull and the shrieks of the manta itself as skin and structure failed to withstand it. After a while there were screams from the crew, as well, and Khalia appeared on the bridge to do what she could.

I had no time to think about anything else, even to consider how the fight was going. After a few minutes Palatine removed me from the shields and put someone else in charge, transferring me to a weapons station where I could recover.

I remember Cadmos's console exploding and the marine being hurled backwards across the floor, his sleeves on fire. He'd been unconscious by the time they were put out, but the stench of burning flesh had filled the room, making it smell as though the Inquisition had been at work.

I remember the moment when a desperate Sagantha ordered all torpedoes launched to try and even the odds. It was, to all intents and purposes, the moment when the battle stopped being a contest and became a slaughter.

Another fireball, and *Shadowstar*'s remaining consort vanished. Four Council mantas destroyed in the space of half an hour, to add to the two crippled wrecks we'd left in the ocean.

With no torpedoes left and half our pulse cannon out of

action, Sagantha could only try and evade, and keep on course for Tandaris while trying to avoid the battle cruiser's pounding and the debris from the destroyed mantas.

It was only then, with flames on the bridge itself, that my weapons station was knocked out and I sank back into the nightmare inside *Crusade*.

Sagantha was hoarse from shouting to be heard over the din; Palatine, her own console gone, was trying to fight the fire in the corner. I stumbled out of my chair and went to help her, almost falling on to my face when another torpedo slammed into the armour. Shields were long gone, the crewman who'd replaced me lay unconscious on the floor with burns on his hands.

There was still a chance we might get away. Both reactors were operational, but our only hope lay in heading out and down, a potentially fatal move with so much interior damage.

'We'll not get to Tandaris,' Sagantha said, when I asked. 'We might not even get to live through this.'

Our enemies had lost four ships. *Shadowstar* itself had sustained some damage, but they'd succeeded in eliminating us, leaving my mother and Hamilcar in the city with only the help that *Aegeta* could provide. Not much against the eleven Council ships remaining in the Inland Sea. If only we knew what their plans were. It was too late to wonder about that now. Just as we managed to put the fire out, someone grabbed both of us and pulled us out into the short corridor leading to the well. I knew who it was even before I saw her.

'We have to distract their attention,' Ravenna said urgently. 'We take a searay, we head for Tandaris. Tell them what we're doing, so they have to break off and follow us. *Shadowstar* is damaged, they won't be able to match our speed.'

'We'll get . . .' Palatine began.

'It gives them two targets,' she went on, the words

almost running over each other. 'There's enough room, but please, hurry!'

Each of the escape rays had more than enough room to fit the entire crew, so if a few of us took one of them, actually told *Shadowstar* what we were doing . . . Palatine nodded, ran over to Sagantha and explained as quickly as she could.

'Yes,' Sagantha said. 'Head out to port. Take some people with you, I don't care who. Just go!' He shouted around the bridge, telling them what we were doing.

Tandaris. If we were going to reach there, we needed people who'd be useful. I remembered talking to the crew in the dormitory only a few hours ago, the fierce loyalty they seemed to have developed for Amadeo. If we didn't take him with us now, there was no point in having brought him, and even if he immediately betrayed us there was little more damage he could do.

I found both him and Oailos, and we ran for the exit, across the well and down to the searay bay. Half the lights were out, and while nowhere near as bad as *Valdur*'s last hours, it was still a scene from a nightmare.

Oailos slammed the hatch of the searay behind us as Palatine and I climbed into the pilots' seats.

'Does this thing have a name?' Palatine asked, powering up the reactor.

'*Crusader 2*,' Oailos said, reading it off the bulkhead. 'Does it matter?'

'Of course it does,' said Amadeo, unexpectedly. 'In Thetia, all ships have names, even little rowing boats.'

'*Apostate*,' Ravenna suggested. Amadeo and Palatine nodded approvingly.

'*Apostate* it is,' Palatine said. 'Engine active, reactor online . . . *Crusade*, we're ready to go.'

'Godspeed,' Sagantha said. 'We'll try and cover.' Nothing for Ravenna, not a word about what had happened. He had other things on his mind.

I felt the clank as the door sealed and the bay doors ahead of us began to open, sliding apart with their usual frustrating sloth. The mechanism had to be simple to work if the ship was damaged.

Apostate moved slowly out of the bay, then gained speed as we cleared it and left *Crusade* behind. Palatine sank her hands into the pads and accelerated us outwards, heading dangerously close to the manta's wing as she brought the engine up to full power. I put the shields up and hoped *Shadowstar* wouldn't have time to hit us before we veered too far out of range.

'Give it a moment or two before we send anything,' Palatine warned. We dived beneath the starboard wing, then the searay's wings began to work. We'd be about as fast as *Crusade*, smaller but less powerful relative to our size. Enough to keep ahead of *Shadowstar* for a few minutes.

'Now,' Palatine ordered, when the distance between us and the damaged manta had widened to a mile, and we began arcing off towards the shore, into shallower waters where the battle cruiser couldn't follow us and we might be able to make our way to Tandaris relatively unscathed.

I activated the comm and aimed the signal at the huge black mass of the battle cruiser behind us.

'*Shadowstar*, this is Cathan,' I said conversationally. 'You've managed at the cost of four of your own ships to damage a Domain prize and kill a few Ilthysian crewmen. I hope you're proud of yourselves, and I'm the sure the Pharaoh will remember your gallant action when she reaches Tandaris.'

It was sheer bravado, nothing more; we had no guarantee of outrunning the battle cruiser, but we had to divert her fire away from *Crusade*, give her time to repair, perhaps limp into Tandaris or head for a safer port in the Ilahi Islands.

'Your trick will not help her,' Ukmadorian thundered a moment later – entirely predictably.

'He only needs to outwit you, old man,' Ravenna said, in a voice dripping with contempt. 'Your mind's going if you thought you could deal with me so easily.'

Now, belatedly, *Shadowstar* began to turn towards us, her stream of fire on *Crusade* lessening. It would have been child's play to destroy the searay if there had been another ship left in Ukmadorian's force, but there wasn't. We had shown what a terrible weapon *Crusade* could be, and it had been the Council's bad luck to be on the receiving end.

'All of you, strap in tightly,' Palatine ordered. 'Quickly.'

Ravenna and the two men did as they were told, belting themselves into chairs in the aft cabin with a view through to the aether tanks, so they at least had a clue what was going on.

Palatine accelerated, squeezing the last power she could out of the reactor, and banked in towards the cliffs only a mile or two to starboard. The bottom was shelving upwards now, only a hundred yards deep or so and rising.

There was no more fire from *Crusade* as she limped on, now behind *Shadowstar* and trailing steam from a leaking reactor. There were more ships in the water behind her, and for a moment I thought they might be Council ships. Too small, though – at least one of the casualties had managed to get her crew off in time. That at least was something to be thankful for.

Only fifty yards of depth now, which was too shallow for *Shadowstar* to operate in, but Palatine kept on, diving through the line of a coral reef and into a channel beyond, safely out of range of anything the Council could throw at us. We moved up enough to be able to see over and confirm that *Shadowstar* was keeping station out to sea, penning us close to the cliffs. To try and engage her in this would be even more hopeless than taking on *Meridian* directly outside Kavatang.

Palatine sat back a little and relaxed slightly, although still concentrating on controlling the ship.

'We should be fine now, at least for a while,' she said. 'Cathan, can you call up the charts of the area ahead and see how far this channel goes? With any luck, it'll go all the way to Tandaris.'

It took me a few minutes following the line of the coast in the aether tank, in the greatest possible detail. The shore was fairly straight, thankfully, bending slightly south until it fell away abruptly, heading due south the last few miles to the city.

Damn. No cover by the headland; the reef ended there and gave way to a bed of sharp rocks similar to those around Perdition's Shore, only on a smaller scale.

Not a problem for mantas, of course, because there was no reason for any sane captain to head west of those rocks. The channels for mantas led north into the centre of the Inland Sea.

Ravenna took over the controls for a few moments while I showed Palatine.

'Not good,' she said, frowning. 'Ukmadorian will have worked this out by now, he'll move to cut us off when we reach the headland.'

On the other side we might be able to outrun him, I saw, but there would be a space of a mile or two when he'd be able to close the range. That would be all the opportunity he needed.

However long we stared at the map, nothing could change that.

'I suppose,' Palatine said finally, 'as a last resort we could leave the ship, climb up the cliffs and walk to Tandaris.'

I glanced back into the cabin, where Oailos and Amadeo were waiting. Palatine, Ravenna and I would all be able to manage the climb – especially since the weather out there was fairly good. Oailos was probably strong enough to cope, but Amadeo? With no ropes to help us, we'd be forced to leave him behind. And forfeit a potential advantage when we reached Tandaris. He and Oailos together could probably create enough chaos in the city that Council and Domain would be equally hampered.

Nothing else presented itself over the next fifteen miles or so, following the almost invisible channel of sun-dappled water between the coral and the cliff, sometimes squeezing through gaps so narrow that I was afraid the wings would break off. The sea was alive with fish and reef-dwellers, everything from shoals of tiny silverfin to shark and the odd juvenile leviathan.

The greatest blessing was that, since we were only six or so yards down, there was light, the first daylight I'd seen for a week, and it was wonderful to see the reflections of the waves on the sandy bottom below us through the clear blue of the water.

Shadowstar had pulled away, taking the most direct route possible from here to the headland in the certainty that we would keep as close to the shore as possible. They were right, of course, since we couldn't afford to try anything else, and after losing her for a few minutes, we caught sight of *Shadowstar* in the treacherous sea off the headland.

'That's odd,' Palatine said, a moment later. She was back in control again for the most difficult part of the run. 'Weapons fire?'

They must be engaging *Crusade* again. The fear that we would never see any of her crew again returned.

'I shouldn't have left,' Oailos muttered.

'We need your help,' said Ravenna. 'It's as simple as that.'

I sank my hands into the aether pads and linked up with the ship, extending the sensors as far as I could, to give us an idea of what was going on. Those were definitely flashes of weapons fire, and *Shadowstar* was replying . . . turning, even as I watched, to fire at an assailant beyond my field of view.

I tried to project *Crusade*'s course parallel to the coast, work out whether she could be the other ship, but it didn't seem likely, not unless Sagantha had managed to get that third reactor hooked up to replace the damaged port one. Not a good idea, given that he had a chance to use the fire-weapon again.

My frustration grew along with my worries as we worked our way to the end of the reef, closer and closer to open water, until we finally reached a point that gave us clear view all the way out to sea this side of the headland.

'Thetis!' Palatine said. 'Where did they come from?'

At least seven mantas that I could see were engaged in battle and from the weapons fire at the extreme right of our sensors, there had to be at least two more out of sight. I could just about hear the sounds through the hull, and as Palatine brought *Apostate* almost to a standstill we stared at the battle in disbelief.

Shadowstar was very close to the headland at the moment, moving into dangerously shallow water to steal a march on her opponent.

'Can you identify any of them?' Palatine asked.

I enlarged the picture as much as possible, trying to get a look at the horn colours – they were at least visible in water this shallow. *Shadowstar*'s opponent was a normal size manta, turned away from us at the moment. Wait until she came round . . . there.

Orange.

I checked three others in the hope that I'd mistaken the orange for red or gold, but I hadn't. At least two more of those ships also had orange colours.

'Domain,' I said finally.

'Good riddance,' Oailos said, peering over my shoulder to get a better view into the tank. 'If they all kill each other, so much the better for us.'

'But they may well stop when *Crusade* arrives and decide to deal with her first,' Ravenna said. 'The Council's still out for our blood, and the Domain know she's been stolen.'

'We'll have a few minutes of grace if *Shadowstar* is far enough away,' said Palatine. 'We have to pick the right time.'

So we waited just inside the reef, open water ahead of us, while the two fleets dealt out death and destruction to each other, trying frantically to get what tactical advantage there was in such shallow water. It was naval warfare at its most brutal and unsophisticated, confined to only two dimensions and reduced to little more than a slogging match. Both sides seemed evenly balanced, and from what I could pick out of the scattered comm traffic from both sides, neither felt they had the upper hand.

Ithien, Khalia and I had all come here with the hope of avoiding further slaughter, but it seemed the issue had been taken out of our hands by the Council and the Domain. The same gnawing fears were working on me again — what if the courier had run into either of these fleets?

Gods, I had to get to Tandaris, to end this awful suspense as much as to help bring all this to an end.

'We go!' Palatine announced, suddenly accelerating away from the reef. The seafloor dropped away here, but she didn't pull inshore to take advantage of the shallows, instead swinging around to pick up as much speed as she could before we entered the currents around the headland.

'Cathan, shields — for what they're worth.'

I expected to feel the now-familiar shocks as soon as I took control of the shields, but of course we weren't under fire, not yet. *Shadowstar* was now quite a way out, surging towards the surface while her opponent — a slightly bigger ship this time, certainly not the same one — was skimming the bottom, clouding the water and her opponent's sensors with billows of sand. Much as we had at Kavatang.

The battle still seemed to be fairly even, about ten ships involved in all, and there wasn't a huge amount of debris. Perhaps one ship destroyed so far, although it was impossible to tell on which side.

Another ship, a long way behind . . . heavens, it was *Crusade*. Surely they couldn't be planning to sail through this hornets' nest? I tried to warn them, but the sand was clogging the comm line now, and I couldn't get a signal through the distortion.

It was too late to go back, now that *Shadowstar* had seen us.

It would be tight, and I felt myself tense as we approached the headland, trying to work out whether we'd get round it in time or if they'd cut us off.

'Evading!' Palatine said and wrenched the ray sharply over to one side and down: a moment later, I saw the trails of torpedoes shoot overhead and slam harmlessly into the cliff. That had been a shot at extreme range, and frighteningly accurate. Please, let them be running low on weapons at last. They couldn't have an infinite supply.

As ever when time was so important, those last minutes as we approached the headland seemed to take forever, and with every yard the battle cruiser and its armament were drawing closer.

She opened fire less than a minute before we would have rounded the headland, and Palatine swerved *Apostate* violently to starboard, a turn so sharp I felt as if my stomach had been left behind.

Then the first globules of orange pulse fire slammed into the shields. I wanted to scream and pull my hands out of the pads! Thetis, it was painful! I felt as if my hands had been rubbed raw and then scraped with wire wool, and the sensation was getting stronger with every subsequent hit.

Somehow I held on as the seconds dragged by and the searay flailed, *Shadowstar*'s attention not even diverted by the return of the larger Domain ship – *Redeemer*, I thought she was called. At least the comm messages we were getting from other ships were addressed to that name, and she was mostly between us and the rest of the Domain squadron.

There was a moment of blessed respite as Palatine took

us behind an outcrop of rock, enough to shield us for a few seconds. Then I noticed an even larger Domain ship cutting under a damaged Council manta, heading straight towards us.

'That's *Theocracy*!' I warned as we emerged again into the torrent of fire, more intense now that *Shadowstar* was almost as close as she could get, perhaps a hundred and fifty yards away.

'Cathan, detach!' Palatine ordered, as the shields flared and I felt the volume of fire reaching critical levels. There was a terrible sound like metal screeching against metal, and I pulled my hands out of the aether pads, just too late to avoid the first surge.

For a second, pain engulfed me totally, and I lost track of everything but the sounds of pulse fire on the outer skin, the cries of alarm from Palatine and Ravenna. Then, mercifully, it faded, and I slumped back in the chair. Someone was running needles over my skin, digging as deep as they could without drawing blood, and in so many places at once. It was a struggle even to open my eyes.

'We won't last,' Palatine said, an edge of desperation to her voice. 'We haven't enough space to draw clear.'

Apostate lurched downwards, escaping fire for a few seconds until *Shadowstar*'s gunners readjusted their aim. I peered into the tank, wondering why so much of it suddenly seemed to have turned black.

'Elements!' Palatine shouted. Something slammed into the roof, pushing us further down, and the fire stopped. Even the light from the surface was cut out.

This was it, then. Why now, when I didn't even have time to talk to Ravenna again?

But it was only for a split second that I expected the roof to descend on me with the weight of the water above it, because the shadow passed and for a second I saw a manta outlined at an incredible angle against the silver-blue of the surface, her white underside like a sloping roof above us.

471

For a few seconds she remained between us and *Shadowstar*, and then she twisted back towards her proper angle, veering away towards the battle as we raced along the far side of the headland, gaining a crucial few seconds on *Shadowstar*.

But in giving us those few seconds, *Crusade* had sealed her own fate, as ships from both sides began firing into her, breaking off their combats with each other to pulverise the ship that both sides wanted destroyed.

Ravenna and the others came forward to stare into the aether tank, watching Sagantha bring his ship round in a final, doomed turn through the far side of the enemy fleet, firing as he went. Almost all of them were turning now, firing what weapons they could bring to bear.

At last her guns fell silent, and there was no more fire, no way for her to respond to the torrent of pulse fire and torpedoes being poured into her. *Apostate* was in clear water now, only *Shadowstar* behind us, but all eyes were on the aether tank and the scene behind us. I linked with the ship again to see more clearly, hoping against hope that she could somehow survive.

But it was too late. A jet of white flame shot from the engine vent, followed moments later by more, shooting out of the windows along each side of the ship. Her shape seemed to distort, hidden for a second behind the wing of a Domain manta trying to get clear.

For a second longer the shape held, then it became a silhouette and was consumed by an incandescent fireball that spread outwards, ripping the ship in two. Before it had even died down there was a second, smaller explosion from the weapon's reactor. The fire spread outwards as it dissipated, engulfing the luckless Domain manta which somehow managed to stay in one piece, and then it faded, leaving only a storm of bubbles and an expanding ring of debris. It was too sudden, too numbing, for me to feel any grief yet. It was the ship I'd seen destroyed, reduced from a thing of beauty into a debris field, only a wing left intact like the severed limb of a corpse. Not the people. That realisation would come later.

'They were true martyrs,' Amadeo said.

But we didn't have time to stop and mourn. The Council mantas must have warned their fellows and even their Domain enemies that we were from *Crusade*'s crew, because within a moment or two both fleets, except for the Domain manta damaged by the explosion, were heading in towards the city.

This time it would be our turn, and not even the few seconds Sagantha had given us would be enough over the five miles remaining to the city. I could see the edge of the undersea harbour on the aether sensors, so close but so far.

'The cliffs fall away in a mile or so,' Ravenna said. 'We should steer inshore and abandon ship. It'll only be a mile or two to the city.'

'I think I'll have to agree with you this time,' Palatine said. 'We may find she's blown from under us, though.'

They could see what she meant in the aether tank. Still spread out over a few miles, most of the fleets wouldn't be in range until we reached the harbour. Leading the others, though, the demonic pairing of *Theocracy* and *Shadowstar* was gaining on us at a tremendous pace.

'We've done what no-one thought possible,' Ravenna said slowly. 'The Domain and the Council have found something they fear enough to put all their enmity aside. I suppose it's an achievement, of a kind.'

Still linked with the ship, I couldn't see her expression, couldn't tell whether the tone in her voice was her old coldness or resignation.

I looked backwards with the sensors, trying to work out if we'd make it to the shore in time, and started. There was another ship suddenly, coming in from the side with what looked like a dark cloud trailing behind it. Thetis, it would be in range in less than a minute!

But the intruder didn't change course, she was coming in almost directly across the line of the fleets' advance, trailing – trailing what?

Neither of the two leaders opened fire. Instead they veered up to let the newcomer pass behind them; practical, I supposed, since she was almost on a collision course. I thought there was some comm traffic from her, so she must have been transmitting a message, but we were too far out of its direct line to hear.

Only then, with the intruder literally a mile behind, did I see what she was trailing, as cables parted from the stern and a vast cloud of floating seaweed filled the water directly behind the leaders.

By the time the fleets realised what was happening, it was too late. They slowed as the weeds swirled round them and turned the water green, engulfing them and their consorts with thousands of fronds that waved in the sunlit waters until they fastened on to the hulls and refused to let go.

Arching round beyond the guns of the fleet, well out of range of the entangled ships' few working weapons, *Aegeta* turned in towards Tandaris, and now I heard Vespasia's triumphant voice over the comm, wishing us good luck and saying she'd meet us in the city.

Their consorts held fast among the weeds, *Theocracy* and *Shadowstar* were left to press on alone.

CHAPTER XXXII

Bathed in the warm glow of the late afternoon sun, the white columned houses of Tandaris clustered on their hillsides in front of us, climbing from the harbour to where the sandy rock of the Acrolith rose like a sentinel above the upper city. There were other colours too – cobalt blue and the green of palm trees, but it was the red orichal on many of the buildings that stood out. Rearing above the agora, the Temple was painted entirely orichal red, the only building in the city that was allowed to be.

I'd stopped for breath a few hundred feet from the walls, the last point where I could see the city properly before the rock outcrop in front hid it from sight. I looked back, waiting for the others to catch up. In the surf behind us, black smoke billowed from the burning *Apostate*, a beacon on the shoreline that was visible for miles in the clear air. Out to sea, two V-shaped wakes arrowed ominously in towards the undersea harbour, still side by side despite their enmity. They were almost there now, only delayed by the dance Palatine had managed to lead them before we abandoned ship. We were only a little behind *Theocracy* and *Shadowstar*, at least we would be if we reached the city soon.

'You should go on,' Ravenna said, more out of breath than Palatine or me, but not lagging as badly as Oailos and Amadeo, who stumbled up now.

'We stay together,' Palatine said. 'There may be trouble at the gate.'

I would have been all in favour of running on, but I waited another minute until they moved off again, over-took them as we finally reached the road that led down and ran along the coast below the rock outcrop to the Sea Gate. It hadn't been repaired in the four years since we'd ridden out along here on our way to Perdition's Shore, and I had to keep my eyes on the road, careful not to trip in a rut and twist my ankle. At least I was running in the wonderful warm heat of a clear evening, not through that wretched jungle in the middle of a storm.

We slowed to a walk as we approached the Sea Gate, which was open, but guarded by two marines, un-armoured and wearing Tandaris colours – violet and silver with a black border.

'Who are you?' they demanded. They must have watched us disembark from the ship and run along the edge of the water to the road.

'Those two mantas are both Domain,' Palatine said. 'They're coming in to try and take over the city.'

It was a more useful answer than I'd have come up with, given that these men might be loyal to the Council.

'Who's in charge?' she went on.

The older one smiled. 'Our people, for once. You'll find someone in the palace, it would be best to warn them.'

'Aren't you Thetian?' the other asked Palatine suspiciously.

'Dissident,' she said proudly. 'Banished by the Emperor.'

'If you're an enemy of the Emperor, you're a friend of ours,' said the other. 'Not that he matters very much now anyway.' The guard drew a finger across his throat and motioned us through.

'Be careful,' said the second man. 'We've got all the Thetians trapped in the harbour, you don't want to be seen as one of them.'

We thanked them and walked through the gate, the colours on it looking even more faded than I remembered. The detailed gold key patterns marking out each step were barely visible against the red paint.

The city inside was at first glance as I remembered it, like Ilthys in an indefinable way, although the architecture was so different. Tandaris was a much more colourful place, and the occupants of the first house we came to had painted their porch columns in vibrant red and blue, a splash of colour against the house.

'Quiet, isn't it?' Ravenna remarked, glancing up the street ahead of us, a wide avenue with plane trees planted down either side. There were few people around, only the occasional child leaning out of a window and craning to look towards the centre of the city.

'Either everyone's keeping their heads down, or they've gone into the centre,' said Palatine. 'We should start heading up, if we don't want to run into Council and Domain people from the harbours.'

It was four years since I'd ridden out of that same gate with the others, heading for Perdition's Shore and a meeting with my brother. Not a night I wanted to remember, nor to be reminded of.

I hadn't been in this part of the city much, but here and there were things I thought I recognised – heavens, it all looked so different in the sunlight! I remembered it as a place of storms and cold, the square houses with their porches and galleries shrouded by wind and rain, the people huddled in cloaks against winter storms.

But I had never seen it this empty. I glanced through a gap between two houses to the citadel, which still flew the Thetian flag. Most of the road below it was hidden, I couldn't make out what was happening.

The Council was already in control, which wasn't a good start.

We reached a side-street, but I stopped the others before we turned off.

'We should split up,' I said. 'Oailos, Amadeo, neither of you are wanted by the Council, so you can go about freely.' I paused, wondering whether it was worth

477

arranging a rendezvous, but Palatine solved the problem for me.

'Cathan's right. There's no point in all of us staying together. You two go off and find as many people as you can. Tell them what happened in Ilthys, just be fairly subtle about it or the Council will get wind of what you're up to.'

'Tell them what you told me in the mess-room,' I said. 'Some of them might listen.'

'Some of them might try to kill us,' Oailos said with a shrug. 'Still, they need to hear it.'

'Do you know anyone here?' Palatine asked them.

Amadeo shook his head, but Oailos said, 'Possibly. Not very well, but there are one or two people, certainly the masons' guild . . .'

'Good. The oceanographers should help you.'

The two men paused. 'Good luck,' Oailos said after a moment. 'All of you.'

'And you,' Ravenna said, with her faint smile.

Then the two of them set off, walking briskly down the road towards the crowd.

Oailos had never lived anywhere but Ilthys, but I suspected he'd be able to blend in well enough among the population. Tandaris wasn't a particularly unfriendly place, unless it had changed very much in four years.

We made our way up the stepped side-street, heavy with scent from a clematis which had taken root by an upturned stone and colonised one entire wall. The paving stones were broken and uneven, more so when we reached a small square at the top with palm trees growing from it. There should have been children playing, or a few old women, but no-one appeared or even challenged us.

We worked our way up through unfamiliar narrow streets, trusting only to our sense of direction. After a while we had to go down again into the dip between the two hills, and we crossed another wide avenue with trees even taller than those by the Sea Gate shrouding apartments built in the same style as the rest of the city. The road reminded me oddly of Taneth, except that Taneth streets would have been crowded with people.

There were a few people in the streets, standing around uncertainly in groups, and a small party of armoured men in the livery of the Citadel of Earth, green and brown.

They didn't seem to be stopping anyone, but citizens were coming up to them, presumably to ask what was going on. Shops behind the row of plane trees were still open but deserted.

As we walked out between two plane trees into the shaded central avenue, a tall black-skinned man, who was keeping a wary eye on what was happening, came over to us.

'You're not from the city, are you?' he said. 'Do you know what's going on?' He was perhaps in his fifties, hair just turning to grey, and his robes were fairly expensive. A merchant of some kind, with a manner that reminded me of Hamilcar.

'No,' Palatine said. 'There was a battle out at sea between the Domain and the Council.'

'The Council? You mean the heretics?'

Palatine nodded, and went on with what had become our cover story, at least until we met someone who recognised us.

'I see,' he said. 'Well, that helps a little.'

'Do you know anything more?' she asked.

'I come to do business and find myself in the middle of a revolution,' he said ruefully. 'I know they have blockaded the Grand Fleet in the outer harbour, and that its high commanders are trapped in the temple. I also heard that there are people claiming the throne – an Empress Aurelia, and perhaps also a man the Council are supporting. More than that . . .' He spread his hands 'I haven't been able to find out.'

At least Aurelia had arrived, thank heavens, and this

man hadn't heard of her capture. I wondered who else there could possibly be, what the Council was up to. The Thetians would never accept some upstart placed by the Council. A Tar'Conantur, perhaps, but where would they find one? Palatine's mother Neptunia was the only one not with us now, and she was an ageing recluse.

'Isn't the fleet doing anything?' Ravenna said.

'That officer over there told me that his superiors are just keeping the fleet where it is for now, using magic and mines, so it can't get out.'

That made sense, at least. I felt myself tense as one of the Earth officers came over to investigate.

'Who are you?' he asked us.

It was the merchant who replied.

'Fellow travellers like myself, wondering what is going on,' he said. 'All we hear is rumour.'

The officer looked at each of us levelly. He didn't have the bearing of a professional soldier, he was too smooth and poised. Maybe I was reading too much into this.

'All you need to know is rumour,' he said. 'Two of you are Thetian. What are you doing in Tandaris?'

'We're with you,' Palatine said. 'Crew of *Rhadamanthys.*'

'Why are you here? She was guarding the northern passage.'

'She isn't any more.' We were all bitter enough at what had happened anyway for our story to sound convincing. 'We ran into a Domain ship with a mage on board. Some of us made it to the searays, then we ran into the rest of the Domain fleet just outside the city. I've no idea where Laeas and the others got to.'

It was an extra spice of detail, but I doubted he knew all the members of the other orders.

I'd underestimated him. 'Captain Chlamas?'

Laeas had specifically said both Chlamas and the captain were out of the way. It was an old trick, but thankfully one we'd been able to spot.

'The captain's dead,' Palatine said. 'Chlamas wasn't in command, he was injured and they took him on the other ray.'

The officer nodded. He had to be Ring of Eight, or at least one of Tekla's men. Not merely a heretic recruit, that was certain.

'Your Councillors aren't here yet,' he said. 'They were on *Shadowstar*, I don't know if she's made it in yet.'

'She was a few moments behind us, I think.'

He asked one or two more questions, then directed us on our way up to the palace. To my relief, he didn't detach a man to accompany us, and I was glad when we left the avenue behind and moved up into side-streets on the far side, heading for the agora about halfway up the hill.

'Where are we actually going?' Ravenna demanded, as soon as we were out of earshot. 'Ukmadorian and his vultures will be here by now, and we're just wandering around the city like idiots. We came here to help Aurelia, then for Thetis's sake we should do something.'

'The Citadel's blockaded,' Palatine mused, 'and from what he said, I think there must still be Domain people in the Temple. So the Council doesn't control quite all of the city. And they can't exactly have agents in every house. We need to find some of these Thetian hostages and free them so as to make life more difficult for the Council.'

'Unless they're all being held somewhere in the centre,' said Ravenna. 'In which case there'll be a heap of mind-mages with them.'

'The whole place is probably overrun with mind-mages,' said Palatine. 'We need to find some people who know the city well, and who are prepared to help us.'

I wondered who might still be here after four years, having survived the Domain purges. I stopped at the next intersection and glanced at the drawing on the wall that indicated the street name. Street of the Maenads; I didn't remember it. Although . . . no, that had been Street of the Mermaid, closer to the harbour.

I asked the others how far inland we were, but neither of them knew.

'Why do you want to know that?' Palatine said.

'Tamanes lives in the Street of the Mermaid,' I said. 'He's an oceanographer, so surely he'll be sympathetic.'

'If he's not working as a penitent in the middle of nowhere,' said Ravenna. 'I suppose it's worth a try, unless it's very much out of our way.'

It was the time I was chiefly worried about. With every minute that passed the Council would be consolidating their hold on the city, and who knew when the Thetian fleet trapped in the harbour might decide to surrender in order to save its captive crews.

If, of course, the Council had any intention of accepting a surrender. Surely they wouldn't destroy the Fleet in harbour? That would be disastrous, since it would bring Thetian vengeance down on them more swiftly than anything else.

Of course, they probably wouldn't need to worry about Thetian vengeance once the ships in the harbour were out of the way. Even after the losses *Crusade* had inflicted, their fleet would be more than strong enough to defend the Archipelago against anything a divided Thetia could throw at them. It was that division that made the difference, the lack of a strong leader, but still, there was an element of this plan missing. We should have got more out of Sagantha, but it was too late now.

We hurried on through the city, occasionally passing groups of people. We kept our heads down and went our way, looking as purposeful as we could and staying in the back streets wherever possible.

We found the Street of the Mermaid by sheer luck in the end; we might have searched for it another half an hour. Then we had a new problem: I had no idea where

Tamanes lived. Palatine and I kept out of sight while Ravenna enquired at the nearest house.

'Down there,' she said, when we came back. 'He's still in the city.'

That was a relief, at least, but people were starting to give us suspicious glances as we walked along the street, and I wondered how long it would be before someone stopped us to ask why Thetians were at large in a rebellious Archipelagan city.

Tamanes didn't live with his House, but in an apartment in this street that led almost directly down to the harbour, at times so steeply that it turned into steps. I could see all the way down to the water where fishing boats were anchored by the quay. Presumably the oceanographic station was nearby, although I couldn't remember exactly where it was.

The concierge, a gruff man in his sixties, was sitting on the steps below the porch with his stick beside him, calling out questions to passers-by.

'Is Tamanes in?' Ravenna asked.

'What do you want?' he asked and I wondered whether I'd seen him before. I couldn't remember meeting him, but then it had been a while ago.

'His help, if he can give it.'

'He's not in,' the man said brusquely. 'You can go away.'

That was it!

'Even a fellow oceanographer?' I said, moving to one side so he could see me. 'Two of us are Guild members, and I ate lunch with Tamanes and Bamako in your restaurant a few years ago.'

'Don't remember everyone who ever ate there,' he said. My guess had been right.

'When Sarhaddon arrived,' I said. 'You warned me not to let people know I was an oceanographer.'

He squinted at me for a moment, then got up and went

inside, hardly leaning on his stick. The door closed with a crash behind him; a few flakes of paint fell off the crumbling porch in a little puff of dust.

We stood there waiting for a moment, not sure whether he'd come out again.

He didn't. The door opened more gently this time, and a hand beckoned us in.

It was fairly dark inside the hallway, and the interior was as shabby as the outside. There was just enough light to see a man of about thirty in the light blue tunic of the Oceanographic Guild.

'Cathan?' he said hesitantly.

'Yes, Cathan,' I said. 'We need your help, Tamanes.'

He looked first at Palatine and then Ravenna. I'd told her the story of what had happened, so she knew how much he'd helped with the plan to rescue her, even if his role had meant he'd stayed in Tandaris rather than riding to the coast with us. If he had come on that journey, I doubt if he'd still be alive.

'I'm Ravenna,' she said. 'Not Pharaoh.'

'Who else can be Pharaoh?' Tamanes asked.

'Whoever wants to be,' she said. 'Thank you for your help. I'm a few years late with my thanks, perhaps, but I'm here.'

'And so are all sorts of other people,' the former restaurateur said. 'They've said nothing about you.'

'This is Cleombrotus,' said Tamanes. 'A friend.'

There were footsteps on the rickety wooden stairway, and a petite Qalathari woman with black hair came downstairs, her expression as haunted as Ravenna's was so much of the time.

'Alcie,' Tamanes said. 'You remember Cathan and Palatine; this is Pharaoh Ravenna.'

Alciana nodded. She looked as nervous as I remembered her, the oceanographer Tamanes had called timid, who had worried about the consequences of a Crusade.

'Why are you here?' she asked, echoing the suspicious Cleombrotus. 'It's good to see you again, but you wouldn't have come here if everything was all right. Why don't you go to the Council? They'll protect you from the Domain.'

'The Council only serve themselves,' Ravenna said. 'I got in their way, so I'm their enemy now.'

'Then why should you deserve our help?'

'Because I owe it to them,' Tamanes said. 'The Council doesn't like oceanographers any more than the Domain. I don't have any influence, any standing, though. What do you want?'

'We need to break the Council's control of the city,' said Palatine. 'Easier said than done, I know, but do you know anybody not linked with them, people who might be willing to help us?'

'The Domain,' Alciana said harshly.

'Merchant Houses,' I suggested. None of us had any idea where their offices were, and hadn't been willing to ask in case it incurred extra suspicion.

'Canadrath, of course,' said Tamanes. 'But they sell weapons to the Council.'

The weapons we had arranged, straight from my father's mines in Lepidor.

'Hamilcar might have gone there,' Ravenna said. 'Seeking his own kind. Even if he's moved on now, he could well have visited them at some point.'

A few Canadrath factors and maybe a couple of marines wouldn't help us very much.

'Canadrath are popular here, but that makes the Domain suspicious of them. And you'd best be careful, feelings are running high at the moment.'

'Against the Thetians?' I said.

He nodded.

'Are they that bad?' Palatine asked.

'Not as such,' Tamanes said, 'but they stand for the

Domain as much as the Emperor. We never used to see Thetian fleets in these waters, and now they've come to reinforce Domain power when we start to oppose it. They came to stamp out any signs of dissent ahead of Sarhaddon's arrival.'

And Sarhaddon was here now, although whether he had a chance of achieving anything in a Council-dominated city was another matter. His Venatics were probably far more use than any number of Sacri would be.

'No-one has very large forces,' said Palatine. 'If people are sympathetic to the Council, though, we have problems.'

'If people don't like the Empire we have problems,' I said.

'Why does that matter?' Alciana asked. 'I thought you were loyal to the Archipelago.'

'I'm Thetian,' Palatine said. 'We came for the fleet, to take over Thetia and protect the Archipelago.'

'The Archipelago can protect itself,' she said angrily. 'Four years ago you brought in Sarhaddon and his preachers, because you believed it was best for us.'

'As I recall, so did you,' I said. She'd been very much in favour of Sarhaddon when we'd talked in Alidrisi's house above the agora after Sarhaddon's first address.

'You knew he couldn't be trusted.' She stared accusingly at me, neither of her two companions intervening.

'I believed he was trustworthy. So did the Emperor.'

'We could have done better without either of you interfering in our affairs. The Thetians are no better than the Domain, they're just more polite, more subtle. Leave the Archipelago to sort itself out.'

Tamanes shook his head. 'This is Pharaoh, Alcie. She's Archipelagan, she needs our help. If the Council want to get rid of her, then perhaps the Council have their own agenda. We always knew that people like Alidrisi and Sagantha did.'

But both of them were dead now, one at the hands of

the Emperor's men above Perdition's Shore, the other less than an hour ago, along with everyone else on *Crusade*.

'Help them on your own,' Alciana said. 'I'm staying out of this.'

'Alcie . . .' he began, but she brushed past him and went back upstairs.

'Times aren't easy,' said Cleombrotus.

Tamanes watched her go with a troubled expression. 'Things haven't gone well since you left,' he said. 'We've lost a lot of people as penitents; we've never seen any of them again. I'm assistant to the Master now, we're down from twenty oceanographers to nine.'

The situation here was worse than I realised, especially if someone as young as Tamanes was holding such a post.

'We shouldn't stay here long,' Palatine said, looking uneasy. 'They might come looking for us.'

'So where do you go?' Cleombrotus asked. There was silence.

'How well respected are Canadrath?' Palatine said. 'Do people really see them as sympathetic?'

'Hard to say,' Tamanes replied. 'About as sympathetic as any Tanethans can ever be, put it that way. The weapons sales are secret, of course.'

Naturally. Canadrath wouldn't want word of their activities to get back to the Domain; Tanethan Houses had been dissolved for less in the past.

'The Canadrath offices, then,' Palatine said. 'Can we get to them without running into hordes of Council troops?'

'I'll show you,' Tamanes said, turned to Cleombrotus. 'Please look after Alcie.'

'Of course,' said the old man. 'Watch your back. Out of your league here.' He seemed incapable of talking in full sentences.

'I'm always out of my league,' Tamanes said. 'Like the rest of the Guild.'

Even as he turned to open the door, I heard footsteps

outside, and a moment later the sound of knocking. It was painfully loud in the confined space of the hall, and I almost jumped.

'Open your doors in the name of the Council,' said a muffled voice outside.

'Quick!' Cleombrotus whispered. 'Tamanes, into the basement with them.'

Tamanes put a finger to his lips and led us quickly along the corridor, through another door and down a flight of steps. The air was close down here, and when Tamanes pushed us all through a cupboard, a false back and into a tiny room beyond, it was even more oppressive. There was hardly room for the four of us once he'd shut both doors behind us.

'I knew this would happen sometime,' Tamanes whispered, sounding strained. 'I just never thought it would be anyone but the Domain.'

We stood there, squashed in the darkness in the tiny space. The stone above us was too thick to hear any footfalls, and time dragged by agonizingly. It became harder to breathe, and got hotter and hotter.

Finally I heard the sound of people coming downstairs, voices calling out and the sound of the other two doors being opened.

Then the cupboard; somebody swung the door open and I felt a welcome draught of air. Someone poked at the assorted equipment stacked in there.

'Nothing,' said a voice after a moment. 'I think the old man must have been telling the truth, or maybe he told them to go away. You're sure it was this house they were followed to?'

There was a pause, a rustle of paper. 'Certainly.'

'There's a door up at the back here,' someone else called. 'Unlocked. This must be where they got out.'

'Damn,' said another. 'Very well. We'll do this the old-fashioned way.' He must have turned away, because I had to strain to hear his next words. 'Tell the Tehamans we need them after all.'

I thought they'd found us after all, because their voices became much clearer; it took me a moment to realise that Tamanes had found and opened a vent which let us hear sounds from the floor above.

'Is it a good idea to let the jaguars out in the city, sir?' asked the man who seemed to be second-in-command. 'They're not used to cities.'

'We have no choice,' said his superior. 'We're ordered to find these people. The Tehamans know what they're doing, or they wouldn't have brought the animals.' He paused, and I heard the sounds of people walking. 'As for these two . . .'

Oh, no. I closed my eyes, but I could still hear the conversation upstairs.

'They were aiding traitors,' the lieutenant said.

'We don't want to kill them here,' the commander said. 'No-one will believe it was the Domain.'

'May I offer a suggestion?' said another voice, a woman's this time.

'Of course, *Illuminatus.*'

'We have made arrangements for a number of people to simply disappear. After interrogation, of course. We will take them out of your hands, and you need not worry about them any more.'

'Fair enough,' said the commander. 'Where do you want to take them?'

'We are using the oceanographic station for the time being; it serves no other purpose as long as we are in control.'

'Fine.' He sent off two of his men as escorts, and a moment later there was more scuffling, the door banged. There were no sounds of protest; Cleombrotus and Alciana must have been gagged.

'There's nothing more for us here,' the lieutenant said.

'The Tehamans can find those traitors for us,' said the commander. 'We have five more houses on the list.'

I heard their footsteps receding, voices dying away. We waited a few more moments, but there were no further sounds from upstairs. Finally none of us could stand it any longer, and we ran out, back up to the hallway. It was almost dark now, and there were no lights in the house.

I could still sense Tamanes's stricken look, and I couldn't look at him. We'd brought this on all three of them.

'I'm sorry,' Palatine said finally.

'There's nothing you can do,' Tamanes said bitterly. 'All these years we took precautions to make sure the Domain never got us, and then you bring the Council and those vultures down on us. She was right, wasn't she?'

None of us answered for a moment, and it was Ravenna who finally said, 'Yes.'

'There's nothing I can do for them, not now,' he said. 'Except join them. The three of you have ruined me the same way you've ruined the Guild and the Archipelago. I can see why the Council wants you out of the way. And I want you out of Cleombrotus's house. Go!'

He pushed at Palatine, the nearest. 'Goodbye!'

'Tamanes,' she began, but he only shouted something I couldn't make out. I turned and opened the door, the others following me down the steps as it slammed behind us, out into the twilight streets of the city.

'We're like a plague,' Ravenna said, staring up at the darkened house. 'Bringing misery wherever we go.'

No-one said anything for a moment. I hadn't thought I could feel any more wretched than in those last hours on the ship, but what had happened here was far worse than Ravenna's detachment. She was right, of course. We seemed to have spread violence and death over the Archipelago, and we'd as good as killed Alcie and Cleombrotus simply by being there.

I set off numbly up the street, stopped and waited for the others to follow.

It was only as they caught up with me that I heard the cough of a jaguar from a road up to the right.

CHAPTER XXXIII

'There they are!' someone shouted, and we broke into a run, sprinting up the narrow street and diving into the first side-street we could find, trying not to trip up on loose paving stones. They'd been watching the house – worse, they must have followed us there in the first place.

I didn't have time to curse my own stupidity. Shouts rose from behind us, calls of 'Catch the traitors!' ringing between the narrow walls. Not that they'd find many people back here – why were they bothering, when they had the jaguars?

The jaguars. Even the thought of them was enough to make me pick up speed, narrowly avoiding a nasty fall when I came to an unexpected step. We wouldn't be able to outrun them for very long, even in an environment as unfamiliar to them as this. They were some way behind us, but not enough.

I wasn't even sure where we were running to. There was a blockade on the road up to the Acrolith, so that was out of the question, and virtually the whole city was controlled by the Council. Thetis, where else could we go?

I'd exhausted my initial burst of speed now, and I could hear the sounds of the running cats behind us, their claws scrabbling on the rocks. I took another turn, only to find myself in a wider, main thoroughfare with far too many people in it, including a group wearing armour and hoods scattering everyone in front of them.

Palatine gave a shout of alarm and swerved into Ravenna; both of them tripped over and went sprawling on the stones. A second later it was my turn, something cannoned into me from behind and I couldn't keep my balance, only just managing to put out a hand to prevent any serious injury. Something flashed by in front of my, a blurred feline figure, and then it turned and was facing me, golden eyes gleaming in the light from the street's flamewood lamps.

Then jaws closed around my ankle, tight enough to warn me without drawing blood, and I fought to suppress panic. I couldn't bolt, not hemmed in like this.

'At last,' said one of our pursuers, but his voice trailed away as the other group of men moved up. Veiled, their curved swords drawn, at least ten Sacri surrounded two men in Domain robes – one black and white, one red and white. Their faces were those of ascetics, utterly devoid of fear even faced with the four or five big cats that prowled around us.

'I was under the impression that your people were allies of the Domain,' Amonis said softly, speaking over my head to the leader of the hunting party. 'Yet here I find you collaborating with heretics. Even if you are hunting down other heretics, I find your lack of loyalty disturbing.'

Another voice replied; Memnon's.

'We have no loyalty to you,' he said. 'We merely allowed you to think that we did, because it suited our purposes. Tehama chooses its own friends.'

'And its own enemies, it seems,' Amonis said. I could just see him looking down at me, a yard or two behind the nearest jaguar. 'At least there you choose wisely.' He looked up again, over my head at the Tehamans – I couldn't see how many they were.

'Even your presence here defiles the Archipelago,' said Memnon. 'Go home before it is too late for all of you.'

'Brave words from a cowardly people,' Amonis replied. 'Your disguise is gone now, we know you for what you are. Your godless Commonwealth will not survive us.' He made a motion with his hand and the Sacri moved forward. One of the jaguars growled, baring its teeth at the holy warriors.

'What are you doing?' Memnon said. I heard the rustling of cloth from behind me, but the jaguar's teeth and claws held me pressed against the dusty stones of the street. Amonis did not move.

'These heretics are within our jurisdiction,' said the other man, the Venatic. He was considerably older than Amonis — perhaps one of those who had been with Sarhaddon that first day in the agora.

'Does it matter who kills them?' Memnon said. 'We may be enemies, but on this, as you said, we are agreed.'

'We are,' said Amonis, with a curt nod. 'Unfortunately, *Domine* Sarhaddon does not want them killed yet. I cannot disobey him.'

'You must obey him,' the Venatic corrected.

'I think not,' Memnon said. 'Kill them,' he ordered his fellows.

The jaguars closed in, but the Sacri were faster. Swords flashed, but the cats moved out of the way with astonishing speed, and my ankle was released. I felt a thin trickle of blood running down one foot, but ignored it and pushed myself to my feet. The nearest Sacrus lifted me up forcibly, almost throwing me towards one of his fellows as others formed a ring around us, keeping the Tehamans outside.

'You live,' said Amonis to Memnon, 'because I have been ordered not to take life. You would be advised to use your remaining hours wisely. Ask Ranthas for His mercy on you and your people.'

There was a look of hate on the mind-mage's face, but I only caught a brief glimpse of it before the nearest Sacrus dragged me back and the others formed up around the three of us.

Why had they bothered? What did Sarhaddon want so badly, that he'd sent Amonis out with orders to rescue us? Amonis, of all people.

The Tehamans moved away, their jaguars slinking after them into the shadows of the side-street.

Amonis turned to us, his expression no more pleasant than Memnon's, and I felt all the old fear come flooding back, remembering my own helplessness at the Retreat and the dam. Pawns, again, after those few brief weeks of deciding our own fates.

I closed my eyes for a second. *Never again.* I would not be afraid. We were still, against all the odds, alive.

Amonis must have mistaken my gesture as a sign of fear. 'You do well to fear us,' he said venomously. 'I look forward to breaking you on the rack.'

There was nothing to choose between them. Amonis and Memnon, Midian and Ukmadorian, Drances and Sarhaddon were far more alike than my brother and I had ever been. I had no excuse for not seeing the members of the Council for what they were, only my own stupidity.

It was Ravenna who responded, without a trace of fear in her voice. 'Is that all you can think of? Nothing about the glory of Ranthas, because that's irrelevant. Fear you? I can only despise you.'

Amonis tensed with fury, but the Venatic laid a hand on his arm. 'Your vows, *Domine* Amonis. Remember them.'

Barely able to suppress his rage, the Inquisitor had to clench his jaw shut, and his fury was directed as much at the Venatic as us. It wasn't normal for Inquisitors to be put under the authority of any other order, but then this situation was anything but normal. My mind was racing, but I couldn't tell what they wanted us for, or why they'd postponed the inevitable.

'You will come with us to the Temple as *Domine* Sarhaddon has ordered,' Amonis said finally. 'Your fate will be decided there. Centurion, tie their hands.'

One of the Sacri, his only distinguishing mark a gold flame on his robes, motioned to his men. Beyond the circle of holy warriors, Archipelagans stood by uneasily – I was sure there were greater numbers of them than before. The only light now was from the flamewood lamps fixed to the buildings at intervals along the street.

As one of the Sacri brought out lengths of rope, Ravenna held her wrists out together in front of her, barely sparing Amonis a glance, and she made no move to resist as the Sacrus bound her. Palatine gave her an odd look before doing the same. I had no idea how much of an effort it was to do that until I followed suit a moment later, still afraid even though I'd resolved not to be. Ravenna had always been braver than me.

When they'd finished, Amonis had the Sacrus loop the loose ends together so he could lead all three of us like leashed animals as we went along.

'Most hunters are afraid of the quarry, not their hunting cats,' Ravenna said. 'At least, those who go hunting prey their own size.'

'And most people slaughter their cattle close to the house, so they don't have to carry the meat all the way back. The cows walk willingly to their own deaths.' Amonis said. I hadn't expected that much self-control, simply another threat.

'An expert on agriculture,' she said contemptuously. 'Perhaps you should go back to the Halettite river mud.'

'Be silent,' said the Venatic, motioning curtly to the centurion. As the others fell into line, the man leading us jerked on the rope and we stumbled after him, following the two priests at quite a speed up the hill. Crowds of people on either side craned to see what was happened, and I could sense their hostility. There was no way to tell whether it was aimed at us or the Sacri.

'I think we should go in by the side entrance,' the Venatic suggested, as we reached the top of the street and turned in along a short road that led to a corner of the agora.

496

'I think not,' said Amonis. 'We will show the rabble that we are not afraid of them.'

'That was not *Domine* Sarhaddon's intention.'

'It was His Grace's intention,' Amonis said, glad to get the upper hand for once. 'These heretic scum need reminding that we still hold power here.'

'We may not for long, if you behave like that,' the Venatic snapped.

Amonis refused to be budged, and the Sacri tightened their ranks around us. I couldn't see over the two priests' heads – both of them were too tall – but even before we came into the agora I saw the glow of the torchlight and heard the sound of a crowd.

Surrounded by the veiled holy warriors, we pressed into the edge of it as we entered the agora. People fell away on either side as they had done in the street, no-one willing to face up to the masked killers. The chatter of voices became a muttering, louder from the people further back who felt protected.

The two priests pressed on behind their guards, and the man who led us pulled the rope in to shorten the gap between us and him. Still no-one made a move to attack the Sacri. I felt my heart beating faster, hammering against my chest. For Thetis's sake, they hated the Sacri, why wouldn't they attack? Once inside the temple we'd be at the mercy of Midian and Sarhaddon – what were Palatine and Ravenna thinking of?

Ravenna caught my eye and bowed her head, mouthed *Council*. I wasn't sure we stood any better chance out here, and when I could see the crowd's faces they didn't seem sympathetic – but then they were too busy trying to show the Sacri how much they loathed them without bringing down reprisals.

No-one was rash enough to risk those reprisals, and we moved through the crowd unmolested, although the muttering rose in volume. Ahead, people stood on the crimson walls above the Temple courtyard, looking out over the crowd. The walls, built with blank half-columns in an effort to make the structure blend in a little, were higher than I remembered, or had that just been because I'd seen them from a balcony before? I couldn't tell.

Double doors in the square gateway swung open just as we approached, then closed again. There was a small gatehouse inside, and a short passageway, then we emerged into the colonnade of the Temple courtyard, lit by flamewood lamps fixed to the columns on the inside. The holy fire – or at least the holy fire that ordinary worshippers were allowed to see – flickered in the centre, and behind it was the towering red mass of the main building with its tall, thin windows and battlements on top.

Two more Venatics stood waiting just inside the colonnade, hands folded inside the sleeves of their robes.

'You were successful?' one of them said. I recognised his voice: he was the man who'd spoken with Sarhaddon on that first day. Ninurtas, Prior of the Venatics and deputy to Sarhaddon, who was thirty years his junior.

'Yes,' said Amonis. 'I have brought them here as you asked, and now I will take them to see the Exarch.'

'The Exarch is busy,' Ninurtas said. 'These prisoners are to be brought to Sarhaddon as he instructed.'

'They are heretics,' Amonis said. 'They are under the authority of the Holy Inquisition. You cannot deny that.'

'I do not. However, you have been ordered to bring them to Sarhaddon. I find it troubling that you do not obey your vow of obedience except when it suits you.'

'I am a loyal servant of my Order and of Ranthas,' Amonis said stubbornly. 'They should be put to the question.'

'They have already been sentenced,' Ninurtas said, a note of finality in his voice. After a moment's hesitation, Amonis nodded curtly, gave the Venatic the briefest of bows and stalked off across the courtyard, robes swishing around him. All but two of the Sacri also left, heading along the far side of the colonnade.

Ninurtas said nothing more, but indicated to the remaining Sacri to follow him and set off in the other direction. Not waiting to be dragged along, we walked behind them. I could still hear the murmur of the crowd outside, and from the left side of the colonnade I saw a group of figures on the wall, some of whom didn't look like either Sacri or priests. Thetian officers, perhaps, those who'd been separated from their ships?

There would be more up in the Citadel, but I still knew nothing about Hamilcar, or Ithien. Where were they? Had they fallen into Council hands – surely Memnon would have told us, if only to make his victory more complete? And despite *Aegeta*'s action outside the harbour, Hamilcar could still claim to be on the Domain's side as well as the Council's. Palatine had mentioned at one point that three or four Great House mantas had been seized by the heretics over the years. Ukmadorian couldn't know Hamilcar and Ithien were now our allies, although Aurelia's presence would give the game away.

Ninurtas led us through a narrow doorway in one corner of the colonnade and along a passageway, the walls built of dressed stone but bare of paintings or hangings. We were still just inside the outer wall of the Temple, if I reckoned rightly – a far thicker wall than I'd expected it to be. It was more like a fortress than a temple, although that hardly came as a surprise.

We went down a short flight of steps and finally came through another broad doorway into what had to be the Temple fire-hall, the main room below the sanctuary. I looked up, following the line of the massive columns to a flat-vaulted roof from which three iron chandeliers hung.

The Sacrus stopped and unknotted the rope he'd been

using as a lead, then he and his fellow went back outside, closing the doors behind them.

Feeling very small inside this monumental building, I didn't notice the third Venatic at first, a small figure standing beside another fire in the apse at the end. I stared at him for a moment, and even though the room was quite gloomy I could tell who it was – by the way he held himself, the set of the shoulders.

He wasn't cowled in this holy place, and I saw his face clearly as he walked down the steps and along the black marble floor towards us. He made no sound at all as he moved, even though an echo rang between the columns when he spoke.

'You have come a long way,' he said after a moment, 'and made more enemies than I could have imagined possible. It is hardly a surprise that you end up my prisoners again.'

'Do you take the credit for that?' Ravenna said, forced to look up as he came closer. 'You rely on everyone else to do your work for you. Orosius, the Inquisition . . .'

'All have their uses,' said Sarhaddon. 'Is that all the pride you have, that you were an Emperor's captive instead of mine? Are those scars worth it?'

She didn't flinch. 'I'm still alive. I'm still the same person I was, despite all you and your vultures have done. We've escaped you every time. Is that something you're proud of?'

'It doesn't worry me.' He looked much older, forty-one instead of the thirty-one I knew him to be. He had the drawn features of an ascetic, but his eyes were still as alive as ever, boring into each of us in turn as if he could lay our souls bare.

'Why did you bother saving us?' Ravenna asked. 'After all this time, you should have known it was better to let the Council kill us.'

'I wanted it this way,' Sarhaddon said.

She shook her head. 'No, we did. It was our decision to come here.'

'You have an odd view of *decision*,' said the Venatic who'd been with Amonis. 'It was Ranthas's will that you be brought here, and against Him there is no appeal.'

They were both right, in a way, but I was beginning to understand why Ravenna had submitted so meekly – or rather, that she hadn't submitted at all.

'We're your prisoners because we chose to be,' she said evenly. 'And because you chose to take us prisoner. There was no god involved.'

'Even here you speak heresy?' Ninurtas said, sounding more vehement than either of the others. There was a quiet menace in his tone, but none of the violence that characterised the Inquisitors.

Ravenna shrugged as the two of us stood by. I wasn't sure what she was doing, and neither was Palatine, so we kept silent. It wasn't a pleasant situation to be in, and I was barely managing to keep my fear in check. Only the resolve that I would not be someone else's pawn, and the additional resolve of not giving in when Ravenna was so strong. More proof, if I needed any, of the vast gap that lay between us that I'd tried to ignore.

'It seems I can't speak anything else,' she said. 'I'm a heretic in your eyes because I don't follow Ranthas, I'm a heretic to the Council because Cathan and I came up with an idea of our own. And to both of you because I don't believe even in those things you and the Council agree on.'

'Your heretic Council has nothing in common with us,' Ninurtas said.

'You both believe there are eight gods, that each has their own element.'

Ninurtas turned to Sarhaddon. 'See, she convicts herself out of her own mouth. She is a heresiarch. Why do we waste our time with her? We should burn all three of them, now.'

'That would be a mistake,' Sarhaddon said. 'They have their uses.'

'No,' Ravenna interrupted, before Ninurtas could respond. 'Isn't it enough to be a guide of souls, do you have to own them as well?'

'Ranthas has made us His agents on Aquasilva,' Ninurtas said. 'Your soul belongs to Him, while we are merely intermediaries. You know better than any that even the most imperfect vessel may serve some useful purpose.'

'Whatever I say, I'm damned,' she shot back. 'Does anything matter? If you're going to burn me, you'll burn me whether I confess and recant everything or keep on believing that everything in the Book of Ranthas is a lie.'

Ninurtas's face darkened, but Sarhaddon gestured for him to keep quiet. 'I concede you're right, but our business is saving souls, not damning them.'

'You were ready to damn us quickly enough,' Palatine said, unable to keep quiet any longer. 'You came offering peace; the words were hardly out of your mouth before you handed us over to Orosius.'

'You wouldn't have recanted,' Sarhaddon said. 'I knew that then, I know that now.'

'So why do you keep us alive?' Ravenna demanded.

'Do you want to go to the stake?' Sarhaddon asked her. 'You seem terribly eager.'

Ravenna shook her head. 'Of course I don't. But we've thrown ourselves on your mercy in the middle of a Temple full of Inquisitors who want to kill us. Why did we do it?'

The question seemed almost to take Sarhaddon aback for a moment, because she was twisting everything round, stretching the truth to the limits.

'You chose us over the Council,' he said. 'Despite everything we've done, you chose to put yourselves in my hands rather than die at the Council's. If, as you claim, it was your choice, then you came here to save your lives. Martyrdom isn't for you, is it?'

'Can you really say that?' she said. 'After Lepidor?'

'Things change. You change. You came close to death once and you don't want to again. Which means, of course, that you have surrendered your free will to me.' He gave a thin smile. 'You've made it obvious why you're here, and that you're hoping to live through this. It's not a very subtle approach, to use death as a threat all the time, and it doesn't always work, but you've just told me it'll be effective. Thank you.' He stepped back slightly, enjoying Ravenna's discomfiture.

She said nothing for a moment, then, 'It's in your interests for us to live. You gain nothing by having us brought back here to be burned, when the Council could have disposed of us for you. Why go to all that trouble?'

Sarhaddon's voice when he spoke again was very different, as if an Inquisitor had suddenly taken over his body and driven out some of the subtlety.

'Let me make it clear,' he said, 'before anything more is said. I have played along with you because I wanted to, and it has gained me some useful information. Do not be deceived. You humiliated *Domine* Amonis at the dam, and in doing so you wounded the pride of the Inquisition as a whole.

'If it suits my purposes, I will hand you over to them without thinking twice. You will tell them anything they, or I, or anyone else, asks you.'

'You're not Tehaman mind-mages,' said Ravenna.

'No, we're not. I think I should perhaps explain. The Inquisition has a technique it uses in certain situations for extracting information. It only works on those people who are loyal to their friends and their families. If I have you put to the question, Ravenna, the Inquisitors will not touch you, or harm you in any way. You can refuse to answer as

503

many questions as you want, and you won't suffer.' He paused, every bit as implacable as Amonis or even the Council people. 'What will happen is that Cathan, or Palatine, or both, will suffer instead. If you choose not to say anything, they will undergo whatever the Inquisitor wants to do to them, and nothing they say will have any effect at all.'

We should have expected that. I could read Ravenna's sudden fury in the way she tensed up, and knew with a sudden sinking feeling that whatever this contest had been, she'd just lost it. I could understand.

But of course, this had happened before. I remembered very vividly the courtroom at Kavatang, the incredible surge of pure rage that had been triggered as they were putting me on the rack. It had been their treatment of Ravenna that had done it – *and she'd been reacting to what they were doing to me*. The same effect, only I had more latent magic.

There had been three or four mind-mages in Kavatang, there could be many more loose in Tandaris tonight – but I'd dealt with them in Kavatang without a second thought.

But my sudden elation faded a moment later, in the silence that followed Sarhaddon's words. Even if I managed to overwhelm the Sacri and the others in the Temple, we'd be alone in a hostile city, and the Tehamans would know where we were.

The surge of hope died away completely, replaced only by a blacker depression, and I found images rushing through my mind unasked, of the Inquisition torturing them in my place. The stone table, Amadeo hung on wires from the wall, leaving scars that Khalia had said would never fade.

The thought of either of them going through that at Amonis's whim was ghastly. Worse than ghastly; it was hideous. And Sarhaddon knew that. Just as both of us knew the two women were stronger than me, in mind and, well, in body too, I supposed, given what Ravenna had endured.

'Neither Midian nor the Inquisitors will have you burned out of hand,' Sarhaddon went on. 'You have valuable information stored in your heads. If you burn, all three of you will first go through what I've just described. Midian will give his Inquisitors a dispensation to break their own rules for torture, because he wants revenge as much as the rest of them.'

It was an unexpectedly honest admission of what had driven Midian all these years, but I hardly noticed it.

'They will not be gentle, and at the end you will die in excruciating pain. Probably one after the other, so that at least two of you have the chance to repent before you are burned.'

Ravenna stared wordlessly at him as he closed the trap around us, as I looked down at the floor, remembering that horrible dream.

This lies ahead of you still. I will see you in Tandaris.

'You have a choice,' Sarhaddon finished. 'You can choose what I have just described.'

He stopped, obviously waiting for one of us to speak. I did, eventually, since neither of the others had.

'Or?' was all I could say, my throat too tight to form any words.

'Or you can join the Venatic Order, swearing on the others' lives as well as the Book of Ranthas. The Inquisition cannot touch any of our number; that is part of our constitution. Your crimes will be absolved, of course, as you are accepted back into the Domain, and you will obey me in everything.'

What did he mean? He would gain something by that, but I couldn't tell what. He would control us utterly, because I knew as well as he did that Ninurtas would be looking for any opportunity to denounce us. The older man was a brilliant preacher and instructor, from what I'd heard, but from meeting him today I thought I knew why he had been made second-in-command, even though he seemed to disagree with Sarhaddon. The hard-liners on the Council of Exarchs had insisted on putting someone they could trust near the top of the Order to ensure its loyalty and prevent it becoming too independent.

That didn't really matter. It was both the most difficult and the easiest way out, because it would be a total surrender to the Domain and a way of ending the misery of being everyone's target. If we could trust Sarhaddon, of course.

'Or there is a third path you can take,' he said. I looked up again, to find him staring straight at me. 'None of you will come to any harm, in fact the opposite, and you will be free of Midian's power for good.'

This was what he wanted, why he'd left it until last. Torture and death, or absolute obedience, or . . .

'What is the third choice?' I asked.

'You will know in a few minutes. For now, if you will follow me outside, I have something to show you.'

CHAPTER XXXIV

One of the Venatics rapped on the doors, and the two Sacri came back inside. They made little more noise than Sarhaddon, even with the echoes in this place.

'Untie them,' Sarhaddon ordered, 'and then come with us to the walls.'

They gave the briefest of bows. I was glad to be rid of the ropes; Sarhaddon presumably thought he could trust us now.

What was the choice? What did he want from us? As we followed the Venatics and the Sacri out of the hall, my brain was running round in circles trying to guess. It was something to do with me, not with either of the others, but that was little comfort to me.

We retraced our steps along the corridor to the colonnade. There the noise of shouting from outside hit me with renewed force after so long in the near-silence of the hall. There were more people in the colonnade now; detachments of Sacri moving purposefully around, and three or four Temple servants – all Equatorians, of course – carrying bundles out of the gatehouse and across the courtyard to a door on the far side.

'There are a lot of Sacri here,' Ravenna whispered as we walked along the colonnade. 'More than usual.'

'Have you been here before?' Palatine asked.

'After the Tehamans captured me,' she said, with a note of finality. None of us wanted to say any more.

We followed the Sacri into the gatehouse and up a wide staircase – the Qalathari version of a spiral – to the walkway along the top of the walls. The crowd sounded even louder here, and I looked over the oddly carved battlements to see it filling the agora. A few people were carrying torches, but mostly the only illumination was that provided by the street-lamps.

The walkway was wider than I'd imagined, certainly broad enough for a two-horse chariot to have driven down it. Not that there were any chariots in Tandaris, but evidently the architects of this Temple had used the Halettite model. There were no lights up here, and when the nearest of a large group of people started walking towards me, it was a moment before I recognised him.

'Sarhaddon,' he said. The voice I knew at once, and glanced uneasily at the three Venatics, all frail and diminutive beside the big Halettite who'd spoken. 'What's this I hear about you appropriating my prisoners?'

'Midian,' Sarhaddon said, giving only the slightest of bows. By any standards the Exarch of the Archipelago was Sarhaddon's superior, yet the Venatic didn't bother with *Your Grace*.

I could see Midian's furious expression in the reflected light from the courtyard as he saw the three of us. Amonis was standing beside him now like a shadow.

'They are condemned heretics, Your Grace,' he said. 'Loose in the Temple, and not even bound.'

'Indeed they are heretics,' Sarhaddon said. 'That doesn't stop them being useful to us. And orders are orders.'

The Exarch's eyes narrowed. 'Accidents happen, he knows that. We should kill them and be done with it.' *He* would presumably be the Prime.

Midian was as unsubtle as ever; an overbearing thug. Perfect for his post, in the Domain's view. The red and gold robes, the cylindrical cap with the flame symbol on it – they were only trappings. Midian was a Halettite nobleman, trained as a warrior and with as few redeeming features as most of his people – among whom I counted the late Emperor as well as the Prime and most of the higher clergy.

'A word, Your Grace, if I may,' Sarhaddon said smoothly, drawing the Exarch away from us before Amonis could protest. They walked over to the courtyard battlements and conferred in low voices for a couple of minutes. Sarhaddon was explaining something to the Halettite, and although Midian seemed to accept it, he wasn't happy.

'We will go on with it,' he said loudly as they came back, 'unless the situation demands otherwise.'

'At the moment all is well,' Sarhaddon said.

'Perhaps,' was Midian's answer. The Exarch went over to talk to a pair of Inquisitors, while Sarhaddon led us over to the group. Several of them turned round as they saw us, and stopped me in my tracks.

'Who are these?' said one man – a Tanethan, with a Merchant Lord's beard. He wore a light cloak over his robe. I'd met him before, although he wouldn't remember me. Lord Hiram, whose House was among the biggest in Taneth. Beside him, looking as unruffled and urbane as ever, Hamilcar Barca. No surprise there. The others were of similar standing – two Thetian admirals, two senior Pharassan officers and another who looked like a high official of some kind. A Mons Ferratan who I assumed held rank of some kind, some other Equatorians.

But it was one of the last to look round that drew my attention, a stocky man with a short, neatly trimmed beard wearing a black cloak over the dark green with stars of an admiral of Cambress.

'I thought you might recognise him,' Sarhaddon said.

The Cambressian gave me an odd look, then moved forward as the other officers looked on curiously. At least one representative from every major power, I noticed.

'Gentlemen, these are our guests,' Sarhaddon laid a slight emphasis on the word, making it clear to the officer what he meant. 'Palatine Canteni, Ravenna Ulfhada and Carausius Tar'Conantur.'

There were indrawn breaths from many of them.

'You had another name last time I met you,' the Cambressian said, 'I remember you, it was just after my ship had been attacked by a black pirate manta.'

Ravenna gave a very faint smile.

'In Oceanus,' I said, remembering a summer afternoon nearly seven years ago, and a Cambressian captain with a ready smile. 'Xasan Koraal. Your first officer, Ganno, was there, and a Mons Ferratan. And I'm still Cathan Tauro.'

The smile faded. 'Ganno went down with the *Lion* at Poralos Atoll. I've seen Miserak again a few times.'

None of the others said anything, and even Ravenna looked surprised. I felt my eyes stinging, and blinked back sudden tears. Not so much for the friendly Cambressian officer I'd hardly known, but for what I'd been, and for my travelling companion that day.

Xasan shook his head, lost in thought for a moment. There was a curious expression on Sarhaddon's face as he studied us.

'Odd how these things happen,' Xasan said, taking advantage of his colleagues' silence. 'I know we were repairing after whatever it was decided to attack us, but I remember how peaceful and civilised everything was. Just a trip up the Oceanian coast to show the flag here and there, conclude a trade deal or two. Catch anyone behaving like that now.'

As he spoke, images came floating up from some corner of my mind. The harbour in Kula, sleepy and almost deserted; the food and the wine in the palace of my father's friend Count Courtières. Sailing south to Pharassa with a talkative acolyte due to begin his training in the Holy City.

Even as these memories came to me, I caught Sarhaddon's eye and knew, in that moment, what the other choice would be. Both of the others would already have guessed, but my lapse into self-pity had clouded my reasoning for a moment.

Sarhaddon smiled thinly, able to read me better than I could myself. His introduction had been very pointed, although it would only have been a matter of time before the Thetian saw my resemblance to Orosius.

'Nephew of the late Emperor?' Hiram asked suspiciously.

Sarhaddon answered for me. 'Nephew of Aetius, brother of Orosius.'

'This is a worrying development,' one of the Pharassans said. 'We were under the impression that there were no more Imperial heirs.'

'Ranthas would not allow such a thing to happen,' Sarhaddon said. 'The Empire can't be without an Emperor.'

'It is at the moment, unless you count the Empress in the Acrolith,' the Thetian said. I felt my heart leap with relief. My mother was still safe then, had presumably taken refuge in the Acrolith. He hadn't mentioned captivity of any kind.

'My fleet is trapped in the harbour,' the admiral went on, staring into the crowd below.

This must be the commander of the Grand Fleet, Alexios, and his companion – not an admiral I saw now, but a captain – was probably his chief of staff, flagship commander, whatever. I wondered how the two of them had ended up here rather than blockaded in the Acrolith with Charidemus and Aurelia.

As they watched, the crowd moved aside to let through a group of people coming down the road from the Acrolith. They stopped before they reached the level of the agora and were allowed to move to the front of the crowd. The noise died away.

'The leaders,' said the Mons Ferratan. 'Now we find out who they are.'

'Not just the leaders,' Xasan said, pointing. 'Look, there are soldiers all through the crowd, they're assembling over there, and just down there. See the plumes?'

511

There was silence on the parapet as we waited to hear from the Councillors – although most of the men present would have no idea who they were.

It wasn't Ukmadorian who stepped forward, not surprisingly, but another man, an Archipelagan as far as I could tell, wearing the grey robes of the Citadel of Wind. Of course he would be an Archipelagan, because this was as much about independence as religion – for some at least.

'People of Tandaris,' he said, his voice ringing out over the square, 'we have returned! We have come back to liberate the Archipelago from the Domain *once and for all*!'

It was hardly very inspired, but there was a roar of acclamation from the crowd that took minutes to die down and let the man speak. He must be Ukmadorian's opposite number as head of his Citadel.

'We have thirteen mantas guarding the harbour, we have trapped twenty-four Thetian vessels here and nine more in Pharenos. When those ships are ours, the Archipelago will have a Navy to make the greatest power in the world tremble!'

Another roar. He was nowhere near as good a speaker as Sarhaddon, but then tonight he didn't need to be. And a fleet of nearly fifty war-mantas, including battle cruisers, was more than Cambress would have mustered for a full-scale war against another continent – not that such a thing would ever occur.

'For now the Thetians are powerless, their fleet is trapped in the harbour. We will transform them from enemies into allies, and when the time comes we will welcome them as fellow warriors against the Domain!' He moved round as the crowd shouted its approval, and he looked directly at the parapet where we all stood. 'Exarch Midian, Preceptor Sarhaddon, those walls will not keep you safe. We will storm your Temple and destroy it, we will purge the Archipelago of every last priest and Inquisitor and send them to die in the flames they have condemned so many of our people to!

'You cannot hide! You cannot seek to thrust your puppet Pharaoh upon us.' He moved again, back to the crowd. 'Our Pharaoh has betrayed us! She has taken the side of the Domain, she has collaborated with them to bring destruction on her own people. Now she stands with Midian and Sarhaddon in the Temple, planning her rule over you as a tyrant with the Domain's help! Will you accept such a ruler?'

As the Tandarans began to shout, 'No!' Sarhaddon turned to Ravenna.

'It seems they've covered every eventuality,' he said. 'You're a false Pharaoh to them now, and how many know better? It's a shame, I suppose.' But his voice told us all clearly that it was no such thing as far as he was concerned.

Ravenna stumbled back, white-faced, as if someone had stabbed her. Palatine caught her as she gave Sarhaddon a look of pure hatred. '*I am not a puppet*,' she said, barely able to speak. She moved forward again as the noise from the crowd died down.

'I am not a puppet!' she shouted out at the crowd. 'I'm their prisoner!' Thetis, how it must have galled her to say that.

'She lies!' the Councillor yelled. 'If you are a prisoner, why you do stand there with them? An odd prisoner, let out on the battlements without ropes or chains. Where have you been all these years? What have you ever done for the Archipelago? Kill her!'

They didn't give her a chance to reply, but took up the chant. 'Kill her! Kill her! Kill her!' She shouted over them, but then a stone flew up and hit the battlements a few cubits along, and Sarhaddon had two of the Sacri pull her back from the parapet. The shouting continued, swelling in volume as more makeshift missiles were thrown, and the officers moved behind the battlements where they could be sure of keeping out of the way.

'They're not . . . it's not . . .' Ravenna shouted, then stared down at her hands, untied by Sarhaddon's order only a few minutes ago. The Venatic smiled coldly.

'Althana!' Ravenna said. 'Thetis, Tenebra, *why*?'

'Listen to your own people howling for your blood,' Midian said, appearing suddenly behind Sarhaddon. He might have been smiling, but the beard and the darkness prevented me from reading his expression. 'My apologies, Sarhaddon,' he said. 'You have destroyed her without even laying a finger on her, which is . . . commendable.'

Ravenna staggered again, put a hand out to stop herself from falling and stumbled against the wall.

'Kill her! Kill her! Kill her!' The people in the agora kept up the chant, shrieking for the blood of their Pharaoh as the Councillor spurred them on, his voice inaudible to all but a small section of the crowd. It didn't matter.

'The affection of the mob is a fickle thing, isn't it?' Sarhaddon said. 'You shouldn't have hidden all these years, or they might be acclaiming you as Pharaoh instead of thirsting for your blood. It's too late now. Too late for anything.'

Ravenna looked up, not at him but at me, and for a moment I couldn't breathe. I'd never seen such loss on anyone's face. The reserves of strength that had carried her through everything had failed her at last.

I couldn't even say anything, because there was nothing I could say. Sarhaddon had spoken the truth for once. Whatever happened, after this, her dream of becoming Pharaoh was finished. In those few seconds she had been labelled a collaborator and a traitor, and no-one would ever forget that.

If she hadn't spoken, admitted who she was, there might still have been a chance, but with the people she had dedicated her life to saving from the Domain howling for her death in the torchlit square, she knew as well as Sarhaddon did that it was over.

Palatine let out a yell and leapt past Ravenna to attack Midian, but the Sacri, as ever, were too quick and too strong. She didn't reach him or have a chance to fight; one stopped her and kicked her in the back of the leg, slamming a hand down on her shoulder to force her to her knees, then twisting her arms behind her back. The other pulled out the tether and tied her hands behind her.

Midian glanced over the wall. 'Take her on ahead,' he instructed. 'Keep her secure, we'll want her later on.'

One of the Sacri nodded, pulled her up by her collar so hard she nearly choked, and half-dragged her after him along the parapet.

Ravenna was leaning against the wall now, head buried in her hands and oblivious to what was going on. I closed my eyes, unable to bear watching this any longer. I felt sick.

'We are nothing if not efficient,' Midian said. 'We could add *assault on an Exarch* to her list of crimes, but there's no point. Ranthas, why you Thetians think you can let a woman do anything at all never ceases to amaze me.'

The Thetian admiral stiffened. 'Treat a man like that and expect him to do any better,' he said curtly.

'He probably would, as long as he wasn't a perfumed popinjay,' the Exarch said. 'Present company excepted, Admiral Alexios.'

'I'm sure my men are included in *present company*,' the admiral said. 'Are you doing anything to rescue them? They can't fight mages.'

'Watch and listen,' Midian said, turning back to the square, where the grey-robed Councillor was speaking again, pausing only for cheers from the delirious crowd.

'Join us, people of Tandaris!' he said. 'Already we have rid the world of the butcher Emperor. Who says that only the Domain can launch Crusades? Join us in ours to rid the Archipelago of them, to burn every temple and every

Inquisitor, to make us a free people again, a people who can hold our head high among the nations of Aquasilva and say *We are Archipelagans*!

'We will worship whichever gods we want to, we will bury our dead as we see fit, and we will not be hunted and enslaved by a bunch of ignorant Halettite peasants!'

I think I was the only one who heard the Thetian captain's muttered, 'Hear, hear,' above the noise of the crowd.

'Our men are ready by the harbour, ready to seize the ships that will bring the Archipelago to glory and victory, and make Tandaris the capital of the greatest nation on Aquasilva! They will help us destroy this monstrosity that for too long has blighted our beloved city, and you shall have the support of every mage the Council can call on! Let us destroy it!'

'DESTROY!' the crowd roared. They obviously weren't ready to yet, because the orator kept on as more Council soldiers moved into position.

'Can they take the Temple?' Xasan asked.

Midian shook his head. 'They might try, but we have more protection than you think. The city itself will be our hostage.'

'What do you mean?'

'We brought you here to show you what we face in the Archipelago, but we've taken precautions of our own,' Midian said. 'The Elemental Council has been planning this for years, you've seen what it's capable of.'

'And so?'

'You will bear witness to what really happened here tonight,' Sarhaddon said. 'All of you. We won't have destroyed an innocent city or be accused of having butchered thousands of law-abiding citizens.'

'Tandaris has been making trouble for years,' Alexios said, 'but what do you plan to do?'

'Make an example of it,' Midian said. 'By morning, the

heretic resistance in the Archipelago will be over. The Council; Tandaris; all the leading heretics.'

'Everyone in one place,' said Xasan. 'I suppose it makes sense. You brought us here to save your reputation, then you tell us that you planned this?'

'We didn't plan it. We knew of the plot, even the attempt on the Emperor's life which we tried to stop. His death was unfortunate, but whoever succeeds him will inherit a cowed Archipelago.'

'You mean to destroy the city,' Alexios said. 'I refuse to be part of this.'

'You have nothing to do with it,' said Midian. 'I thought Eshar had turned your Navy into a professional service, not produced officers who are no better than the women they fawn over.'

Was he being this offensive on purpose? The admiral held the balance of power in the city, as commander of the Grand Fleet. If he sided with anyone against the Domain, there would be nothing anyone could do.

'We are a professional service,' said Alexios coldly. 'We do not murder civilians.'

'Very enlightened of you,' Midian said. 'But these are heretics. Animals. You've seen them, they even turned on the leader they adored. How trustworthy can they be?'

'And when your men start slaughtering them, what of my sailors? Will you leave them to die as well?'

'We have companies of Sacri ready,' Sarhaddon assured him. 'As soon as the mob is committed to an attack on the Temple, we will send the Sacri to pick off the enemy mages and free the harbour mouth.'

The casual way they were discussing mass murder was sickening. Unnoticed, I slipped round to stand beside Ravenna, but she didn't seem to notice my presence.

'So how will you teach them this lesson?' said the Pharassan diplomat, who sounded as if he approved of this. Knowing the Pharassan court, I wasn't particularly

517

surprised. I'd been present at the Congress which had elected the present King – elected was perhaps the wrong word – and he was an out-and-out fanatic.

'Why, with fire, of course,' Midian said. 'It is Ranthas who will punish them, we are merely his intermediaries.'

'Your mages are helpless,' Xasan pointed out.

'We don't always rely on mages,' said Midian. 'I think it's time we put the Temple shield up. They'll start using magic soon.'

The Sacri ushered us back from the parapet as one of their fellows walked into the gatehouse, and a moment later I heard a deep, low humming and sparks flared from the shield-guides at the corners; a second later the blue glow spread along the outside of the battlements and up beyond the Temple, enveloping the whole building from the walls to the pinnacle of the hall in an aether-blue glow.

'It'll take their mages a while to penetrate that,' Midian said with satisfaction.

'Can aether shields keep elemental magic out?' Alexios asked curiously. 'I've never faced it before, so it was never a problem.'

'It's Fire,' said Amonis. 'Superior to any magic they can throw at it. Both a spiritual and a physical defence, and their mind-mages can't interfere with it.'

'I wouldn't be too confident,' the Thetian said. 'If I was in their place, I'd know about the aether shield, I'd have come up with some way to deal with it in advance.'

Midian shrugged. 'They can whip up a crowd, but they'll have to use force to break the shield down.'

'You brought us here to show what a danger they pose to us all, Your Grace. As a strategist, I'd say it was unwise to underestimate your enemy.' His eyes narrowed. 'Could they have siege weapons?'

'The only siege weapons here belong to us,' Midian said. 'You're too nervous, Admiral.'

'We shall see,' Alexios said, deliberately turning his back on the Exarch.

'Perhaps our prisoners know more than they're letting on,' Amonis offered. 'They were, after all, creatures of the Council until recently.'

'And until recently they were both in your custody,' Sarhaddon said.

Amonis held his ground. 'We don't know whether they discovered the Council's plans. Have you allowed me to interrogate them? No. You keep them back for this secret purpose of your Order's, when they could have vital information.'

'We don't need their information,' Midian said. 'They are of no consequence.'

'They why aren't they being punished?' Amonis said. 'His Holiness sent us to the Archipelago with a mandate to crush this heresy once and for all, and here we have three of the most notorious heretics in our hands. How can we justify this behaviour when we come before Ranthas's justice? One at least is a heresiarch, not a mere heretic.'

'The girl is too,' Ninurtas said. 'She denies that there are eight gods, she claims that we have common ground with the Council.'

Midian, who had been losing interest, turned back abruptly, motioned to the Sacri to move between us and the officers. 'What?' he demanded. 'Sarhaddon, explain.'

For the first time I thought I spotted concern on his face, and I felt the fear returning. Whatever Sarhaddon wanted to do with me, there were a great many here who opposed his plans vehemently.

'She attempted to brazen her way out of captivity,' Sarhaddon said. 'In an effort to do this, she attempted to contradict me as outrageously as she could think of.'

Midian shook his head, and when he spoke again his voice was much tighter, much less hearty than usual. 'Amonis, take them below and interrogate them. Find out

519

if this is true, and come back up to me. Do not let them come into contact with anyone else. Sarhaddon, your plan will have to wait for now.'

Ravenna looked up at him. 'Too late, Midian,' she said. 'The world already knows.'

'And find out if that's true,' Midian added. 'I release you temporarily from all obligations to follow the rules of interrogation laid down by the Domain universal. You may do penance for this later.'

As I was dragged off again, cold fingers of fear running up and down my spine, I thought I could see the Exarch's hands shaking.

CHAPTER XXXV

'I'll tell you whatever you want to know,' said Ravenna as two Sacri in gold-trimmed cloaks pulled the cell door back into place behind them, sealing us in the long, ill-lit underground room with Amonis and two more Inquisitors. In the gallery, a level above with barred windows looking down on to us, Midian and Sarhaddon stood with Ninurtas and two or three others. All of them, including the Sacri, were of the highest ranks of their orders.

'You'll tell us what you want us to hear,' Amonis said. 'The two aren't the same.'

I could see that she was still shattered from what had happened on the wall, broken by the malice of Sarhaddon and the Council. 'Ask me.'

'I will,' said Amonis. 'I'll simply give you an incentive to tell the truth.'

It was me he chose, as I'd known it would be. I was stripped and tied by the wrists to a rail running across the room above head height, dangling more than a foot above the floor. I could hardly breathe, but a moment later two of the other Inquisitors began tying weights to my ankles, dragging me down further. Struggling to support my own body and the weights, every breath became an effort, every time a little harder to force in all the air I needed. I couldn't speak, there was too little air.

'If you answer our questions quickly and truthfully, your friend may survive,' I heard Amonis say. 'If you pause, or lie, more weights will be added. Eventually he will suffocate.' He stared pitilessly at Ravenna.

'You didn't need to do that,' she said, her voice barely audible.

'Speak louder,' Amonis said.

She repeated it, a frail figure standing in an open space surrounded by the Inquisitors and their instruments of torture. I kept my eyes fixed on her, not wanting to think what else they could to do me – or to Palatine, secured in the far corner.

I heard a pen scratching, and glanced up into the gallery to see Ninurtas standing at a writing lectern now, transcribing the interrogation.

'What is your name?' Amonis demanded. 'Your formal name.'

'Raimunda Ulfhada Selessis di Tolosa.'

'And your title and station?'

Her voice almost broke as she answered. 'Pharaoh of Qalathar by descent from Orethura Selessis di Tolosa.'

'And your age?'

'Twenty-six. You know all of this, why are you asking me?'

'Shorten the formalities,' Midian said. 'We may need to evacuate at some point, and I want this to be cleared up by the time we do.'

Amonis nodded. 'That will be enough. Very well. Prisoner, do you believe in Ranthas as the one holy, true and undoubted god of Aquasilva, Lord of the most sacred element Fire?'

'No.'

'What part of this truth do you deny?'

'It's not truth, and I deny all of it.'

'*All of it?*' Amonis said. 'You deny that he is Lord of Fire?'

'Yes.'

'Which false elemental god do you worship?'

She paused.

'More weights,' Amonis ordered.

She protested, but the Inquisitors ignored her, and I felt myself dragged down even more. The pain in my wrists

522

was unspeakable already, as if my hands were slowly being pulled away from my arms – which they more or less were.

'None of them,' Ravenna said. 'I don't worship any of them.'

'Have you ever worshipped any of them?'

'Tenebra of the Shadows,' she said.

'When did you cease to follow this heretical cult?'

'I don't know – little by little.'

'That is not a satisfactory answer; I will ask you once more. When did you cease to follow this heretical cult?'

'About two weeks ago,' she said. 'If you must have a time.'

'Do you believe that Tenebra of the Shadows is the only goddess?'

'No, and I never did. I believed in all eight of the elemental gods, and I worshipped Tenebra.' She looked round at me again, then back at Amonis. 'Can't I just tell you to save time?'

'You will answer my questions,' Amonis insisted. 'If you want to volunteer information, it will be recorded, and I'll move on if it answers the question. You say *believed*. Do you no longer believe that the elemental gods are . . . true?'

'No they aren't,' she almost shouted. 'I don't believe in any of them! Not Ranthas, or Tenebra, or Althana – none of them are real.'

There were stunned looks among the priests on the gallery, and Midian looked visibly worried.

'What do you believe?' I was sure this interrogation was going more quickly than it should have done, remembering how long our trial had taken at Kavatang. They didn't have much time, and they knew it. But Midian had been so confident the city would be destroyed, what was he waiting for? Why did this worry him so much?

'I'm not sure,' she said. 'I just don't believe there are eight elements.'

'How many do you think there are?'

'I don't know. Please believe me. If I did, I'd tell you. There aren't eight because they're all parts of the same thing. It's an artificial division, separating Fire and Water and Earth and all the others.'

Even Amonis looked shaken now. 'So you believe that there are no separate elements?'

She nodded.

'And no separate gods?'

'Whatever the gods are, they aren't the ones we've been worshipping.'

'You deny even your false elemental gods?'

'There are no elements,' she repeated.

'Track everything down,' Midian ordered, cutting across Amonis's next question. 'Work out how she came to think like this.'

Amonis bowed. 'Prisoner, why do you believe there are no elements? Is it because you are a woman, that you cannot see the realms of Fire, and Water, and Air, all around us? Only one has its god, but none here would deny that the others exist.'

'Of course they exist,' she said, 'but not as individual elements. What is steam? Water or Air? Which goddess rules it?'

'The false elements are by nature impure,' Amonis said. 'They mix, their edges blur and their gods must concede to each other. This is why Fire is the one true element, and its god the one true God.'

Midian appeared relieved, but Sarhaddon was intent on Ravenna, ignoring his fellows up on the balcony. Ninurtas finished the sentence and looked up expectantly.

'I could use the magic of two elements,' she said. 'Shadow and Air.'

'Exactly,' Amonis sounded puzzled that she'd put that in. 'And because of that you were doubly cursed, by the effect of the false elements and being at a point where they mixed.'

'*All* the elements,' she said.

'Fire is separate and above any of the others,' he insisted. 'Fire consumes them and drives away the darkness, but it's separate.'

'It isn't,' she said.

'Where is there an example? The simplest novice in a good seminary knows about the impurities of the other elements, but you can't mix Fire and the others.'

'It's not as bad as I thought,' Midian said, now back to his old form. 'Find out how she came to this conclusion.'

'You know about our storm-magic,' she said, turning to the Exarch and not waiting for Amonis to phrase the question. 'I realised that Storm was just as plausible an element as either Water or Air – but in that case, what's the point of adding elements? There are so many places where they all collide, we'd only be reclassifying what already exists.'

'The impurities explain these flaws in the heretical system,' Amonis said.

I was hardly able to concentrate on them over the waves of agony that were engulfing me from wrists to feet. My back felt as if it was being slowly distorted beyond repair, and Thetis, it was so hard to breathe.

'Who came up with the idea for your storm-magic?'

'I did,' she said.

'You're lying,' Amonis said, without hesitation. More agony, as the Inquisitors slung extra weights on to my feet. The muscles in my shoulders were screaming protest, felt as if they were about to tear.

'I'm not.'

'Just one more weight,' Amonis said. I tried to protest, but it used up air in my lungs and I had to gasp in breaths, feeling my air supply being inexorably cut off.

'We both did,' Ravenna said desperately, looking down. 'Or rather, it was his idea. I just had the time to think about it.'

Why had she said that?

'So you're both heresiarchs,' said Midian softly. 'I know where this came from now, and that at least it is something we can deal with.'

'The Guild?' Amonis said.

'Yes,' Midian replied, nodding deliberately. 'The Oceanographic Guild.' He paused. 'Who knows your heretical thoughts?'

'The world. I told you.'

'How can they? You've been out of our custody for barely a month, don't delude yourself.'

'You won't listen,' Ravenna said. 'When you said there were no impurities, that fire was separate – it isn't.'

'As I told you,' Amonis said coldly. 'You have no examples.'

'No examples, but I can use fire-magic.'

For a moment there was silence.

'Did you expect us to believe that?' Amonis demanded. 'More weights.'

'No!' she shouted. 'Please, I'm telling the truth, let him be.'

'Wait.' It was Sarhaddon, speaking for the first time. He looked far more disturbed than any of the others were.

'That's impossible,' Amonis said.

'I've done it,' she said quietly. 'Three times.'

'She must be lying,' said one of the others on the balcony. A mage, from his robes. 'Fire and the other elements can't be mixed.'

'Test her,' Midian said. 'Amonis, apply the aether whip to the other prisoner and see what her answer is then.'

I suppose it was a measure of how deep the scars of Perdition's Shore ran that Ravenna actually knelt then, facing Midian and the others in the gallery.

'It's true,' she said. 'I beg you, don't use it.'

'She lies!' the mage said, raising his voice.

'How can you tell?' Ravenna said, still on her knees. 'Let me show you!'

'She wants to use her foul elemental magic to kill us all,' said the mage. 'Can't you see?'

'What chance do I have of doing that?' Ravenna said.

'He's right,' Midian declared. 'You're trying to trick us. Amonis, I believe you know what to do.'

Amonis nodded to the Sacrus, who marched over and held Ravenna where she was. I followed Amonis round with my eyes as he retrieved a whip with a thick, bulky handle from a rack nearby and uncoiled it. A moment later I saw a blue spark flicker up and down the blade.

'How many?' Amonis asked Midian. Held immobile by the weights, I couldn't even move as he walked round behind me.

'Twenty,' the Exarch said.

I braced myself, knowing that the pain could hardly get any worse. I heard the swish of Amonis's robes, then an inarticulate shriek from Ravenna and the Sacrus fell back slightly.

Magic flared in the room, and I saw fire flash through the air, pain flare on my back as I tried to avoid it. I screamed and felt the air leave my lungs. I couldn't breathe in again, there wasn't enough air; I felt myself choking.

I saw the Sacrus push Ravenna over, but by then I was beginning to suffocate, my vision becoming worse and worse, as I tried in vain to breathe.

Then, blessedly, I was lifted up, and gulped in air, trying to get as much into my lungs as I could before whoever it was put me down again. The weights were still dragging, but at least when I was dropped a moment later, I had enough air to cope.

It was a minute or so before my vision came back, and the babble of voices died away. The Exarch was on his feet, shouting for order amid a group of stunned clerics, while one of the Sacri had his sword at Ravenna's throat. It had been his companion who'd lifted me up, on whose orders I couldn't be sure.

'Silence!' Midian roared, and the voices died away. I looked round as far as I could, saw Amonis pouring water over his right hand, helped by one of the other Inquisitors. Whatever had happened must have burned him as well. The pain in my back was intense.

'What happened?' the Exarch demanded, turning a withering look on the mage. 'She used fire-magic, didn't she?'

The mage almost wilted, then pulled his robe closer around him and said, 'Your Grace, she is a heretic, she can't have.'

'Don't tell me what I didn't see,' Midian bellowed. 'You said it was impossible. She's just committed the greatest heresy we know of, one so vile that it isn't supposed to be possible. Tell me how she did it!'

'Your Grace, I . . . I don't know,' the mage said, taken aback for the first time. 'You said it yourself, it isn't possible.'

'But she did it. What does this mean?'

'It means,' said Ninurtas, 'that she can break virtually all the rules we know about. She's the most dangerous heresiarch we've ever seen.'

'But who else knows?' the mage asked. 'What if she's infected others with this heresy?' He motioned to one of the Inquisitors, who walked over to where Ravenna knelt with arms pinioned and the Sacrus's sword at her throat.

'How many people saw you do this?' he demanded.

'About five thousand,' she said, her face a strange mixture of defiance and resignation.

The Inquisitor glanced up at Midian, asked. 'How? Where?'

'In Ilthys,' she said. 'About a week ago. In the main square, after the city had been put under Interdict.'

'She must be lying,' the mage said, but Midian quelled him with a glance. A shaken Sarhaddon was standing looking down at us.

'If only we still had the Tehamans,' one of the Inquisitors said. 'They've broken her before, they should be able to tell for us.'

'We don't,' Midian said. 'Find out the old-fashioned way.'

The Inquisitor glanced over at me, then down at the weights. 'We can't put on any more now, he'll suffocate.'

Midian shrugged, and I felt a stab of panic. No matter how bad this was, I still wanted to live, I could still hope we had a chance of accomplishing our original objective.

'That would be unwise,' said Sarhaddon, the first words he'd spoken since that moment when the whip had burst into flame in the air and shattered two hundred years of carefully constructed theology. 'She loves him, and that's the only hold we have over her.'

'Try something different,' said Midian. 'Cut him down, and torture the other woman instead.'

'What's the point?' Ravenna said. I saw a thin line of blood trickle down her throat as the Sacrus tightened his grip slightly. 'I'll only do the same.'

'But can you?' said Sarhaddon. 'You didn't use your magic until Amonis tried to use the aether whip, when you could surely have called on it earlier?'

The mage looked over at him. 'I can't help. Our mind-mages and the Tehamans are both covering this room, she shouldn't have been able to do anything.'

'But what if she can break through the limits only when she's desperate?' Sarhaddon said, spotting in a few seconds something it had taken us hours to realise, and the rest of the world seemed not to have noticed yet. 'We were going to use the whip because it was used on her, and it was only when she realised Cathan was actually going to feel the same that she managed to use it. Yes, I'm right, I can see from their expressions.'

Thetis, it was as if we were transparent to him. Was there nothing any of us could do?

'Just leave him alone and I'll tell you what happened,' Ravenna said. 'It's not worth my trying to lie to you.'

The Exarch paused, obviously preferring to have some control over how the interrogation went, but after a moment he nodded.

'Cut him down if he's on the point of suffocating, but not before,' he ordered. 'Now, Ravenna, you will tell us.'

She nodded, and as the Sacrus moved his sword slightly away she told them, haltingly, what had happened in Ilthys – or at least as much as she was willing to let them know. My vision began to shrink again, and my head was hurting as well now, I wasn't sure why. I couldn't feel my hands any more.

'And how many of those in Ilthys have come to the same conclusion as you?' the Inquisitor asked finally.

'I don't know,' she said, but her slight hesitation had given it away.

'You do,' he said. 'Your Grace, she needs some encouragement.'

'The survivors of *Crusade*,' she whispered. 'In the city, now. But there will be others, and I asked the Ilthysians to let the world know before I left.'

An ashen-faced Exarch looked down at us, his bombast gone. Sarhaddon was standing utterly still, his expression inscrutable.

'We should kill them,' Amonis said.

'That will gain us nothing,' said Midian shakily.

'It should be done, Your Grace,' Amonis insisted. 'Before they can infect any more.'

'It will already have spread.'

'We lose nothing by killing them,' Amonis went on, persistent as ever. 'We should, now, while there are no witnesses, before the delegates or any of the Temple servants hear the sedition. That way we protect at least some innocents from this foulness.'

'Won't you understand?' Ninurtas said. 'This is not a

matter of heresy any more, of protecting ourselves and torture and burning. Can you imagine what the world will do when this is discovered? What the Council will do?'

'We can destroy the Council,' Midian said. 'Tonight, as planned. That'll at least give us one thing the less to worry about.'

'The Council can't threaten us any more,' said Sarhaddon heavily. 'Only *they* can.' He pointed down at Ravenna and me, and at a shaken Palatine helpless where the Inquisitors had tied her.

'Only the Council has mages,' Midian said. 'If their mages can learn how to use Fire as she's done . . .' The Exarch covered his face with his hands for a moment. I could hardly believe this had happened, the contrast between the Midian above us and the man who'd more or less ground us underfoot on the parapet. And not by weapons, or fleets, or anything else . . . it was surreal.

I didn't have time to think about that. Each breath was becoming harder and harder again, and I knew I'd be reaching suffocation point soon. Every part of my body seemed to be awash with pain, and it was an effort to even keep my eyes open, almost as much as to breathe. Someone cut me down, for Thetis's sake! I didn't care what else they did to me, as long as it was something different.

'If there are only the two who know, we should destroy the city, kill everyone,' Midian said.

Ninurtas shook his head. 'All those Ilthysians saw it, though, and sooner or later someone will realise.'

'Then we'll move on to Ilthys and obliterate that as well,' Midian said. 'Maybe we can still stop the contagion from spreading, and if not . . . it'll send a clear message to the rest of the world. With the Thetian fleet under our control, it won't matter whether there are a few lunatics preaching this heresy.'

'That's what we've said about the Council for two

hundred years,' Ninurtas pointed out, moving over to stand by the Exarch. 'All it needs is one charismatic person to take up its cause, set himself up as a prophet and tell the world what happened in Ilthys, claiming it was a message from whatever god he believes in.'

'Then we will kill him and any who follow him,' Midian said, standing, his confidence flooding back. 'We, the servants of Ranthas! We will not be brought down by the lies of some false prophet! *This cannot be.* Whatever we have seen today, whatever happened in Ilthys, it was a lie. We have seen the work of Ranthas all our lives, we have had His truth revealed to us by Temezzar, and yet we're ready to believe this girl's trickery? What have we been saying these last few minutes?

'We know what those Tehamans can do, isn't it clear that they've been playing with our minds, working on us to believe that this . . . creature and her heretic friends can challenge the truth that Ranthas laid down for us? Are we such cowards, that we're ready to give up at this?'

'Your Grace . . .' Ninurtas began, but the Exarch cut him off with a furious hand motion.

'We have been deceived enough today,' he said. 'There is no argument, there is no crisis.' He looked down at Ravenna. 'You have condemned the citizens of Tandaris and Ilthys to death,' he said. 'I will not tolerate heresy. Not the Council's heresy, not yours, nor the attempts of your forgotten people to meddle in world affairs once again.'

As the Exarch paused, his expression as grim as it had ever been, I finally realised what had happened, the conclusion Midian had drawn – and the part of my mind that still functioned was astonished that he'd had the intelligence to work it out.

'No doubt your people were celebrating their success in getting you inside the Temple, but I will spoil their celebrations before they die along with the rest of the city. We know they exist now, and soon the world will know as well. It is time the world was finally rid of the three of you, and everyone concerned will be better off for it.' He looked over at the Sacri. 'Kill the three of them, but without shedding blood; we want no pollution here.'

I felt a spasm of terror, watched in disbelief as the Sacrus holding Ravenna put his sword down, motioned over one of the Inquisitors who unlooped his belt and handed it to the holy warrior.

More weights were fastened on to my feet, and I gasped for air again as the Sacrus wrapped the rope around Ravenna's neck, ignoring her feeble protests, and twisted it tighter. She tried to tear it away with her hands, but it was already biting into the skin, choking off her breath.

'Your Grace, wait a moment,' I heard Sarhaddon say, and the Exarch barked a command. The Sacrus stopped, looped his hand through the makeshift garrotte to better pull it tight as Ravenna struggled vainly against his grip. I felt a slight lessening of the pressure as his fellow lifted me up, but it would only be a momentary reprieve.

'What now?' Midian demanded.

'Perhaps destroying every trace of this isn't the best way to proceed. We consider this a Tehaman illusion, a deceit to spread dissent within us. But what if it is the voice of Ranthas speaking to us, showing us the way to discredit the heresy for ever?'

'So what do you propose?' Midian asked. 'Be quick.'

'What they would have us believe,' Sarhaddon said carefully, 'is that because they can use fire when our faith says they cannot, all the gods are false. But that's only one interpretation. We could use them to show the world that the elemental magic, the elemental gods, can be stripped down to corruptions of Fire.'

'That's a dangerously heretical view,' Amonis said, but Sarhaddon ignored him.

'This is a matter of faith, your Grace,' Sarhaddon said, and even in this state I could hear that he was changing his line of attack very subtly. 'Ranthas may work good through evil vessels, such as the captive heretic mages we use for our own purposes. He has used these fallen vessels to reveal one of His truths to us, that His fire lives in all things, it is only the corruption of man and his refusal to see this that creates the elemental magic. That all magic is Fire, but some of those who wield it have been twisted.'

It was a struggle to follow his reasoning as I tried to breathe, but I could see understanding beginning to dawn on one or two of the faces as they all stood looking up at Sarhaddon in the gallery. Including Ravenna, possibly the only person in the room who might be able to keep up with him.

'Think of it,' the Venatic went on. 'Instead of killing every last elemental mage, we capture those who are most tractable and cleanse them, make them into our vessels. These two and their companion will of course be the most notorious, but there will be others. We need not merely speak any more, try to win people over with words, but prove to Aquasilva that the elemental magic really is nothing more than a perversion. Tonight we crush the Council, and in the months that follow we disseminate this new truth of Ranthas.

'This is a chance, Midian, to see in your Exarchate not just the destruction of the Council, but public proof to everyone from the Prime to the lowliest peasant that the heretics were *wrong*. The remnants of the heresy will be recruited to serve us, and they will ensure the extinction of their faith once and for all. We need not spend those vast sums on armies and fleets, only select those of the prisoners who will be useful and turn them to the glory of Ranthas.'

I looked up at Midian, my head still spinning with the effort of trying to keep up. Sarhaddon had explained it as clearly as he could, but it was still touch and go whether the Exarch had kept up.

If only he could keep his anger in check.

'This sounds like a recipe for disaster, Sarhaddon. It may be a good plan, but these three heretics will remain at large.'

'Not at large,' Sarhaddon said. 'Under our control. I'll explain in more detail later on, when we have time.'

'I'll hear you out,' the Exarch said after a moment. 'We have work to do now, so you'll have to wait a while. Leave the prisoners down here, though if they're still alive, I should like them to watch the destruction of the Council. Whatever happens, they should see it.'

A moment later one of the Inquisitors stepped up on to a block and began untying my wrists, as the other unfastened the weights from my ankles.

Being lowered to the floor a moment later was, if anything, more painful than being hung up, then the Inquisitors and the Sacri filed out, two of them sliding the door into place behind them. Amonis made sure I caught his last look of venom, and I knew there was one man who would not be arguing on Sarhaddon's side.

CHAPTER XXXVI

Too drained to move, my hands useless, I had no idea how long I lay there on the floor of the cell with my head resting on Ravenna's knees. She'd untied Palatine as soon as the priests left and I gave up trying to concentrate, sinking back into a sea of pain and a struggle for breath. My hands were numb, I couldn't so much as twitch a finger.

'Why is it so important to stay alive?' Palatine asked eventually. 'Aside from the obvious, I mean?'

Ravenna must have whispered the reply so any guard wouldn't hear, telling her we'd made a promise to the dying Salderis, an oath that took precedence over almost all others – except, of course, that the Domain claimed it had the power to release anyone from an oath if they chose. It was one of the rights they'd arrogated to themselves, and one that many people still wouldn't accept.

'Makes sense,' Palatine said bitterly. 'Even if it means living as creatures of Sarhaddon?'

'Yes.'

'You don't owe her any favours.'

'We might owe Sarhaddon some.' Ravenna sighed. 'I should have seen that coming. Of course, he was too clever just to let such an idea pass, to mindlessly try and crush it as anyone else would have done.'

'As Midian still wants to do.' Palatine paused. 'The awful thing is that if Midian isn't convinced, and if he executes us, the Domain might still fall. If he follows Sarhaddon's plan, then it'll probably become stronger.'

'Are you sure?' Ravenna asked. I closed my eyes, and their voices seemed terribly far away.

'Midian and Lachazzar never realised that if you try to

crush something and fail, even by a tiny margin, it just does more damage. Everyone would realise that it's a threat to the Domain.'

'Not a fatal one, though,' said Ravenna. 'They're simply too strong, and in the process of trying to eradicate it, Midian would kill thousands more people. They've come to think that force can solve anything.'

'At the moment, they're right.' Palatine shivered; we were several storeys below ground here, and the night's heat didn't penetrate this far down. The pain was too bad for me to notice the cold, but Palatine didn't know that.

'Better put your tunic back on, if you can bear it,' she said, sounding slightly less distant now. 'They said they'd want us outside, and you won't even be able to walk if they come for us.'

I hated not even being able to dress myself again, but I couldn't move at all until they'd put my tunic back on and massaged a little of the circulation back into my hands and feet. The line of gashes on my back where the burning whip had hit still stung terribly, but there was no water in the cell and nothing we could do about them.

I was more or less able to walk with their help when the Sacri came back and heaved the door of the cell open.

'You will accompany us,' one of them said. 'Don't attempt to use your magic, you will be dead before it can help you.'

They didn't bother with anything as sophisticated as the bracelets Orosius had used, but Midian was taking no chances. The Sacri fitted each of us with garrotte collars, a barbed line leading behind them so that whoever was holding the end could simply pull hard and choke us. Remembering Midian's words earlier, I guessed that if he decided against Sarhaddon's proposal, they would be used to kill us. Without warning.

As we walked along the rough stone passages, surrounded again by Sacri, I felt as if they were already tightening the rope little by little, although it was probably just the after-effects of the torture. From what I'd heard, the pain they'd inflicted on me was mild, and even with my limbs aching and feeling distorted, I could believe it.

We passed dozens more cells, their doors shut, but the Inquisitors had other things to do at the moment; they would be up with the Exarch, involved in whatever plan he – or Sarhaddon, more likely – had thought up.

At last we came out into a wide, vaulted corridor and I heard the shouting of the crowd again, a distant roar beyond the outer walls that grew louder as we walked out into the courtyard.

By the time we'd reached the parapet it was deafening, coming from all sides now that the mob was too big to be contained within the square. It was frightening, a vast animal gradually surrounding the Temple, encircling it with human tentacles.

For the first time I understood why Abisamar had acted the way he had, why he'd been so heavy-handed. Only the walls and the gate protected the people in the Temple from being torn apart – and now I had to number the three of us with the priests, because the crowd would show no mercy to anyone not locked up and obviously a prisoner.

If they ever got in. It was hard to believe, looking out over the torchlit agora, that they wouldn't, that this creature out there didn't have the power simply to crush the Temple under its own weight, but the Council had weapons of its own. The leaders were still there, on the speaking platform across from the Temple. More of them now, one orator just reaching the climax of a speech.

'When are they going to stop talking and do something?' Palatine wondered. 'They're wasting time.'

The Sacri around us, who presumably knew what was going on, didn't bother to reply. I moved slightly to one side, so I could hear the orator on the platform – Drances, I realised a moment later.

'And so it is that this night, in this city which has too long been the heart of the Domain's power, we will set ourselves free. Not just from the Domain, but from the ancient enmities which have divided us for so long, Archipelagan against Thetian against Tehaman. Here we stand, the leaders of the Council who have fought against the Domain for so long. Tehaman, Archipelagan . . .' He paused as the other Council leaders came to stand around him. '. . . and Thetian.'

The roar of the crowd died for a moment as more figures came on to the platform, naval officers surrounding one particular man in white and blue, whose features seemed familiar.

'I give to you a new Emperor, a man who will not stand by and let the Domain rule his lands for him, who will not drown his throne in the blood of innocents. All hail Emperor Arcadius!'

'Gods,' Palatine whispered. 'He survived.'

I was stunned for a moment. So there was another Tar'Conantur, presumed dead at the hands of Eshar's assassins but evidently very much alive. The former Viceroy of Oceanus hadn't taken his attempted murder lying down.

So this was what the Council had in mind, a man who would attract the fleet's loyalty and rule Thetia in alliance with them. A replacement for Eshar none of us had considered for a moment, but who must have been working with the Council at least since Orosius died.

The trim, grey-haired man in Imperial white and blue saluted the crowd solemnly.

'I join with you tonight,' he said, his voice not as rich or impressive as Drances's, 'to right the wrongs done to my country by the tyranny of Reglath Eshar, the Halettite peasant who called himself a Thetian Emperor, and his Domain allies. I have suffered too at their hands, as has my country, and I promise you the Thetian fleet will stand with me, will follow me and aid us in ridding the Archipelago of the Domain once and for all.'

The crowd was for a moment uncertain, then erupted in acclamation.

'This makes everything different,' Palatine said. 'They might succeed.'

'Midian seemed very confident, though,' said Ravenna uneasily. 'He must have known about this.'

I couldn't see Midian and the group of officers on the far wall, which was frustrating and probably deliberate. I knew they were still there; I'd noticed them from the courtyard, but the Exarch certainly wouldn't want the officers to come into contact with us any more. I wasn't quite sure why Sarhaddon had introduced us to them in the first place, what he'd hoped to achieve by doing that.

Arcadius was speaking again, but only briefly. He was an administrator, not an orator, and Drances was much, much better at it – unsurprising given the Commonwealth's history and the way it worked.

The Council would be short of resources, though, unless they'd managed to disembark men from the ships offshore, and they didn't have siege weapons. Midian had strongly implied that he did, but where were they? And why had neither side acted?

Finally, I saw a flurry of activity in a side street, as the crowd moved away to create an open space around an odd wooden construction – a catapult, I realised a moment later. Far less advanced than a pulse cannon, but easier to make. Technically, that was, but how they'd created one in a city under Domain occupation was another matter.

No, not one, I saw then, two. Another had been trundled up on the far side, but at both points it was too dark to see anything properly, and I couldn't tell how the machines worked or what the ammunition was.

Someone nearby barked a command and I saw a squad of Ranthas soldiers running along the parapet carrying

Thetian longbows. *Thetian*? Ranthas soldiers didn't use Thetian bows, and in any case few Thetians joined the Domain's forces. Anyone so disposed would have gone into their own navy. Something was seriously amiss here.

More Ranthas soldiers and some Sacri, carrying rough sacks that bulged as if full of stones. And at the corner of the walls, by the edge of the aether shield, some more soldiers in thick gloves were uncovering an odd contraption, linking it to the wire that steadied the aether current.

'Be silent,' said the nearest Sacri, as Palatine looked about to say something, 'or die.' I felt a slight pressure on the line, and my collar slid a single notch tighter. There had been little enough slack to start off with.

I took the point, stayed still and watched the Domain's plans unfolding around me, unseen by anyone outside the walls. Twenty or so of the archers were standing along the front wall now, either side of us. The would be more beyond the gatehouse as well.

This had been planned, I thought. There was no way this was the normal garrison of the Temple, or that the defence was improvised. There had to be another element, probably the artillery, because all these archers would be useless with so many Council mages around. The mages held the upper hand at the moment, along with Arcadius and his control of the fleet – if indeed he did control it, and his announcement hadn't simply been a bluff. It was more likely that he'd won over a few ships and officers while the rest were waiting to see how things fell out.

They were the wise ones. The activity in the Temple was slowing down now, as most of the troops seemed to be in position. The archers had strung their bows and nocked arrows; now many of them had removed the veils they wore, to aim better. One nearby turned to look over at us, a hint of curiosity in his face.

He was Thetian. These men might not even be Ranthas soldiers, but Thetian marines or Imperial Guards, and they must have left Thetia before Eshar died. So they'd been planning something even then.

In the square, the men on the platform were looking over at the Temple in silence. One waved over at the catapults, and I heard the sound of the first stone being released, flying over the heads of the crowd to crash into the wall above the gate with a jarring thump. The crowd had been careful to leave a zone directly in front of the gate, perhaps on the Council's advice, and it was there that the stone fell, followed a moment later by a second. The cheer that accompanied the impacts seemed to hit us with as much force as the stones themselves

The aether shield couldn't stop these missiles, it was only good against energy weapons or magic, and I was willing to bet that Midian had never expected them to use something as primitive as catapults. They were aiming for the door, the weakest spot.

Four, five impacts, the noise louder each time, and still the priests did nothing. Encouraged, one of the Air mages began trying to weaken the aether shield by sending a very localised tornado at the corner support. The metal wire thrummed as it was bent out of shape, but held.

Then I heard a *whoosh* behind me, and three or four of the Sacri instinctively looked up. Feeling pressure on my collar again, I didn't follow suit, but a moment later a starburst exploded over our heads, a golden signal firework.

There was no cheer from the crowd as the next rock slammed into the gate, sending more tremors along the wall. Thousands of faces turned to the sky, suddenly afraid and wondering what the rocket might mean.

I knew, and even if I could have told them, it was too late.

Seconds dragged by, the crowd wavered even as Drances egged them on. Then I saw flashes from the hill just beyond the city, followed by a screeching sound and three dull thumps.

Two houses just beyond the square exploded, showering masonry on to their neighbours as gouts of fire roared up from the ruins. A second later, another shell hammered into another house more than a street away. Columns of smoke and dust leapt into the air.

I felt the Council mages' power unravel, their efforts falter as they tried to avoid the masonry or stared in disbelief at the carnage the pulse cannon were wreaking. An aether shield over the city might have helped, but Tandaris didn't have one. If it had, the controls would have been in the Temple.

'They'll destroy our city!' one of the Council leaders shouted. 'We must storm the Temple, it's the only way to stop them.'

'There is no other way!' Midian shouted as the crowd wavered, aware that it was trapped in a far worse situation that its cousin in Ilthys. There was a backbone of Council troops, true, but most of these people were ordinary citizens of Tandaris, sick of Domain persecution and stirred up by Drances's rhetoric.

Now they would pay for the Council's folly.

'I will allow no heretic to go unpunished!' Midian roared. 'Tonight your Council and your heresy will be extinguished for ever!'

More flashes. I wanted to look away, but kept my eyes on the city in horrified fascination as three more shells descended. Two more houses crumbled, one into a street leading out of the agora, and I silently screamed at the destruction they were wreaking on this city. Even as I watched, one of the neighbouring houses wobbled and fell, sending a cascade of masonry and timber that engulfed one of the catapults and the edge of the crowd.

But by then another shell had landed, and whether it was superbly aimed or merely hideously unlucky I would never know.

It exploded on the rear of the speaking platform,

incinerating dozens of people in a brief fireball. As if in slow motion I saw the Council leaders consumed, the figures of Drances and Arcadius hurled outward into the crowd along with chunks of marble from the platform, shattered and blackened. I saw the Tehaman fall into the crowd, people trying to get out of the way, then beginning to run frantically as they realised what was going on.

The light from the last explosion died down, and with it went the last workings of the remaining Council mages. Many had been on the speaking platform, confident that their powers could protect them.

Even before we had a chance to recover, the shield hummed and lines of blue fire sped outwards from the corners towards pockets of Council troops. Aetherised harpoons, giving the equivalent of an aether surge to anyone they touched. Fatal, with this much power behind them.

Then the shield was down, and the Thetian archers stood up and began firing rapidly and deliberately at the Council troops, the mages, anyone and anything that stood out. They were, at least, not trying to cause indiscriminate slaughter, but the damage already done was bad enough.

More pulse impacts, this time over the other side. They missed the second catapult but destroyed four or five buildings in a cluster. For the love of Thetis, when would they stop? When would Midian be content?

The archers continued to fire, although when the pulse cannon thumped again their shells fell down by the harbour, presumably targeting the Council troops on guard duty there. It was a small mercy in the carnage. I could see bodies now in the agora, some horribly burned from the impact of the pulse cannon, others still moving or plucking feebly at arrows in their bodies.

I felt sick, tried to turn away but my collar tightened again, the Sacrus said, 'Watch.'

I heard a battle cry from the street to the right of the

Temple, the noise of a hundred men or more shouting in unison, and answered a moment later by another from the left-hand side.

'*Aezio! Aezio!*'

'*Tanais! Tanais!*'

Even among all the horror of the destruction of Tandaris, that moment would be one of my clearest images, as two columns of blue-cloaked soldiers marched at a run into the agora, shields locked in front of them, their scallop helms gleaming in the firelight. A mage of Water tried to throw them back, but a moment later he fell, pierced by six or seven arrows from the parapet. There was no cover for the remaining Council troops in the square, now trying to make a last stand by the catapult. Some had managed to get away down a street to the right, but the Thetians outside the Temple weren't worrying about them yet.

Halfway down the right-hand column, a silver dolphin stood high on its pole, above a square of blue cloth with the golden numeral *IX* on it.

For the first time in two hundred years, the Ninth Legion went to war. The Thetians around us – on the battlements and in the square both – were Imperial Guards. Which could only mean that Eshar and his Domain allies had planned this from the beginning. And, very probably, that they had staged Eshar's death to draw the Council out, to make them show their hand and concentrate all their force in this one place so that the Domain could deal with them all at once.

Below the standard, three white-plumed officers surrounded another whose only distinction from the rankers was his size. He towered head and shoulders above the officers, a massive figure holding a heavy sword as if it were a toy and, like his men, as he burst into the agora he was singing. I knew the words but not the tune, and it was a song I remembered from the History, a song Carausius had heard as the legions marched to Aran Cthun more than two centuries ago. Marched under the command of the man who led them now: Tanais Lethien, Marshal of the Empire.

The front line of the Ninth slammed into the Council troops with a shock I could almost feel from up here, the Thetians keeping a tight formation as the enemy line buckled. Across from them, the other column was disappearing into a street beyond at a slightly slower pace, moving round to take the main body of Council troops – down now to less than a hundred – in the rear.

Even before they came surging round the corner, the slaughter was nearing its end. Two mages, Earth and Shadow, had managed to create a small dent in Marshal Tanais's line for a while, but they had fallen to new soldiers pushing forward to take their comrades' place. I knew both the mages' names – Sorghena and Jashua; the latter had been one of my instructors at the Citadel.

Then the last of the Council troops were dead, and the Thetian columns instantly reformed, one heading further into the city while Tanais and his men returned to an almost empty square. There were more Legionaries in the city, or at least soldiers loyal to the Domain, because I'd caught a glimpse of more fighting going on further away.

But it wasn't really fighting, because the issue of this had never been in doubt. All that remained now was the destruction of the city, which wouldn't be completed while there were Domain troops in it.

Eyes wet with tears, I was finally allowed to look away as the Sacrus holding my collar relaxed his grip slightly.

The pulse cannon had ceased fire now, and the world seemed eerily quiet after the deafening sounds of the last few minutes.

Quiet enough for me to hear Sarhaddon approaching, to turn and see my own death written in his face.

'The Exarch has decided that it is better not to be too

clever,' he told the Sacrus. 'However, he feels it would not be politic to execute them in sight of the observers. Take them down into the guardroom, but do not under any circumstances kill them until we join you. After the trouble they have caused us, the Exarch wishes them to be given a shameful death in the Halettite way.'

The Sacrus bowed. 'As His Grace commands.'

There would be no reprieve then.

I will see you in Tandaris.

I was too numb at everything that had happened, shocks piling up on each other, that I didn't resist as they walked me to my death. I hardly noticed anything, not even whether the others were as shocked as me. Dimly, I saw the figure of the Exarch of the Archipelago watching us from the far wall.

We never got as far as the guardroom, never had the chance to suffer the final humiliations Midian wanted. As we crossed the courtyard, a figure suddenly stood up in the colonnade, by the inner wall, and started running away.

One of the Sacri guarding us shouted in alarm, but he was too late. A second later there was a massive detonation, and after a moment of teetering, the outer wall shivered and fell inwards on to the courtyard.

CHAPTER XXXVII

As the wall fell, the Sacri let go of our collars and threw us to the right, away from the plummeting wall. For the second time that day I fell badly on to the stones, bruising my arm and side, but all that hit me was a wave of masonry dust and a deafening concussion. Other people across the courtyard and on the wall were knocked down, and even the Exarch staggered, although he was high above us and big enough to stay on his feet. My collar had tightened again and I had to gasp in air, hoping that it wouldn't constrict any further; after what they'd done to me earlier I couldn't get to my feet either.

'Cathan?'

Ravenna appeared above me, grasping my shoulders to try and pull me upright. I saw the bodies of three or four Sacri lying under the trailing edge of the wreckage, and . . . Council troops pouring in through the breach in the wall.

'Their leaders are dead,' Ravenna said. 'And we're dead if we stay here.' She shouted over at them, a desperate appeal for help that was joined a moment later by Palatine's.

'Kill those men!' Midian shouted. 'And catch those prisoners!'

'You have to stand!' Ravenna said. She tensed, then stood and pulled me to my feet, steadying me for a moment as I wobbled. There were forty or fifty at least of the invaders, including at least one mage – and a figure in a smoke-blackened naval uniform.

We stumbled over towards them as arrows began to sing, and the mage – Water, I thought, although I didn't know her – swept three or four archers off the battlements.

Belatedly, I remembered what I was capable of, and it was more than easy enough to summon a surge, to turn round and blast torrents of raw power at the Thetian archers. The rain of arrows thinned as I flung men back against the parapet, sent one of the fire-mages hurling back over the parapet and into space. A second later Ravenna joined me, with the sense to use Council magic instead of fire-magic. We didn't want the Council troops to think we were Domain after all.

And then the man in the blackened uniform came up – alive, impossibly alive – and pulled us backwards even as we continued to sweep the battlements. The observers had ducked out of sight, the archers had fled, and Ravenna had dealt with the few people left alive in the courtyard.

I started hobbling back towards the breach, Sagantha helping me over the stones, when a figure in white and red ran up, holding a fighting stave he didn't know how to use. Behind us, some of the motley assortment of Council survivors had produced bows and were shooting up at the parapet.

'Cathan!' Sarhaddon shouted, trying to make himself heard over the din. His robes were more sand-coloured now, from the dust that had fallen on him. 'Don't leave! You must kill Midian!'

It was such an astonishing thing to say I stopped dead for a moment.

'He wants us to stop!' Palatine shouted, but for once I kept my head, remembered the running man in the colonnade.

'Sagantha, did your men blow the wall?'

'What? Oh, no, we didn't. We were trying to escape down that side-street, heard it fall. We still have a chance, but you're too exposed here.'

'I ordered the wall blown,' Sarhaddon said, closer now. Ravenna was still raking the battlements, but I knew Tanais and his troops were nearby, and I couldn't blast my

way out through an entire city. Although . . . some of the
Council people did have explosive charges, and I flinched
as a thrown charge brought down part of the interior
colonnade on the other side.

'Why?' I shouted. Two of the Council troops began
moving down towards him, swords drawn.

'He'll destroy the Archipelago, and that will bring the
Domain down. I knew that, I tried to save you but he
wouldn't listen, he ordered you executed. I blew the wall
to give you a chance to kill him. You're trapped in the city
still.'

'Why should I believe you?' We were close enough
now to talk in normal voices amid the chaos of the
courtyard that had become a battlefield.

'You want to kill him. Please!'

But then another voice broke in, ringing across the
courtyard.

'Ninth, to me! Sacri, the Temple is in danger!'

Sarhaddon was the only one who didn't look stunned,
the only one who didn't looked up in horror and amazement as a group of armoured figures appeared in the arch
of the gateway, silhouetted against torches in the square
beyond. Ninth Legionaries in cobalt blue, surrounding a
man who should, given his position, have been wearing a
helmet.

Who should have been dead in the sanctuary in Mare
Alastre. I'd been right.

'Archers, fire on the Thetians!' Sagantha ordered.
'Now!'

Two or three of the archers had been felled by return
fire, but now they shifted it as more Ninth Legionaries ran
in from the square, forming a shield around and over their
Emperor. Their very alive Emperor, whose plan, as I'd
suspected, this must have been. His and Sarhaddon's.
Midian wasn't clever enough.

Ravenna jumped past me and grabbed Sarhaddon,

pulled him towards her and brandished a knife that I recognised from Kavatang. Sagantha's, grabbed from his belt as she went past.

'We will kill the Preceptor!' she shouted.

'You are surrounded,' Midian bellowed from the parapet. 'You cannot escape. Your Majesty, I beg you, kill every last one. *Domine* Sarhaddon, you must be ready to give your life for the Faith?'

Sarhaddon was the only man in the entire city who would even think of sparing our lives. Then one of the archers just above us nocked another arrow to his bow, drew back, and shouted, 'Are you, Midian?'

Then, in the second before the Exarch could react, he fired. A Thetian archer, trained from birth in the only form of combat most Thetians ever practised, a man who had lost so much at the hands of Exarch and Emperor.

I heard the *thunk* as Ithien's arrow plunged through brocade to take the Exarch in the chest. For a moment Midian seemed to be unhurt, then he swayed.

'This is heresy . . .' he said, and lost his balance.

He fell forward, over the edge of the parapet, to land in the rubble of the colonnade with an unpleasant crunch.

The answering arrows found their mark in Ithien before I could raise a shield over him, before I could do anything to stop them. He cried out, then blood gurgled in his throat.

'Ithien!' I shouted, not taking it in for a moment. Ignoring the pain in my hands and feet, I scrambled up the rocks towards him, reached him just as the woman next to him laid him against the rocks.

Ithien looked up at me, struggling to speak. Two arrows had punctured his lung, another his thigh, and there was already blood pouring over the stones. I could see the pain he was in, but there was nothing I could do.

Palatine ran up, knelt down on the other side of the dying Thetian.

'I stole your revenge,' he said finally, with a terrible effort. 'Say goodbye to Ravenna for me.'

Palatine nodded, took his hand. His fingers clenched weakly around hers for a moment, and for an instant the pain of losing him almost overwhelmed her. She squeezed his hand, but he was too weak to smile.

'You were a good friend,' she said. 'And a true republican.'

'You too,' was all he managed to say. 'Live for me,' he whispered. 'Live . . .'

I closed my eyes then, as he died, and only opened them again a moment later, aware of an unexpected silence around me. We shouldn't have taken this time, but nothing seemed to be happening.

She lifted his hand up and kissed his fingers before they slid out of her grip, then laid his hand back on his chest and closed the brilliant eyes. There was no blood on his face, and as the muscles relaxed it seemed as if he was moving.

'Goodbye, Ithien,' I whispered. A brightly dressed man on a magnificent horse, riding out of the Sea Gate of Ilthys in the morning sunshine to save a friend from the Domain, the only man I'd ever met who'd stood up to an Inquisitor.

'Ilthys will give him the burial he deserves. If it can,' said the other woman, who I realised, belatedly, was Persea, my friend and lover from the Citadel, the last of Sagantha's archers left standing.

I stood up again as Palatine knelt over the body of her oldest friend, looked down the pile to where the Emperor and his men waited, the tableau frozen as I remembered it.

The Emperor was a soldier. He had us trapped; it did him no harm to allow us to mourn a fallen friend.

We wouldn't be able to keep that last promise of Ithien's, though. Tanais and his soldiers now blocked the street beyond the wall, and three or four Domain mages had gathered, ready to strike. This was over, then. Unless . . . unless Sarhaddon had meant what he said for once.

I turned to face Reglath Eshar, Aetius VI, as he stood among the tense ranks of Ninth Legionaries in the courtyard of the Temple.

'You have defeated us,' I said, feeling oddly calm now everything was clear. Persea looked at me for a moment with the lopsided smile I remembered. 'There is no more heresy, except in the minds of those you've trapped here. And Sarhaddon has shown us, at least three of us, that everything we believed in was an illusion.'

'An illusion?' the Emperor asked, very clearly. I could just hear the sound of battle from somewhere down by the docks, but everything else was very still, including the heretics clustered with us on the mound of rubble.

The Domain mages came alert, hands raised to strike.

'Mages, leave this man alone,' said a hoarse voice from above and behind us. 'Let him do this.'

'Who are you?' the Emperor demanded.

'I am Amadeo, acolyte of the Venatic Order. Let this man speak, for through him the truths of Ranthas are revealed.'

Ravenna relaxed her grip on Sarhaddon long enough for him to look up and see Amadeo, standing with Oailos at the top of the rubble pile.

'He is indeed an acolyte of my Order,' Sarhaddon said, 'although I thought he was dead.'

'These former heretics rescued me from the Council's tortures,' Amadeo said. 'They are agents of Ranthas, for He determined that one of us should see Him work through them.'

'Continue,' Eshar said.

I tore part of the hem off the remains of my tunic and laid it on the palm of my hand, as Ravenna had in Ilthys. She still bore the faint scar, although it would fade with time. It was an effort to keep my hand in that position, and my wrist was in agony, but I somehow managed to hold it as I drew on my concentration, poured magic and heat on to the scrap of cloth, more and more.

It seemed to take for ever, long enough for people to shift and look uneasily at each other. And then, finally, it burst into flame. I held my hand as motionless as I could, feeling the flames spread over the cloth and singe my hand, then found myself unable to keep it going even though the agony from my palm overwhelmed everything else, and finally I cried out and let the embers drop, drew a little water from the air to soothe it.

In Ilthys, Ravenna had used this to try and bring down the Domain. I didn't have that luxury.

I noticed the 'observers' over in one corner, expressions on their faces ranging from worry to incredulity. Two or three Inquisitors and Venatics were left, and six or seven priests were attending to the body of Midian, but even their eyes were on me.

'You are not the first to have seen this,' I said, lifting my voice to carry over the silent Temple. 'There were thousands of others, others who will spread the word across the Archipelago that any mage, not just the mages of Fire, can use the element you hold sacred. Or at least many of you, those who haven't devoted your lives to the overthrow of the Domain.

'After what we have done, all of this may not matter to you. But I ask you to remember that however much we have been fighting over politics, over land and ambitions, we have also, at least nominally, been fighting for the souls of Aquasilva, over dedication to the gods our ancestors believed in, and their ancestors. The Council forgot that souls were supposed to matter. The Domain almost has!' I was taking a risk there, but this whole speech was a risk. And besides, since Ilthys this could not be forgotten, could not be swept under the carpet, could not be ignored. The flames that Ravenna had lit there now stood for the souls of Ilthys and all those who would hear their message. All those who would die if Midian's path were to be followed.

554

'To all intents and purposes, tonight this conflict is over. The Council is destroyed, its power broken. There will be no more Citadels, no more training and indoctrination such as we received, no more leaders or organisation. Only scattered people throughout the world, dwindling with each generation until nothing remains.

'So Fire has won, but as we have fought we have discovered something else, something that can mean a great many things. The fire I called now, the fire Ravenna called in Ilthys, should not have been possible. The world knows this now. Midian believed he could stamp it out, but had he not been blinded by hubris he would have seen that was impossible. It was Sarhaddon who realised that this might give the Domain the chance to redeem the souls that it has lost.'

I had gone as far as I could, as far as I dared, and now we would live or die by what Sarhaddon said. Not just the few dozen of us who stood encircled in the Temple courtyard, but the people of Ilthys, all those who had spread the word across Aquasilva. If Ravenna's rejection of all the elements became established as another heresy, the whole cycle would begin again, only this time there would be followers truly across the world, and the wars would become civil wars. Beside the slaughter that would follow, the truth was a small price to pay.

Nothing lasted for ever.

Ravenna reluctantly let Sarhaddon stand up, and the dust-covered Venatic sketched a bow to the Emperor before looking up at me, his gaze boring into mine. For a second he was silent, contemplating, then he began to speak, his astonishing voice so much richer than mine or the Emperor's, more powerful even than Drances's.

'Every true believer knows that a few times in our history, Ranthas has spoken to us through His prophets, by directing His mortal agents to the benefit of His faith or to reveal truths that He sees fit to reveal. We also know that

His work may still be done through the agencies of evil, through corrupt vessels that we would dismiss.

'But never have the two been combined. Never has a revelation come to us by a path so strange as this, through the vessel of heretic mages, those we consider corrupted beyond redemption. They have shown us a greater truth, one that Ranthas has decided we are wise enough to understand. The truth that there is only one Power, only one God, as we have always known, but that all the elements are part of Him. He is the being who controls our destinies, a being whose primary appearance is in the flames of a fire or a star, the Lifegiver of the world, but He is more than that.

'We may see Him through everything, because all the elements are His creation. We could not live on a world made entirely of Fire, any more than one entirely of Air or Earth. They are all facets of Him, all parts of a greater whole that we worship as Ranthas. The flames are His purest form, but not his only form. If we embrace this truth, we may bring many who have lapsed back into the light of His redemption.'

Sarhaddon's voice changed subtly. 'If we do not, if instead of accepting this as His truth we turn our faces from it, persecute those who have the sight to accept it, then we shall have war. Not the pure cleansing of a true Crusade, but a civil war of the Faith, fighting our own fathers and brothers, people in our cities and our homelands who have understood where we have not. There is no glory in a civil war, no victor, no honour. Only Death can win.'

He fixed his gaze first on the observers, then the Emperor, a still figure in the middle of his legates. A trim man, bigger than the rest of the family but still not tall, his skin dark from years of campaigning. Eshar the Butcher, warrior of the Faith. Halettite at heart, a friend of Midian and Lachazzar.

We had done our best. It would depend on him now, a

556

devout man called to judge a question beyond his interests, but one that could save the lives of thousands or plunge Aquasilva into civil war. I had done the most I could, steered the last Tar'Conantur Emperor towards a choice that gave us a glimmer of hope in the darkness ahead.

Eshar said nothing for a moment, waited as gusts of wind tugged at the Ninth Legion's banner and the sound of a collapsing building rumbled across the city.

'I am not a theologian,' said the man, the enemy on whom, after all this, our fates hung. I could not forget that. It was the lives of Ravenna, Palatine, Persea and Sagantha as well as all those others that I was bargaining for. With a man who had killed so many, whose purges had robbed Thetia of her brightest stars.

'I am a soldier and an Emperor and a follower of Ranthas,' Eshar went on. 'I was the last before either of the others, and I have spent my life fighting for my two countries and my Faith. Now I have an Empire to rule, an Empire that must be strong in war. That is the way to survive, but it is not the way to live.

'I believe that Ranthas watches over my Empire, even though for centuries it followed a goddess who is an abomination to me. And I can believe that all these centuries He was indeed watching over Thetia, even if my people only saw him through their own confusion. My ancestor Valdur took a step towards the truth, and now I will take another. Preceptor Sarhaddon, I think you speak the truth, and that these mages are indeed the voices of Ranthas.'

Hardly daring to believe what I'd heard, I took a deep breath, saw Ravenna look over at the Emperor.

'Come over here,' the Emperor ordered, pointing at me, then raised his voice to carry over the mound of rubble. 'Marshal Tanais!'

I picked my way shakily down the pile as the Emperor ordered more light from the fire-mages, and four blazing beacons sprang up, forming a square in the centre of court-yards. They were more used to ceremony than anything else, these mages.

'You too,' Eshar said, gesturing at the others. 'Put your weapons down, I give you my word that you will not be harmed.'

Slowly, one by one, I heard weapons being put down on the rocks as they obeyed, wondered if any of them believed or understood what was happening here.

I almost fell as I finally reached the stone of the court-yard, grabbed at an offered arm and looked up, a moment later, to see that it was Sarhaddon's.

Leaning on the Venatic's shoulder, I limped across to stand in front of the Emperor just as the Marshal, a titanic figure in his antique Legion armour, strode across to Eshar's side. I should have expected him to side with a soldier Emperor. Aware of how precarious my position still was and might become, I knelt on the stones in front of him, an honour that this man would expect. The stone was warmer than I expected against bare knees.

'You are my nephew,' said Eshar in an entirely different tone, a moment later. 'I was told you were a weakling. What I've seen here tonight doesn't bear that out.'

This close, I could sense some of the same magnetism Palatine had, but it was more tightly controlled, less immediately obvious.

'Midian and I were wrong,' Sarhaddon said. 'He isn't. He's a survivor.'

I knew Sarhaddon was playing his own game here, but it was close enough to mine that, for now, we were work-ing together.

'Will you serve your God and your Emperor with all your heart?' Eshar asked, unexpectedly.

'I will,' I said, with only the slightest moment's hesitation.

'And you will return to the true Faith, make public

558

remission of your sins and be accepted back into the holy Domain universal?'

Considering the seven years I had spent fighting the Domain and its followers, I was surprised I was able to agree at all. How I could I had no idea, but to sacrifice anything for a Faith I no longer believed in would be beyond stupidity.

Eshar reached down and took my arm in a military handshake, wrist to wrist, to pull me back to my feet and stand beside me while he asked the same questions of all the others.

'I will absolve them,' Sarhaddon said, when they'd agreed.

'They must publicly renounce their sins,' Eshar said, 'but they've agreed to that.'

From what I knew of that ceremony, normally applied to people who had committed terrible crimes while still remaining within the Faith, it was a ritual submission and absolution, but nothing like the public humiliation reserved for heretics under penance.

'I hereby declare all those present pardoned and absolved of any crimes they may have committed under the laws of the Empire and the Archipelago. As a condition of their absolution, they will serve the Empire or the Domain for five years in whatever capacity Sarhaddon or myself shall decide. I call upon two of those here present to witness what I have said and done here.'

Now I realised why he'd called the Marshal over.

'So do I, Tanais Lethien, Marshal of the Empire, bear witness.'

Alexios was the second, but the witnessing was a formality. There were too many important people here for the Emperor to go back on his promise.

There was silence for a moment, then Eshar turned to Tanais. 'Go, take command of the battle and finish it quickly.'

'We should give as many heretics as possible a chance to recant,' Sarhaddon urged. 'The more who can be turned to speak for us, the more we'll be believed.'

'That makes sense.'

'Your Majesty,' Sagantha said, and the Emperor scrutinised the smoke-blackened figure carefully. 'Might I suggest that Tanais takes some of these survivors with him, it may help to end the battle more quickly if the remaining Council troops see that they can be spared.'

'Tanais, arrange this. But don't show any mercy to the fanatics who are left.'

'As you wish,' Tanais said, with the briefest of nods, and turned away to speak to Sagantha.

The Emperor looked at me for a moment, then smiled, something I hadn't expected. 'You're called Cathan, I'm told?'

'Yes, Your Majesty.'

'We're speaking informally,' Eshar said, taking my elbow and leading me out into the courtyard beyond the circle of his guards, over to where Midian's body lay. 'I can see you're being careful, but I don't like flattery.'

I nodded, wondering where all of this would end. Half an hour ago I had thought this man dead, a month ago I had counted him among my bitterest enemies. But then little was ever achieved by pursuing a feud to its bitterest conclusion. The Tar'Conanturs had a habit of doing that, and little good it has ever brought them.

'Who was the man who died?'

'Ithien Eirillia,' I said.

'I see. A friend of yours?'

'Yes.'

'I couldn't have allowed anyone to kill Midian and not pay for it. But he's dead now, and his worst act against us turns out to have been beneficial, because it harms those treacherous Tehamans more than anyone else. I'll forgive him his crimes and allow him to be buried as you wish, provided that you end the revolt in Ilthys and any ringleaders who aren't included here make remission with you. If the revolt finishes without my having to deploy troops, I'll be satisfied with the bargain I've made tonight. Is that clear?'

I nodded, noticed absently that although Eshar used the royal plural on paper, he didn't bother with it in conversation.

'You'll leave as soon as Tandaris is subdued . . .' he began, but was cut off as a figure in black and white appeared between the pillars of the fallen colonnade. Ninurtas followed him a moment later, looking apprehensive.

'Your Majesty, you must not do this!' Amonis said, wild eyes filled with hatred. 'He is a heretic and corrupt, he will always be a heretic! He traffics with foul powers, he is no agent of Ranthas but an agent of evil, and so is his accomplice Sarhaddon! This Faith he tells to you is a monstrosity, a perversion of the truth.'

'You heard what I decreed,' said Eshar coldly.

Amonis still stood there, hands hidden within the sleeves of his robes. I shivered, as if the night had taken a sudden chill. Amonis was an uncomfortable reminder of how close the past actually was. 'He has poisoned your mind, my lord!'

'Enough of this!' Eshar snapped. 'Guards, remove him!'

I didn't know why no-one else spotted it, but as the guards stepped forward I saw a glint in the sleeve of his robe as he waved his hand again. Death rode with this man, a death I'd managed to avoid a few minutes ago . . .

'He has a knife, Your Majesty!' I shouted, moving between the Emperor and the Inquisitor.

'You are an enemy of the Faith!' Amonis screamed.

For a few seconds, everything moved in slow motion. I felt someone cannon into me, Ninurtas throwing his weight at me. Ankles weakened by the Inquisitor's torture,

I crumpled underneath him, agony flaring across my left side as I hit the stones. Ninurtas had a knife too, was scrabbling to get it out while I was too dazed with pain to respond.

Above us, the Emperor's arm was moving towards Amonis, but the Inquisitor's hand flashed out, drove the knife into the Emperor's chest.

I heard Eshar's cry of pain, a shout of 'Treachery!' from somewhere in the distance. Ninurtas had freed his hand, and for a moment the knife shone into the torchlight as the Venatic reared up, stabbing his blade down towards my stomach.

Pinned by his weight, I couldn't move, tried instead to grab his hand, but felt my wrist giving way. For a second I saw my own death in the fall of the blade, then I somehow managed to knock his aim off.

A moment later a hideous pain tore through my shoulder and I screamed at the shock of it. Ninurtas's hand was covered in blood as he tugged at the dagger, more waves of agony sending out every time he jolted it. Above us, the Emperor staggered as Amonis stabbed him again.

Please, let the wounds not be fatal! For the love of Thetis, he couldn't die now! He was our last chance to stop the fundamentalists, to even hope for peace in the Archipelago.

I heard a shout much closer, but Amonis didn't take any notice, drawing back his hand to stab Eshar a third time. Ninurtas raised his knife again, then jerked convulsively. His face drew back in a terrible rictus of pain, and I saw a sword sinking into his back.

The knife fell, point-first, slashed through my tunic and between two of my ribs, but it didn't have the force to penetrate far, even when Ninurtas in his death throes knocked it out a moment later. I struggled to move away from the ghastly spectacle of the dying Venatic.

Amonis had nearly completed his third stroke when

Tanais's sword virtually cut him in half.

There was blood everywhere, the stink of entrails and death, pain and more pain as someone forcibly dragged me out from under Ninurtas's body, gashing my legs on the stones. I didn't care, I was so glad to be free of the horror.

Only of this small horror, I saw, as the Emperor fell into the arms of one of his guardsmen and another hacked at the already dead Amonis. Unable to stand, I crawled over, trying to block out the carnage around me, but I could tell from the way Eshar's head hung that the Emperor was already dead.

It was the second time I had watched an Emperor die at the hands of the Domain, and the second member of my family in less than an hour.

But none of them, even Orosius, had mattered as much as this man here, for all that he'd been an enemy.

'He is dead!' Tanais said, bloody sword held in one hand. 'The Domain has killed our Emperor!'

'Revenge!' someone shouted. And with that single word the tragedy of Tandaris was complete.

I looked down at the dead Emperor as the unnamed Legionary cradled Eshar's head, weeping openly in the debris of the Temple, then around to where the entourage stood.

'They are faithless,' Tanais said.

'They are murderers!' Palatine replied. She had remained kneeling by Ithien's body all this time, but now she stood with a drawn sword. 'How can we trust them? They killed Orosius, now they kill Eshar who kept faith with them. Did you hear the Inquisitor? He called the Emperor a heretic because he had the vision to accept a new way where they didn't. They will destroy us if we let them.'

'But we won't,' Tanais said. 'Legion, kill every last priest in this city. Preceptor Sarhaddon we will spare. End the battle with the Council, but make sure that not a single

Inquisitor or Sacrus remains alive within the walls of Tandaris.'

It was Tanais who gave that fatal order, but if he hadn't spoken, Alexios, or Charidemus, or one of the Ninth's officers would have. Tanais had been the Emperor's deputy tonight, and he had the authority now. But they would have obeyed those orders had he been the newest lieutenant rather than the oldest general of all.

I didn't watch Tanais kill the remaining priests, didn't have the heart for any more slaughter. The Thetians were enraged, and not all the restraint in the world could have prevented them that night. From the moment Eshar died, the future was set down as if it had been written in stone.

Charidemus had gone with his men, and even the guardsman near me had laid Eshar's head gently down before drawing his sword and running after his comrades. Only Tanais and a few others under Alexios and a Legion officer were left, and they surged into the interior of the Temple in search of more priests. I was left alone beside the corpses.

It was Hamilcar and Xasan who came over to me, lifted me up and between them carried me over to the centre of the courtyard, past the white-faced Pharassans. Xasan pulled off his cloak and they laid me down on it, almost unconscious from the pain in my shoulder.

'There was a healer with us earlier,' Sagantha said. 'We left her in a safe house, I'll go and get her.' Three or four of the other heretics ran after him, but the others clustered round me until Xasan told them to give me some space.

'He'll live,' the Cambressian admiral told them a moment later. 'I'm no healer, but I can't smell poison on the wound, and it's not fatal. Just painful.'

I tried to shut out the pain using the void in my mind, but it was too intense and after a moment I opened my eyes again, stared up into the smoke-smudged night sky. I lost track of time for a while, didn't notice people coming and going until Khalia finally arrived and poured a substance on the wound that felt burning cold for a moment, but then banished the pain and made my whole shoulder and arm go numb.

I was capable of speech again when Tanais returned, but Khalia had cautioned me not to move.

Khalia repeated Xasan's impromptu diagnosis, and I saw the Marshal's relieved look.

'He needs to be moved,' she said. 'I have to clean the wound, and I can't do that out here.'

'We have field attendants here, they're used to carrying stretchers. I'll send some of my men to find them, we'll requisition one of these houses. I'm glad you're here, Khalia, at least I know he's in safe hands and not with some local quack.'

I thought the offhand comment rather pleased her, but I couldn't be sure. They knew each other from the Imperial court, of course.

'I couldn't save him,' I whispered, feeling nothing now but a black despair. 'There will be war.'

'Yes,' said the Marshal a moment later, 'you're right. A war on a scale none of you have ever seen, or even imagined.' He stared off into the distance.

'It was inevitable,' Ravenna said. 'From the moment Lachazzar become Prime.'

'Not so.' Sagantha looked a hundred years older tonight. 'Cathan and Sarhaddon might have succeeded. It's ironic, Eshar was the most warlike Emperor in two centuries, yet if he'd lived, he would have brought us all peace.'

'A peace under Domain rule.'

'Peace has its price, Ravenna,' said Tanais heavily. 'The price Cathan and Sarhaddon proposed was a light one for so many lives.'

'Is there no hope at all?' Khalia asked.

It was Alexios who answered. 'No. The Domain's

Emperor is gone, and his successor will be one of us here tonight. We won't forget, and the Domain won't forgive us. Not after this slaughter.'

'You saw how Amonis reacted,' Ravenna said, looking around the circle of weary faces above me. 'For all the hopes we had, would Lachazzar and the fundamentalists have accepted that proposal as anything other than heresy? Of course they wouldn't.'

'Even if there was no chance,' said Sagantha, 'it doesn't make the path ahead any brighter. There will be a Crusade, a Crusade to make the previous ones seem like raiding parties, and it will engulf everyone from the Tiberian Islands to Thure. And because we are fighting for souls, for beliefs rather than simply politics or territory, it will be bloodier than any before. Except the Tuonetar War, and all of us have read the descriptions from either side. None of us can really imagine how terrible this will be.'

My gaze met Palatine's in the sudden silence. She reached down, took the hand that still had some feeling in it.

'I failed,' I said, before she could speak. 'Don't try to pretend otherwise.'

'Most wouldn't even have had the courage to try,' she said.

Out of the corner of my eye, I saw two white-cloaked men running up carrying a stretcher.

Tanais nodded, raised the hilt of his sword to his face. 'I salute you.'

'I don't deserve it.'

'The Marshal thinks you do,' said Alexios, 'so you do.'

They moved aside to let the stretcher-bearers through, and I heard Tanais exchange a few words with another subordinate. 'We'll take him to the palace,' he said. 'The city still isn't safe, we can't afford to lose him.'

Khalia nodded, and I endured the pain as the two men shifted me as gently as they could on to the field stretcher.

Tanais left a few men behind to relay messages, but all of the others guarded me as I was carried up through burning Tandaris on the night that the last road to peace was closed for ever. Clouds of smoke drifted overhead and blackened people ran through the chaos of the streets. I thought I could hear thunder in the distance, but even if it was only collapsing buildings it was a reminder of what had happened here tonight, and a dreadful harbinger of the future.

EPILOGUE:
THE GHOSTS OF PARADISE

Western Harbour, Selerian Alastre
Six months later

We stood at the end of the quay, a lonely group of figures bathed in the golden light of sunset, and watched the manta leave. We followed its wake out of the harbour and beyond, into the water of the Sea of Stars, until it turned out of our sight and was lost to view.

And upon all this godless nation of heretics and infidels, pagans and idolaters, this race of people who in their folly have turned away from the guiding light of Ranthas we do hereby call the wrath of His vengeance . . .

For a moment no-one said anything, then Palatine moved past Sagantha and walked slowly out to the very end of the quay, below the unlit beacon, to stare out into the west. None of us made a move to follow her.

. . . by the authority given us we, the General Council of the Domain meeting in Taneth this Festival of Ranthas, do hereby resolve that for the salvation of souls and the glory of Ranthas the one true God and Lord over all Aquasilva . . .

My gaze rested on the lonely figure at the end of the quay, still holding the scroll in her hand. Not even the dictates of formality had overcome the unruliness of her hair, and a robe sat oddly on her, as if it didn't really fit despite the best efforts of the tailors.

. . . decree this heretic land of Thetia anathema and accursed, excommunicate in its entirety from the blessing of Ranthas, and from all its people great and small we withdraw the protection of

Ranthas, save those who may fight beside us in this holy cause . . .

'The City is waiting to hear, Palatine,' Sagantha said. 'People will have seen this, be wondering what has happened.'

For a moment Palatine didn't answer, then she swung round.

'Let them sleep one more night, Sagantha. They deserve that at least.' She turned away again, lost in the ocean. I wondered how she could look out into the glare with unshaded eyes.

'No. They've been waiting long enough.'

. . . and from all nations we lift the yoke of the tyrants, all obligations, tribute and obedience formerly owed. From its ruler, the excommunicate apostate Palatine, we strip all titles and rights, all authority that the Lord of Heaven gave to her ancestors, and from her subjects we lift all obligations to obedience. Those who within a period of ninety days are not reconciled to the Faith . . .

The envoy hadn't even set foot on the quay, simply handed the scroll to the waiting Imperial aide and stood by until he had seen Palatine read it. He would have been acting on specific orders there, although I didn't know the significance of it.

'May I have your leave to tell the High Command?' Alexios asked.

'And the Assembly?' said its leader, the grey-haired Aurelian Tuthmon.

Palatine nodded. 'Call them together. I'll speak to them in an hour.'

The two bowed in acknowledgement and walked slowly back down the quay, their distended shadows stretching far out over the quiet water.

. . . this call we make, to all nations and empires, to all peoples and races under His bright sun, that they shall come and gather in arms in this city of Taneth by the thirtieth day of summer next year for a Crusade against these godless islands of Thetia and the Archipelago . . .

A pair of seagulls swooped low over the water, their harsh cries breaking the unnatural silence of a harbour that was normally so busy. It was as if the whole city had turned its eyes aside from us at this moment, knowing what was in the scroll the envoy had brought.

. . . and so we request, require and command that all available men, ships and money be given to this great expenditure, that the quarrels of nations be put aside, that all may act in a spirit of concord for the duration of this great undertaking, so that in His blessed name we shall be victorious.

Signed by the hands of those present at the Twelfth General Council of the Domain, on the seventh Festival of the primacy of Lachazzar in the blessed year two thousand seven hundred and eighty one by the Calenda Annalis, to be sent to every corner of the earth and every last island on the face of the waters, in the name of Ranthas.

Four of us remained with the Empress now: Sagantha, Persea, Ravenna and me. Sagantha, who had miraculously escaped by taking the other sea ray through the ring of debris after *Crusade* was destroyed. All the others who'd been with us on that dreadful night were gone now, except for Alexios. All scattered across the known world as friends or enemies, all tainted by the very fact they had been present.

Some, I knew, I would never see again. Amadeo and Oailos, gone together into the heart of the Domain's new power to try to spread the message of Ilthys, to tell the world what the Domain wanted to suppress. They had had no illusions about their chances of survival, heretic strangers in a strange land.

Hamilcar, still high in favour with Lachazzar, had been charged with the mammoth task of organising the Crusade, an advantage greater than any of us had hoped for, but he'd have to move quietly, to work against it in secret. Hamilcar was no martyr, he intended to live through this whatever happened, for his sake and that of

570

his House. It was easy to forget how many people worked for a Merchant Lord as powerful as Hamilcar, how many lives depended on him.

Then there were the sailors: Charidemus and Xasan, neither of whom I really knew, who would soon be facing each other across a battle line. Laeas, now holding a commission in the Imperial squadron based around Ral Tumar. The sacrificial pawns.

My mother, passed over in favour of Palatine because of what had happened, and what we were facing, she had returned to her island, promising to come and see us again. I still didn't know whether she regretted missing the throne or not. There was so much I didn't know about her, might never have the chance to find out.

And then there was Sarhaddon, for whom that night in Tandaris had been a final defeat, Midian's victory from beyond the grave in the game the two of them had been playing. They'd kept the conflict between them hidden so well that only with hindsight had I been able to see the tension, the power struggle that had flared into hostility with such tragic consequences.

And only with hindsight had I realised that Sarhaddon, for all his treachery, had never wanted this. A Crusade had been the last thing on his mind, something his Venatics managed to prevent for four years, sacrificing a few thousand Archipelagans for the safety of the majority. That had been, perhaps, the hardest thing for me to accept afterwards. Even though he'd wanted me dead with every part of his being, we'd shared that common aim, and in the end it had bridged the gulf between us, a thin line over an uncrossable abyss.

Though you may hear dark things of me, though some of them may even be true, I will keep faith with you, Cathan. I will not forget what we might have done together. I promise this, and may my soul burn for all eternity if I betray you as I betrayed so many others.

'Will you be speaking to the Assembly tomorrow?' Sagantha asked, as Palatine came back to stand with us again.

'Tonight, when the lamps in the Octagon have been lit. The whole city.' That was unprecedented, even in Thetia, but it didn't surprise me. Palatine needed all the support she could get, and while appealing to the people of the capital – who were, given its relative size, the heart and soul of Thetia – might have unforeseen consequences in the long run, that was a risk she had to take.

'What will you tell them?'

Palatine would work on that speech herself, rather than delegating to one of the orators she'd employed. She had given up her dream to take the throne as we urged her, but she insisted on at least keeping appearances going, of reconvening and talking to the Assembly – or, as the Thetians called it, the Praesidium. When the crisis was over, she'd said, then she would try. Too little from a republican, but the times demanded it.

It was a bitter end to the hopes of the last republicans, but all of us knew that Thetia needed leadership now, not the confusion of a new government. The Assembly had been given its own tasks, and we could only sit and hope that it would fulfil them, that Palatine wouldn't be forced to reduce it to a powerless relic again.

'Did you know two more ships came in from Taneth this afternoon?' she asked, unexpectedly.

'Of course. More refugees?'

'Yes. One of the ships was so old it was leaking at the seams, the engineers took one look at it and said it had sailed for the last time. Nothing new there, but Aurelian spoke to some of them. They're scholars, most of them – seventy or eighty, along with forty or fifty oceanographers and all their families, packed on two mantas.'

That must have been a ghastly crossing, two months or so from Taneth with two or three times as many people as the mantas were designed for.

'They've purged the universities then?' Persea asked.

'Purged the universities, burned thousands of forbidden books, closed every oceanographic station, offered rewards to those who enforce the laws of Ranthas most strictly in their territories. Except for the oceanographers, it would be normal. Nothing they don't do every generation or so.' But her voice gave the lie to that, and we all knew it was different.

I clenched my fists to stop my hands trembling. That no-one else could forgive. What was happening to the Guild was my fault, mine alone. For two centuries the Domain had left the oceanographers alone, making examples of a few more heretical ones, but treating them – with a few exceptions such as Salderis – no worse than anyone else. They had even cooperated on joint projects such as *Revelation*.

All across the continents now, oceanographers would have been hounded from their homes, arrested, driven into exile.

All because of me.

Ravenna caught my eyes, but just then Palatine spoke again.

'What will I tell them?'

'This is not a matter of nation against nation, for it never was. It is no longer simply a matter of faith, of our right to worship. It has even gone beyond being about our right to exist.

'They show their true face now, they prove that above all they want to take away the right that all humanity has, a right that we were never given, a right that we have had from the beginning of time. The right to know our own history, to peer through the veils of ignorance around us in search of the truths we know to be there. The right to lift ourselves above the ignorance that they would condemn us to because, Honoured Presidents, Citizens of Thetia, it is their interpretation of the will of Ranthas that we belong there.'

The citizens of Thetia were there in their tens of thousands, packing the Octagon to watch the Empress give her address from the balcony of the Assembly, looking out over a city of lamps and torches, over the great blue-tinted aether arclights burning around the Octagon.

'They come with flames, not just to burn our bodies and our souls, but our minds and our hearts, to erase from the world the knowledge that we hold and our desire to rise beyond the servitude they assign to us. Their flames are not the flames that hold back the night, the flames that give life to the world, but the darkening flames of tyranny and despair.

'They stretch out their hands across the sea and order us to obey them, tell us that it will bring us salvation, but when in our history have we known a lower point? When my predecessor came to the throne, our fortunes had fallen farther than we have ever known. Our Empire was little more than a shadow on the waters, a memory of glory. Our houses were crumbling in ruin, our greatness was faded.

'These years have been hard for us, I know, but at least we have begun to climb again, to drag ourselves up towards the heights we once held. To hope that we can recreate the Thetia of our bright morning two hundred years ago. Not to turn back the clock, but to move with it, to see the future in the same tones as the past.'

With this news, she didn't need to be a great orator to hold them, only a Thetian speaking to Thetians on the day they had heard that Lachazzar intended to wipe all of us from the face of the waters.

'The Domain would deny us that future, but more than that, they would deny all of Aquasilva that future. They would plunge us back into a dark age of ignorance and superstition, an age before cities and aqueducts, before gardens and fountains and wine, silks and spices, all the things that make us a civilisation rather than a few barbarians in the mud of a dark age, at the mercy of witch-doctors and shamans.

'Yesterday, more than a hundred oceanographers and scholars came to us from the continents, fleeing the Domain's purges. Tanethans and Cambressians, Oceanians and Equatorians, they came to us because they have nowhere else to go. Because, whatever we were before, we have become the last refuge for them. Not only for them, but even for those priests who followed their hearts and the true image of their god rather than the malice of the fundamentalists.

'We have made our peace offer, Citizens, and you have heard their reply. You have heard their intentions. There is but one course left to us, the darkest course of all. For two hundred years we have lived at peace. Now we are threatened once again, by an enemy beside whom the Tuonetar seem enlightened, an enemy with the resources of four continents behind them.

'We must stand firm, Thetia. We must stand firm because if we do not, then there is no hope anywhere. You know the alliance of nations ranged against us and our Archipelagan cousins. It is a war of far greater magnitude than we could ever have feared, but now that it is come, *we must survive*. We must survive because we owe it to ourselves, our families, to Thetia and the Archipelago. But above all we must survive so that our civilisation survives, so that we have the time for drama and poetry, for opera and sculpture, the time to educate our children in more than the dogma of a vengeful god. So that we can educate our children at all rather than see them dragged away to live their lives as slaves in some corner of a forgotten continent far from the sea.

'This will not be a war as any of us have known, not

575

simply a war over territory and prestige as we fought against Cambress three years ago. It is not enough to place our trust in Mother Ocean, to believe that the sea will defend us as she always has.'

There was a murmur of astonishment at Palatine's open heresy, but it was followed by a louder shout of approbation, of praise that she had at last dared to break a centuries-old taboo and mention the goddess that all Thetians still worshipped in their heart of hearts, even if only in their love of the sea.

'We must create our own ocean around us, a firebreak to protect us from the torches and the stakes. An ocean to protect this last bastion of freedom and knowledge against the darkening flames that surround us. That is what we fight, Citizens. Remember *the darkening flames*. Remember that it is no longer enough to go on as we have done, but that we must rouse ourselves from the sleep of years and drive back the flames, extinguish the fires and put an end to the despotism of men who would destroy everything for the sake of a half-seen god. Will you stand with me, Thetia? Will you stand with the Archipelago against the firestorm?'

For a second there was silence, then a deafening acclamation, a roar that surged outwards from the centre of the crowd, thrown up by a hundred thousand throats. There were twice as many people in this vast square as lived in the whole of Tandaris, and the noise was staggering. Standing behind Palatine and to one side of her, I felt the noise hit me like a wave, saw the Empress gravely acknowledge the crowd's vocal salute.

'AVE PALATINA! AVE PALATINA!'

That was part of what I had turned down, but even as the citizens of Selerian Alastre roared their approval, I felt other memories intruding. The crowds in Ilthys and Tandaris, the scenes that must have played themselves out in Taneth, hundreds of thousands gathering to demonstrate their devotion to the Faith.

576

Palatine was using their weapons against them, because they were the only weapons we had. But as I listened to the crowd, I felt a shudder run through me.

We are going the same way.

I wondered how many of them would realise, once they had left the crowd behind, what was facing us. Most, I suspected, because this was Selerian Alastre, and for all the Navy's traditions, perhaps because of them, the Thetians were not a warrior people but a mercantile one. Only Taneth could compare, and Thetia's long reach had made the world forget how much it still thought of itself as a city-state, how much Selerian Alastre *was* Thetia.

And would be for how much longer? We had to face the Domain, and because of that we had to make sacrifices – sacrifices which would betray everything that Palatine wanted us to fight for.

We would take ourselves into the night.

The crowds dispersed, eventually, and so did the Assembly and the admirals. For a while Palatine stood conferring with Tanais, surrounded by a circle of the officers who seemed to be the Marshal's protégés. A few around my age, some more about twenty years older; those who'd been at the Naval Academy during his last two visits.

Eventually they finished, and Tanais despatched a few of the officers while the others followed him and the Empress downstairs.

As for the Presidents, some left with the Empress; others drifted away in small knots, leaders from the same clan alliances talking quietly. The new Assembly was an odd mixture of the very old and the very young, because Orosius and Eshar had taken so many of the middle generation. Two of the Presidents weren't yet twenty-five, another was eighty-nine and had been clan President before, thirty-five years ago.

Then they were all gone, and only two people remained

with me on the long, curving balcony around the grand Assembly building. The arclights faded, and only the flamewood lamps were left on.

'You must do it,' Vespasia said, as the three of us wandered a little away from the doors, to a place we could be sure no-one was listening. '*Aeon* is still there, waiting for us.'

'It'll only make things worse,' I said.

'It'll end this before it begins,' Ravenna said. 'We take *Aeon* off Equatoria, wait for a storm and the Holy City will be gone in a few hours. Lachazzar, the Primes, most of the Sacri . . . all the leaders.'

'And terror will breed terror,' I insisted. 'It'll only harden their resolve to go on, the remaining Exarchs will have all the material they need to whip up a crusading fervour. Then what will you do? Turn the storms on Pharassa and Cambress?'

'Cathan, you've said it yourself, you've heard Palatine say it.' I could hear temper flaring in her voice. 'This war will destroy all of us. If we can end it before it begins, so much the better.'

'And ignore Salderis's warning?'

'Salderis's warning was an attempt to scare you into claiming the throne. We can't sit around and debate this any more. We don't even have time to find a few pathetic Tuonetar survivors as Salderis suggested. The Tuonetar don't exist, they won't know anything about the storms or how they were made.'

'They don't,' said a deep voice, 'but I do.'

So quiet, none of us had heard his footsteps, giant though he was.

The three of us looked up at him, a formidable figure in a cobalt blue uniform. Tanais, who had served Aetius in the Tuonetar War. The only man alive, unbelievable as it was, who had seen Aquasilva before the storms.

'How?' Ravenna asked.

'Because I was there,' said Tanais. 'I will tell the three of you this because of what you know, what you've managed to discover without any knowledge of what really happened, but you cannot tell anyone else. Palatine already knows, but never mention it to her or any other person, no matter how much you trust them.'

'Why not?'

'Because it would destroy the Empire,' Tanais said.

Then I felt a dreadful chill run across my skin, and I forgot the warmth of the night. For a second before he began to speak, I knew that neither of the others had grasped what he was about to say. Not even Vespasia, although we'd talked about this on the docks of Ilthys. The greatest question of all about the storms.

Why?

Why had the Tuonetar committed an act that doomed their own civilisation to destruction even if they won the war?

Now I knew the answer.

They hadn't.

'The Skyeyes don't only see the weather,' Tanais said, 'they affect it in some way. I don't know the specifics, none of us ever did. It was beyond our capacity to understand, but not beyond our capacity to use.' I wondered if he'd ever connected the weather system with the odd fast-moving stars, but I thought not. That wasn't where his interests lay.

'The accounts you've read in Carausius's *History* are a lie. We didn't find *Aeon* floating in the open ocean, we took her from the Tuonetar, as we took their other facility behind Mons Ferranis, although the city didn't exist then. She was their flagship, much older and much more sophisticated than the rest of the arkships, and even they didn't fully understand her.

'We never cleansed the Tuonetar presence from *Aeon*, we simply struck a bargain with the ship itself – yes, the

579

ship had intelligence, of a kind. The intelligence to run itself, to keep all its complex systems running indefinitely.'

His story was becoming more and more incredible, more and more horrible for me because I knew where he was going. And I knew that he had to be telling the truth.

'We were able to use her for those last few years as a transport, a city under the ocean, but we never really possessed her. Never saw what the Skyeyes represented until we discovered that we could communicate with them, and so affect the way they worked. And by then we were losing the war, badly. The Tuonetar were more advanced than we were then, ahead even of the technology we've developed now, although not by as much, and we couldn't stand up to them.

'There was no magic involved, only Carausius's intellect and our help – Aetius, Cidelis and myself. Only Tiberius was ever told, and he never passed it on. Because we understood so little, we thought we had to do far more damage than was necessary, and we wrecked the Skyeyes. They still see, but nothing more. And whatever control they'd exerted was gone, so the weather was left to its own devices.'

The two women had gone white, and I reached out a hand to steady myself on the balustrade as the weight of what Tanais was saying broke over me like a mental tidal wave. I'd realised, but it was far worse to hear him actually saying it.

'We ruined the climate and started the storms, the four of us, because we realised that whatever happened, Thure and the Tuonetar would lose. They did; Thure is now a desolate icecap, the Tuonetar are gone . . . and Thetia is still here. Even without our sack of Aran Cthun, the Tuonetar would have been destroyed, they might just have taken us with them because they knew what we'd done.

'I don't know what will happen if you try to control the storms using magic, but my guess is that you'll only make it worse. If you can do it and blame the other side, as we did, then Thetia will survive again. Which is, after all, what matters.'

'Why did you tell us this?' I managed to ask.

'Because I heard from Palatine what you wanted to do, and knew I had to tell you before you found out. And to stop you thinking that the Tuonetar mages had done it. If you use magic on the atmosphere, you'll be the first ever to do so, and I can't predict what will happen. But if it saves us all, then perhaps it's worth it.'

The Marshal gave us the briefest of nods and then walked away, back into the night. I saw two men join him as he went back through the doors into the building, presumably guards to stop anyone eavesdropping. Ninth Legionaries both. It wasn't only the officers who revered him.

So Sarhaddon had been right, that day in Tandaris which seemed suddenly so long ago. It was all a lie, from the elements to the Archipelagan Paradise to the heroes of the past. More distorted even than the Domain's lies, but the Domain had never uncovered the greatest secret of all.

The other two were ashen, and I knew that I probably looked the same. Vespasia, who'd never had the heretic training but who had read the *History*, knew a lot of the Archipelagan past from the years we spent with her, looked as stunned as Ravenna.

All those deaths, all the damage that the storms had done over the years, the need for protection that gave the Domain its power – heavens, the obliteration of an entire ancient civilisation and the near-extinction of another – Thetia had caused them.

'Not Thetia,' I said, without realising I was thinking aloud. 'My family. The Emperors.'

The loathing I'd felt for my family, the horror at what they'd done, came rushing back. Sarhaddon's first speech had been questioning the *History*, painting Aetius and

Carausius in markedly different colours. Of course the *History* had been biased, because Carausius himself had written it, but none of us had ever realised that. It was taught to us as the truth, part of the religion, so of course we didn't question it.

'That was two centuries ago!' Vespasia managed to say. 'You're probably more closely related to me than you are to them.'

'Unfortunately not,' I said.

'Don't be an idiot,' she said, spurred into life. 'You can't live by what your four times great-grandfather did any more that the rest of us can. It's absurd. I know this is ghastly, but it's the past now.'

'It isn't, though,' I said. 'Don't you see? Most people don't care any more about history than they do about the Bank of Mons Ferranis and its fortunes on the merchant exchange.' The Mons Ferratans were famous for banking only for the richest – powerful clans, plutocrats and governments. 'They might have an interest in it, but it never affects them.

'The storms are another matter, because they condition so much. The way we can build our houses, the places we can found our cities, the times we can make journeys, whether we survive those journeys – all of that is important, and all of that is determined by the storms, especially on the continents. It was the reason the Domain could never soften their line on the Tuonetar any more than in their histories, because people still hate the Tuonetar for what they did. What we thought they did.'

'And if the world ever knew that the Tar'Conanturs and the Thetians were behind the storms, Thetia wouldn't survive five minutes,' Ravenna said hollowly. 'The world is still paying for what Tanais and Carausius did, and they won't forget that.'

Even in telling us Tanais had taken a terrible risk, because he could never be absolutely certain that we wouldn't be taken and tortured by the Domain if the war went badly. It wasn't something they would ask, but there was always the possibility that one of us would break and tell the interrogators to make the pain end.

No. Tanais intended for us to use it as a weapon, wanted to us to come to terms with what had happened before we found *Aeon* and the incriminating evidence. Once the war was over, it wouldn't matter, and . . .

And we, most likely, would die tragically but heroically in some minor skirmish.

I was taking this too far, and dismissed the thought from my mind, but it refused to go away. Tanais was a law unto himself, loyal to Thetia above everything. I'd seen the way the Navy and the Legion treated him, the fervour and the adoration he inspired among so many for whom he was the embodiment of Thetia and its history. Tanais was a living part of history, a very tangible and visible link to what the Navy considered its glorious Imperial past.

I told the others the conclusion I'd come to, and was disturbed to find that Ravenna, the most politically acute of us by a long way, agreed with me.

She also raised the spectre of what else Tanais knew but had kept to himself, what other secrets the Marshal guarded from everyone except himself and the Emperors – or maybe, in some cases, even the Emperors. He'd despised my brother; I doubt he'd have shared many of his secrets back then.

And now this meeting had gone far beyond its original purpose, and the three of us had been marked out by what the Marshal had told us, the dreadful knowledge all three of us carried. To the burden of knowing that war would be coming he'd added this one, assuming that our loyalties were certain.

Like Palatine's.

My family's legacy still ran deeper than any of us could have imagined.

'I'm not one of them,' I said quietly, remembering that

Ravenna had more than once turned on me for this. 'Even if only because I'm too weak.'

'You still bear their name,' she said, implacably. 'You're still the last person on Aquasilva who has a chance to carry on their line. Palatine won't marry, she expects you to now. She's Empress, she has to think about the succession because it's part of her duty.'

'Enough of a duty for her to get married herself?' I asked.

'I doubt it. But that doesn't matter. At the moment, there's no question of her marrying, two members of the family left and no future in sight. Of course the Imperial line has to go on. You still have the name, you're still unmarried. And the longer you leave it, the greater the pressure will get until you cave in, as you do to everything else.'

'Not on that,' I protested.

'Really? Is it that different from all the other things you've caved in on?'

I felt my cheeks burn as Vespasia tried to intervene.

'You're being too harsh on him, Ravenna. How well do you know him? Even Sarhaddon admitted that he isn't weak.'

'He can stand up for himself,' she snapped. 'And Sarhaddon said he was a survivor. That's not the same, in fact it's very different. The people who tend to survive are the weathercocks.'

Finally stung into action, I said, 'You know that's not true.'

'Then prove it,' she demanded. 'Cut yourself off from the family.'

'And tell the whole of Thetia that I don't support the Empress? How do you think Tanais will take that?'

'Tanais wants you to find an Exile girl and marry her. You know that.'

'I'm legally obliged to,' I replied. That shook her,

because she hadn't known it was a legal requirement. Nor had I, until concern over it led me to consult the Imperial archives, and discovered that the tradition did, in fact, have a legal origin dating back to Aetius the Founder. In its unsuccessful effort to suppress the Exiles' influence, the Domain had tried to make sure the law would be forgotten.

'Well, go on then! What are you waiting for? Produce yet another generation of Tar'Conanturs, another pair of Imperial twins who'll divide the world between them and destroy even more of it than you and your ancestors have managed. Perhaps they'll be female, because heaven knows a pair of girls are overdue, and then *nothing* will stop them, because incompetence doesn't seem to run in the females.'

'What do you want me to do? To change my name, set myself aside from Palatine at a time Thetia needs to see us together, that would be stupidity of the first order.'

'Don't you dare say,' Ravenna interrupted, stepping towards me and jabbing her finger into my middle, 'don't you dare say you have no choice. The more you vacillate, try to excuse yourself from having to do anything, the more you show that everyone was right. You may for once have been decisive and capable in Tandaris, but that doesn't mean you actually are. I can deal with the storms on my own, and I have the experience under Salderis that you insisted on. I can walk away and leave you, try to solve this myself without having to cope with you and your weakness, or we can go on as a partnership. At the moment you don't qualify to remain as a partner.'

'Just making a gesture won't be enough,' I said, meeting her gaze this time. 'It doesn't accomplish anything, since we're trying to work in secret. The course we'll have to take eventually goes against both Domain and Empire, but we can't reveal that so soon.'

'So you leave things as they are and try to please both sides.'

'So we end this as soon as we can, Ravenna. Before it consumes all of us, before it drags Thetia down into the darkness too.' Perhaps I sounded grandiose and empty, but I didn't care. All I needed to do was to get the message across.

'End what?' she demanded. 'The war?'

'The storms. We don't use them as weapons, at least not directly. We go back to *Aeon*, we spend as long as it will take trying to work out exactly what happened, and we put an end to the storms for ever. And once we've done that, we make sure it can never happen again by putting an end to the Empire as well.'

There was silence for a moment after I'd spoken. The other two stared at me disbelievingly.

'That could take lifetimes,' Vespasia said. 'And how can you be sure?'

'It could, but it won't. We leave the Empire to get on with its own affairs, to fight off the Domain as best it can until we can unravel the storms. And when they're gone, even if the Domain's grand alliance is still in place, things will change. The other powers, starting with Cambress, will realise that the Domain has no more real power over them. They'll hold with the Faith, of course, but it'll be just that: a faith.'

'And the Empire?' Ravenna asked finally. 'Yes, why do we have to end that exactly?'

I wondered if she was waiting for my reply simply to pour scorn on it, but I answered anyway.

'To stop my family or any other doing the same thing again. It didn't win them the war; the march on Aran Cthun did that. It merely ensured that the Tuonetar would be obliterated. And once the storms are gone, the Emperors are gone and the world can forgive, we tell them what Tanais told us, so that there are millions of witnesses to stop its ever happening again.'

'You don't think on a small scale, do you?' Vespasia said.

'No, but at least he thinks,' said Ravenna, with the faintest trace of a smile. 'And stands up for himself.'

I felt a surge of anger as I realised what she was saying. 'You were *testing* me?'

'Of course. I had to know, Cathan. Evidence of my own eyes, scientific method. That was all I meant with that talk about gestures and the family. Of course it's a bad idea. You need to take steps to ensure you're not forced into marriage with someone who'll actually give you children, but it doesn't matter. Your plan . . . needs improving, but I like it. It seems Ithien survives in you more than in Palatine.'

None of us said anything for a while after that, because the memory of his death was still close. All of us had been at his state funeral in Ilthys, though I'd been too weak from blood loss to stand and had had to be carried to the ceremonies in a litter. We'd buried him at sea in the old Thetian fashion, in a coral garden off the bay where he'd boarded our ship such a very short time before.

By the time she spoke again, my anger was gone, as she might have known.

'I needed to do that, Cathan,' she said. 'To prove that we were equals again. For a while I thought you were my superior, then for years my inferior, but at the Citadel I thought we were on the same level. You've convinced me again.'

'Are there any more tests I need to pass?' I asked, still slightly bitter.

'None that I'll throw at you.' She turned to look out, over the city with its lamps and domes and gardens under the summer stars that gave it its official name. 'It's odd, you know. I was brought up under Shadow in Tehama, I always found shadow-magic the easiest, and though now Tehama and Ukmadorian have turned on me and I realise that shadow-magic isn't really any different from the others, it's still special. I still prefer night-time. Even here where it's so light.'

'There are places you can go in the city where it's properly dark,' Vespasia said.

'Where?'

'Around the far side of the hills, by the cliffs on the north coast. The ground's too steep for anyone to have built there, so it's all a kind of vast wild garden, a cove or two. Not really wild and deserted, like all those atolls down in the south, or the long dune shore with the forests behind it, up in the north-east – but for the Citadel, it's dark.'

'Will you show me where it is?'

'Gladly,' Vespasia said. 'Darkness for you and swimming for Cathan and me.'

I felt a corner of my mind thinking, *This should have been Palatine's to show us*, and almost cried. Once it would have been, but Palatine was Empress now, she had other things to occupy her time.

So I could tell myself.

We walked slowly back along the balcony of the Assembly building, through the great galleried spaces of its interior and around the chamber of the Praesidium. Thetia had been a republic once, four hundred years ago when it had been little more than the city of Selerian Alastre and a few dozen outlying villages.

I could feel the age in here, the antiquity of a building that still, in some ways, was the heart of Thetia. Here the Assembly had met for close on seven hundred years, through three fires and the sack, here each new Emperor or Empress until Eshar had been confirmed and accepted by the clan Presidents.

It had become little more than a ritual, one Palatine chose to revive, but once it hadn't been. I thought of the Statue Gallery in the palace, with effigies of every single Emperor looking down at me, centuries of malevolence and hatred.

No matter what had passed in this building, it could

never equal what my family had done.

Then we walked out of a side door and down some steps into the deserted Octagon, through the heart of a city now at war again, a city with the shadow of a Crusade hanging over it.

And of the storms, even in the empty skies above it.

We stopped in the centre of the Octagon, by the great fountain there, and sat on its stone rim, splashing ourselves with a little of the water to relieve the night's heat. Letting the sound of the water wash over me, I lay back along the rim and stared up into the summer sky until I saw what I was looking for, the fast-moving point of light crossing the heavens from north to south until I lost sight of it behind a dome on one of the hills.

I pointed it out to Vespasia, who'd never seen it before, and Ravenna, who'd been with me that night on the Citadel island in the far south. I told both of them what it was, because I hadn't had a chance to so far, and was pleased to see that both of them agreed with me. We had seen the Skyeyes, all three of us this time.

But the memory of that night by the sea wasn't enough to lift my mood entirely, not even when the three of us walked off towards the harbour and Ravenna laced her fingers through mine. It would be because there was no-one except Vespasia to see, I knew.

I didn't feel the same way about that. In this city, in the heart of the world, its history was all around, and I could feel eyes on us even if Ravenna couldn't. Disapproving eyes, somehow knowing what we intended, frowning at our defiance of their laws and the threat to their existence.

Eyes not of humans but of the legacy we still had to overcome, the shades that Salderis had named and Tanais still personified with all the tradition and weight of the Thetian Empire – and its Empress – behind him.

The Ghosts of Paradise.